WHEN *Paris* WHISPERS

a novel

MARIANNE C. BOHR

Brother Mockingbird Publishing

Also by Marianne C. Bohr

The Twenty: One Woman's Trek Across Corsica on the GR20 Trail
Gap Year Girl: A Baby Boomer Adventure Across 21 Countries

Library of Congress Control Number: 2026932477

Cover Design by: Alexios Saskalidis
www.facebook.com/187designz

For information please contact:
Brother Mockingbird, LLC
www.brothermockingbird.net
ISBN: 978-1-960226-34-1 Paperback
ISBN: 978-1-960226-35-8 EBook

To Joe, as always, because even before I say it, you're the one who whispers, "Let's go to France."

"Life shrinks or expands in proportion to one's courage."

—Anaïs Nin

Prologue

PARIS

April 1981

Fresh from a shower, Freddie gestures with her mug, a wave of black coffee splashing to the floor. "How could you have embarrassed me in front of my friends like that? Are you really so clueless?" She puts down her coffee and begins to pace.

I take the pile of her clothes I just folded and set it on her bed.

"You're a dull little wallflower Cat, with no panache. The innocent intellectual with no common sense who can't let loose for some fun." Freddie pulls her towel tight at her side and sneers. "You're actually the dullest person I know."

She picks up her coffee and sips. It looks like she's trying to smile, but it doesn't quite reach her eyes. An abyss opens between us, one that was always there but that I haven't fully acknowledged. I seethe as I slam my mug on the counter and hear it crack, coffee leaking.

Freddie says, "Easy now—"

"Do you realize how cruel and shallow you are?" I jump in. "You never have anything good to say about anyone." A wave of my hand accidentally knocks over the floor lamp, but I leave it. "All you talk about is yourself and all you care about is yourself. You used me just to have someone to kick around."

Her eyes narrow and her lips curl. "I swear to God, you make it so easy, you sanctimonious twat." She sets her mug by the bed and pulls her towel snug around her chest.

I say in a low near growl, "You hate that Vincent flirts with me, that he might even like me—"

She's up in an instant, her towel falling to the floor, her hands lunging for my neck. I quickly step aside and she crashes into the wall. She spins around, her blue eyes wild. "You boring, neurotic bitch!" She steps back, loses her balance, arms like a windmill, and falls on her bed, bumping her mug on the nightstand. Coffee flies, staining the wall like blood spatter. She tries to get up but tangles in the bedclothes, slips off the mattress and falls forward, bare ass in the air. The pile of laundry teeters and then tumbles on top of her.

I look down at Freddie and suppress bubbles of nervous laughter.

"Goddamn you, Cat Gray," she says from the floor, teeth clenched. "You skinny, uptight loser!"

I resurrect all the resentment I've bottled up for years. "Never once did you say I'm sorry for all the times you let me down."

Freddie stands, wriggles into a pair of panties from the floor and clomps to the closet. She slips a mottled mango muumuu over her head, transforming herself into a psychedelic nightmare.

"Freddie Fucking Forestier, I'm done with you."

She points at the door and screams, "Nothing of mine is yours anymore! Not my friends, not my flat, and certainly not Vincent!"

She grabs a madeleine, and hurls it, hitting my belly while laughing. Another madeleine flies and smacks my head. "I swear to God, you think you're so special-—speaking perfect French and acting all smart. Well, you're not so special and no one likes you."

"You're just jealous, Freddie."

She bolts across the room, jumps onto the bed behind me and grabs my braid, yanking my head back. I struggle, arms flailing. Then I feel a rhythmic, sawing pressure at the base of my neck. A sound like... ripping...Oh God… Oh my God, she's cutting my hair! I scream as my foot finds the bed and pushes off. I reach back and touch my long, thick braid, hanging by threads.

Freddie steps back, holding her bread knife high. I open my mouth but nothing comes out. My hair. My long blond hair...gone.

Part One

PARIS

March 1981

Chapter One

When I was little, my father read me Ludwig Bemelmans's picture book, *Madeline*, so many times that I knew every word by heart. I even came up with my own story beginning: "In an apartment in Paris at the end of the hall, lived a girl named Catrine who was curious and tall." It was one of dozens of titles I kept on my bedroom bookshelf. Most had belonged to a grandmother I'd never met and many were in French.

I devoured story after story about French farm children who churned butter in Normandy and made cheese in Burgundy. I read about mademoiselles in embroidered aprons, lacy coifs, and noisy wooden sabots who lived in Brittany, and about irresistible Gigi in turn-of-the-century Paris. My favorite was about a little girl, Nanette, who got lost in a turreted chateau outside a Breton village. Each story made me feel more connected to my invisible Francophile *grand-mère* than my own mother, with whom I was usually at odds.

From the age of five I knew I would go to Paris when I grew up.

Just before I started high school, Dad took me to the coffee shop Mother said was too expensive and I ordered my first café au lait. Unable to deny me, he bought me my first caffeinated brew. He didn't have to say, "Don't tell Mother."

When he set a steaming bowl of foam before me, I inhaled the rich, creamy scent and then took my first sip of heaven. Dad laughed at the mustache it left on my upper lip. Just then, a tremulous alto poured from the café's speakers.

"Édith Piaf," Dad said. "They called her the Little Sparrow, *le piaf.* As tiny as you are tall."

I loved her voice. It made me want to cry. "She lived in Paris?"

"Of course."

I added Miss Piaf to what I knew about Paris and wondered if my grandmother knew her.

With new flavors on my tongue and Piaf's lyrics encircling us, I asked Dad, "What was my grandmother like?" I didn't often ask him about his parents because I could tell it made him blue, but I knew there was more to the story than that he had lost them too soon.

He sighed and looked out the café window. "Well, she loved studying French and spoke it well. She and I read La Fontaine's fables together when I was a boy and then Maupassant's stories when I was in high school. I tried to guess the endings because there was almost always a twist."

I had organized my grandmother's books alphabetically by author, from Bemelmans to Hugo and La Fontaine to Zola, and I'd read them all, even those whose French was difficult and caused me to miss some of the meaning. The world of French writers fueled the fantasies Mother called my wasted delusions.

"What else?" I ask.

"She was warm and sweet and smart. Tall and blonde with wide-set brown eyes. A lot like you. In fact, just like you."

I saw his eyes mist over but I urged him on. "Her name was Catherine, right?"

Dad wiped his eyes. "Yes, Catherine. But everyone called her Cate and she didn't like it. Wanted people to call her by her full name, pronounced the French way—Catrine. Like yours."

I sipped my café au lait and imagined myself in Paris with Édith Piaf and *Grand-Mère*. Sometimes I pretended I was a princess in the

French court or a protégé of Georges Sand, debating politics in cafés. I took myself to Paris, far away from Mother, almost every day, because I knew imagining was the first step to making dreams come true.

But it took me a long time to figure out who and what I was. It took pain, longing, rejection, and loss—a major loss that nearly crushed me—but most of all it took courage.

Coco Chanel once said, *"Une fille doit être deux choses: qui et ce qu'elle veut."* A girl should always be two things: who and what she wants. I heard her sometimes, her voice faint, her accent intoxicating. She told me, *Just do it, Catrine. Be who you want to be.*

Finally, I listened.

Chapter Two

The pilot's announcement jars me from my fitful excuse for sleep. "Ladies and gentlemen, we're beginning our descent into Charles de Gaulle airport... *Mesdames Messieurs...*"

I pull my backpack from under the seat and stuff in my copy of *Let's Go France*, dog-eared and highlighted to near meaninglessness. Once again, I review the directions for getting to my high school girlfriend Freddie's flat, trying to keep anxiety in check.

As I disembark, I imagine Dad, his steady hand on my shoulder, at my college graduation, less than a year ago. "You can do this, Catrine. You'll find your way to France." Just the thought of him gives me a needed boost. Dad always said I belonged in France and I hope he was right. "You're a dreamer and a doer. You'll make it happen. Don't let anyone, including yourself, hold you back."

It was just last month. Dawn on a seemingly ordinary Friday. I was about to leave for work when the phone rang. The news was a gut punch. I remember the quiet whir of the kitchen ceiling fan as I listened to the foreman but hardly grasped the details. Dad had driven the factory's truck through the night to Trenton for a delivery. In the rain. He'd made it back, but had fallen asleep in the truck's cab, the engine idling in the enclosed warehouse bay. Cardiac arrest triggered by toxic fumes.

My throat tightened as if not breathing could reverse time. I dropped the phone, stumbled out the back door and collapsed on the stoop. Grief exploded in my chest and tears gushed—huge, quivering sobs I was sure would never stop.

After the call, I felt adrift with no anchor, sleepwalking through the next week, handling arrangements while Mother's priest friend, Father Ceinture, saw to the funeral, and she fielded condolences. When it was all over, she did shed some tears but then blessed herself saying, "The good Lord always has a reason." But I was inconsolable, a boiling waterfall of tears spilling down my cheeks, my chest raw as if lined with shards of glass.

The evening after Dad's funeral, I grabbed the afghan from the couch, curled up in the recliner where he used to read to me, pulled down his plaid shirt draped over the back, and rolled it like a pillow. I buried my face in the flannel that still held his scent. He'd taken part of me with him when he died. And I knew then that I had no more excuses for not leaving.

I dab at my eyes with a tissue, look around, and see the airport signs in French, remembering where I am. *Look at me, Dad. I'm in France! I summoned all the courage you told me I had and left. I finally left.*

But as I approach passport control, I hear Mother go on about the nastiness of French men and my emotions sink again. "Pay attention, Cat. Foreign men will always take advantage. Hold your wallet close. Can't be too careful." Her words cut me sideways and my confidence wavers. I've barely been out of suburban Virginia. Why do I think I can live in Paris?

And then I rally, remembering all the years I've dreamed of being here. I dismiss images of Mother's frown and return my thoughts to the realities of getting to Freddie's.

I fly through airport arrivals and cash some traveler's checks. But finding the shuttle to the city center has me walking in circles. I'm eager to loosen my jaw and speak French, so I approach an airport guard. While I don't understand every word of her fast directions, they get me to my train.

Once seated, I look out the window, anticipating my first glimpses of the Parisian horizon I've pictured for so long. I lean back and relax to the mellifluous sounds of French around me. I need some sleep, but force my eyes open so I won't miss a thing.

The train soon glides through the tangle of tracks and into the Gare du Nord. The grimy, graffitied concrete walls lining the approach take me aback. An old man at the end of the platform hawks up a gob of phlegm, spits it into the track bed, and then swigs from a brown bag. Not exactly the Paris I've been imagining. But then I step off the train and gaze up at the soaring glass-and-cast-iron roof of the station. It's as beautiful as I pictured.

I take a deep breath, scan the signs for the metro, and descend into the subterranean labyrinth. I wend my way around corners, and follow the signs through long, white-tiled tunnels as they merge with ever-longer ones. It all seems so easy and I'm already feeling like a Parisienne. I reach my platform as the subway cars, jam-packed with morning rush hour commuters, fly into the station. The crush of the crowd is fierce, until the doors open and I'm ejected at my stop.

I climb the stairs to the street and am Audrey Hepburn in *Sabrina*, unable to stop grinning. Pedestrians hurry past and I hear the distinctive wail of a French ambulance, the one I've heard so often in French movies. I peer into the window of a patisserie, at the lines of pastries covered in chocolate, mocha, and strawberry. The smells almost lure me in, but I must find Freddie's flat before I succumb to sugar and cream.

Adrenaline pulses as I follow the directions I'd memorized. I turn a corner and a primary-colored, tinker-toy building looms. The four-year-old Pompidou Center. It appears inside-out with exposed pipes, tubing, and exhaust ducts. Its quirky design makes me smile.

Several blocks later, after weaving down dim, narrow lanes lined with boutiques where early-rising shopkeepers wash sidewalks and windows, I reach number eight on the rue de Montmorency. The brown door with grimy windowpanes looks nothing like the picture Freddie sent. Where is the monumental wooden portal, shellacked to a shine, with a heavy brass knocker I expected? I should have known—Freddie and her exaggerations.

I glance up and down the street to get my bearings. From the direction of the Pompidou Center, a young man in sweats walks towards me and smiles. I nod as he passes. Hardly the rude male Parisian Mother told me to expect. I swing my pack around, take out my notes, and let the bag drop to the pavement. Yes, Freddie said it was number 8.

When I look up at the number again, I'm shoved powerfully and fall forward, my knees and hands smacking the cement. A guy races down the street, my pack in tow.

Chapter Three

"Goddamnit" I scream.

I get to my feet and take off after the thief who disappears down an alley. I turn to follow and see my pack in the gutter ahead. My jeans, journal, and underwear are strewn across the alleyway. Breathing hard and on the brink of tears, I stop and turn back to collect my things. All my tee-shirts are now dirty, and my one dress sports a grimy boot print.

You will not cry, Catrine.

When I emerge from the alley, I lean against a shop window and slide to a sit, my thighs against my chest, so angry to have been so naive. My palms ache and my bloody knees sting through my torn jeans. Eczema has pestered me since elementary school and right now, it's on fire. My finger tracks the blazing scar left by so much scratching along the back of my hand—a rough, puckered line, ring finger to wrist. As I sink into self-pity, my hand flies to my buttoned chest pocket.

The swell of my wallet and passport remains. I close my eyes as Mother's warning rings in my ears. For once, listening to her was the right thing to do. "Be vigilant. Paris is foreign and dangerous."

No matter my fantasies, maybe I don't belong here.

My head on my knees, I beseech my grandmother as I do so often. *Should I return to the airport and go home? Was this all a terrible idea?* I never receive an answer, but this time I do hear a voice...

"A vaincre sans peril, on triomphe sans gloire."

I whip my head around to glance up at the shop window. Whoever is quoting the seventeenth-century playwright, Pierre Corneille, has just answered me. To win without risk is a triumph without glory.

But there's no one there. The sign on the door says *Fermé*. I look up and down the street. Who said that? I decide it was just my imagination. *You're exhausted. You were just mugged. And now you're concocting voices.*

Freddie is working today and swore she couldn't get off. Maybe if I were her best friend and not just a sidekick, she'd have managed to meet me. I take out a tissue to wipe tears that finally fall. I must get to Freddie's ASAP. I stand, jittery, lift my pack, and walk back to the sorry entrance of number eight. Her letter said to buzz the concierge. But there's no buzzer anywhere. I knock loudly. When there's no response, I look back up at the number.

On closer inspection, I see that the number is actually a 3. Some joker changed the stenciled numeral with paint, turning it into an 8. I manage a chuckle and turn to restart my search. A doorway on the next block mirrors Freddie's photo: a magnificent wooden door surrounded by an elaborate stone arch and, to the right, a blue tile with a perfect 8 in white. I push the doorbell, hear a buzz, and then snap back the heavy bolt. I pull and pull again on the door grip, until I see the brass plate: *Poussez.* Push.

I wrestle with the heavy wooden door until it gives way and I step into the foyer. The concierge appears lugging a garbage bag ready to burst. She looks me up and down, reinforcing what a mess I am—jeans ripped with blood-stained knees and my long hair in frizzy tufts. Bleary- and teary-eyed, I struggle to decipher her rapid-fire French.

"Who are you and what do you want?"

I fall into the chasm between school French and real-life French, but manage to spit out my name and that I'm staying with Freddie Forestier. She scowls and I realize I've forgotten to pepper my sentences with "*madame*" out of respect. "*S'il vous plaît, madame,*" I add. Her face softens and she points to the plain white door on the left. Digging into her apron pocket, she hands me a long, brass key. She says something about "Fréderique told me," "another tall American," and "do not lose it."

"*Je comprends, madame.*" I understand. "*Merci, madame.*" She and her trash slip out the front door.

Freddie has been writing from Paris every few months since we finished college, extolling her expat exploits and asking me to visit. "My flat is in the Marais, the hottest quartier in the city. I swear to God, you would love my place."

But, when I turn the key and open the door, I see that the fabulous flat Freddie raved about is a dark efficiency. Her family has money but it's obvious they're not funding her life here. It's also clear my arrival didn't inspire her to clean. Dirty clothes are everywhere, shoes litter the floor, and worn socks are clumped in a corner. A single sheet and blanket sit heaped on a bare mattress with a note on top. *Bienvenue* is written on heart-shaped paper in red crayon followed by, *Home by eight. Enjoy breakfast. Freddie.*

The red heart transports me back to the first day of high school. I was used to the sting of adolescent cruelty, classmates mocking my height and studiousness, and laughing at my juvenile clothes. They were always too small for my lanky body and more appropriate for someone half my age. I once overheard someone in seventh grade say, "What she's wearing must be her little sister's with those silly black buttons up the front."

"You mean the smarty pants girl who sits in the back with her hair hanging in her face? Total trailer trash."

At lunch, I used to read alone at a corner table in the cafeteria, eating my sandwich, drinking milk from a box. The librarian let me spend recess in the library window seat, my skinny stork legs drawn to my chest, a novel at my feet, as classmates played outside.

Starting in ninth grade, I arrived extra early so no one would see Mother drop me off in her beat-up Datsun on her way to the shoe polish factory and warehouse where she and Dad both worked. It also meant I could sit in first period by myself for a few minutes, watching everyone else arrive. I always dreaded the looks I got when "that tall girl" walked into class.

Someone I'd never seen before sashayed into Honors French early. She was chubby, voluptuous, and almost as tall as I was. Her confidence oozed from every curve and her body had matured years beyond mine. She had light blue eyes, like an eerie Arctic canine, and under a floppy felt hat her face was framed by curly auburn tresses cascading over her shoulders. She wore clothes that would have looked ridiculous on others, like the tasseled scarf draped over her tunic. A flouncy, tie-dyed peasant skirt swirled around her middle and a beaded necklace accentuated her bouncy breasts. She was a hippie chick, a ginger-haired Earth Mother, while I was a flat-chested square in my white Peter Pan collar, black pants, and loafers, my long hair woven into two thick braids along the sides of my head.

She dropped a baggie of cookies tied with red ribbon on Monsieur Loisel's desk, plopped down in the seat in front of me, and turned around. "*Salut*! I'm Frédérique, Freddie for short. I swear to God, your blonde hair is gorgeous. Let's hang out." She leaned over, elbows on my desk, giving me her full attention.

My mouth fell open and I could feel my cheeks redden. I hid my hand beneath the desk so the angry pink eczema wouldn't show. Someone was actually speaking to me. All my life I'd wanted friends and I assumed my unrequited yearning would continue through high school.

I managed a smile. "Okay."

"So…what's your name?"

"Catrine. Catrine Gray."

She nodded, smiling. "Ah, like Catherine, in French. Well, I'll call you Cat."

"If you don't mind, I like to be called—"

"Nope. It's Cat. So cute."

I swallowed further protest. Mother called me Cat, which I hated, but maybe Freddie was right and it was cute.

As other students drifted into class, some who had bullied me since elementary school, Freddie pulled another bag of cookies with a cardboard heart attached from her macramé bag and set it on my desk.

"Homemade. My own recipe with ground almonds. I love to bake but give a lot away so I don't eat too much myself." She winked and patted her belly. "I still do, of course. Tonight, I'm making coffee cake. What's your favorite fruit?"

"Blueberries, I guess…"

"Then I'll add blueberries. Bring you some tomorrow."

"Okay. But only if you want to."

"So, you like French?"

"I love it. Especially literature. How about you?"

"I mostly like the pastries, not the language so much. But my mother's French, so I have to take it. She spoke to me in French when I was little, but I was never very good." She prattled on about her passion for baking and Paris and said she visited with her mother every July. "We stay with my mother's sister, Tante Mathilde, and my cousin Vincent." Her American father sometimes joined them, but usually couldn't because of his law practice.

I smiled and nodded, still stunned about the conversation. But high school wasn't middle school and perhaps our shared Francophilia magically dissolved the social barriers I was used to. Perhaps freshman year would mark a change.

"I'll get a flat and work in my aunt's boutique while I go to pastry school. It'll be good for my gypsy heart." She patted her chest and tossed her hair. "I swear to God, you should come with me."

My mouth dropped open again.

"None of my friends take French, so you're it. One day, you should take classes at the University of Paris—the Sorbonne. My cousin Vincent just started there."

Freddie stopped and sat back. "You know, you're actually kind of pretty. That hair and those brown eyes. But you should wear bright colors—for positive energy—and something more than gloss. You have great lips!"

I heard little else of what she said about boys and makeup, having stopped at "kind of pretty." Mother always said I was too tall and my eyes were too big and far apart to be attractive.

The bell rang and Monsieur Loisel strode into the classroom. I opened my notebook and wrote: An auspicious beginning to high school. One day I'll not only go to Paris, I'll also go to the Sorbonne, no matter what Mother says. I tucked the cookie bag's cardboard heart into my notebook.

Still tired and now hungry, I look around the apartment. There's a kitchenette with a small stove, tiny oven, and mini-fridge to the right inside the entry. Breakfast remains are on the counter, including homemade blueberry muffins still in their tins, two missing. She must have baked them to welcome me. I take one and inhale half in one bite, so I grab a second.

A filmy horizontal window sits high above the bed on the left, and a steel rod bolted at each end to the ceiling serves as a closet. A bathroom with a cheap mirrored medicine cabinet filled with French slimming creams, includes the tightest shower I've ever seen. The living space is too snug for me to practice yoga, but I can't complain about a free place to stay.

I clear the floor at the foot of my bed, unzip my knapsack and make small, neat piles of my belongings. I wrap my fingers around the well-worn, talismanic Eiffel Tower key chain in my pocket, its geometric design pressed into my palm, take it out and hang the key to Freddie's flat on it. It's been my lucky charm since I was ten, a party favor from a classmate's birthday party that had an "around-the-world" theme. We each got a brass key chain from a capital city, and mine was a mini-Eiffel Tower. Of course, I knew it was in Paris because of *Madeline*. I've treasured it ever since.

I drape the linens over the mattress, undress carefully, peeling my jeans from my bloody knees, and squeeze into the shower.

Bliss, until the hot water runs cold.

I find a dry towel in the laundry basket and wrap it around me while I bandage my knee. I slip on Dad's Allman Brothers T-shirt—the one I gave him for his birthday last year. I scrub and rinse my jeans in the sink, and then hang them to dry.

I'm so exhausted that the assault now feels like a blurry nightmare. I arrived in Paris so optimistic and want that feeling back. Maybe things will look better after a nap. I clean the kitchen, count my money, funds for ninety days, and finally crawl under the covers.

Chapter Four

A determined knock yanks me from the depths of sleep, my limbs impossibly heavy. It takes a moment for the fog to clear and to realize it's my first wake-up in the City of Light.

As I come to, the tang of dirty laundry disrupts my delight. Again, a rhythmic series of knocks. Raprapraprap. I rub my eyes and stumble from bed, managing the four steps to the door.

Did Freddie forget her key? Or is it the concierge. Oh, God, I'll have to speak French half asleep.

"*J'arrive,*" I say as I fumble with the lock. I finally get the latch to click, swing the door open, and am face to face with a handsome man wearing tortoise shell glasses and a close-lipped smile. There's something familiar about him. He's wearing black slacks with a jacket slung over his shoulder, a crisp white shirt, and gray tie. He's even taller than I am—over six feet and those blue eyes...I could swim in them.

"*Bonsoir,*" he says, folding into a theatrical bow.

I now I recognize the angular face of Freddie's cousin from Christmas pictures she shared of him, his brother, and his mother—Tante Mathilde—over the years. "*Ah, Vincent Lanier!*"

"*Oui, c'est moi.*" He smiles, nods, and reaches to shake my hand. "*Enchanté.*"

He's attractive in a lazy kind of way. His dark mop of hair, short in back and longer in front, brushes the rims of his glasses. He's a few years older—twenty-five, twenty-six?—and rake-thin with well-defined cheekbones. I rub my sweaty palms on my hips realizing I must look like an unmade bed.

But I can't let him stand in the lobby. It's dark and smells of stew, although Freddie's flat isn't much better. Stepping aside, I say, "*Entrez.*"

His quick glance down at my legs reminds me that all I'm wearing is a rock band T-shirt barely covering my bottom. I must have pillow wrinkles across my cheeks, my hair every which way, and my cheeks burn as I cross my hands over my braless chest.

Vincent says, "*Désolé,*" and then changes to English, his accent thick. "Freddie told me you will arrive today, and I know she will work late. I only want to assure your arrival is okay."

"What time is it?" I wrap my arms tighter.

He pushes up his glasses with his index finger. "It is only seven. You would like some dinner?"

My stomach grumbles a noisy assent.

"A brasserie is on the corner. Outside, you go right. Come when you will be ready." He steals another peek at my legs. "I'll wait for you. *À tout de suite.*"

He slips away. The door closes. I uncross my arms, and bend over giggling, hands on my thighs. Nothing like this has ever happened to me before. But then I see the cuts on my knees. Did he notice?

I pull off my tee and toss it on my mattress. There's only one thing to wear that's better than my jeans. I shake out my long-sleeved black knit shift and smooth it on the bed. I wet a facecloth and wipe away the boot print. I wash my face, and then tug my brush through my long, crazy hair.

When I was seven, gap-toothed with a sun-bleached summer mane, Mother tugged and tore at it and then pulled the elastic over my tangles before she'd loosened a single knot. I was convinced she hated me because my hair was nothing like hers—brown curls cropped close by her own hand. Mine fell to my waist, and I refused to let her near me with her shears.

I looked like my dad with my full mouth and lips, slender frame, and tall stature that, by the time I was twelve, put me in my Dr. Scholl's a head higher than Mother in her heels. I always looked for something to physically link us, like the shape of my eyes or the curve of my calf, but I gave up quickly, my oval face so different from her square German jaw.

I weave my blond strands into a braid, wondering about Vincent. Even if my hair looks acceptable, will he notice my tarnished Timex and worn black dress?

In the bathroom, I open a drawer filled with Freddie's blushers and lipsticks and borrow one of each. A few swipes of pink will do me good. I slip on my patent leather flats and take a last look in the mirror to practice a smile.

I smooth my dress with both hands and step out of the building as a duo of motorbikes whizz by. I walk to the corner feeling a giddy combination of self-consciousness and glee. I'm about to have my first meal in Paris. With a man. A handsome French man. Me, who's never even been on a date.

Despite the late March chill, Vincent waits for me at an outside table under a yellow awning. A sycamore towers over him, its knotty roots punching through the pavement. He stands as I approach and leans in to kiss me on both cheeks. My first ever *bisous.* I take the seat he pulls out for me as he gently tucks the label into the back of my dress. Did he notice it's from Sears?

"*Merci,*" I manage.

"*De rien,*" he says, sitting back down. He cocks his head. "I want to tell you the very first thing, I will not allow you to pay for your first meal in Paris. It is *un cadeau.*" A gift.

I protest but he insists, and so I leave the ordering to him. I haven't eaten since the morning, hunger twists, and I know almost anything will taste good. "We'll both have the steak-frites," Vincent tells our waiter and then points to a listing on *la carte des vins.* His French leaves me limp. There's a surefootedness about him that begins to eclipse my anxiety.

He asks about my arrival and what I think of Paris so far.

I pause, adjusting my dress as I think about my skinned knees and the guy in sweats, but push that aside. "I'm still pinching myself," I say, pushing my hair off my brow and wondering if he can see me trembling. "I've dreamed about Paris for so long. I can't believe I'm actually here." I must sound maniacally chirpy.

The server returns with a bottle of red, shows Vincent the label, and—*squeak, pop*—pulls out the cork. He pours us each a glass after Vincent samples the wine and nods.

"*Santé*," he says. I echo his toast as we clink. I take a taste and by accident, smack my lips.

"You like the wine!"

"It's delicious." I take another sip. "I know little about wine, but I do know this tastes very good."

"You will learn much about it because now you are in France. This one is from Syrah grapes in the Northern Rhône. It will be perfect with our beef."

I take my journal from my pack and note it. Northern Rhône, Syrah, steak. I put the end of the pen between my teeth, waiting to take more notes.

"*Tu es écrivain*?" Vincent asks. "Freddie did not tell me you are a writer."

He pours more wine. As I sip, my muscles loosen, warmth slipping down my arms.

"I'm actually more of a reader. Of French literature. But I do record lots of things. I wrote a lot in college, and sometimes I write stories. But I wouldn't call myself a writer."

"Maybe with this taking notes *habitude* you will become a writer, and I will say, 'I dined with Cat Gray in Paris once...'"

The sincerity in his voice puts me further at ease. "Maybe," I say, smiling. "But would you mind calling me Catrine? My full name?"

"*Désolé.*" He reaches across and touches my hand. "Freddie always calls you Cat."

"She and my mother. But I don't like it much."

"Catrine, *alors.*" He raises his glass. "*Tchin tchin* to your perfectly French name. Where did it come from?"

"My grandmother," I say. "She's part of why I came to France."

"Are you close?"

"Oh, she and my grandfather died when I was a toddler."

He shakes his head. "*C'est dommage.* We lost my grandmother several years ago. I miss her, but cannot imagine life without my grandfather. *En fait*, I would say we are best friends."

"You seem to have a tight-knit family. I know you and Freddie are close as well."

"She is my preferred cousin and we talk a lot. She has said to me some things about you. That you speak French more better than her."

"I suppose..." I say, blushing. Instantly, I'm back in French class. Freddie's and my last names began with consecutive letters, hers the melodious Forestier and mine, the dull Gray (even Grey with an "e" would have been an improvement). We sat alphabetically by last name, one behind the other, and always did projects together. I chose the subject, did the research and writing, and she did what came naturally: the bravado of the presentation.

It didn't take long for me to realize Freddie's approach to education was the path of least resistance—more concerned about partying than intellectual pursuit—and the only reason she was in the honors class was that her French mother insisted.

"You have to help me, Cat. I swear to God, *Maman* will kill me if I get less than a B."

While Monsieur Loisel said I had a good accent and a facility for verb tenses, my speech was tentative and halting, not wanting to risk mistakes. At the other end of the spectrum was Freddie. Her French flowed freely, peppered with Franglais, but with no self-consciousness about how American she sounded. Freddie's nerve was the opposite of my reticence, and I was in awe of the easy way she carried herself. I was just happy to have a friend, especially one as popular as Freddie.

Vincent snaps me back to the present. "So, perhaps we should speak French now?"

I try not to appear nervous. "I'm out of practice since I've been away from the university for a year, but yes, I'd like to. I'm hoping to take conversation classes at the Sorbonne. Freddie said you went there."

Vincent nods.

"If you'll be kind while I warm up, *oui, on parle français*," I say.

He winks and switches to French. "Yes, I will be patient with you, if you will be patient with my English. *D'accord*?"

I nod, my eyes on his mouth, reading his lips as I want to catch every word. Or maybe it's just their softness that draws me in. I focus again on what he's saying and find I have no trouble understanding his carefully enunciated French.

"Do you work nearby?" I ask.

"Yes, my bank is close and not far from my flat. When I'm not traveling to see clients, I always have lunch here."

"So close to Freddie's flat..."

"Yes, I found her place for her because she wanted to be near me. We like to be together and I love that she's always laughing and looking for a good time. Ever since we were little, she liked to be the center of attention."

"And you?"

"Oh, I was always in her shadow."

Soon after I met her, Freddie told me she knew her colorful personality was her superpower. She added, "My mother told me, 'You'll need to rely on your personality to make friends, Fredérique, because no one likes the fat girl.'"

My eyes widened.

"My French mother weighs like two pounds so I know I embarrass her."

"Embarrassed? That can't be true!"

"You're just being nice, Cat. I heard *Maman* admit it to my dad." Freddie's lip quivered. But soon enough she snapped back to her devil-may-care self, which is how I always saw her. She invited me to her pool party the summer after freshman year. She made a groovy impression in her tie-dyed bikini, while my body made none at all in my tank suit the color of mushrooms.

When I was with Freddie, it felt like the air around her hummed. She moved through the world as if she owned it. I found myself trying to match her pace as she pranced around the pool, breathless and a little dizzy from the effort. Being caught in the pull of her gravity helped soften my awkward edges and allowed me to believe that if she wanted me around, I must have something to offer.

She did a cannonball off the diving board and landed amid giddy screams. She lost her suit top in the plunge but didn't care, climbing out of the pool swinging the stringy triangles above her head with no hint of modesty. "C'mon, Cat," she called as she dove back in and then tossed me an inflatable flamingo.

"I can't swim."

The waiter arrives and sets down our dinners, followed by a basket of bread. I lean over to take in its yeasty smell, take a slice, and bite. Perfection. I pick up the utensils, fork in my left, knife in my right—French style.

Vincent asks in English, "Do you understand me until now?"

"*Pas du tout*," I say and he laughs.

"You understand nothing?"

"Damn," I say. "I meant *pas tout*—not everything." I shake my head at my gaffe, self-doubt bubbling.

"*Hé, dis donc*," says Vincent. "Many people mix those up. It is no big deal. You say this, yes? No big deal?"

I nod, but it's hard to shake the embarrassment. More wine helps.

Vincent asks me questions about English expressions and is patient with my French, letting me take the time to find the right words. My mouth is now sticky with Syrah and salty from the frites, and I thank him for dinner. "I'll never forget my first night in Paris."

"Me not either," he says, reverting to English. Again, he reaches over, but this time takes my hand and kisses it. I've felt unattractive forever, but right here, with Vincent, I feel beautiful, and it's a brand-new sensation. I feel myself blush and I suppress a giggle.

The waiter arrives to pour more wine. I tilt my head to the side when I hear, "*L'attention à l'autre est la plus rare et la plus pure des formes de générosité.*" Attention is the rarest and purest form of generosity. The voice of philosopher Simone Weil is as clear as the evening sky but no one's there. Hearing the voice this morning, I was in a fog, but I can no longer blame jet lag. And I can't tell Vincent.

He says, "*Alors*, since you studied French literature at university, tell me what you like to read. Finance was my specialty, but I prefer letters to numbers."

"If you like literature so much, why finance?"

"I'm good with numbers and it made my parents happy. But I have a plan. To start a building company in Normandy with my grandfather and being a banker will help. But I do love literature, so for now, we will speak about words."

We're soon discussing our favorite writers, and I tell Vincent that in addition to seeing sights like the Eiffel Tower, I'm anxious to visit literary landmarks. "Like where Hugo and Colette and Proust lived. And Hemingway's neighborhoods, and where Balzac's *Le Père Goriot* took place. The *rue Neuve-Sainte-Geneviève*, where the boarding house was."

"Well, you speak to the right guy. Have you looked for that street on a map?"

"Not yet, but—"

"You will not find it." Vincent tells me one of his literature classes visited quartiers all over the city where either stories took place or authors lived. "It was my favorite class. Not many people know the *rue Neuve-Sainte-Geneviève* was an actual street, but they changed the name. It's in the Latin Quarter and is now the *rue Tournefort.*"

"Is the boarding house still there?"

"Most historians agree that number thirty on *rue Tournefort*—a tall house with gray shutters—was Balzac's inspiration. If you go to the northwest corner of *Tournefort* and *rue du Pot-de-Fer*, you can see the name etched on the ancient stone wall: *rue Neuve-Sainte-Geneviève*."

My hands fly to my cheeks. "That's the best secret ever!"

Vincent shakes his head. "How can you possibly be my cousin's friend? Freddie wants nothing to do with anything 'literary.'"

He tells me about his relationship with his cousin, what they've done together since she moved to Paris after college almost a year ago, and how protective she is of him, even though he's four years older.

"I understood when I was young and visited her in America. I didn't speak English well, but she still wants to protect me." Vincent laughs, shakes his head, and says in English, "She likes to keep her two eyes on me. It is silly, I know, but she is a funny one, our Freddie."

"Yes," I say, taking a swig of wine. "A very funny one."

"But you, Catrine, you are not like her." He leans in. "You are guarded, I think, like maybe you're hiding something?"

I look down at my lap and twist my napkin. "There's nothing very interesting to hide. Please, let's talk about you, not me."

Vincent shrugs and smiles. His eyes search mine but he doesn't push, and I'm tempted to tell him about my father's recent death when a brazen voice interrupts. "Well, aren't the two of you just *le tout Paris*."

This voice is not in my head, it's Freddie's, and she's wrapping her arms around Vincent from behind, kissing his neck noisily. She has the same tousled tresses, the same flourish, the same wild blue eyes.

"*Bisous, bisous, bisous*," she says and then leans over to grab my shoulders and plant three kisses on alternating cheeks. She turns to Vincent. "Figured you'd be here. Where else?" She looks at me. "Cat, I swear to God, I'm so happy you're finally here in Paris!"

She pulls a chair close to Vincent, reaches to take a French fry from my plate, and pops it in her mouth. She grabs a glass from an empty table and pours herself some wine.

"So, the two of you seem awfully cozy," she says, looking pointedly at me. "Fill me in. I want to know *everything*."

Chapter Five

I must let Mother know I'm safe in Paris, so the following day I head to La Poste to make an international call. On my walk, I pay close attention to what women are wearing. They seem so put-together, most in dresses and skirts along with leather pumps and cute purses. I look down at my jeans and brown boots and feel my pack on my back, knowing no one would ever mistake me for French.

But then I turn a corner and am jarred by the sight of a woman in a natty pea green jacket just like the one Mother wears almost every day she goes shopping. I loved that jacket as a child and thought it was beautiful, just like her. But as I got older, I realized her coat was badly pilled and her uniform of button-up, short-sleeved, calico blouses had dingy armpits and gaped across her chest. They probably fit her as a young wife, but what had become her ample bosom now strained the seams, yet she refused to buy new ones. Her perfectly carved calves, her "flawless gams," as Dad called them, were forever hidden under polyester pants. The only time I saw them was when she wore a dress to church, where I accompanied her weekly for Saturday confession and Sunday mass without complaint, pretending her religious dogma didn't chafe against my need to question everything.

The telephone clerk could be the French pop singer France Gall's twin with her blond pageboy. I give her the equivalent of twenty dollars in francs and Mother's number. She points to a row of confessional-like wooden booths along the wall. "The one on the right." I open the door, pick up the receiver, and breathe deeply. I hear a ring tone on the other end: buzz-buzz-stop—buzz-buzz-stop, and then, "Hello."

"Mother?"

"Where are you? Are you safe? I've been crazy with worry."

The sound of her voice inflames my eczema, triggering an urge to scratch.

"You didn't even bother saying goodbye to your own mother. You have a sacred duty not to abandon me. Would Jesus have done that to Mary? It wasn't very Christian of you." She clicks her tongue.

"Please, let's not fight. I'm in Paris, with Freddie. Like I wrote in my note."

"I can't believe I'm talking to you in Paris, France. What were you thinking going there? Come home and all is forgiven. I've been imagining the worst. You with all those foreigners. Have the men bothered you?"

"Mother," I say, steadying my voice as I recall the assault but refrain from mentioning it. "I'm fine. Freddie's cousin, Vincent, has been very nice. He bought me dinner last night."

"Well, you never know with those people. I hope he's a gentleman and didn't load you up with alcohol. I don't trust that family. Always thinking they're better than everyone else."

Years of experience tell me that across the ocean, her brow is furrowed. It's useless to argue with her.

She continues, "Being around strange men is an occasion of sin, I've always said that. You haven't drunk the water, have you? You'll end up with diarrhea. You can't be too careful. You know, Rose Marie—from Catholic Daughters—said her and her husband," (why can't she ever get the grammar right? It's 'she and her husband') "were pickpocketed when they went to Rome. At the Vatican, no less."

"My time's almost up. Twenty dollars only buys a few minutes to the U.S."

"Twenty dollars! Highway robbery. The French will always overcharge you. Write a letter next time."

The clerk knocks on the booth window with a one-minute warning.

"I have to go, Mother. I only wanted you to know I'm fine and not to worry."

"How can I not worry when you're gallivanting around France, spending all your money, and eating disgusting things like frog legs and snails?"

I'm sure she's wrinkling her nose. "I haven't tried either but when I do, I'm sure I'll like them."

"Well, I hope Freddie's being nice. She hasn't always been, you know, and I doubt you'll make new friends. I mean, how could you in a foreign country and all? When are you coming home?"

"I'll write. Next week."

"Be careful. And Be-A-GOOD-GIRL."

As usual, Mother has the final word and I'm left with eyes brimming. I heave a sigh, leave La Poste, and take a long, circuitous route back to Freddie's to calm down. I cross the Seine to the Latin Quarter, sit outside at a café that faces the river, and order a café noisette. Just as my coffee arrives, an older man passing on the sidewalk gives me a leer and I return to Mother's parting imperative. "Be-A-GOOD-GIRL" pulls me back to a Saturday night when I was twelve. She and I watching television. I said I thought Kurt Russell, who played a cowboy on Walt Disney's Wonderful World of Color, was cute. My first shiver of adolescent sexuality caused a low ache in my pelvis, along with a tickle. "Those eyes and those dimples. He's totally dreamy."

"Careful," she warned. "Be-a-good-girl."

I pictured the words in capital letters: A-GOOD-GIRL. I'm going to hell, I thought, dismissing the dangerous daydream.

From then on, Mother made me terrified of boys, declaring my body a tripwire. But that didn't square with what she'd said about no boy wanting someone so tall. She told me I was skinny as a pencil with spindly legs, a flat chest, and no decent curves. I heard her tell Dad I was "physically ungifted," followed by, "Thank God she has her books."

But then I turned thirteen and practically overnight, went through yet another growth spurt, my body stretching and shifting. I sprouted downy hair in private places, dissolved in tears at the slightest provocation, and pimples erupted across my nose and chin. I started wearing a training bra because Mother said it was a sin to show your nipples. I often caught her sizing me up, shocked at how I was changing. It was as if she never expected me to grow up. I knew she was uneasy with my exceptional height and maturing body and would be unable to explain a woman's hidden passageways and what would soon stain my underwear. She believed everything about the human body led to sin and so refused to talk about it.

But she did buy me a pamphlet at the Catholic bookstore.

For the first time, I worried about how others saw me. I compared myself to the soft, cute girls at my school, and I looked nothing like them. My features were too obvious, eyes too large, nose angular, and my sharp knees and elbows protruded from gangly arms and legs.

But enough of those thoughts. I drain my drink, pay the bill and wander among the buildings of the Sorbonne, knowing I'll be back soon to register for a class, and then around the Panthéon on the Montagne Sainte-Geneviève. On the rue Mouffetard, I pass an open-air market and marvel at the colorful selection of fruits and vegetables. At home, I always went to the farmer's market, the one in the church lot. I bought fresh produce so I wouldn't have to eat Mother's cheaper, less-than-healthy canned varieties. She told me I was frivolous for spending my money on things that took up so much room in the fridge. But every time I shopped there, I thought of open-air markets in France, hoping I'd experience them one day.

Just a couple weeks before leaving for Paris, I ran into Dr. Rousseau, my high school guidance counselor, at the market. As I bagged my blueberries, I heard her familiar voice, and when I turned I saw her short, spiky gray hair, cat-eyeglasses, and thin frame waving from behind a pile of potatoes. "Catrine, hi!"

I waved back and finished my purchase as she approached. She kissed me on both cheeks, then pulled back to look at me. "You're all grown up and how pretty you are. I thought for sure you'd be living in Paris by now."

"That's the plan," I said, my face flushing. "But some things got in the way."

Her bright smile faded. "I heard about your Dad. I'm so sorry. That must have been incredibly difficult for you and your mother." She touched my arm and I felt tears well. I nodded, trying to swallow the lump in my throat. "Are you okay?"

I nodded unconvincingly. "I just miss him."

"I'm sure you do," she said, her smile back. "But he'd want you to move on with your life. Especially after doing so well at college."

"Yes, he would. I'm sure I'll get to France soon."

"Hey, congratulations, by the way. Salutatorian of your class. All of us at the high school are so proud of you."

"Thanks, Dr. Rousseau. It means a lot coming from you."

"Are you still working with your mother? At the warehouse?"

"Afraid I am." I could tell from the almost imperceptible shake of her head she was disappointed.

"Well, it's so nice seeing you, but I have to run."

"And I have yoga class."

"Don't forget, Paris awaits." She leaned in for a quick hug. "*Au revoir*, Catrine."

"*Au revoir*," I echoed as she disappeared under an oak and into the parking lot. Her admonition about Paris nagged.

My purchases loaded in the trunk of Mother's car, I sat behind the wheel scratching at the eczema on the back of my hand and thinking about how Mother had never valued my academic achievements. On the last day of seventh grade, she'd wiped her hands on a dish towel, sat at the kitchen table, and glanced at my perfect report card.

"Straight As," she said, a hardness shadowing her face as she lowered her glasses. I waited for a dig to diminish my grades. It would come.

"Let's thank God you did good."

Well, I said to myself. *You did well.*

"But it's not like you were taking advanced math or anything."

In my mind I added, that's because you wouldn't let me take the honors course. She'd seen no need for algebra II, especially for a girl of twelve, sowing seeds of failure before I even tried. Affirmation of my academic effort would have to wait for Dad, and he was away.

"You'll be a secretary and bookkeeper like me," she said, her mouth in a firm line. I wanted to scream, I'm not you and have no intention of being you! But I stayed silent as she continued.

"You'll have to rely on organizational skills and arithmetic. It's not like you have much of a personality. I mean, why else don't you have any friends?"

Mother looked away and I'd retreated to my room and scratched at the flaring eczema patches on my hand until they were red, raw, and bleeding.

Hands on the steering wheel, I saw that my eczema was still there, but less raw now. I no longer believed I wasn't smart enough for upper-level classes or whatever else I might strive for, but I still lacked at least one essential ingredient for shaping my life: courage.

On the ride home from the market, I remembered the many evenings I had looked through my murky reflection in the bedroom window to the muddy creek running lazily behind the garden. I'd imagined it becoming the wide Potomac, flowing into the Atlantic and all the way to France. As I turned onto our street, I heard Dad's voice. "It's time for you to go, Catrine."

Then I thought about Freddie calling the previous week because she'd heard from her mother that he had died. After a few cursory condolences she said, "My roommate, Odette, just moved out. You know that extra bed won't be empty long. You said you saved a bunch, so come live with me. You know your father would want you to."

"I don't know..."

You can stay as long as you want. Until you figure things out. Rent-free."

I gulped. "Really?" It was almost too good to pass up. "I don't think

I can leave my mother right now. I promise I'll come, next year?"

"Yeah, yeah. Whatever. You're a coward, Cat."

"Freddie!"

"You're almost twenty-three. Make the move."

I hung up in hot tears, angry because she was right. My spreadsheets showed exactly what Paris would cost and I had enough for a few months, but I wanted to live there.

I parked on the street in front of our house since the driveway was full because Mother was hosting a Catholic Daughters meeting. I slipped in the back door with my market bags. The house smelled of stale coffee and I heard Mother from the living room. "…thinks she's doing well at work because she's smart. It's actually because she's my daughter. The executive secretary to the warehouse foreman. I got her started on the assembly line when she was in high school. She's been there for so long, of course, they promoted her to junior accountant."

One of the Catholic Daughters asked, "Will Cat keep living here? That would be nice. You know, so you won't have to live alone."

"She'll probably always be here. Where would she go?"

I stared into the open fridge, the chill cooling the sting of her words.

"She's young. She must want to do something."

Mother gave a little laugh. "She has some hifluting ideas about living in France but she's much too timid to make the move."

Highfalutin, Mother, I whispered as I slammed the refrigerator door. Hard.

"Cat, is that you?" she called, now the solicitous, saccharine-voiced mother for her blessed audience. "Come say hello." When I didn't respond, she pushed open the kitchen door, her fake smile twisting into a mocking glare reserved for me.

"Come. Say. Hello. You can spare a minute. Or are you too good for my friends?" She grabbed my arm, hurting me as she tugged.

"Stop!" I cried, for all to hear as I broke free. "I'm putting my groceries away." Mother fumed while I folded the grocery bags, opened the closet, and piled them on the shelf.

"Let's go," Mother said, once again grabbing my arm.

"No." I yanked my arm and then my gym bag from the closet, the mop crashing to the floor. "I'm going to yoga." She gave me a hard stare of silent disapproval. The back door slammed behind me as I stormed to the car, my upper arm throbbing.

I slid behind the steering wheel, fired up the engine, and drove to the hot yoga studio. The 105-degree room smelled faintly of eucalyptus. Halfway through class, I got into Vrikshasana, tree pose, standing my ground, and staring at my reflection in the mirror that lined the wall. I heard Dad's voice in my mind again. "It's time for you to go."

I wriggled to the top of my mat for Ustrasana, camel pose, sweat trickling down my spine. I went up on my knees, hands at the base of my spine. My head fell back and I dropped my hands to my heels until the pattern on the back wall focused.

"Ustrasana is a key to our heart chakra," the teacher said. "And helps us accept things or leave them behind."

Gravity eased me deeper into the posture, my abdominals loosening.

"Emotions are easily blocked. A relationship's end, the pain of abandonment, and even unkind words can choke our feelings."

I thought about working at the warehouse, living with Mother, and the truth that my life would keep draining away if I stayed. And then something stirred low in my belly. Was it courage? It crawled into my chest and throbbed in my throat, but then I was suddenly nauseous. I released the pose early and folded into Balasana—child's pose—to slow my hammering heart. Then I rolled onto my back and into Savasana—the sweet relief of relaxation.

Sweat trickled from my temples into my ears. I couldn't fully let go so I sat up, soundlessly opening my aluminum water bottle. But the cap dropped, spiraling metallically across the wooden floor. All eyes turned. I mouthed "Sorry," rolled up my mat, retrieved my cap, and fled. As I slipped around the building to the parking lot, the cool wind felt good as it hit my clammy body.

I sat in my car gripping the steering wheel. Rage flared so hard in my belly I could taste it, and then my emotions exploded, sobs bursting. The hard lump in my chest finally let go on another wave of nausea. I opened the door and retched. It was awful, but it brought relief. And clarity. Suddenly, I was sure. "It's time for you to go."

Mother waited in the living room. She stood and started to speak but I cut her off. "I'm leaving," I said calmly, holding my yoga mat like a shield. "I'm going to Paris."

And for the first time, I saw her sharpness blunt. Her posture slumped and she dropped to the couch, palms on the cushions beside her.

"How can you leave me now that I'm all alone?"

"You're not alone, Mother. You have your house and your Church and your blessed Catholic Daughters and Father Ceinture."

Her mouth opened and then closed, as if she thought better about what she'd planned to say. Her face was impassive, but her jaw clenched as I disappeared into my room, and quietly shut the door.

I called Freddie before dawn the next morning to say I was coming, and she shrieked. I pictured her jumping up and down in her trendy flat, her ample body jiggling as she twirled herself in the curlicue phone cord.

That night, I went to sleep reciting: "In an apartment in Paris at the end of the hall, lived a little girl named Catrine who was curious and tall."

Two weeks later I rolled my clothes tight, one piece at a time, and squeezed them into my brown backpack. I tiptoed into the kitchen and looked out the back door, to the patio where Mother was napping on her new chaise lounge next to a bed of yellow daffodils, their trumpets newly opened. My bitter knot of rebellion, the one that had metastasized over the years, kept me from waking her and saying goodbye.

I pulled on my new Frye boots and composed my note:

> I'll be in Paris, staying with Freddie. Will let you know when I arrive. I do love you.
>
> Catrine

I checked my room one last time, picked up my ticket, and wrapped my favorite gray and yellow scarf around my neck. I doubled back for Dad's flannel shirt hanging on my chair and threw it on over my white tee and jeans.

Chapter Six

Freddie takes a few days off work and parades me around to her bohemian hot spots, putting me on display, and introducing me to everyone she knows at the cafés. "Meet my friend, Cat."

I say, "*Salut, je m'appelle Catrine. Ça va?*"

They say hi but no one pays me much attention. I quickly learn that contrary to her claim of having so many French friends, many of them are actually American and British, not interested in speaking French at all.

"I swear to God, you're such a drip," Freddie says, rallying her mates and smiling as she puts her arm around me. "You'll have plenty of time to speak French, Cat—just not with us." After a few feeble attempts, I abandon the effort and do my best to fit in.

When I ask her if Vincent will ever join us, she waves me off. "He's on one of his 'very important' business trips, as usual."

Freddie doesn't seem to want to talk about Vincent—at least not to me. And after first avoiding my polite then curious questions about her studies at pastry school, she finally admits she dropped out after only six months. Her French was weak and the long hours, in addition to her shifts at Aunt Mathilde's boutique, put a crimp in her social life. Her parents were not happy. They had been paying for a bright one-bedroom flat overlooking the Seine while she attended class, but once that ended, their funding dried up.

But she brushes it off. "Being around all those sweets wasn't good for me." She pats her hips. "You know I already eat too many—can't help myself. And those religious things—I'm addicted."

She must mean *les religieuses*—choux pastry buns filled with whipped cream and dripping with chocolate.

The last of Freddie's days off is my one-week mark in Paris. After repeated requests, she finally takes me by the boutique on the *rue Vieille du Temple* so I can see where she works and meet Vincent's mother, Mathilde. "It's an okay shop," Freddie whispers. "My aunt's had it for like thirty years and she designs most of the merchandise. But I swear to God, she doesn't exactly have an eye for fashion anymore. I keep asking her to let me buy from other designers. But at least I get everything wholesale."

"*Bonjour*, Catrine," says Tante Mathilde, coming from the dressing room. "*Enchantée*." She reaches out to take my hand. "Vincent told me all about you."

"*Bonjour*, Tante Mathilde, *et merci beaucoup*," I say. I continue in French, telling her it's so nice to finally meet her and see her shop.

"I'm impressed," says Mathilde. "Vincent said you speak French *comme une vraie française*, and he was right." Like a real French girl. I blush and she turns to Freddie.

"Frédérique refuses. I'm afraid she doesn't like it when I correct her mistakes."

I decide to switch to English. I don't need Freddie teasing me further for speaking French. I tell Mathilde her shop is lovely, and she tells me I can have the same discount as Freddie. Eying me up and down, she says, "I have some sundresses that would be perfect on your leggy frame."

Perhaps my taller-than-average height isn't a defect after all. I'm grateful, even tempted, but my finances require me to be frugal, so I say, "Thank you, but I'm hoping to travel a bit around France, so I'm saving everything I can."

Freddie flashes me a look. "Paris not enough for you? You're leaving me?"

My face reddens.

Mathilde clicks her tongue. "A girl with a plan is a wonderful thing."

Freddie ignores her as she grabs her hair and swoops it into a knot atop her head.

Mathilde reaches behind the counter and pulls out a shopping bag. She hands it to me.

"*Pour toi*," she says softly. "A welcome gift."

Freddie twists around and glares. "You never gave me anything for free."

It's Mathilde's turn to ignore her.

I sneak a quick look in the bag. "Yellow's my favorite color!"

"I didn't know, but they will look lovely with your long blonde hair." She leans in to touch cheeks. "Keep in touch, Catrine. And let me know if you need anything while you're in Paris."

"*Merci*, Mathilde."

"Let's go," says Freddie. "We're meeting friends for drinks." She grabs my wrist and pulls me out the door. "Let me see what's in the bag," she adds, taking it from me. She digs around and hands it back. "Guess I can't borrow it. No way that blouse will fit me."

As we walk along the rue Saint-Antoine, I think about Mathilde's sundresses, look at the flashy clothing Freddie's wearing and the vivid displays in the shop windows. I recall how every August until I was in high school, when Mother took me back-to-school shopping, she'd say, "Only things in black, white, and beige."

Great, I'll look like a nun, I always thought.

She'd add, "It'll be easy to pair things up and you'll need less clothes."

And I'd bit my tongue. *Fewer. I'll need fewer clothes.*

Mother knew yellow and gold were my favorite colors but deliberately ignored my preferences. I had to buy myself a pair of jeans, a gray and yellow scarf, and a golden tee, with my babysitting cash—the sole patches of color in my monochrome wardrobe. But even now, it's hard for me to wear bright colors, thinking they'll draw attention to my height.

But that's going to change with Mathilde's blouse.

Chapter Seven

The day after visiting Mathilde, Freddie returns to work full-time and I'm free to explore the city on my own. Her shift starts at one, so she sleeps in while I get up and head out early.

I pinch myself as I walk across the Seine on the Pont Notre-Dame and then the Petit Pont to the Quartier Latin, feeling so much more Parisian than the day I arrived. I enter the iron-grilled doorway of the Sorbonne's main building, wondering if Vincent walked down this very hall, and sign-up for the last spot in a three-week French conversation class that starts the following Monday.

I feel rather jaunty in my daily uniform of jeans and boots with the addition of Mathilde's gifts: dangly, beaded earrings and a bright yellow blouse that goes perfectly with my scarf. I cross back over the Seine to the Île de la Cité and marvel at Notre-Dame's iconic façade, deciding to save seeing the interior for a rainy day. I buy a jambon-fromage baguette sandwich at an awninged kiosk and sit in the flower garden behind the cathedral to eat. As I watch French children in the playground I'm surprised that I understand their every word. After my sandwich, I take the bridge to wander along the Île St. Louis and buy noisette ice cream at a place called Berthillon, a must-do mentioned in my guidebook. Licking what tastes like heaven, I stroll back to the Left Bank.

The Boulevard St. Germain is bustling as I steal quick looks into one celebrated haunt after another, none of which I can afford: Les Deux Magots, Brasserie Lipp, Café de Flore. I make my way to the Saint-Sulpice church and the Luxembourg Gardens, studying my map and highlighting the places I've visited. It's almost six when I finally return to Freddie's flat. I take a shower, pour a bowl of cereal, and read for an hour. Freddie arrives as I crawl into bed at nine.

"Get dressed. Club time," she says.

"I can't, Freddie. Too expensive. And I want to be up early to see the Eiffel Tower."

"Such a wuss," she says, hands on hips. "No fun at all. Carpe diem, I say." As she redoes her makeup she scoffs at me. "You know the Eiffel Tower will just be a bunch of tourists and North Africans trying to sell you junk, right? It's why I never go." She grabs her poncho and stomps out into the night.

The next morning, I take a bus along the river to the Champ de Mars. Springing off the bus near the Pont d'Iéna, I freeze where I land, my eyes locked on the tower...well, towering in front of me. Yes, there are crowds, long lines, and orange construction netting, but I only have eyes for the tower. I slowly scan the one thousand feet from its pedestals to its tip. As I take in the intricate, lacy ironwork, my chest tightens, and for a moment I forget to breathe. I can hardly believe I'm here.

I spend the rest of the day at Gustave Eiffel's masterpiece. First, I wander around at ground level from the École Militaire to the Place du Trocadéro, circling the lawns, gardens, and fountains below, and then I take the elevator up to the final stairs. My breath catches as the wind tousles my hair. I'm here, in the city of my dreams!

The day is crystal clear and all of Paris stretches out for miles, like a brilliant tapestry unfurled just for me. Montmartre's hill and the white Sacré Coeur Basilica is far, far away, the spires of Notre Dame rise along the Seine, the black Tour Montparnasse dwarfs the buildings below, and the Arc de Triomphe marks the end of the Champs-Élysées. As I gaze out at Paris's creamy white buildings, I imagine amorous adventures unfolding beneath terraced roofs.

Prolonging my experience by taking the diamond plate stairs all the way down, I recall the early criticism of the tower. French creatives like Guy de Maupassant, Charles Garnier, and Alexandre Dumas disdained the—to them—visual atrocity, yet they often ate lunch in the café at the base. Maupassant reportedly said, "It was one of the few places where I could sit and not actually see the Tower."

But I can't get enough of it. Hours later, famished from all my wandering and stair climbing, I stop at a boulangerie and choose an Orangina and a *pain bagnat* stuffed with salade niçoise, a combination of tuna, black olives, tomatoes, hard boiled eggs, green beans, and anchovies—all drizzled with olive oil and vinegar. Far from a mushy tuna sandwich at home.

A tall, thin man in African dress approaches me where I sit on a wooden bench. As Freddie predicted, he offers his wares, but I don't mind—and can't resist. I buy a six-inch tall brass Eiffel Tower to go with my key chain. I'll put it next to my bed so it'll be the last thing I see before I sleep. The African man wanders off in search of his next tourist as I tuck the little statue into my day pack.

Chapter Eight

I jump out of bed Monday morning for the first day of French class at the Sorbonne. As usual, Freddie snores loudly as I get myself ready and slip out quietly.

I practically skip my way to the Latin Quarter and the *rue des Écoles*. Behind a series of arches, the colossal grilled doorway is daunting. Again, I think of Vincent. Did he often come in through these doors? When I find the classroom, I marvel at the high ceilings and tall windows, amazed that these buildings have been here as a university for over 700 years. I choose a wooden desk and the professor arrives, tall and slim, and asks us to introduce ourselves. I learn that my eleven classmates are from around the globe—Australia, England, Brazil, Sweden and Japan. We'll meet for four hours every morning, Monday through Friday. My shyness melts in the company of international companions with common interests. French is our lingua franca and so even outside class, it's all we speak.

Freddie and I rarely cross paths once classes start at the Sorbonne. At least not in a waking state. I'm gone before she gets up and then in bed long before she's back from clubbing. But on the first day of the second week, she forces herself up early for a doctor's appointment and before I'm out the door for class, she says, "You're such a goody two-shoes, Cat, studying in Paris when you should be partying."

I try to take it on the chin. "I'm just trying to expand my horizons. Intellectually. Meet other people—"

She glares at me. "I'm not enough for you? Not intellectual enough? And what about everyone I've introduced you to?"

I bite my lip. "They're great. But that's not what I meant and you—"

"You act all shy and diminutive but you're really just a snob, aren't you."

My cheeks flame. "Freddie! That's not—"

She laughs.

Then she points mockingly at my journal, which has a romantic watercolor of a Parisian streetscape on the cover. "You really think that's in Paris? A little juvenile, no?"

I open the door to hightail it to class, but she lets loose another arrow.

"By the way, the wine you bought at Monoprix was crap. I know you're pinching pennies but can't you spring for something better? Or is that too much to ask the girl who's living here for free?"

I dash away without a word. I know she can evict me at will and I can't afford that, so I double down on being the perfect roommate. I buy a nicer bottle of wine at the end of each week, pick up warm croissants most mornings and am careful to leave the flat in impeccable order: bed made with crisp hospital corners, pillows fluffed and perfectly placed, dishes done, bathroom sink and mirror polished, and clothes neatly piled. But what did the trick with Mother doesn't seem to impress Freddie.

On the Wednesday afternoon before classes end on Friday, she returns and I'm on my bed, memorizing cooking terminology for class. She insists we go for coffee, bitterness behind her words. I'm not in the mood but agree, not wanting to aggravate her.

Coffee arrives and Freddie gets right to the point. "I asked you to come to Paris for how long? And now that you're here, you desert me within a few weeks?"

I take my time undoing the wrapper of the butter cookie on the saucer. I dip it in the coffee and let it dissolve in my mouth. It's not a madeleine and is hardly a Proustian moment, but it gives me an excuse to delay responding. Do I say that now that I'm here, I prefer time on my own to time with her? She drums her nails on the table.

"Sorry, Freddie. I'll do better." I hate that I sound so hesitant. And to my ears like I'm lying.

She looks at me long and hard, but then her face lightens. "Listen, some of us are going to the beach on Saturday. Come along with us and I'll forgive you."

My stomach tightens. I'd made plans with my classmates for dinner at the Sorbonne caféteria, the Resto U, on the rue Soufflot, and then wine on the banks of the Seine to celebrate the end of three weeks together. I really want to be with my class, but I fear what Freddie will do if I reject her again. I know I have to go if I want to restore her trust. My only solace is the hope that Vincent might also be going to the beach, but I dare not ask. Still, I feel a need to explain myself.

It takes all I can marshal to say in one breath, "You know I've wanted to come to France for like, forever, and I'm so, so thankful you're letting me stay with you, and I really appreciate it, but I came to learn as much French as I can and I'm sorry but I'm supposed to see my classmates..." I exhale. "But, I'll tell them—"

"Are you kidding me? A bunch of people you barely know? I swear to God, I thought our friendship meant more to you. I thought you'd be grateful for the invitation but forget I even asked."

She stands and grabs her shawl from the back of her chair.

"Wait, Freddie..."

But she storms away, her peasant skirt swishing, leaving me with the bill.

I never got to say that yes, I would go to the beach after all.

There's no Freddie when I return to the flat, but there is a note in French under the door.

> *Coucou*, Catrine,
> Did Freddie tell you we're spending the day in Étretat on Saturday? It's really warm for April and you must come. My friend, Gaston, will drive. Pick you up at nine.
> Vincent

Vincent is going! I run my finger over the words. Three days away. My heart thrums against my ribs and Mother isn't here to tell me why I shouldn't go. The prospect brings goose bumps. Does Freddie know he invited me?

She returns that evening and ignores me as I sit on my bed licking chocolate from an eclair she made. I manage to say, "I'm coming with you this weekend." I pause to take another lick.

She stops, her back to me, but then moves to the fridge. "Whatever." She takes a swig from the orange juice container, goes into the bathroom, and shuts the door.

Chapter Nine

On the three-hour drive to the coast, I'm folded into the back, my knees knocking the seat in front of me, Freddie and I smushed together with some beach gear. Vincent's childhood friend, Gaston, drives. He's squat and thick with long, badly cut hair, too-tan skin, and painfully crooked teeth. The edges of his ears are littered with rings and his unbuttoned shirt reveals thick, black chest hair. His presence dominates, making me feel small even though I'm many inches taller. He has a smoker's cough and reeks of Gitanes and I wonder how he and Vincent became friends. I suppose some might think the same about Freddie and me.

Gaston glances in the rearview mirror as if he knows I'm sizing him up. His dark eyes lock on mine and I freeze. "He has a temper," Freddie had said when his car pulled up. "Be polite and invisible. Should be easy for you."

"Cookie?" he asks, leering as he raises a buttery biscuit Freddie baked for the ride from a paper bag. I slam my eyes shut and turn away, wondering if he's still looking.

Before we're even out of the city, Freddie's head drops back, her mouth opens, and the snoring begins. I lean my head on the window, pretending I'm asleep as well, but I sneak peeks at Vincent, sitting up front. He's in profile to me, and I detect the shadow of weekend stubble on his chiseled jaw. I listen to the chatter in the front, hoping to learn more about Vincent. I piece together something about Gaston's job at a bar and a girl he met, but they have their own rapid, clipped language, most beyond my grasp.

As we cruise closer to the English Channel, I think about swimming, water, and sand—the story I told Freddie years ago. How old had I been? Five? At Delaware's Rehoboth Beach.

Mother sat reading *Good Housekeeping* in Bermuda shorts and a madras blouse. No revealing bathing suit for her. Did she even have a belly button? She never, ever left her midriff exposed.

Muggy heat blurred the line between sea and sky and sweat trickled down my back. "Come in with me," I begged. "Please?" When there was no response after repeated appeals, I turned and went on my own.

Foamy-edged waves tickled my toes, the water rushing around my ankles creating little whirlpools. I loved the feeling as it sucked at my soles in retreat.

But then without warning, a rogue wave slammed me to the sand. I gulped saltwater as wave after wave pummeled and then the undertow dragged me deeper into the roiling water. As I dug my fingers in the sand, strong hands grabbed me and whisked me back. I stood, sputtering through strings of wet hair. I expected Mother, but it was a man I didn't know.

He stooped. "You okay?"

I bobbed my head.

Where's your family?"

I couldn't speak for the coughing but pointed to a red umbrella. Mother hadn't even noticed I was gone.

I must have drifted off, because I awaken when we slow, leaving the autoroute. We're close since I smell the tang of the sea, sharp and briny, and hear gulls. In minutes we're in Étretat, fishing village turned seaside resort on the Channel, with its apron of pebbled beach stretching across a break between Normandy's limestone cliffs. To the south, I recognize from pictures and paintings, the *Porte d'Aval* arch and *L'Aiguille*, a slim pillar rising from the sea. Atop the rock face to the north is a stone chapel in a sweeping meadow. I wrote a paper on Monet's paintings of Étretat's chalky coastline at college. What luck that of all the northern beaches, this is the one we've come to.

The car jerks to a stop at noon. Freddie wakes as her macrame bag falls to the floor, its contents scattering. "Shit," she says. "Thanks, Gaston for braking so gently." She stretches her arm across my neck and yawns loudly. I help her gather her things—lipstick, a mirror, tampons, a chocolate bar, and a condom…really? She snatches up a magazine clipping about the grapefruit diet. "Give me that."

We've parked next to a car that carried part of our extended group—five other young people in bright beach colors now leaning on the bumpers. Gaston waves and the two girls wave back. Like Freddie, they wear flowered sundresses, pastel flip-flops, and wide-brimmed straw hats. They look like they stepped out of a magazine. Even the boys. Vincent wears shorts, a pastel polo shirt, and brown buffalo sandals. Only one girl stands out from the rest. Odette, who arrives in a third car, alone, wearing a purple felt fedora, cropped black pants, and a black tee. Then there's me in my drab neutrals—khaki shorts, a white tee, and sneakers—looking like an anemic beige pebble among colorful stones. Freddie flits among them all, exchanging *bisous*. Her tresses are long, loose, and curly as usual, but this morning she can't stop tossing them side to side. Today's rendition of "Look at me."

"We're here!" Vincent calls open-armed into the refreshing edge of ocean air and the cacophony of seabirds swarming the boardwalk. "How lucky are we that it's so warm? It's almost never like this in April." He helps me and our gear out the door. "I love this place, but it's years since I've been. With my brother and grandfather when we were teens. He lives close, near Dieppe."

Putting on saucer-sized sunglasses, Freddie interrupts. "And you, Cat?"

I blink, startled by my name. "Me, what?"

"Happy we're at the beach?" She gives me a dark look, meant only for me, and then turns and smiles broadly for the others as she rattles off their names. "You remember Emma and Paul, Sophie, Simon, and Odette—from the café a couple weeks ago?"

When I nod, they give me half smiles and then go back to linking arms, drawing Freddie into their embrace, and talking among themselves in English.

They're all British except Odette, a twig of a girl at five-foot-nothing with narrow hips and a small chest.

She breaks away from the group. "*Salut*, Catrine." She offers friendly *bisous* and only then do I realize the other girls didn't. Were they this cool to me before, or has Freddie been filling their heads with her frustrations about me?

Odette's dark eyes dance under the edge of the purple hat that completes her outfit with simple elegance. She's the only one I recall talking to on my café tour, and the only one who's ever called me by my proper name. She's the one who lived with Freddie right before I got to Paris. As when I first met her, I'm struck by her silky black hair in a pixie cut and angular, film noir profile, cigarette dangling from her lips. A plume of smoke rises beside her and then vanishes in the bracing wind. She says in French, "Your hair is such a pretty blond in the sun, Catrine. Glad you came."

"And I didn't know it was so long," says Vincent, joining us. "Last time I saw you, it was tied in the back." He remembers.

Our group gathers coolers overflowing with food and drink, and baskets stuffed with towels and blankets for our day at the shore. Jubilant revelers are scattered along the strand and music pulses from the boardwalk. We step down to the gravelly beach and traipse towards the gently whitecapped water. The sun shines brazenly in a piercing blue sky.

"Best view—over here!" Freddie directs us to the right, very close to the shoreline, flicks open a quilt, which gets bunched and tangled, and says with a pout, "Vincent, help." He sidles over, smooths the quilt over the sand, and then repeats the motions with several other blankets.

I avert my gaze from the channel's gray-blue water, a mere ten yards away. Yes, I agreed to a beach outing, but has Freddie picked this spot to set me on edge, knowing my fear of water? My throat closes, so I sit on the blanket, my legs folded to one side, and look back at the boardwalk while Freddie orchestrates our picnic. She assigns me a basket. I take out the bread—thick crusty loaves—and easily slice them with her razor-sharp bread knife. The others open pots of pork rillettes from Tours and pâté from Perigueux.

Freddie calls to Vincent, "Where's that Champagne and those flutes I told you to bring?"

He stands, reaches into a huge sac, and pulls out glasses, two bottles and a magnum. "Time to celebrate," he says. Freddie digs out a package of sliced ham from a wicker basket along with at least six kinds of cheese, including an enormous wedge of Gruyère. Emma flips open containers of olives and tapenade while Vincent hands out flutes and then uncorks and pours the bubbly. The whole picnic dance is a study in casual elegance.

I've never been part of an outing quite like this, a grown-up field trip of sorts. With gourmet refreshments. I observe their flirtations and soak up their badinage. When I catch Vincent looking at me, our eyes meet, and the playful warmth in his gaze makes me blush. In high school, flirty looks were always aimed at Freddie. Her big personality, piercing blue eyes, and striking auburn hair drew attention. But in college, I also started getting looks. I always assumed it was my height, but maybe I was wrong.

Vincent kneels near me and slowly pours Champagne into my flute before continuing to circulate, filling glasses. I sip the bubbly, my first ever, willing it to loosen my tongue as the fizzy liquid tickles its way to my belly. I've read so much about the proper way to drink sparkling wine but have so much to learn in the real world. The girls in this group look as if they've been sipping bubbles since they were in diapers. They delicately stick bites of crust spread with *rillettes* and cheese into their mouths. They lick their lips and make sucking runny Brie from their fingers look sexy.

I take an olive and pop it in my mouth. I lean back on my elbows as I chew, feigning ease.

Paul notices. "You like olives, Cat?"

"I do. But until I came to France, I never knew there were black ones, and that the green ones don't grow stuffed with pimento." I laugh at myself.

"Huh," says Paul, nodding slowly, but clearly my point is lost on him.

And then Sophie, a pale-haired girl with balled-up features, throws her head back, curls bouncing, and hoots. Freddie gives me a sidelong glance and then joins her, their laughter carrying an edge of derision. Are they talking about me? I flush from chest to ears while the eczema scar on my hand flares red. All my classmates at the Sorbonne liked me. What am I doing wrong with these people?

But then I lock eyes with Vincent, standing behind Freddie. He gives me a supportive smile and shrugs. My shoulders loosen, and the tightness in my stomach begins to melt away. He's on my side. I watch him make the rounds, bottle in hand, until it's empty. I can't look away from his cheekbones and jawline. I watch how his mouth relaxes when he chews, his wrist twists as he raises his glass, and his legs tense as he stretches them into the sand. The other guys seem immature and silly in comparison. My stomach flutters just below my ribcage.

Freddie catches my coveting eye. A muscle in her cheek twitches as Vincent refills my glass again. He drops to my side smelling spicy and clean, like he's just come from a shower. I feel a frisson of attraction as I fixate on his blue eyes, strong hands, and thick brown hair. My cheeks are suddenly hot. He reaches for a chunk of baguette and makes me a perfect little sandwich of Brie and ham.

"I want one too," Freddie says. Again, with a pout. "But make mine bigger. With more ham."

She takes the sandwich and her empty glass, calling to no one in particular, "More bubbly!"

"So, real Champagne," I say to Vincent in French. "My first taste.

Of any sparkling wine, actually." The bubbles have gone straight to my head, and suddenly everything feels a little brighter, a little funnier.

"Well, you are starting with the best."

"The wine of kings, the king of wines, yes?"

He nods. "Maupassant."

"He's one of my favorite authors and now I know his words are right."

"Well then. *Santé* to your first Champagne." We clink glasses and as I take a long sip, Vincent winks. "Speaking of quotes, have you heard this one? 'Great love affairs start with Champagne...'"

My color rises and confidence surges as I finish the quote. "... and end with tisane." I cock my head. "Balzac."

He laughs. "Not many people know the second half, but then again, Catrine Gray, you are not many people." He switches to English. "You are in a league of your own. This is the phrase, yes?"

He gets the phrasing right, but I'm not sure it applies to me. He pushes a stray hair from my temple, tucks it behind my ear, and then touches my cheek. I think of him touching me elsewhere. My face reddens and my chest tingles.

His gaze lingers on my face for a moment and then he takes a sip of Champagne. He finally says, back to French, "Maupassant was born not far from here,"

"I knew it was Normandy but forgot exactly where," I say, and a deep pang for my dad smarts with the memory of reading the author's stories together.

"Tourville-sur-Arques, near my grandfather's farm. My brother and I used to play in the woods behind the chateau where his family lived."

"I told you I never knew my grandmother, and I didn't know my grandfather either," I say. "But I like hearing about your grandparents." I look to the sky to steady my sadness.

"Speaking of those who are gone helps to keep a part of them alive. Do you know their names?"

His sentiment very nearly melts me as I nod and say, "My grandmother was Catherine—a real Francophile. My dad said I looked just like her. But we don't have any pictures of her."

"And your grandfather's name?"

I run my fingers through my hair. "Étienne. Étienne Gray. The French version of my father's name, Stephen."

But you don't remember your grandfather at all?"

I shake my head. "My dad said he looked just like him and that he was kind and generous, just like my dad."

Vincent reaches over, puts his hand on mine, and then joins me in looking up at the cloudless cobalt sky. He says, "I'm so sorry you never got to meet them." He turns to look at me. "Wow, that sun is hot. Your face is bright pink. This will cool you down." He picks up the cold bottle of Champagne and holds it to my cheek and then touches it to my wrists before refilling my glass.

"Only half. Don't want too much to ruin my initiation."

Freddie has been deep in conversation with Gaston and Simon but seems to overhear this last thing I say, because she gives me another sidelong glance as she intones. "Cat-the-Cautious." She purses her lips then adds, "Wouldn't want to lose control, would we?"

Vincent laughs. "Says the queen of losing control."

But Freddie frowns. "And Vincent-oh-so-proper is getting a bit touchy-feely."

"Cool it, Freddie," he says, all humor gone.

But then Gaston jumps in. "Only half for Cautious Cat," he sing-songs.

Vincent turns to me. "Ignore them." But I feel kind of sick. He reaches over to touch my back. "You're getting pretty hot. We've been out here over an hour already and you're all flushed." He picks up a container of sunscreen, rubs some on my arms, and dabs my cheeks. He takes his jacket to cover my shoulders as Freddie stands and blocks the sun.

"Here," says Freddie, tossing Vincent a tube of lotion harder than she needs to. "Do my back."

He rolls his eyes but rises to oblige.

The bubbles in my head make me sleepy and so I lie back on the quilt, drape Vincent's jacket across my torso, close my eyes, and stretch my arms high. I brush my hands over the warm pebbles, sift them through my fingers and then dig into the soft sand below.

I hear a footfall at my head and see Emma lean down. "Punching above your weight?" She stands and walks away.

Chapter Ten

I wake up from a nap under building cloud cover and check my watch. Two-thirty. I slept for over an hour. I stand, hands shading my eyes. Where is everyone? Only Paul remains, arms akimbo, face down on the far blanket. I take Vincent's jacket and drape it over Paul's painfully red back.

The funk of weed wafts from a trio of dreadlocked teens sitting further down the beach, the pungent pong floating over the remnants of our lunch. A crooked line of empty bottles tilts in the sand and seagulls dive and bicker over leftover scraps. I draw my wind-tangled hair, thick with salt and sea spray, in front of my nose to breathe in the smell, and then lift it to twist and secure it in a knot.

I spy Freddie and Vincent well down the beach, walking towards the *Porte d'Aval* arch, her hand on his shoulder. I watch until they're tiny shapes, wading into the water. I do a brief yoga flow on the blanket to generate energy for exploring on my own.

Emma's put-down echoes as I leave my pebbled post. I reach the boardwalk and find a plaque marking where Monet stood and painted. I turn to look up and down the alabaster coastline, marveling that I'm seeing what he saw when creating his masterpieces. A sign points to a steep stairway winding up the chalky cliff to the north and the Chappelle of Notre-Dame-de-la-Garde. As I start the ascent, I test myself on French seaside vocabulary, repeating the words out loud—*les mouettes; une vague; une promenade*—and then I hear my name.

"Catrine! Wait up."

It's Odette. She joins me on the stairs. "Hiking to the chapel?"

"Yup."

"Okay to join you?"

"Sure!"

"I walked up the south side with Sophie and Emma, but all they're interested in is talking about people they don't like, so I left them."

I turn to point down at the commemorative plaque on the boardwalk. "I took some time to follow Monet's footsteps, right where he painted."

"He did more than eighty canvases there."

"I have three of his Étretat prints above my desk in Virginia."

"I absolutely love him. He and Renoir are my favorites."

"Me too. Plus Sisley."

"I just finished promoting a book on contemporary artists, but I prefer the Impressionists." Odette tells me she works for a publisher of art, architecture, and literature. She'd prefer to be in editorial, but publicity got her foot in the door. "I do love my job, especially because I get to work at home sometimes, usually when I have lots of writing to do. Though that was hard when I lived with Freddie…"

"How long were you with her?"

"Couple months. The chaos made me crazy. There was no room for a desk and she woke me up when she came home at all hours of the night."

"I hear you. She hasn't changed her ways."

"So, Catrine—did I detect a bit of a connection between you and Vincent? It's what the girls were starting to talk about on the walk."

"Oh, no! I guess we didn't hide it very well, did we? Before things go further, is there anything I should know about him? Is he really as nice as he seems?"

"He's a total sweetheart and has had lots of girlfriends. But no one for more than a couple months. He's a fun guy but is serious about his career and has an intense, intellectual side. Lots of girls don't like that part."

I file away the nugget. He sounds perfect to me.

"Would you mind telling me about the others? Sophie, Emma, Paul, and Simon. You all seem close."

"We've known each other forever because we grew up in the same neighborhood and went to the same school. We're almost like siblings."

"All Freddie told me was that they're fun and she likes hanging out with them. Maybe tell me one thing about each?"

"Okay, so Emma didn't get into university, still hasn't gotten over it, and loves being in Freddie's shadow. Follows her blindly. Sophie's the same. Will do anything she says. And well, Sophie's had one bad break-up after another, the last one this week. She's one of those girls who always needs a guy. Paul and Simon are into soccer and rugby and drinking in whatever British pub they can find in Paris. Paul doesn't run too deep, but Simon's actually studying for a master's in public health. He's a nice guy."

We stop to catch our breath, close to the top of the climb. Odette steps off the stairs to pick some wildflowers and hands me a posy in her tiny hand.

"Thanks," I say. "So pretty." I tuck them in the waistline of my shorts. "And Gaston?"

"Sorry about him. I heard what he said earlier about being cautious. Seems to me coming to France on your own is anything but cautious. Gaston's insecure and compensates by trying to be tough. He told me once he hates being short. Maybe it's that. Or maybe he's just an immature jerk sometimes."

We continue up and then take the path that cuts through the sweeping meadow blanketed by red, yellow, and purple wildflowers to the chapel. Odette tries the latch but it won't budge. "*Putain*," she says, rattling the door. "It's locked. I really wanted to go inside." We walk around the side and peek in a window.

"Maybe we should head down," I say. "The sky's getting ugly." I point to the ominous gray clouds scudding quickly from the north above the now leaden channel and towards us.

Odette tells me to go ahead. She wants to take some photos by the cliff and will be down soon.

Descending the stairs on my own, I see Vincent climbing. He's shirtless, his polo squeezed in his hand. I stop to watch him and then continue. We meet in the middle.

"Hey!" he says when he sees me. "I'll walk you down."

"Don't want to go to the top?"

"Only came up for the exercise. And hoping I'd see you up here." He puts his arm around me briefly and I smell his earthy perspiration. We start the descent. "So, where you been?" Last I saw, you were fast asleep."

"Guess the Champagne went to my head." I repeat what I told Odette and point below to the boardwalk and the Monet marker.

"So, in addition to our language, literature, and film, you like our artists as well."

"I like everything about your country." I pretend to lift a glass. "You already know I like your wine."

He grins. "You should be a French ambassador, or maybe write articles about everything you love here. Hope I'm on your list." He winks, and I don't know if he's being playful or serious, so I try to match his flirty edge.

"Every time I see you, you move farther up. But, I don't know..." I move my hands beside me, palms up, weighing the options. "Champagne, Monet, Vincent…"

"Van Gogh? I know you love artists, but him more than me?"

At first I laugh, but then stop my step, chin on my fist, as if pondering his question quite seriously. "I think I need more time with you to decide." I force myself to hold his gaze.

He tosses his head back and laughs. "I'll see what I can do about that."

Sunlight low on the western horizon peeks below dark clouds and sparkles on the water. Early evening settles softly, but as shadows lengthen and daylight drains, the wind kicks up. Vincent stops to put on his shirt and I want to say, "Must you?"

Back at the blankets, I slip into Dad's flannel shirt and wrap it tight to ward off the chill. Sophie and Emma return and I ask about their hike.

"Good views," says Sophie.

"And you?" Emma asks.

I tell them about Monet and the locked chapel. Emma pulls a face.

Sophie shrugs and says, "Whatever lifts your skirt." She takes a swig of Perrier, passes the bottle to Emma, and they head to the water's edge.

Paul, awake now, sits with Simon, talking sports. Freddie, Gaston and then Odette soon appear. The April sun sets below low clouds that stain the sky, purple and black like a bruise on the horizon. Darkness finally descends and the temperature plummets. Freddie announces with a clap of her hands, "Bonfire time!"

Fifteen minutes later, we sit ringing the blaze, shoulders touching, wine again flowing. The flames whoosh in the wind and bath our faces with warm light. Vincent sits next to me and whispers, the tickle of his breath in my ear. "Light is the most important person in the picture." He turns to look at me and touch my cheek.

"Monet, of course," I say.

Freddie must have seen Vincent's touch, because she stomps over and pulls him up to sit by her on the far side of the circle. She runs her fingers through his hair as if he's a child. Hiking up her multi-colored, striped caftan to her hips, she exposes her sunburned knees and thighs as she leans into him. He shrugs for my benefit and I echo the gesture. I make meager attempts at small talk with Sophie beside me, but she responds with grunts and I surrender. Gaston chatters to Odette, so I simply watch the flames dance as I listen to the cheerful babble around me while firewood snaps and shoots sparks skyward. The fire deepens to an orange glow, blue at its core.

Freddie starts a story I can't hear because the fire crackles loudly but a moment later, laughter erupts.

"What was that like?" I hear Emma ask.

"Only like the hottest sex of your life!" Freddie says, cackling, and then looking at me. "Oops." Her hand flies to her mouth. "Forgot Cat's here. She wouldn't understand. Still has her V-card!" All turn to me.

Gaston says, "No way!"

Heat floods my face and I'm desperate to make myself smaller. Could she embarrass me any more cruelly?

The pop of yet another Champagne cork shifts the focus. Freddie, too drunk to twist the stopper has yanked the thing out. The liquid effervesces over the bottle as she raises it to her lips and pours, the bubbly spilling out the sides of her mouth and darkening her dress. Everyone laughs as they empty what's left into their glasses.

Vincent says, "The weather's seriously changing. I just felt a raindrop. We should pack up and—"

Freddie jumps to her feet. "Hasn't changed yet! Who wants a cold final swim?" She pulls off her caftan and everyone but me strips to bathing suits, leaving their clothes in a pile.

Vincent takes off his eyeglasses and turns to me. "Come in?" He crouches down, picks a yellow buttercup from the sprigs Odette gave me, still at my waist, and tucks it behind my ear. "*S'il te plaît*?"

"You go. I'll watch our stuff. Besides, the water's too cold."

Freddie slinks over. "How would you know? You never even put your toe in."

I look down.

"Darn," she snickers, banging her head with her palm. "That water thing..."

I mumble, "Screw you, Freddie."

Vincent says, "What water thing?"

"Nothing. It's nothing." I wave him away.

Vincent stands. "I'll stay with Catrine."

"The hell you will!" Freddie grabs the glasses from his hand and tosses them to me. She loops her arm in his, pulling him hard. "You promised we'd do a polar bear plunge."

He stumbles and looks back. I mouth, "Go," and wave my hand. Freddie always wins in these moments, demanding without grace and taking without permission, believing all is hers.

Gaston says to me, “Watch our blankets? Shouldn’t be tough.” He snickers at his own stupid sarcasm as they all splash into the water. Immediately, the fierce current sweeps them south towards the arch and I now feel raindrops.

I button my shirt and carefully place Vincent’s glasses in the front pocket. I lean back on my elbows, extend my legs, and point and flex my toes. Closing my eyes, I imagine myself fearless, gliding into the icy water with everyone else, cool waves sliding over my skin, my hands finding Vincent. But then Freddie’s face appears in my mind, and Vincent’s slips away.

The daydream dissolves as the timed lights along the boardwalk blink on. I look to where a squall twists not far from shore. The sea is meaner now, no longer flat as swells slap the shore. The rain kicks up and the air feels charged, a storm about to let loose. I stand, hands on my hips trying to spot the intrepid swimmers well beyond the light. Surely, they see how quickly the weather has shifted? Why aren’t they coming out? The wind grabs the wilted buttercup from behind my ear and it disappears.

Rain now falls light but steady, so I stack and fold our things by the fire and cover the piles with quilts. I stand looking down the now deserted strand and feel the ever-building wind with both hands on my head. Finally, Odette, and Vincent run out of the water, shivering as I hand them towels while they warm by what’s left of the fire. The others lag behind them.

A shout rips through the air. “Cat!” It’s Freddie, her voice severe. “Where are the car keys? I swear to God, you better have them.”

“Why’d you move our stuff?” screams Gaston, his face contorted with rage.

I say, “The storm…I thought it would help us leave quickly.”

“But the keys!” Gaston is livid, hands slicing the air. “I buried our keys in the sand. Under the pink quilt so we wouldn’t kick them away. It’s what we always do. But now you’ve fucked up and lost them!”

Paul rushes up, his British accent thick, “For fuck’s sake! You’re kidding me."

I fight lightheaded panic as tears build. Gaston grabs a flashlight from his rucksack, and storms away. Vincent looks at me and then Freddie. "It's not her fault. She didn't know." He asks me for his glasses, but when I pat my pocket, they're gone.

"They were right here. In my pocket."

"Don't worry. I have an extra pair at home." He turns and quickly follows Gaston to the far side of the fire. I see them drop to their knees, scooping sand and piling it behind them.

"Nice," Freddie says with a withering look. She follows the beam of Gaston's flashlight with long strides, her arms pumping. The others follow and join in pawing and digging.

Down on all fours, I pat the sand around the piles, desperate to find Vincent's glasses. Feeling them crack under my knee, I press my lips together, trying to ignore the hollow feeling opening in my chest.. I tuck them into my bra and join the others to find the keys.

After much swearing during a fifteen-minute, sand-flinging pursuit, Freddie unearths our buried treasure. She jumps up, jangling the set of keys victoriously. Everyone cheers and high-fives her as I remain on my knees, hands in the sand. I stand slowly and help lug stuff to the car. I grab Vincent, apologize, and hand him his badly damaged glasses. He takes them with a tired smile. I think we're all done with the drama.

Rain pounds in diagonal curtains and the wind screeches on the drive home. I try to relax but tremble with tension and cold, scratching my hand until my fingertips are sticky with blood. My mother's voice rises like a tickle in my throat.

"You're a bore, Cat, and unremarkable." It's what she always said.

For so long, I thought things would be different if I could just get to Paris. I'd have friends who found me interesting and I'd be confident and happy. But I'm just a tired cliché—one more lonely girl seeking a new life in Paris. Maybe it's time to go home.

As I relive the lost keys fiasco I begin to wonder… Why would anyone bury the car keys? Why not put them in someone's purse or zip them in a beach bag? And why not tell me? Since I was new. Was it a set up? Or did they assume I'd sit there like a loyal puppy obeying orders because Freddie convinced everyone I don't have a mind of my own. Maybe she hasn't convinced Vincent yet, but she's clearly trying hard. And me breaking his glasses hasn't helped.

Gaston pulls up to Freddie's flat and dumps our stuff on the curb in the rain. Vincent gets out to help, but when Gaston calls him and starts to pull away, he jumps back in the car. I try to wave, but as far as I can see he didn't even look back.

The fight gone out of me, I drag the bags inside. Freddie has left the shlepping to me and by the time I'm through the flat door, she's already in the shower using up all the hot water. When she's done, I use a tepid trickle to rinse the sand off my feet and crawl straight into bed. Freddie slices a baguette, loudly sawing, to make a sandwich. But soon, she too is under the covers, snoring and whistling while my toes search for cool spots between clammy sheets. Tired as I am after the fresh, salty air, sleep eludes me, sneaking around hazy margins and then scooting away. I toss unsettled, the room humid, my skin sticky. I plunge down chasms of slumber only to have them broken as I shudder awake. Why am I here? Did Freddie only invite me so I'd be a dull surface off which she'd shine brighter—the blasé background for her flashier self?

I awaken after fitful sleep when daylight streams through the window, thin and pale as skim milk. How will I ever get through this day and what do I say to Freddie?

Chapter Eleven

While Freddie sleeps in, I take a long, hot shower, quietly make a pot of coffee, and slip out to the laundromat to wash our heap of wet, sandy clothes. Doing a bit of penance might ease her fury.

When I return with the basket of clean laundry, Freddie's in the bathroom and the freshly baked madeleines on the counter have the flat smelling like a bakery. I stand by my bed, carefully folding our things. She comes out in a cloud of steam, wrapped in a towel that barely reaches around her, and shoves past me to refill her coffee. She sits on the edge of her bed and begins clipping her toenails, white shards flying.

"I'm really sorry I messed up yesterday," I say. "It wasn't my intention."

"Intention or not, it's what you do."

My stomach twists as I fold the final piece of laundry. I mindlessly weave my hair into a tight, heavy braid.

Freddie stands and gestures with her mug, a wave of black coffee splashing to the floor. "How could you have embarrassed me in front of my friends like that? Are you really so clueless?" She puts down her coffee and begins to pace.

"No one told me—"

"I'm sure Gaston did."

"I thought he was mocking me, telling me to stay put. He made fun of me all day." I take the pile of her folded clothes and set it on her bed.

"My God, why wouldn't he? You're a dull little wallflower Cat, with no panache. The innocent-intellectual-with-no-common-sense who can't let loose for some fun."

But that's not who I am at all. At least that's how a *Seventeen* magazine personality quiz labeled me when I was thirteen. I've kept the result—my very own epithet—tucked away inside and summon it when I need to feel strong. Before thinking, I say, "You're wrong. I'm a Curious-Intellectual-with-a-Streak-of-Rebellion."

Freddie pulls her towel tight at the side and sneers. "For chrissake, do you hear yourself? A rebel? You're an observer. Never joining in. Never doing anything remotely radical. You're actually the dullest person I know."

She picks up her coffee and sips, smiling coldly, as if she enjoys insulting me.

My throat tightens, and I blink hard, trying to make sense of what she just said. "If I'm such a bore, why'd you invite me in the first place?"

She plops back down on the bed, her thighs spreading apart the towel. "I never actually thought you'd come *mademoiselle* scaredy-cat. Get it? Scaredy. Cat."

She laughs at her own joke as an abyss opens between us, one that was always there but that I hadn't fully acknowledged. My head is about to explode. I can no longer hold it in. My body tenses as hurt and confusion morph into rage.

"You invited me every year thinking I'd never come?" I seethe as I slam my mug on the counter and hear it crack, coffee leaking. "What kind of cruel experiment was that?"

"Easy now—,"Freddie says.

"Do you realize how cruel and shallow you are? You never have anything good to say about anyone." A wave of my hand accidentally knocks over the floor lamp, but I leave it. "All you talk about is yourself, all you care about is yourself, and all you want is to be the center of everyone's attention. You use people. You used me just to have someone to kick around."

Her eyes narrow and her lips curl. "I swear to God, you make it so easy, you sanctimonious twat." She sets her mug by the bed and pulls her towel snug around her chest.

I say in a low, near-growl, "You hate that Vincent flirts with me, that he might even like me more than—"

She's up in an instant, her towel falling to the floor, her hands lunging for my neck. I quickly step aside and she crashes into the wall. She spins around, her blue eyes wild. "You boring, neurotic bitch!"

She pushes off the wall and her naked body comes after me again. But I stand my ground and shove hard against her shoulders, my height and reach advantages. She steps back, loses her balance, arms like a windmill, and falls on her bed, bumping her mug on the nightstand. Coffee flies, staining the wall like blood-spatter. She tries to get up but tangles in the bedclothes, slips off the mattress and falls forward, bare ass in the air. The pile of laundry teeters and then tumbles on top of her.

I look down at Freddie and suppress bubbles of nervous laughter.

"Goddamn you," she says from the floor, teeth clenched. "You skinny, uptight loser!"

I calculate how quickly I can grab my things.

She swims from under her delicates, grabs her mug and tosses the coffee dregs at my freshly laundered yellow blouse hanging by my bed.

I resurrect all the resentment I've bottled up for years. "You barely gave a damn when I lost my father and only cared about me when it was convenient for you. Never once did you say you were sorry for all the times you let me down."

Freddie stands, wriggles into a pair of panties from the floor and clomps to the closet. She slips a mottled mango muumuu over her head, transforming herself into a psychedelic nightmare.

She snatches my now-stained blouse from its hanger. "You know Mathilde only gave you this yellow piece-of-shit-de-résistance because no one else bought it, don't you? It's hideous and I never want to see you or this ugly rag again." She pitches it across the room.

"You can be sure you won't, Freddie Fucking Forestier. I'm done with you and done being your lackey."

She points at the door and screams, "Out of here, right now. Nothing of mine is yours anymore! Not my friends, not my flat, and certainly not Vincent!" Her face is scarlet, curly strands of hair stuck to her lipgloss. She wags her finger at me. "He's my cousin and my friend and don't you even think about contacting him."

She grabs a madeleine, and hurls it, hitting my belly. She laughs half-crazed, on the edge of hysteria. She waves her other arm high, brandishing her bread knife like some wild commando. Another madeleine flies and smacks my head. "I swear to God, you think you're so special—speaking perfect French and acting all smart. Well, you're not so special and no one likes you."

"That's not true. Vincent likes me and that kills you, doesn't it?"

"I want you gone." She pummels me with the last three madeleines.

"You're jealous, Freddie. He's your cousin for God's sake. It's gross."

She bolts across the room, jumps onto the bed behind me and grabs my braid. She yanks my head back. I struggle, arms flailing. Then I feel a rhythmic, sawing pressure at the base of my neck. A sound like... ripping...Oh God… Oh my God, she's cutting my hair! I scream as my foot finds the bed and pushes off. I reach back to my neck to where my hair was and touch my long, thick braid, hanging by threads.

Freddie steps back, holding her bread knife high. I open my mouth but nothing comes out. My hair. My long blond hair... gone.

I stand, lunge forward and whack her arm until the knife goes flying, skittering across the floor. I'm shaking, my chest heaving. Freddie massages her arm where I hit her and her blue eyes are wide as if she can't believe what she did.

But then her gaze darkens and the corners of her mouth turn up into a demonic sneer. "You got what you deserve." She stomps to her bed and grabs her macramé bag. She pulls her knit poncho from a hook and slips into sandals. "Be gone before I'm back, bitch." She slams the door behind her.

Chapter Twelve

Silence rings in my ears. "Oh God," I finally sob. "What did you do?" I feel boneless as I sit on the bed and cry audibly and then hysterically until the buzzing in my head subsides. I swallow a lump in my throat.

Terror takes over and I drag the plastic chair in front of the door to jam it beneath the latch. Madeleines squish under my feet as I move to kick the knife deep under the fridge. My legs give out and I slump to the floor. I put the heels of my hands to my eyes, but the harder I press, the faster tears flow. I lower my head between my knees to hold myself together. I've lived so long with such quiet seething. Then rage finally boiled over. And now this humiliation. I give over to more sobbing until I hear distant footsteps in the foyer. I hold my breath.

The steps move away and I'm finally able to calm my breath. I force myself up, and totter to the sink. My braid hangs heavy, pinching my hairline where still attached. I take scissors from a drawer and do what I must. I reach behind my neck, close my eyes, and snip the hairs. Quickly. I pick my severed plait from the floor, run my fingers along the ridged weave as I cradle it limp on my palm. I rake my fingers through what's left of my hair, touch the ragged ends, and know I'll never forgive her. Ever.

I must get out of this flat.

I stuff my things, coffee-tainted yellow blouse and all, in my backpack. I grab my toiletries from the bathroom, careful not to look in the mirror. I coil a rubber band around the severed end of my braid, shroud it in a length of plastic wrap, and then zip it in my pack's top pocket. I pin back my hacked tresses with two barrettes, leave the key on the counter, and hoist my bag to my back. I slide the chair from the entry and before I slip out, crush what's left of the madeleines, leaving the mess for Freddie. I take a deep breath in the foyer, momentarily fight back nausea, and then escape out the big wooden door, letting it slam behind me.

I have no idea what to do or where to go. Most of the people I met in French class are gone. And the few that are left are probably mad I didn't go to the final celebration. Why did I invest so much time and energy in Freddie? Didn't a part of me know she couldn't be relied upon? And even if her crazed anger cools, and I doubt it will, I know for a fact mine won't. Ever. She's ruined everything. I touch what's left of my hair. I'm on my own now.

As I adjust my pack's straps, feeling very alone, a voice seems to call from across the street. "*L'homme ne peut découvrir de nouveaux océans tant qu'il n'a pas le courage de perdre de vue la côte.*" Man cannot discover new oceans unless he has the courage to lose sight of the shore." André Gide? Can it be I'm hearing voices again? Am I to be lonely and crazy? The words themselves are helpful though, and so, with nothing left to guide me, I gather my resolve, cross the street toward the disembodied voice, and proceed to put several neighborhoods and a river behind me while I sort out what the heck to do next.

I relocate from the Seine's Right Bank to the Left and find a youth hostel near the Place de la Contrescarpe with a vacancy and bunk-bedded dorms—the fourth one I try from the list in *Let's Go*. It's cheap and clean and will be home for however long it takes to find a new flat. I will not go back to Freddie's. I will not fly home with my tail between my legs. I will not give Freddie or Mother the satisfaction. I'm on my own, but I can do this. I'll get a job to pay for rent and stay as long as I like.

Lionel, the cute Australian at the hostel's front desk, his long brown hair falling to his shoulders, gives me a funny look when he checks me in. He's probably staring at my lacerated locks but is too polite to say anything.

"What brought you to Paris?" I ask as I fill out the registration form.

"I finished uni last December and am doing a gap year in Europe. But I partied way too much in Greece. Ran out of cash so here I am for a few months."

"So, I'm not the only one with money problems," I say, smiling. I can tell he likes me by the way he leans in and smiles back. Until Vincent, I rarely had any male attention. Have I changed since I arrived in Paris?

"Why are you in Paris and how long are you here? At the hostel?" Lionel asks.

"Only a few days, I hope. Until I find a flat. It's my first time in France and I want to stay as long as I can. So, I also have to find some work."

"I'll let you know if I hear of vacancies. Owners often ask me to post them on our board." He looks down at my form and gives me a little salute. "See you round, Catrine."

"See you. And thanks." I give a wave and walk down the bright hall to the women's dorm. My first task is to wash my yellow blouse. A little vinegar and dish soap from the hostel kitchen do the trick. I hang it to dry from the bunk frame near my pillow. I skip dinner and collapse in my upper bunk.

Tomorrow, I'll deal with my hair.

Chapter Thirteen

For years I've put off cutting my hair but now the decision's been made for me. Mother would probably thank Freddie for her troubles. She always told me, "Men like long hair, so a shorter style is better—less temptation."

But I'm determined to make the best of what happened, hoping a *coiffeuse* can fix my severed tresses. I ask the young French woman in the bunk below mine if she knows where I can get my hair styled. She suggests I try the budget salon—*le salon de beauté*—that caters to students. "It's close. A few blocks away." She gives me the quick directions.

I cross my fingers and head out. On my way, I pass a wine shop whose window displays bottles of the red wine Vincent and I shared the night of my arrival in Paris. It hits me that I don't know how to get in touch with him to properly apologize and offer to pay for new glasses. He didn't appear angry two days ago, but I'm sure he's upset with me and it's why he never even said goodbye. We had such a nice walk at the beach and I absolutely want to see him again, but maybe not so soon. I'll let some time go by while finding my own place. I'm actually tentative about facing him after my blunders and who knows what kind of lies Freddie concocted? Certainly, he'll believe his cousin over me. I push away the thought and resolve to swing by the boutique when Freddie's not working, hoping her stories haven't poisoned Mathilde against me.

As I approach the salon on a cobblestoned street tucked behind the Sorbonne, I hear a voice behind me.

"*Une femme qui se coupe les cheveux est une femme qui s'apprête à changer de vie.*" I turn side to side and see only sidewalk.

"It's Coco," the voice continues. "Coco Chanel."

In the distance I hear tinkling laughter, like a Disney fairy. "Coco. Coco Chanel."

Could she be right? A woman who cuts her hair is about to change her life? Maybe a change is exactly what I need.

Emboldened, I enter the salon. On the wall is a picture gallery of famous French women, each with a signature hairstyle. I focus on the photo of Mireille Mathieu, from the Ed Sullivan Show, sporting a bob. I point and ask the young *coiffeuse*, "Maybe something like that?"

An hour later, I spin around to see my reflection and gasp at the young woman staring back. Her face is framed by a stylish, jaw-length cut, her neck graceful, her brown eyes soft. "Wow," is all I manage. For the first time my face doesn't look too thin nor my eyes too big. The shorter style swept back from a side part makes my blonde hair look like it's been highlighted. Is it really me?

"Now make it your own," the hairdresser says. "So you look like yourself and not a famous singer. You have a pretty face so you mustn't hide it." Her fingers brush my roll of Mireille Mathieu bangs to the side and smooths the back of my sleek new bob. She squeezes my shoulders and puts her face next to mine as we look in the mirror together. From nowhere, my eyes fill.

"It looks nice," I say, shocked I believe it. And yes, maybe even a little pretty.

I wander from the salon, bound for nowhere in particular, swinging my new bob. With no hair to impede them, the earrings Tante Mathilde gave me sway in unison and it's a surprising new sensation. I turn down streets and cut around corners, catching my reflection out of the corner of my eye as I pass shop windows and cafés.

It's almost May and the afternoon breeze is warm as I duck into Shakespeare and Company, the renowned bookstore on the Left Bank across the Seine from Notre-Dame. I inch across creaky wooden floors and through the maze of shelves jammed with books and journals. I stumble on a corner dedicated to French fashion and find an illustrated biography of Coco Chanel with an appendix of her maxims. I sit on the bottom rung of a library ladder and run my finger down the entries: first page, second page and there it is on page three—A woman who cuts her hair is about to change her life. Let's hope you're right, Mademoiselle Chanel.

Back at the hostel, I ask for Lionel and am told he's off for the next two days. I then scan the bulletin boards and copy down addresses of flat owners seeking tenants. I look at a dingy basement studio and a few cramped student flats with three to a room near the Sorbonne. I'll settle on one if I must, but even thinking about them makes me blue. Gray, overcast skies don't improve the picture. As if to deepen my mood, when I walk around the Pantheon a bloated cat with jaundiced eyes darts from behind a parked motorbike and jumps on a garbage can to watch me. It opens its mouth wide and hisses, and a sudden whiff of dog *merde* makes me watch my step. Paris can be downright depressing.

On my second day of searching, I follow up on flat listings posted at the Sorbonne, but they yield nothing. They've already been taken or they're dark and stink of cigarettes.

My third morning, however, dawns hopeful when Lionel approaches me at breakfast.

"Good news," he says and hands me an address. "This flat is a fifteen-minute walk and the owner is anxious to rent it. It just came in and I haven't even posted it yet. I wrote you a recommendation on the back. If you get there right away, it's yours."

"*Merci*, mate!" I say as I take the letter and push away my tartine. I get up to leave and this time, I give him a salute and then step around to give him a hug.

"By the way," he says, "your hair looks great."

I blush, thanking him as I sweep my bangs to the side and tuck a tuft behind my ears.

The six-story building on rue Monsieur le Prince is a few blocks from the Luxembourg Gardens. I press the buzzer next to the wide ruby door and the concierge lets me in. She introduces herself as Madame Vauquer. Wide-bottomed and wearing a shapeless floral housecoat, she has short hair dyed a purplish shade of red, spiking in all directions around her pale, puffy face. Her build is sturdy, made for hauling heavy things. Her smile reveals a missing tooth, giving her a touch of the sinister. She could easily be a character in a Victor Hugo novel.

We pass through a stone archway leading to a central cobbled courtyard. She points to her apartment on the ground floor, the kitchen door and lace-curtained window looking onto the courtyard. The flat I've come to see, an old *chambre de bonne*—a former maid's quarters—is in the building's eaves up six flights of stairs accessed across the quad. She leads the way and motions for me to follow.

Thinking about the assault on my arrival day, I blurt, "Is this neighborhood safe?"

"Of course it's safe. Would I live here if it weren't?" We pass through a door and reach the stairway. She hits the light switch and the stairwell lights sputter on.

"You go," she says after two circular flights of stairs. "To the top." She's short of breath and coughs, long and loud. "Left side. Door's open."

I practically run up the remaining stairs. The garret flat's ceiling slopes down sharply beside thick wooden beams. It has faded pink toile wallpaper, threadbare linens on an iron-framed bed against the wall, and not one but two windows. It's cozy, with a thick rug I can use for yoga. I open the window to a chorus of impatient drivers leaning on their horns. Across the neighborhood I see a magnificent mosaic of rooftops with red terracotta chimney pots, one melding into the other. The flat has a sink but no kitchenette, but I'll make do with a hotplate and saucepan. I try to forget the shared toilet and shower down the hall. "Perfect," I say out loud, spinning around on one heel.

Back downstairs, Madame Vauquer sweeps the courtyard. I say, "I'll take it."

She pauses and smiles but then her mouth sets in a straight line. "A month's rent. Up front. In cash."

"Deal," I say. I follow her into her little white kitchen to sign the month-long lease. She's nosy in a pleasant, somewhat maternal way, asking question after question as she hands me a pen. "Why are you in Paris? You're a student? You have a boyfriend? Do you stay out late?" I answer her with appropriate reassurances and leave out the fact that I'm looking for work. She says I can use her phone for local calls. Five francs each. Again, cash.

"When may I move in?" I ask, calculating what another night at the hostel will cost.

"You paid me. The flat is yours right away."

I have funds for an additional four weeks. Now, I must find a job.

I return to the hostel with a note and a box of eclairs for Lionel to thank him for his help. He gives me a hug, and says, "So glad I could help." After packing, I put my hands behind my hips, tighten my thighs, and stretch, arching my back into a standing camel pose. I ease out of the posture, pick up my bag, and move to the help-wanted board. I scan a dozen listings for au pair positions and a few for maids, and jot down the numbers for the nanny jobs. It's not how I want to extend my stay in France but caring for children would surely beat mopping floors.

That afternoon, I head to my new flat, but feel I might get sick when I pass a *cordonnerie* with its doors open. The smell of shoe repair shops was one of my favorites until I worked at the factory. The day-in day-out smells of leather, oils, and chemicals, even in the warehouse offices, gave me headaches and now reminds me of what awaits me in Virginia. I will not go back there.

I move into my place, determined to take Coco's advice to be who I want. I hang the big brass key on my keychain and beam as I put it into the lock of my very own room. I enter and fold into Downward Dog on the pink shag rug until my tight calves release and my biceps ache. I drop to my knees, crawl to the bed, and pull myself up to stand. Then I fall, face first, on the mattress, smiling again. I'm in Paris, with a place of my own, a room with a view. Of rooftops perhaps, but they're my very own Parisian rooftops.

On the first full day in my new flat, I explore my new neighborhood for hours: the Odéon Theater, the Luxembourg Gardens, the streets that surround them, and the narrow lanes between the Boulevard Saint Germain and the Seine. By day's end, I'm familiar with every street, café, patisserie, and shop within half a mile.

But all I can think of is Vincent and meeting him for a glass of wine. I resolve to find him, even if I have to risk seeing Freddie. Tomorrow. Definitely, tomorrow. I'll stop at Tante Mathilde's boutique to ask her how to contact her son.

Chapter Fourteen

The following morning, I summon every ounce of bravery I can and walk across the Seine to the *rue Vieille du Temple*. I arrive fifteen minutes before the shop opens at ten and sit with an espresso in the shadows of the café across the street. Mathilde soon arrives, unlocks the door and then rolls up the shades. But then Freddie shows up. What is she doing here? She never works this early. A few minutes later, Mathilde comes out the door and waves down a taxi. Maybe she has an appointment? So much for my first attempt. I leave francs on the table and when a bus stops in front of me, I scurry away, undetected.

As I walk with little energy towards the Seine and the Pont Louis-Phillipe on the way home it hits me. How could I have forgotten? Vincent said he often had lunch at the brasserie where we had dinner. Might I run into him there? I turn on my heel to head back into the Marais. It's likely a foolish hope but I'm suddenly bursting with optimism. I slow my step and take a couple detours through the Place des Vosges and the Centre Pompidou to kill some time. I want to arrive just after noon.

I can't believe my luck. Across the street sits Vincent, his back to me at our table under the sycamore. I feel my temperature rise as I figure out what I'll say. I knew last night but my mind is now blank. I cross the street but stop short when two businessmen in dark suits arrive, shake Vincent's hand, and sit. Well, at least I now know that he does lunch here. But there's no way I'm interrupting their meeting.

I turn and walk to the corner to catch the bus back across the river to *La Poste*, not far from my flat. I call Mother to give her my new address. Even before she answers, I'm scratching my hand.

"I told you it's too expensive to call," she says.

"I'll be quick. I wanted to tell you I moved."

"What happened with Freddie?"

"We had a misunderstanding."

"She kick you out? I told you she only hung around with you because you helped her with French."

"I'd rather not say."

"Was it about paying rent? It's always about money with those people..."

The Queen of the almighty dollar misses the irony.

"Mother. It's not about money and I'd prefer not to talk about it."

"What do you want to talk about then? You called me. Do you have something to say?"

"I wanted to give you my new address in case you want to write."

Silence.

"Okay, well...I also got my hair cut."

"Must have been ridiculously expensive in Paris. What did they do to you?"

"It looks a little like Mireille Mathieu—you know, from Ed Sullivan."

"Of course. She sings 'Ave Maria' like an angel. Father Ceinture has her album." She pauses. "But wait, it's that short?"

I run my fingers through my bob. "I was ready for a change."

"So now you're running around Paris, alone, looking like a French temptress?"

I ignore her taunt and clear my throat. I can almost see her pursing her lips and crossing her arms.

"Where are you staying? Can you afford it?"

"I can."

"They miss you in accounting. I told them you're coming home soon, but they'll only hold your job for a few more weeks. You should feel lucky, especially with so much unemployment."

"I'll let you know," I say with a sigh. I don't dare tell her I'm looking for work here.

"Well, be careful and I'm sure I'll see you soon. Once you realize you made a mistake."

I end the call and think, I've done it, Mother. Even though you'll never give me credit. I've done what I always wanted despite your protestations.

As I walk through a pocket park on my way home, I pass a father sitting on a bench, reading to his daughter. I sit across from them. I feel a pang of longing for Dad and wonder, as I so often have, how he ended up with someone like Mother. They met at a company barbecue. He drove a delivery truck and she was the factory foreman's assistant—the "top girl" at the plant. He said her long, toned legs with delicate ankles and high arches, like a dancer's, caught his eye.

"What else did you like?" I asked once when I made a delivery with him.

"She was always so organized and took care of everything. My route details, our dates, and even before we married, my bills. She made me feel safe and always remembered things I forgot. I'd be a disaster without her."

He paused for a moment and then added, "She was funny and made me laugh."

Mother funny? Maybe behind their closed doors but she was always deadly serious with me.

Dad initially made local deliveries, but right after they married, Mother made him apply for the long-haul position. It came with a raise, overtime, and a healthy per diem.

When I came along ten months into their marriage, Dad was away five nights a week, but it got Mother what she wanted: out of their basement apartment and into the little white house around the corner.

But Mother wasn't satisfied. There was a kitchen to repaint, furniture to buy, chairs to reupholster, a patio to build, and bathroom tile to replace. And every year Mother upped her contribution to the Diocesan

Bishop's Appeal to get her name in the parish bulletin. Dad's miles on the road financed Mother's domestic and religious obsessions. I hated that he was always away, but knew he delighted in his hours on the road, singing along with the Allman Brothers and the Stones, music Mother deemed "too noisy." But over the years I found myself more and more angry at him for not standing up to her and for me.

Once, at fourteen, I dared ask Mother, "Why do you let money color everything?"

She'd hurled back, "Maybe if you thought less about literature and more about dollars and cents, you'd realize what life actually costs."

I swallowed retaliation, knowing it would upset Dad. If I asked him how he put up with her shit he always said, "If she's happy, I'm happy."

Eventually, I'd figured out my own way of dealing with her. Avoiding certain subjects, saying what she wanted to hear, and doing as I was told, or at least pretending to, made my life easier as well.

Dad told me there were things I didn't understand, but he didn't tell me what they were.

Now and then through the years, right before bed, I'd see Dad pull Mother into his arms and slow dance as he hummed a tune. She nuzzled into his neck and once I saw she was crying.

So often she fretted about the Church, like a frightened kindergartener afraid to color outside the lines. Was it a sin for Dad to miss Mass when he was on the road? Did not going to church on Holy Days of Obligation make him a "fallen Catholic?"

"Don't go getting ideas," Mother said. "He's an adult and can make his own decisions, but me and him are responsible for your soul."

He and I, Mother.

Dad often came home from work at dawn because he'd done an overnight haul. One Saturday when I was sixteen, he returned from New York City with a white paper bag filled with bagels and a tub of cream cheese.

"Dear Lord," Mother said. "What are those and what did they cost? They're Jewish things, right?"

She ended up putting most of her bagel back in the bag. "Too chewy for me."

God forbid you enjoy something from someone else's religion, I wanted to say. But she would have replied, "That's right. God does forbid it."

What I did say was, "Well, I like them." I reached for the bag to have another.

Chapter Fifteen

It's the third morning in my flat and I'm feeling confident about being on my own with a new look, my own agenda, and no roommate to please. Though I've not totally recovered from the row with Freddie—the ache deep in my chest tells me so—acceptance has settled. It's been a week and she hasn't tried to find me. She's probably relieved I seem to have vanished into thin air.

I tiptoe down the hall to the shared bath and step into a tepid, half-hearted shower. As I rinse soap from my body, the voice of Auguste Rodin startles me. "*Rien n'est une perte de temps si vous utilisez l'expérience sagement.*" Nothing is a waste of time if you use the experience wisely. I wonder why Auguste has found me naked in the shower rather than Coco, but the sculptor's wisdom gives me a sense of freedom.

I take the bus to the sprawling flea market I've read about—*le marché aux puces*—throbbing with life at the Porte de Clignancourt. The body odor of the young man seated next to me is powerful, but I can't change my seat as the bus is jam-packed. I'm anxious to buy a secondhand raincoat so that not only will I be protected from the frequent downpours, I'll look like every other *Parisienne* in my beige, belted trench. For once I'm pleased to be clad in taupe. I look like a local and not an American.

My job search starts two days later after Madame Vauquer tells me no self-respecting French person would conduct interviews on a weekend. On Monday, I'm hopeful as I swing by the hostel to say hi to Lionel and ask if he's heard of any job vacancies.

"Afraid not," he says, "but check the bulletin board. Something may have come in overnight." There actually are a couple new listings, so I jot down names and phone numbers, and then, with my French flowing freely, make calls from Madame Vauquer's kitchen while she's at the market. Surely, I'll find a family needing childcare for the summer.

But after a long week and a half of inquiries and an occasional, unsuccessful interview, I'm feeling dejected. I decide that if I run out of money and days, I want to at least have created memories of enjoying the lilacs and hidden spaces of springtime Paris, so I cut off my single-minded search by three o'clock each afternoon.

I stroll along the river, go up and down the stairs of Montmartre, and explore narrow medieval lanes and broad Haussmann boulevards, imagining secret gardens and hidden courtyards behind monumental portals. I spend evenings in galleries attending free lectures and reading books on park benches. Beneath dazzling light streaming through stained glass windows, I visit the Sainte Chapelle for a Bach violin concerto, the vaulted ceilings providing perfect acoustics and the woodsy smell of incense warming me. I sit at cafés under colorful awnings and pass time journal-writing and people-watching, my glass of Perrier lasting hours. I exhaust my list of must-see sights and can now identify the arrondissements by number. I've come to enjoy the breeze on the back of my neck, and often lift my hands to tousle my hair. Perhaps because my cut has me looking much less casual, I find myself attracting double-takes from men. I smile coyly and then look away.

One Saturday morning after ten days of looking for work, I'm on my way to Monoprix for groceries. A man on a bicycle passes by on the Boulevard St. Germain and I swear it's Vincent. I hurry to catch up as he stops at a light. But despite the resemblance, it's not him. My heart sinks. I must find him once I land a job.

But the specter of joblessness continues to thrum, raising its ugly head over coffee every morning as I count my remaining francs. My hand shakes and my stomach hurts as I raise my cup. For some reason, I feel the need to find a job before seeing him. And so I cross various Parisian parks with pebble-kicking frustration as I trek past cooing pigeons from one interview to the next.

But on day eleven of my search, I'm optimistic as I leave the Haussmann building near the hills of the Parc des Buttes-Chaumont in northeast Paris. The skinny American wife with a black headband really seemed to hit it off with me. She even told me she liked my hairstyle. The job would be for the two years the family is in Paris. And while I'd prefer working in a French household, if the job keeps me here, I'll accept. Though she says she's seeing two more candidates that afternoon as she walks me to the door, she smiles and touches my shoulder saying warmly, "I'll call you."

Outside, the sun is shining. I don my sunglasses feeling cool and sure I landed the job. Which means I'll try to find Vincent tomorrow. I'm in a mood to celebrate.

The long bus ride home takes me through unfamiliar neighborhoods. After an hour, we enter the Marais in rush hour traffic. The bus slows with a hiss, stops, and opens its doors. I glance out the window. My breath catches. Freddie sits outside a café with a group of friends I don't recognize, a pitcher of beer on the table. I pull my sunglasses down my nose and watch her holding court. The sight of her ginger curls heaped high on her head like a bird's nest hurls me into in a vindictive stew and my blood pressure surges as if I'm back in her flat, the knife at my neck.

While the bus idles, Freddie and friends stab out their cigarettes and drain their drinks. Freddie tilts her beer to catch the last foamy drips and then throws her head back to laugh. I push up my sunglasses but can't release my gaze.

As the bus doors begin closing, impulse overwhelms me. I leap up and stick my foot between the flaps. They fly back open and I jump to the curb. Freddie turns as I stride toward the café tables.

It takes her a second to recognize me. She stands. "What the fuck? You didn't leave?"

I catch her off guard as I raise my open hand. Her hands fly to her face but I stop short of smacking her cheek. If I slap Freddie in public,

I'll be stooping to her level. Still, I feel compelled to hurt her in some way.

"Why would I leave?" My face is impassive, but Freddie's is furious. Her nostrils flare, her blue eyes bulge, and her mouth is open.

"Why would I give up my own place and a new job?"

Her mouth stays open but she says nothing. I turn and walk away, giving a little wave over my shoulder. "Bye, bye, Frédérique."

A few feet away, I hop on a different bus with its doors open. I don't really care where it's headed, as long as it's far from Freddie. The bus continues straight ahead from the rue Saint-Antoine to where it becomes the rue de Rivoli. I smile at the older, handsome gentleman who sits across from me, but when he tries to hold my gaze, I glance away. Mere flirtation rather than invitation.

We reach the Pont Neuf and I get off for the ten-minute walk home. But first, I study the large metro and bus maps posted at the bus stop shelter to see if there's a direct route to the Buttes-Chaumont. Today I went extra-early and was in no hurry to get home, but for the au pair job, I'll need the fastest way there.

My step is carefree as I walk across the Seine, past the Square du Vert Galant to the Left Bank, and up beyond the boulevard St. Germain. I reach the rue Monsieur-le-Prince and enter the courtyard. Madame Vauquer waves from her window where she trims her geraniums. "Someone called. With a message," she says.

I take the note and Madame shakes her head, watching me closely as I unfold it. It's from the American woman. She found a native French speaker to watch their children—what they'd wanted all along.

Merde, alors.

Chapter Sixteen

Sitting with disappointment in my room is not a pleasant prospect, so I turn and leave the courtyard to wander the neighborhood.

And then suddenly, I'm craving a glass of wine, and I'm hungry. Truly hungry. I decide to forgo my normal dinner—bread and cheese on a park bench, or boiled macaroni in my room—and treat myself to dinner at the corner café. Every day on my way home I've been eyeing their prix fixe menu—starter, main dish, dessert and a *pichet* of wine—that, while inexpensive, exceeds my daily food budget. I'll skip a few breakfasts and go without a lunch or two in the little time I have left. I need this dinner. Since fate has determined I may not get to stay in Paris after all.

It's my first ever solo meal out. I open my journal to vent about Freddie and record the details of my meal, feigning ease as I eat alone. The food is delicious—an endive and pear salad with warm vinaigrette and chicken with mushroom sauce. Why does food smell and taste so much better in Paris? Must be all the butter and cream. I put down my utensils, wipe my mouth between bites, and sip some wine to make the meal last longer.

My waiter is a distinguished, efficient gentleman at least twenty years my senior. The wine has relaxed my reserve and so I ask, "I hate to bother you, monsieur, but would you tell me about the wine?"

"It is no bother, mademoiselle. It is our house Chablis."

"I like it."

"Chablis is a region and the grape is always Chardonnay."

I jot it down, my thoughts drifting to Vincent and Syrah.

He smiles. "*Bonne continuation.*"

A middle-aged woman looks in the window, her hands around her eyes and her image summons Mother to my mind. If she were here, she'd tell me it's inappropriate for a young woman to eat out alone. "Makes you look available," she would say. And because I'm wine-fueled, I would respond in my best de Beauvoir imitation. "But I *am* available, Mother."

De Beauvoir's philosophy was one of Dad's and my favorite subjects for discussion, especially during my senior year of high school, when I took a seminar about her novels. It was when I came to understand her thoughts on free will and taking responsibility for your choices. Dad repeatedly told me if I wanted to go to Paris, I would make it happen and that every decision I made could get me closer.

But once, Mother overheard us and rebuked his sentiment. "Aren't you Miss Fancy Pants, still wanting to go to Paris. Virginia not good enough for you? My sister, your Aunt-Dagmar-who-moved-to-Germany, went to Paris once and all she talked about was the girls dancing the can-can. I tell you, it's a den of iniquity."

At least Aunt Dagmar has a sense of adventure.

The waiter refills my wine glass and brings me dessert, a slice of tarte tatin crowned with a dollop of whipped cream.

Half the larger-than-expected carafe remains. I know they'll let me stay at my table to sip my wine for as long as I'd like, and the server won't bring the check till I ask.

After another hour of watching people come and go, overhearing dinner conversations, jotting down new phrases, and enjoying my Chablis, I look up and see twin servers. I focus hard and when the two meld into one, I request and then pay the bill. Feeling woozy and wonderful at the same time, I hold the table as I stand. So, this is what being tipsy is like. Mother always told me being drunk made people mean, but I'm feeling incredibly happy. Weightless but powerful, without a care in the world. Who needs a job anyway?

"Do come back mademoiselle," I hear behind me.

Flush with the thrill of transgression, I turn to say goodbye and the waiter blows me a kiss, his eyes smiling. I hiccup, giggle, and toss him a little wave. Even though he's my father's age, he's made me feel special. More validation that embracing my shorter hair was the right thing to do. As much as I despise Freddie, she may have done me a favor.

But I quickly rethink that.

Freddie did her best to ruin me. I was the one who did myself a favor and made the best of it. This wine-inspired thought makes me admire myself briefly in the mirror behind the bar. You've lived up to your label, Catrine: a Curious-Intellectual-With-a-Streak-of-Rebellion.

I leave the café floating on the waiter's flirtation and decide I need some fresh air. Uncertain on my feet, I walk close to the buildings so I can stop and lean when I need to. I enter the garden behind Le Musée de Cluny, the Museum of the Middle Ages. The clang of the metal gate closing behind me hurts behind my eyes as I sit on a curved stone bench. The sun has set, the lamps are lit, and it's the magical light of dusk—*l'heure bleue.*

My head now feels heavier than I can hold and the bench starts spinning. I slump down, legs extended in front of me, and turn to hang tight to the iron arm. I drop my head back and hear from above.

"*Il faut être toujours ivre, tout est là.*" One should always be drunk. That's all that matters.

Even in my fog, I know it's Charles Baudelaire. I respond, slurring my words. "*De vin, de poésie ou de vertu, à votre guise. Mais enivrez-vous!*" With wine, with poetry, or with virtue, as you chose. But do get drunk."

Oh, Lord. I've followed the advice of a licentious nineteenth century poet renowned for overindulging. I pull up my head and stretch out, the urge to sleep irresistible. The last thing I need is to wake up hungover on a park bench in Paris as a street cleaner passes by at dawn.

The following morning, I have little memory of getting home. My head pounds, I rub my temples, manage to sit up in bed, drink a few sips of water, and then slide back down. There's no way my search for

Vincent will start today. "Never. Again," I say out loud. "Never again, Monsieur Baudelaire."

A couple hours later, my insides churn with sour juices and I must get a cold drink and something in my stomach. My mood, I'll sort out when I feel better.

In a shaded spot of the Luxembourg Gardens near the Medici fountain, I finish an overpriced Coke and bite into a jambon-fromage baguette. The jolt of caffeine and a sandwich to absorb the bile in my belly are exactly what I need. For the second day in a row, my budget be damned. It's the only way I'm getting through the next few hours.

I think about having to go back to Virginia and depression descends. I can only stay in Paris for a few more weeks. I was sure I'd have found a job by now, but maybe I've been too idealistic, too "hifluting," as Mother might say.

Still in the gardens, I breathe in the smell of freshly cut grass and my thoughts drift to Mother and her putting green lawn. She'd be ashamed of me for last night's excess.

"Time for a novena," she would say. "To Monica, patron saint of alcoholics. You know that son of hers, St. Augustine, was a wild one."

It's May 19 and my days are dwindling. I have just over a month left.

The air is calm and the French flag hangs limp atop the Luxembourg Palace. A pigtailed gamine in a pink cap and her papa launch a pretty blue and white sailboat in the Grand Bassin duck pond, a young couple swings a toddler between them, and a trio of runners kicks up a cloud of dust as they jog by.

I exit the south end of the garden in a daze, but then glimpse the newly greening wisteria blanketing the storied Closerie des Lilas brasserie. Renoir and Monet used to dine there, as did Hemingway and John Dos Passos after them. What was it like to belong to the generation that fled to the Left Bank, a beehive of intellectual activity and artistic breakthroughs in the twenties?

Through the vines, I sneak a quick look into the dining room and imagine Jean-Paul Sartre and Simone de Beauvoir, existentialists extraordinaire, having collegial conversation in the thirties, espousing a fresh philosophy of personal engagement.

While I never identified with de Beauvoir and her willingness to live non-monogamously with Sartre, I'm intrigued by their arrangement and want to know more about the post-war Paris of jazz and cafés they inhabited. I draw back from the window, desperate for someone to talk to. Someone like Vincent who enjoys literature, philosophy, and art. I wonder if he thinks de Beauvoir believed in her open relationship with Sartre. Or does he think she would have preferred the wall-eyed philosopher to herself? A professor once told me when the elation of the Allied victory waned, France had to face the reality of genocide and its complicity. Existentialism and engagement helped pull the country from the abyss. Would you agree, Vincent?

But then Sartre speaks to me. "*Si vous vous sentez seul lorsque vous êtes avec vous-même, vous êtes en mauvaise compagnie.*" If you are lonely when you're alone, you are in bad company.

I am not bad company, Monsieur Sartre. I'm just lonesome. And then I remember that he and de Beauvoir share a final resting place only blocks away. I haven't explored the *Cimitière du Montparnasse*, eternal home of so many of France's artistic and intellectual elite, but dare I yield to my mood by visiting a cemetery so soon after Dad's funeral? We often discussed existentialist philosophy and I know he would tell me to go. It couldn't possibly make me feel any worse and a least my day will have a destination.

I pull out my map and start walking towards the cemetery. I continue reflecting on French philosophers, writers and artists—some of whose graves I'll soon visit—and mentally thank the many professors who deepened my appreciation for all things French. At the end of my four years of college, I desperately wanted to move to Paris, but insecurities eclipsed all I'd learned about free will.

"Catrine Elizabeth Gray, salutatorian," the provost announced atop the library steps. I reached for my diploma with trembling hands, and then descended the stairs, tears at the brink.

The balance of the ceremony passed in a blur, but as the crowd dispersed, I saw Dad's handsome profile. He stood tall in the shade of a tree, looking dapper in the white shirt and red tie I'd bought him for the occasion. Mother had refused to get him something new.

"There's my girl," he said beaming, his arms open. He lifted me and swung me around like when I was little and my black gown blew in the breeze. "I am so, so proud of you," Dad continued, his eyes moist.

"Thanks, but where's Mother?"

"Went for the car." He looked at his watch. "Wanted to leave before noon so we didn't have to pay another ten bucks." He put his arm around me and I softened into his embrace. How does he walk this emotional tightrope with me on one side and Mother on the other? However he manages, he does it exceedingly well.

"So," he said, stopping behind the college gate, pulling a brown envelope from inside his jacket. "For France." His voice caught. "Add it to what you've saved."

I looked down. Dad had written, "*Bon voyage, ma cherie,*" in clean, confident script. He'd drawn a mini-Eiffel Tower.

"But Mother... she controls your every penny."

"Not when it's a bonus and not when it's cash."

I hugged him silently and then slipped the envelope in my diploma folder. I held tight to his arm until we reached the curb where Mother sat in the car. She looked out the open window beside her, in another world. She dabbed her eyes with a tissue when she heard us. Had she been crying?

"Dad?" I asked.

"It's been an emotional day for her. She's had some challenges."

As he opened the back door for me I wondered: is she crying because I graduated or is something else going on? But I didn't ask.

We had lunch at a French restaurant and I was sure Mother had first resisted. I'm sure she'd said to Dad, "Why not some nibbles at home?" I pictured Cheez-Its in soup bowls. But Dad had insisted. The nicest place we'd ever eaten was a Hot Shoppes in Washington, DC. No white tablecloths and certainly no linen napkins.

I'd read every article I could find about manners and fine dining. And so, when I saw my parents split their rolls in half, butter each side and leave their napkins untouched on their plates, I knew better. I spread my napkin on my lap first thing, put a pat of butter on the side of my bread plate, and broke off a bite of roll.

Mother ordered chicken and iced tea—the cheapest things on the menu. Dad had the pork loin with cream sauce and a beer, and, at his urging, I had the steak au poivre, despite the price. As the waiter started to leave, I added, "And I'll have a glass of red wine. Please." I could hear Mother's silent disapproval but I knew that to be French was to drink wine with your meal.

Mother's mouth was in a hard line but Dad gave me a thumbs up. "Come on, Hon. It's her graduation. From college."

It was only then that she said, "Congratulations. I know you worked hard for this."

I nodded and managed a quiet, "Thank you." College was the first step in the kind of life I wanted for myself, though I knew if Mother had her way, I'd forever work at the warehouse, coming home in time to do her dishes.

Dad and I savored our meals all the way through our *mille feuilles* and coffee. She, of course, passed on dessert. "There's a half-gallon of ice cream at home."

The months after college were much as before, with the addition of paying room and board. I continued working in accounting at the warehouse, with Mother across the office and Dad often away.

I still spent my free time at the university library devouring articles about Paris and sketching itineraries around France, and at the art house watching French films. Every few paychecks, I pulled the brown envelope Dad had given me from my nightstand drawer and opened the clasp. But despite my growing bank balance, I wasn't convinced I had enough. Or maybe it was Mother's refrain. "Don't expect me to bail you out if you get over there and need money."

Work consumed me. Six days a week I was at my desk, writing to suppliers, reconciling invoices, preparing payroll. They gave me all the overtime I wanted and so I rarely made it home before eight. My boss promoted me to client coordinator and gave me an assistant manager's salary.

"Impressive, Cat," Mother said, as if she were proud, but I knew it was all about the money. About how much she could increase my rent. Which she did. But it was still less than the going rate and so I focused on the getaway a fattened bank account would eventually fund.

A taxi horn interrupts my thoughts as I cross the intersection of the *boulevard du Montparnasse* and the *rue Boissonade*. I pass a café with a yellow awning, the muted, layered banter of late breakfasters a rebuke to my loneliness. It reminds me of my arrival dinner with Vincent. I sigh.

After a few quick turns, there it is: the imposing entry to the walled graveyard, its tombs packed together cheek to jowl. The chestnut leaves whisper in the warm breeze under a blue sky, making it clear spring arrived some weeks ago. The translucent green canopy of the trees, the nubby buds on the bushes, and the tulips in planters give a pointillist effect, as if Sisley and his paint brush had visited. I pause to look up at the limestone pillars and take off my sweater, suddenly warm.

I jot notes from the cemetery map posted inside the walls. It directs me to division twenty and the shared grave of de Beauvoir and Sartre. They're buried side-by-side under a simple slab and headstone. Their long love affair was tumultuous and erratic but maybe the philosophical power couple finally found peace lying in tandem for eternity.

The iron clang of the noon bell from a neighboring church reverberates, followed by another in the opposite direction. I feel them in my bones.

Next, I find the flower-strewn tombstone of American actress, Jean Seberg. I reach up and touch my hair, almost as short as hers. The words of Seberg's character, Patricia Franchini, echo, as if speaking to bad-boy Jean-Paul Belmondo of Breathless fame: "It's sad to fall asleep. It separates people. Even when you're sleeping together, you're all alone."

Is it true, Simone and Jean-Paul?

Deeper into the crowded cemetery, I pass under blossoming Paulownia trees and then pay my respects to others in forever sleep: Samuel Beckett, Eugène Ionesco, and Alfred Dreyfus. But, the tomb of my favorite writer, Guy de Maupassant, in division twenty-six, is elusive. I hear Dad tell me, as he did when I was a teen, "He's a master of irony. A genius." The graves I've found so far share an edge with a walkway, but the short story master was laid to rest in the middle of a rectangular parcel packed with dozens of other tombs, many carved with now difficult to decipher lettering. The sarcophagi are crammed so closely that finding a name in the middle means stepping on someone to get there.

After a futile fifteen-minute search, I walk past tidy patches of peach roses and tiny lilies-of-the-valley and towards a green slatted bench under a broad chestnut to consult my notes. An elderly woman sits hunched at the far end. She wears low-heeled black pumps, like a nun's, and must be very warm. Her black woolen coat is buttoned top to bottom. She rotates her face towards me, revealing faded blue eyes with watery rims and thin lids, and skin so pale it seems translucent. Dull hair, mostly gray, is drawn back in a loose chignon at her neck and below her eyes are dark, purple shadows. Yet behind her gently furrowed face is the hint of a former beauty—the trace of loveliness beneath what remains.

Although clearly she's alone, I gently ask if the space beside her is free.

"*Mais, oui,*" she says with no hint of a smile and then continues in French. "If you don't mind sitting next to a worthless old woman." I hesitate, my mouth open. I've no idea how to reply.

"Sit, sit," she says, slapping the bench.

I take a seat and study my cemetery drawing. It clarifies nothing.

After carefully considering whether she would mind being disturbed further, I say, "*Excusez-moi, Madame*. I'm looking for the grave of Guy de Maupassant but can't seem to find it."

The woman continues gazing ahead and starts rhythmically rubbing her thighs. She doesn't answer. Did she not hear me? I stare at her hands moving back and forth, at the knobby fingers, mottled skin, and unkempt nails.

She eventually turns and stares for longer than the seconds it should take to assess me. "You're a tourist, aren't you?"

At first, I'm sheepish. Just what I need—another bully in my life.

But then my cheeks flush with nerve and I take a deep breath to puff up my chest. "No, I'm not. I live here. "

She raises an eyebrow.

I add, "Not in the cemetery. In Paris."

"Well, your jeans and satchel make you look like one."

My face flushes further, but this time from embarrassment.

Her eyes narrow behind black-framed glasses. "You are English?"

"From the U.S." I look away, fearful to return her gaze.

"Your French is rather good. At least for an American."

Normally I would burst with the thrill of it, but this woman is mocking me.

She says, "Although it is *la tombe*. You said *le tombe*."

My face reddens further. "Thank you for the correction."

She straightens her glasses. "Do you work in the city? Or are you just another romantic with 'American in Paris' dreams?"

"Actually, I'm looking for a—," I begin, but she cuts me off with a nod and a sniff.

"You and all the others."

I turn away, blaming myself for taking her questions as real interest or curiosity. I am so tired of people being mean to me. I'd love someone to talk to but I don't want to waste another minute with this woman. Yet something tethers me to the bench. I gave her no reason to be mean, so why should I slink away and let her get away with her taunts? Since Freddie, I'm done with letting anyone steamroll me, not even this hurtful French stranger.

I feel her looking at me and prepare for another disdainful remark, but instead she says thoughtfully, "I know his grave well, but it's hard to find."

I meet her eyes. "*Madame*?"

"Maupassant's grave. It's through there." She points ahead and to the right. "It has columns and a rectangular crown."

I look to where she's pointing. "*Ah, bon. Merci*," I say, stuffing my cemetery drawing in my pack and then lifting it to my shoulder.

The woman now sits up tall, staring. "Do you know about Maupassant or are you checking him off a list of famous graves like everyone else?"

"I think his work is brilliant. *The Necklace* is my favorite," I say, trying to be pleasant. "Are you a Maupassant fan?"

She snorts and straightens her glasses. "I would hardly call myself a fan. My affection runs much deeper." She pushes a stray wisp of hair towards her bun, but the breeze blows it back across her face. "You say you like *The Necklace*." She flicks her hand dismissively and then pushes up her glasses. "You and millions of readers. It's certainly not his best work. It's a shame so many only know one of his stories. It's like seeing the Arc de Triomphe and thinking you've seen Paris."

Was this woman not as shocked as I was when I read the story and discovered the protagonist's fatal mistake was not losing a piece of jewelry but failing to be honest about it?

I set my pack down on the bench and say, "If you must know, I've read every one of Maupassant's pieces and my analysis of his work was published in my university's literary journal."

Her eyes widen.

"As for *The Necklace*, I'm sure you know the story was revolutionary for the time and imitated by both Somerset Maugham and O. Henry."

At the close of my declaration, a man wearing dark socks and Birkenstocks, and wielding an expensive camera with a long lens, emerges from the patchwork of graves. He whistles as he hopscotches from one marble block to the next before jumping off and disappearing down the path.

The woman says "tsk, tsk," and shakes her head. "It is not respectful. So many come. Day after day. They pick their way through this holy place, noses in guidebooks, unaware that the resting place of the celebrated is also a place of repose for the ordinary."

I tilt my head and look at her. Though my hands are ready to sling my pack's straps back onto my shoulders, her change of attitude gives me pause. Was my tone too harsh?

"Do they not understand how maddening it is to see them here just to check off names on their list of sights-to-see?"

I look down, recalling my own tombstone crisscross.

"Yes, I saw you." She gestures, tracing my path.

"I meant no disrespect."

She shrugs and frowns. "So many young people do things they claim they don't mean and then think an apology erases it all. It's a failure of personal responsibility if you ask me."

But I didn't ask, and the last thing I need is to be on the receiving end of a grumpy old woman's diatribe. I may be a bit lonely, but I'm not that desperate. I turn to go.

"You're leaving so soon?"

Yes, Madame. I must go."

"What about Monsieur Maupassant?"

"*Au revoir, Madame.*" I turn and hasten towards the exit. I'm in no frame of mind to visit even my favorite author.

Chapter Seventeen

I fill the balance of the afternoon with laundry and a wistful visit to the job boards. I've mostly, but not entirely, given up hope that I can stay in Paris as I join pedestrians filling the streets to enjoying the spring evening.

But my miserable morning mood lingers and I walk along the Seine until the sun sets and I'm under soft moonlight. I sit on a riverside stone bench near the Jardins des Tuileries and delight in the pale reflection of streetlamps twinkling in the river, barge windows, and puddles on the quay. The voice of a Spanish tour guide cuts through the evening, telling passengers on a *bateau mouche* to wave to all by the Seine. I wave back. In front of me, I hear the river swoosh against the quay and behind me, in the gardens, the soft strains of an accordion float. Soon I'll no longer be surrounded by such beauty. I'll have to return to Viriginia. To Mother and her puzzling bitterness.

I'd asked Dad once, "Why is Mother so mean?" And though I haven't thought of it for years, I hear his answer clearly. "If you look inside an angry woman, you'll see that she is crying."

"What does Mother have to cry about?" Didn't she have all she wanted—her religion and her tidy little house?

"There have been losses," he said and then paused. "They made her, made us, very sad. One day you'll understand. All you need to know right now is I love your mother. She can be difficult, I know, but never forget she loves us both."

No matter what he said, I didn't feel her love. Only anger and criticism. If she was crying inside, she kept it well hidden.

And then I think of Freddie, certain her cruelty didn't mean she was hurting inside.

But, what about the cemetery woman? Was she mean on the outside because she was crying inside? And why was she there in the first place. Had she lost someone, like I had?

I cut my thoughts short to head back across the Seine to my flat. A young man on the crowded quay near the Pont Neuf hands me a flyer. It offers free entry and a drink at a club with live music off the rue Saint-André des Arts.

If I turn right, away from the river, and then go left down an alley, I'll pass it on my way home. It's only nine o'clock and I'm feeling brave—brave enough for my first visit to a club. Freddie took me to endless cafés, but I always declined when she went clubbing.

I turn on the rue Saint-André where a sputtering red neon sign marks the bar's entry. I push open the metal door papered with performance posters and step down metal stairs into the dim interior with vaulted brick supports. The concrete floor is sticky, the place smells of stale beer, and the light is vaguely orange. My eyes adjust and I see a long bar to the left of the narrow space. A man plays guitar and a woman sings at the far end. It looks like the dancing music won't start until later. Most tables are full, but I find one in the shadows by the entry and order a Chablis.

The duo is performing Pete Seeger's "Turn! Turn! Turn!" in French. I resist the urge to rely on my usual social crutch, putting pen to journal. I will myself to relax, shrug off my coat, loosen my shoulders, and feel the music. My drink arrives as the musicians launch into a Mamas and Papas song, "California Dreamin'." The familiar harmony and reference to the States prick a moment of homesickness but I gulp it down with a mouthful of wine. They continue the sixties set, ending with a string of Beatles tunes, this time in English. They finish, "Let It Be," and I think, one more song, as I'm starting to yawn.

The woman closes her eyes and tilts her head as she begins the haunting strains of "Eleanor Rigby." I listen carefully to the lyrics. The woman's silvery voice rises and falls and I'm moved by the funereal arrangement and melancholy message. An image of the cemetery lady fills my head and I wonder who she is, besides a fellow Maupassant aficionado. Has she been sarcastic all her life? Is she down on her luck? Or maybe she's in a lot of pain? I think of my grandmother and my eyes well.

The performers announce a break. I turn to slip my arms in my trench and freeze when I lock eyes with a slender woman in a black chemise and tan beret coming down the stairs. It's Odette. Besides Vincent, she's the only friend of Freddie's who was nice to me. She sees me and waves. I hold my breath. Is Freddie with her? When I confirm she's alone, I exhale and break into a smile. She approaches my table and its empty wineglass.

"*Salut,* Odette," I say. "Love your beret!"

"What a surprise!" she says, leaning down to exchange bisous. "Join you?"

I open my hand and she takes a seat.

"You look wonderful. And your hair! It's adorable."

"Thanks," I say, sweeping my bangs to the side. "Thought it was time for a change."

"I heard you'd gone back to America."

"From Freddie?" I tilt my head back and laugh. "Nope. Still here. At least through June."

"I'm so glad!" She flashes a smile and I smile back.

"How are you?" I ask.

"Making plans for summer. You know...the old beach or mountains debate."

I flinch at the mention of the beach. I'm dying to ask about Vincent but hold back. Don't want to sound like a schoolgirl. "Two good options."

"Time for another drink? My treat."

"That's so nice. Chablis. Please."

She goes to the bar and returns with two glasses of white.

"So where do you live now that you left Freddie's?" she asks.

"Not far. Just south of the boulevard St. Germain."

"*Chouette*! That's a super cool neighborhood. The publisher I work for is around the corner from here and my flat is nearby. Small, but I do love having my own place. Especially after Freddie." She raises her glass. "*Santé* to almost being neighbors."

"*Santé*," I echo. "And thanks for the wine." I take a sip. "So, tell me about work. Must be really interesting."

"Most days. I'm in publicity and the hours are long, but yeah, I meet some great writers."

"The free books alone would make me want the job." I ask her to tell me more and she explains about sending out advance copies, book launches, setting up author signings, and booking media coverage.

"But I'm actually interested in acquisitions," she says. "You know, finding new authors and books to publish."

"How does all that happen?"

As she reaches into her bag to retrieve something, I look up and see the bar door open and a guy come down the stairs, a waft of weed announcing him. It's Gaston, a joint dangling from his lips. My heart sinks. He stops for his eyes to adapt to the dark, looks around, sees me, and sneers. Odette turns to see what caught my attention but he's snuck up behind her. "Boo," he says in her ear.

She jumps. "I thought you were working tonight."

"Got off early." He reaches into his bomber jacket and looks at me.

"Well, if it isn't Cat," he says, pulling out his wallet and slapping it on his palm. "Nice hair. Freddie says you flipped out after the beach—went all Joan of Arc' crazy and cut it off." He laughs, spilling ash on the table.

"What?" says Odette, turning to me.

I stare at Gaston. "That's what she told you?"

"Yeah. Told everyone."

That means Vincent, too. My fingers curl into fists.

"She didn't tell me," says Odette.

I say, "You know what really happened, Gaston? I bend down and pull my pack to my chair, preparing to go. "It was Freddie who took a knife to my neck and Freddie who hacked off my hair."

Odette's hand flies to her mouth.

No way," says Gaston, looking surprised. He looks to Odette and then back at me. "No shit. Huh." He contemplates for a few moments then nods towards our glasses. "Get you ladies something?"

I'm relieved he seems to believe me, but I don't feel much like lingering. I slip my arms into my coat and tie the belt around my waist. He must take my movements as an affront because he stubs out what's left of his joint into the table and snipes, "Oh, right, you're a one glass girl."

"Fuck off, Gaston."

"Enough," says Odette. *"Imbécile."*

He grins, as if he's scored a point by aggravating us both. He gives a salute and heads to the bar.

"I really like talking to you," I say to Odette. "But can't take him."

"I get it. We've been friends since we were kids, so he's like a brother. But he can be a real jerk. Trust me, I tell him off all the time. Like you just did." She hands me two of her cards. "Let's do this again soon. The two of us." I write my address and Madame Vauquer's phone number on one card and hand it back. I slip the other in my pocket. She says, "I'm super busy this week, but maybe next."

"Definitely."

Gaston returns, a handful of nuts cupped to his belly, and takes a long swig of his beer, foam on his upper lip.

I take a slow swig of my remaining wine, sling my pack over my shoulder, and head for the door.

But before I'm around the corner, Odette calls as she scurries to catch up. "Catrine, wait."

I stop and turn, instantly regretting having left so abruptly. "I apologize. I would have stayed if it weren't for him."

"I haven't seen Freddie in weeks so Gaston's news is a total surprise. You can't leave me hanging about what she did. It's terrible. I know she's passionate, can be a spoiled brat and lies all the time, but I never thought she could be violent."

It's painful to rehash the details, but I manage to summarize.

"That bitch," Odette says. "She could have seriously hurt you."

"I really can't think about it too much."

"Are you okay if I tell Vincent what really happened and that you're still in Paris? Freddie told everyone you went home."

"Sure," I say.

"He's at some banking conference in Frankfurt, but I'll tell him when he's back."

"Freddie won't be happy..."

"When is she ever?" Odette laughs.

"I made a mistake trusting her as my friend."

"Well, now you've made a new one." Odette leans in and kisses each of my cheeks. With a wave, she says, "Call me."

I watch her walk away and allow a flicker of hope to ignite.

Chapter Eighteen

Three days later, I take the metro to interview for a position at an *école maternelle* near the Parc Montsouris. But when the brief interview ends, they tell me that although my French is good, they need a native speaker.

Disheartened, I walk through the park, deciding not to waste time with disappointment. I stop by the lake at a kiosk for a warm *crêpe aux marrons*—sweet chestnut cream. I stand under a peeling sycamore, button my sweater over my tee, and cross "*école maternelle*" from my list of possible positions. The early morning breeze is now a wind, penetrating my inadequate layers, and the skies are under thin clouds filtering the sun to watery light. Parisian weather is so unpredictable right now, some days warm—balmy even—and others going back to early spring temperatures, forcing everyone to don jackets.

I consult my map and see that if I follow the avenue René Coty towards home, I'll end up in Montparnasse. I consider heading back to my warm walk-up but what I really need is companionship, even if it's of dead luminaries. And the cemetery lady sidetracked my search for Maupassant the other day, so I'll give it another try.

Inside the gate, I approach the bench where the woman sat and then head to where she'd pointed: the one with the delicate columns and rectangular crown. Knowing what I'm looking for makes it easy and I find the grave in minutes. His name is engraved in the horizontal frieze: Guy de Maupassant. I circle the tomb and then stand on the path, remembering the hours I spent reading his stories with Dad.

After ten minutes, I bid adieu to my literary colleague and cross the cemetery to visit Baudelaire. I did channel him the other night and decide he deserves a nod. He wrote powerfully and erotically about sex, alienation, and death and he stretched my capacity for exploring dark subjects during a particularly lonely semester in college.

After a visit with the *poète maudit*—the accursed poet—I turn towards the gate but a voice from the trees holds me in place.

La vie est la farce à mener par tous. Life is the farce we are all forced to endure.

But that's not you, Monsieur Baudelaire—it's your libertine compatriot Arthur Rimbaud. He isn't even buried here. Why's he trying to depress me? The thought of the enfant terrible's poetry triggers yesterday's loneliness.

I wander up and down the narrow paths, gravel crunching under foot, and then circle back to Maupassant. The noon bells sound, and there she is: the cemetery lady in her black pumps headed to her bench.

My eyes track her down the path and my eczema itches when I think about how brusquely I left yesterday. But I did love speaking to her about literature, so my steps follow hers. She sits as I reach her.

"*Cette place est occupée, madame*?"

Today, my question startles her. She looks up and shakes her head. She's wearing the same outfit, black from head to toe, and this time I notice that she holds a cane. The marks of age are more pronounced today—bent shoulders, deep-set eyes, and a slight tremor in her hands. We sit on the bench side by side for at least five minutes before I finally ask, "Do you come here often?"

After some hesitation she replies. "Almost every day, God willing. It's only when my legs ache that I miss my morning with Monsieur Maupassant."

She remembers we talked about him. "*Toujours au même heure?*" I ask. Always at the same time?

"Yes. At noon so I can hear the church bells," she says looking beyond the trees. "And it's *à la même heure. Toujours à la même heure.*"

"*Merci.*" I say, shaking my head. "*À la même heure…* "

"You never saw his grave. Have you returned to find it?"

"I did. Thank you for pointing me in the right direction."

"You left so quickly."

"You didn't seem to like me much."

"It was a difficult day."

"Is today better?"

She looks up, something behind me catching her attention. I turn and see a tangle of tourists in sneakers, cameras around their necks, led by a woman hoisting a flag. The group turns to the left, towards Maupassant's tomb, disappearing into the forest of graves.

"Definitely disrespectful," I say, and then look at her. I'm surprised to see her cheeks are wet with silent tears and feel unexpected fondness for her.

"Madame, are you okay?"

"I apologize." She stops as her voice breaks. She pulls a lace handkerchief from her pocket and pats her eyes.

"When I saw you, it was the two-year anniversary of losing my husband. It's painful for us visiting loved ones to see tourists walking on their graves."

"I am so, so sorry." I fight the urge to touch her arm.

"We used to come here. To this bench. After morning classes. We would sit and talk and then go home for lunch." She wipes her face and dabs at her eyes. "And so now I come to visit his grave and talk to him. Tell him what I'm reading and how I'm feeling. It gives my days some form now that I no longer teach."

"You were a teacher? How long has it been since you taught?"

"Three and a half years. Since my husband got sick. If I didn't have him to visit, I might never leave home. Or my bathrobe." She pauses to push her black glasses up her nose. "He's buried in division twenty-six in front of us. Not far from Maupassant. My husband wrote much about him." She pauses to fold her handkerchief and put it back in her pocket. "He also wrote a book..."

"I'm sorry. I assumed you were an ordinary follower."

"Not ordinary, no. But then, neither are you, apparently."

"You and your husband were both teachers?"

She nods, fiddling with her wedding ring. "Professors of nineteenth century French literature. At the Sorbonne."

I knew there was something about this woman. I sit up straighter. "Did you like teaching?" While I fear upsetting her, the curious part of me needs to know.

Her eyes go misty. "I did."

"Would you mind another question, Madame?"

"That's a question right there, no?"

It takes me a moment to recover.

"Second question," she says.

"Why did you dismiss my appreciation for *The Necklace*?"

She uncrosses her ankles. "It's a fine piece of irony, certainly, but it's usually the only story uninformed readers know—its twist ending a punchline. They've never heard of, no less read, any of his other work, much of which is unlike your favorite."

"But his most popular stories are favorites for a reason, don't you think?"

The woman shrugs. "Perhaps."

"I also like *Butterball*. "It is a masterpiece of social criticism with its take on hypocrisy."

She doesn't respond. I turn and see she's staring straight ahead, though her eyelids droop. She rubs her thighs mindlessly, rocking forward ever so slightly. She did that yesterday and here she's doing it again.

"*Madame*?"

This time, she looks up. "I suppose. Both stories are good, with unexpected endings. But you do know we French must always debate things."

I nod, though this is the first time I've experienced it. "And your favorite?"

"Impossible to choose. It would be like picking my favorite student." She cocks her head. "All Maupassant's stories remind me of my husband. I was his editor, so I'm something of an expert on the author myself."

"No wonder you have opinions."

"No one has ever accused me of not speaking my mind."

I grin, although I'm not sure she meant to be amusing. "It's getting cold," I say, rubbing my palms together and then pulling up my hood as it's started to sprinkle. "This weather is crazy, like it's reverting to winter."

"And I must go," says the woman, pulling on black leather gloves as she leans on her cane to stand.

I don't want her to leave. "Madame, I would love to hear more about your husband and his book and your thoughts on Maupassant and being a professor at the Sorbonne and anything related to French literature." I cut myself short, embarrassed, and put my hands, one over the other, on top of my heart. "I'm so sorry. I'm babbling..."

"I am afraid you are."

But I'm not going to easily relinquish the chance to talk with an authentic Sorbonne professor. With a deep breath of courage, I lick my lips and ask, "Would you like to go for coffee? Nearby?"

When there's no reply, I regret my entreaty and give ground. "Or—maybe you're busy..."

But she turns and her face has lightened—slightly. The beginnings of a smile lift the corners of her mouth.

"You don't mind discussing *belles-lettres* with a grouchy old lady?"

Still prickly, but no longer mean.

I smile and extend my hand. "*Je m'appelle Catrine.*"

Chapter Nineteen

At bustling Chez Papa on the cemetery's south side, waiters in black waistcoats and white aprons balance trays as they weave hurriedly among patrons. Our server turns sideways to squeeze between tables, holding our coffees high. He places them carefully. I wrap my chilly fingers around mine.

I stir my *grand crème*, bringing color to the surface, while my companion, Madame Arnoux, sips hers. Her eyes are pale, as if any blue that once brightened them has drained. She tells me she decided to leave teaching behind for good last year while on bereavement leave.

She tells me her fifty-five-year-old unmarried son, Eugène, lives outside Paris in Versailles and visits every weekend. "He's dutiful and cares about me but is busy as a computer programmer. Always in a rush. But not too rushed to order me around."

"Sounds like my mother. She's the bossy one."

"You don't get along?"

"We're fine as long as I don't respond to her slights."

This revelation leads to another and then another. I tell her about our house and neighborhood, my studies and my scholarship, Dad's death, my Francophilia, and coming to Paris. Now and then she corrects my pronunciation and reminds me of vocabulary if I struggle.

"Did your parents support your French studies?"

"My father, yes, but Mother still doesn't understand." I shake my head. "They were poles apart and I've never really understood what held them together."

She sips her coffee and sighs. "Every marriage is unique, and what makes a particular one work can be a mystery."

I try to get Madame to talk about her husband.

"You lost your father and I lost my husband," she says. "But enough of that." She snaps her napkin and smooths it on her lap. "People die and we move on. No use getting sentimental."

"A little harsh, don't you think? I mean, I loved my dad and it's clear you loved your husband. Losing them was difficult."

She shrugs and looks away, tears brimming. She raises her coffee, perhaps to cover her emotions, and so I pick up her reference.

"So, who said that? About not getting sentimental. Stendhal maybe? In *Le Rouge et le Noir*?" I open my journal to record her response.

"It's mine, *ma fille*. Delphine Arnoux. But I'm a realist, like Monsieur Stendhal."

Delphine Arnoux. She's revealed her full name. I close my journal. "Your name is very pretty. Are you named after someone?"

"My grandmother."

"I'm named after my grandmother too!"

"Is she French? It's a good French name and a royal one too. There was Catherine de' Medici, of course."

"My grandmother's name was spelled the French way, C-a-t-h-e-r-i-n-e. But mine is C-a-t-r-i-n-e."

"Maybe your mother wanted to make it easy for Americans to say it the French way."

"Mother never would have thought of that. It was my father. I'm named after his mother and she spoke French. She died before I was a year old. But I have all her books about France."

"And you love my country and my language as a result?"

"They were the start. And there was an Eiffel Tower keychain..."

She looks at me askance. "Tell me about the books."

"My father read them to me, in English and in French. They made me curious about France and taught me lots of words. And I took French in school."

"Do you still read French?"

"I always have a French novel in my knapsack."

"And writing?"

"Everything I've written in my journal since I arrived is in French." I pause to sip my coffee. "Don't know what I'd do without reading and writing."

"Well, don't you sound like Miss Gertrude Stein herself. The Mother Goose of Montparnasse. She said, 'Writing and reading is for me synonymous with existing.'"

"I love that!"

"But enough of things personal. We came to discuss literature. Which is what you do in a café with someone you've barely met." Meaningful pause. "You Americans are so quick to reveal so much."

Has she forgotten it was her questions that got me talking? "Okay then. Literature."

She tells me Balzac and Baudelaire are her specialties, and thus her favorites.

I decide not to tell her about the latter speaking to me. She'll think I've lost my mind.

"I find you grow to love what you know about most," says Madame. "The more I read Balzac, the more I admire him."

"And Baudelaire?"

"A brilliant writer and not only of the neurotic poetry we associate with him. He also wrote essays, was an art critic, and his translations of Edgar Allan Poe gained him recognition in France."

"I had no idea." I reopen my journal.

Madame dips a sugar cube in her cup, lets it fill with coffee, and then nibbles its edges.

"Do you miss your students?" I ask.

She looks at me long and hard. When she speaks, her voice constricts with emotion. "Terribly. But speaking about them makes me sad because they're in the past." She rubs the back of her neck. "The past." Madame raises her cup. "So much sorrow in two little words." Her lower lip quivers, so I wait until she returns her cup to its saucer.

"Will you teach again?"

"Eugène thinks it would be too much."

"Do you always listen to Eugène?"

"Only sometimes." She chuckles. "The rest of the time I pretend to and then do what I want."

It's the first time I've heard her express anything approaching levity. I ask, "What's Eugène like?"

"Ever since his father died, he's become overbearing, constantly lecturing me. He's always angered easily but it's gotten worse. He may be right about teaching, though."

She frowns. A moment later, her lips curve up into a slightly mischievous smile. "About two years ago, right after my husband died, I defied Eugène."

I lean forward, wrists on the table.

"He insisted I live with him in Versailles. I wasn't emotionally strong enough to push back, so I acquiesced when he packed my bag and loaded me in his car."

"Did it help being with him?"

"Initially, all I did was sleep. Barely came out of the bedroom for weeks. But my strength returned and I could fix myself a meal. I missed my apartment and was miserable so far from where Charles was buried."

Her husband's name is Charles. I resist reaching for my journal.

"Eugène wouldn't hear of me moving back to Paris, but I insisted. He didn't think I could live alone. But it was he who wouldn't let me do anything for myself."

"So, you went home?"

"Packed and left a note. Said I appreciated his concern but that we'd be better off living apart. I took a taxi to the train and back in Paris, took the bus home. He shouted at me over the phone that evening but there wasn't much he could do. He delivered the rest of my things the following day. I'd bought groceries and made us lunch to show him I could."

I smile.

"But he treated me like a child. Told me I couldn't have wine with our meal. 'You'll fall and break a hip and then where will I be?' He didn't consider that a glass of Burgundy might be what I needed—a taste of the routine I'd had with his father."

Just then, a teenager slips past our table and bumps the corner, coffee splashing on my journal. She apologizes as I mop the spill with my napkin. I tell her not to worry.

But Madame gives the girl a sharp look and snaps, "*Dis-donc.* You spilled hot liquid on my companion."

I wipe my journal as she scowls. I say, "It was an accident."

"It was rude." She leans on the table to stand. Is she leaving? She points her cane at the sign for *Les Toilettes* and shuffles off, muttering.

When Madame returns, any awkwardness is gone. She taps my notebook. "I know you're a reader but you also write?"

"It's just a journal. But I do sometimes write stories."

"Do not ever refer to anything you create as 'just.' What if the French writers and artists you love believed that about their work. It was 'just a painting of waterlilies' or 'just a story about Normandy.'"

"It's just...sorry. Not 'just.' It's something I do to pass the time."

She points to my journal. "May I take a peek?"

She sees the fear in my wide eyes and adds, "At the jacket. What's inside is private unless you decide otherwise." I sigh with relief and hand her the book.

"You've seen this street on the cover?"

"My friend told me it was a fairytale sketch." Ex-friend I remind myself.

"*Mais non*, it's real—it's the rue Crémieux—in the Twelfth. Its houses have colorful shutters and pastel facades, some with trompe l'oeil drawings."

"Really? I'll have to go see it for myself. Freddie said no place in Paris is that beautiful."

"Who is this Freddie? He does not know Paris if he said that."

"She's my former roommate. Frédérique. Always making fun of my romantic ideas."

"Well, Paris is a romantic city, so why mock the truth?"

"Oh, that's only the start of what she mocked me about."

"This Frédérique doesn't sound like someone you should waste time with."

"I know that now, but I had to learn the hard way." I go on to tell her about living with Freddie, Mathilde and her shop, conversation classes, the beach, and my hair. It's such a relief to share my story, though I leave out mentions of Vincent, not wanting to invite questions, but then I freeze mid-sentence.

"*Zut!* I've gone and done exactly what Americans do." I feel myself flush. "Too personal, too quickly."

"But I also have spoken of personal things. It seems we both need..."

"A friend?"

"Perhaps." She pushes her cup away and I take the cue to put my journal in my pack. I don't want to overstay my welcome.

Madame raises her palm to her chest. "Leaving already? Would you let an old woman drink a glass of wine alone?" She clasps her hands on the table's edge. "Coffee hour is over and so wine heralds the evening. My treat."

She orders two glasses of Sancerre and I retrieve my journal to add what she says to my growing wine intelligence: it's a white from the eastern Loire Valley and the grape—Sauvignon Blanc—is refreshing, and makes a good aperitif.

Our drinks arrive, I take a sip, and confirm that indeed, I do like Sancerre. "It's a little like the Chablis I had last week." I never would have expressed such a mockable opinion with Freddie.

"You have a perceptive palate. A good Chablis can taste quite like a Sancerre."

For the next half hour, Madame tells me about her years in the classroom. I can tell she misses the respect of her profession, her colleagues, and above all, her students. We resume our discussion of nineteenth century writers and agree that *Le Père Goriot* is our favorite Balzac novel.

"I love the main character and how innocent he is at the beginning and understand how he must have felt living in that dusty old boarding-house." And suddenly it hits me. "Wait," I say. "Is that where Eugène's name comes from? Eugène de Rastignac?"

"Naming him after a character seemed fitting for two literature professors." She sighs heavily. "But I'm afraid Eugène's lived up to his namesake—an *arriviste*, at least regarding his bank account."

She closes her eyes as if to end the subject and moves on. "There are infinite literary destinations in Paris and every week, I took a group of students to visit some. Charles often came along." She looks down at her lap. "Cancer ended Charles's life but he is still here." She touches her chest. "Thank God, grief's sharp edges have softened. Like sea glass at the shore."

"So true," I say, thinking of Dad.

"When you grow old with someone, your souls intertwine and eventually you share roots. Like aspens in the American West." She crosses and then uncrosses her arms and a softness descends. Her eyes fill and she touches them with the corner of her napkin. "Yes," she says, leaning back, holding my gaze. "It is good sometimes to talk about when I was a professor."

Now my eyes well. "But you still are a professor. You're just no longer in the classroom."

She shrugs.

I hesitate before asking. "Would you take me out one day to see some sights? I could be your student. At least until I find a job."

She smiles.

I raise my glass. "To Professor Arnoux."

She shakes her head. "I should go," she says as she looks down at her watch. "Eugène calls—four p.m. sharp every day—and I don't want him lecturing me about being out too long." She signals for the check.

I empty my wallet into my palm—barely enough to pay for the coffees—and see Madame looking ahead vacantly, as if she's lost consciousness but with her eyes open. I wait until she looks at me.

"Are you okay?" I say, reaching across to touch her arm.

She pulls back quickly, ignoring my concern. "Shall we meet again on Sunday in the cemetery? To talk more about literature?"

"Yes, I'd love to."

She leaves more than enough francs for our entire bill. I breathe a sigh of relief.

"See you at noon." She stands and moves towards the door, but then turns back and extends her hand. I reach out and she shakes mine, firm and brief. "*Au revoir*, Catrine." She heads out, the tap of her cane preceding her.

Chapter Twenty

I approach the cemetery bench for the third day. Delphine Arnoux sits with her back erect, hands in her lap, hair pinned neatly in a high bun. She wears brown slacks under a taupe trench and comfortable lace-up walking shoes, white like a nurse's rather than black like a nun's. Around her neck, a pink patterned scarf that matches the tulips next to her peeks through the collar of her coat. Pearl earrings dangle from her ears. Her carriage has changed—stronger, straighter, steadier. I can tell she's happy to see me, her face lighting up.

"You're dressed differently," I say as I sit. "You look nice."

"I didn't look nice before?"

"You look happier. And no more black."

"When I have somewhere to go, I dress for it. The sun is out, it's back to being warm, and I thought we would walk. Madame lifts an ankle and says, "I put on my best walking shoes." She winks.

"So, you assumed I would agree to go wherever it is you're taking me?" I ask with half a smile, folding my arms across my chest.

"I could tell from the start, you have a curious mind. And the curious like to explore. Am I right?"

I nod. I'm a "Curious-Intellectual-with-a-Streak-of-Rebellion."

"As Françoise Sagan said, 'Curiosity is where wisdom starts.'" She gets to her feet more quickly than I expect. "Do you want to go, *ma petite*, or not? We're wasting time sitting here."

Her tone is testy, ready to boss me around, but she called me *ma petite*. I guess it's her way and I can play along. I jump up. "Where are we going?"

"How about some literary haunts—American ones. And I made reservations for lunch."

Though she appears steady on her feet, she does use a cane and so I worry she could fall. "Can I help you manage?" I offer her my arm and instantly regret my words.

She shoots me a look, leans on her cane, and heads down the path as her retort. I grab my pack and scurry to catch up.

When I reach her she says "I walk four blocks here and then home every day. By myself. When I want to, I can go quite far. And quickly." She picks up her pace to prove her point. I match her steps, ready to grab her, just in case. We snake across the cemetery under chestnut trees with pink blossoms, circle around the central garden of yellow daffodils and blue forget-me-nots and pass through the gate to destinations yet to be revealed.

We turn left onto the boulevard Edgar Quinet and say little in transit as the street is noisy, bustling with buses, bikes, and pedestrians. Madame is intent on her footing and I on her. As she predicted, I'm surprised at how quickly we put blocks behind us.

She slows when we reach the rue Delambre, a narrow side street lined with boutiques and bistros I can't afford. We turn right and stop well short of the main crossroad of the lively Montparnasse neighborhood.

"You see number ten?" she asks, using her cane to point across the street, nearly hitting a passing cyclist. He responds with the loud ring of his bell.

It's a low-slung storefront painted gray. "That old café?"

"Well, it wasn't always in disrepair, and had a different name. It was a popular drinking spot in the twenties and thirties—famous in part because it was open all night. You've heard of the Dingo American Bar?"

"The Dingo Bar? In *A Moveable Feast,* Hemingway said it's where he met F. Scott Fitzgerald. In 1925, right after *The Great Gatsby* was published."

"Smart girl. I used to come and lean right here on this building. I'd squint my eyes and imagine what it was like back then...but haven't returned in a very long time."

"It must have been fascinating with so many American and British expat writers and artists mingling with the French creatives."

"I don't know who drank more, Hemingway or Fitzgerald, but I do know they spent a lot of time in there." Madame stops to tuck a lock of hair back into her chignon. "I was a young woman in the 1920s and used to pretend I lived inside nineteenth-century novels. It never occurred to me that at the very same time, literary history was also being made here, where I grew up."

I do some quick math. Definitely younger than I initially thought, especially now that I've seen her move. Maybe late seventies? "You must be in a good mood today, Madame. You haven't corrected my grammar once or told me to roll my Rs."

She harrumphs without a smile.

We both lean back, gazing at the old café, its paint peeling. "Why are you so interested in the watering hole of American ex-pats? You're a professor of French literature."

"And you're a fan of French literature and this place interests you. I love all good literature even if the writers are American." She winks.

"Do you like Hemingway and Fitzgerald?"

"I appreciate them. They broke new ground. Hemingway, the minimalist: why write five words when two will do? And Fitzgerald, with his elaborate descriptions. *Et vous*?"

"I never really liked Hemingway's style. I know he broke lots of rules and influenced so many after him, but his writing is too, I don't know, lean, for me."

"And Fitzgerald?"

"I definitely prefer him. More lyrical."

"I guess we'll have to disagree. Hemingway is my man."

"*Vive la différence*," I say.

I follow her across the street, squeezing between cars parked tightly together. We shade our eyes and put our noses to the dusty window of the former Dingo. I picture the American writers on bar stools, sharing a bottle of Champagne. Fitzgerald leans in for a Hemingway war story.

"I'm sure the interior looks nothing like it did fifty years ago," Madame says, "but we do have our imaginations." She looks at her watch. "Our next stop calls." She points to the end of the street.

While we're speaking of literary places, I tell Madame what Vincent told me about the *rue Neuve-Sainte-Geneviève* in *Le Père Goriot*. She confirms it is indeed a real street. Unexpectedly, longing for Vincent moves up from my toes, tingling all the way to my scalp, and I'm lost in reverie while we walk fifty yards to the boulevard du Montparnasse. It's been a month since the beach.

I stop to smell fresh flowers spilling out of plastic containers for sale outside a tabac. When I turn to ask Madame if we're crossing the busy street filled with noisy buses, I realize my companion has stopped several yards behind. She stands still, staring straight ahead, as in a trance, outside the corner café—Le Dôme. Her metal cane clatters to the pavement, her arms loose at her sides.

I rush back. "Madame Arnoux, are you all right?"

She looks past me in silence. As before, she returns to herself after twenty seconds and then looks up as if nothing happened. "Let's go," she says. "More of literary Paris awaits."

"Hold on," I say firmly, taking her arm, but she shakes me away. "We are not leaving until you tell me what just happened."

"If I tell you, you won't see me again." Her words are clipped as she looks down.

To put her at ease, I try to catch her eye by tilting my head. "Who says I want to see you again?"

She looks up, her posture rigid. "Nothing is wrong. It's fatigue."

"But I've seen it. You drift off. And don't say 'just' when you're talking about your health."

"Well, I'm not telling you anything standing here. Let's cross to La Rotonde. Hemingway's favorite. We'll talk over lunch."

I pick up her cane and hand it to her. She appears to have recovered as we walk across the intersection. As I look around, it hits me: Le Dôme, La Rotonde, and Le Select next door. Oh my God! This was the epicenter of Paris's philosophical scene between the wars. I'm right where Picasso or Eliot or Modigliani may have sat reading *Le Matin* to catch up on news and gossip over coffee. An intellectual frisson buzzes up my spine.

We're halfway across the broad boulevard when I take Madame's elbow and this time don't let go. "Thank you for bringing me here," I say. "I've walked all over Paris but not beyond La Closerie to Montparnasse and this crossroad. I'm so grateful."

"I thought you might appreciate it. It is one of my favorite corners because of its past and because I love these cafés. I could sit at a table at any one and watch people for hours." She points ahead with her cane. "La Rotonde awaits."

Chapter Twenty-One

We enter the café under bright red awnings into the scarlet-hued reception. Madame announces our reservation and we're led to burgundy-upholstered chairs at a window table. I think about my thinning wallet and have no idea how I'll afford such a place. My hand starts itching.

But then my companion says, "Catrine." She unfolds her napkin and places it in her lap. "I will only answer your questions if you allow me to buy you lunch." Without waiting for my reply, she suggests she order for me.

While we wait for our plats du jour—*coq au vin* with roasted potatoes and garlicky string beans—over glasses of red Burgundy, Madame insists I tell her about being a curious intellectual.

"...with-a-Streak-of-Rebellion." I flash a smile. "You have to say the whole thing, so it makes sense." I explain about *Seventeen* magazine and how after thirty-six questions, it branded me. "I liked having my own epithet that was unlike how Mother saw me."

"Hmm," Madame says as she straightens her glasses, her eyebrows raised. "So, a magazine helped you figure out who you were and not your mother."

I shrug. "I've never forgotten and it helps me understand myself better. Did you ever wonder when you were younger who you might be?"

"Oh, I think who I am is obvious and immutable at this point. No surprises there."

"You're sure? I actually keep the quiz in my journal."

I reach behind, but Madame stops me, pointing her fork in my direction. "Young lady, I have no desire to play a silly game intended for sentimental teens. I would think you're beyond that."

My lower lip trembles and my face reddens. I take a long sip of water and raise my napkin to my mouth. She's right, of course. It's childish and I shouldn't have spoken of it seriously.

Our waiter sets down our plates, cutting my embarrassment short. Avoiding my gaze, Madame picks up her wine glass.

"*Tchin, tchin,*" I say, raising my glass in a gesture of surrender. She clinks my glass, takes a sip, and then picks up her utensils. She pushes a piece of chicken and a mushroom onto her fork with her knife, and gracefully slides it into her mouth. "Mmm," she says. "Excellent, as usual."

I pick up my knife and fork and lean in. "It smells delicious. But before I start, please tell me why you stop and stare sometimes."

She looks at me and I refuse to release her gaze. Her cheeks flush pink as she lowers her hands. "It is humiliating, you must understand. I do not like to talk about it. I have frightened children with my spells, and don't want to frighten you."

"As you've just pointed out, I'm hardly a child and whatever you tell me will make me less afraid than the unknown."

She draws her brows together, frowns, and pokes at a piece of potato with a crispy brown edge. Finally, she speaks. "You will be one of few people who know." She pauses. "It started when I was an adolescent. I have petit mal seizures. Epilepsy. I briefly lose consciousness and then come back. It never lasts more than twenty seconds."

I sit back in my chair. Epilepsy is serious.

"There. I've told you. Happy?"

"Are they dangerous? Your seizures?"

She slowly and deliberately takes a forkful of chicken, chews, and then swallows. I follow suit. "Only if I'm somewhere unsafe—like the middle of a street. But thank God, that hasn't happened in many years. I can't feel the spells coming on—they hit me a couple times a day—and when I come to, I barely sense anything happened."

Over our meal, I pull Madame's story from her. When she was twelve, teachers told her parents she sometimes wouldn't respond when called on. Her mother knew this wasn't like her daughter, so she took her to the doctor.

"I've had to take medication ever since. It lessens the frequency and severity of the seizures, but they can't be cured."

"Is it genetic?"

"Yes. They ran tests when Eugène was little, but he's fine. Still, Charles and I decided to have just one child."

Our desserts arrive, *tartes au citro*n with fat raspberries on top. Madame's face lights up like a child's as she looks at the pale-yellow rounds. "My favorite part," she says. We take mouthfuls of our citrusy desserts, relish their sweet and sour flavors, and finish with tiny cups of espresso.

"Did the university know about the epilepsy?"

"Only the head of my department and he kept the secret. They would not have fired me, of course—this is France, where academics are practically royalty—but I feared they wouldn't promote me if they knew."

"And so, you were named full professor?"

She nods. "And eventually department chair."

"*Félicitations,* Professor. That must have made you—and Monsieur Arnoux—very proud."

"Yes. Eugène as well. He was finishing high school and invited his friends to our apartment to celebrate. They prepared the food and even made me *une tarte aux abricots*, my favorite. But, that was long ago."

I make a mental note about her preference for apricot pie and then think about the end of my own time in high school. Dad had always told me I was "college material," but Mother ignored my hints about going to the university until one day she screamed, "You're unrelenting, Cat. Think about the money. Your father and I didn't go to college, so why should you?"

I didn't respond but my epithet tolled: I'm a Curious-Intellectual-with-a-Streak-of-Rebellion and I'm going.

By senior year, classmates had visited schools up and down the east coast and a few in Chicago and California. I knew my best hope was a degree from the public university two towns over. One evening, I heard Mother and Dad argue about college in their bedroom. "Fine, Stephen," she said. "She's your flesh and blood. Do what you want."

Was she disowning me? Relinquishing her role as my mother?

They never knew about my visits to the university when I told them I was doing a project at school. I didn't like lying but figured that one wouldn't keep me out of heaven.

The grounds were hardly beautiful. Not an ivy-covered wall or grassy lawn in sight. But I loved the wide concrete stairway up to the library. I sat on the steps for hours, reading and watching college life go by—carefree girls with ponytails and athletic boys in Levi's, all of them laughing and carrying an armful of books.

One Saturday, I returned from campus to an empty house. Dropping my backpack on the counter, I saw Mother's note: Ordering new carpet, then off to five o'clock Mass.

New carpet? Her pocketbook knew no bounds when it came to her crappy little Cape but she couldn't afford my education? And never mind that Dad needed a new car, the trunk of his Maverick held shut by a bungee cord and the front bumper patched with duct tape.

I was convinced she must get off on her little slice of domesticity.

The four years passed in a blur, save one day in late April when a slim number ten envelope from the local university arrived. Dad hugged me hard and wouldn't let go. When he pulled back, he whispered, a catch in his voice, "I'm so proud of you, Catrine. A full scholarship. And there's nothing anyone can do about it."

I looked up at him, my eyebrows raised.

"Not even Mother," he said. "I'll break the news."

He knew if I told her myself, she would think I'd betrayed her.

And then finally, it was May, the last month a hurried haze of exams, helping Freddie pass French, and the lead-up to the prom. Without a date, I stretched out on the backyard chaise lounge in my bathing suit on dance day, merciless Mid-Atlantic humidity pressing down while I listened to the noisy whine of the window fan. I tried not to dwell on what I was missing. At Freddie's suggestion, I'd doused my hair with lemon juice to lighten it further and slathered my body in baby oil until it glistened. I lay back, whirling patterns of colors shifting behind my closed eyelids, enjoying the scent of Mother's garden, soft lilac and sharp geranium, and transported myself to a Provençal field.

Then the screen door slammed. *Stairway to Heaven* blasted on my transistor radio, but the scolding sliced through.

"Don't you get oil on my cushions!" Mother stood on the stoop, hands on her hips. "Father Ceinture's coming for dinner. I don't want stains."

Dad was on the road so we'd economized all week with breakfast for dinner so the good Father could have London Broil.

She continued, "Where'd that apple pie on the counter come from?"

"Freddie. For helping her with French."

"We'll have it tonight so I won't have to buy something." She blessed herself, acknowledging the answered prayer.

"Graduation's coming up," Mother said as she swept the patio.

"Two more weeks."

"You working full-time after?"

I rubbed the back of my neck, thinking about going back to the warehouse day after day. "Why would this summer be any different?" Clenching my teeth, I gripped the lounge chair's arms hard. "At least until I start at the university."

"Well, when I finished high school, I moved out, paid my own rent and—"

"That's what this is about?' I pushed myself up on one hand and shaded my eyes with the other. "Paying rent? You couldn't even wait until after I graduated to mention it?"

I shot up, grabbed my cut-off shorts and tee-shirt, and disappeared around the garage before she could respond. I threw on my clothes, hopped on my Schwinn, and rode for miles to cool down.

The following day, Freddie called to fill me in on the prom and to let me know her parents had booked her summer ticket to France. She begged, "Come with me, Cat."

My longing notwithstanding, I knew Paris was a no. The airfare alone was a nonstarter and so I didn't bother asking. I imagined Dad's gentle but tired reassurance. "What a nice invitation. Maybe next year..."

And so, as I did every May, I stayed silent about summer possibility.

Back with Madame at La Rotonde, we take the final bites of our dessert. I hear the scrape of her chair as she pushes back and signals to the waiter for the check. She quickly pays and swings around to take her cane from her chair. "Shall we walk some more? I have one more address to show you."

Chapter Twenty-Two

We step from under La Rotonde's awnings. "Thank you, Madame. That was the nicest meal I've had in Paris."

"*Je vous en prie.*" You're welcome.

We walk single file past a parade of Parisians carrying plastic bags heavy with produce, cheese, olives, and bread from Raspail's open-air market. Madame walks ahead between the double line of pollarded plane trees sprouting leafy green shoots, their truncated branches like fists thrust to the sky. In my post-lunch torpor, I'm content to be schoolgirl Madeline, following Miss Clavel, the tall, thin headmistress, marching her girls through Paris. It's a role I've always been content with—listening intently, reading voraciously, and completing assignments.

I also enjoyed the satisfaction of work. Just after high school, the warehouse foreman moved me from the assembly line to accounting and I took gratification in organizing files, resolving problems, and emptying my wooden in-box. I had my own desk with a swivel chair just behind Mother. Everyone at work knew I was her daughter, despite the lack of resemblance. The older I got, the more I looked like my Dad, and was pleased his genes were evident.

"Definitely your father's kid," my flirty new boss said on my first day as he took in my long legs. "Same blonde hair, same Greek nose, same wide eyes and cheekbones. And such a tall drink of water."

Was he coming on to me? Mother cleared her throat behind me. "Time for work."

I smiled, scratching hard at my hand, but no words came out. I'd made it through high school with a blank sexual scorecard, but would I now have to deal with my supervisor making moves? He's gross and I'm hardly flattered. But maybe Mother would be pleased, thinking this young accounting manager would make a good catch, given her relationship mantra: "Graduate high school, find a man with a good job, and marry him."

The fall after high school graduation, Freddie went off to an exclusive women's college in New England. I took a bus to the university to register and repeated the commute daily. With each passing year of my studies, Dad was away on ever-longer trips and I minimized time at home to avoid Mother's jabs about my education. *So, how's Miss Smarty Pants today? Feeling superior to your family?*

After junior year, my savings were significant—enough to get me to France for a month. Freddie made her annual plea for me to join her there in the summer (I haven't seen you in like forever), but I knew that when I finally got to France, I'd want to stay for much longer than four summer weeks.

Madame stops before the intersection with a side street to sit on a bench.

"Tired?" I ask as I sit.

"That's usually why one takes a seat."

"Well, I'm in no rush." I pull my feet up on the bench, wrap my arms around my jean-clad shins, and hold my elbows with opposite hands. I close my eyes, feeling the sun on my face.

Madame coughs and I open my eyes. "I lost Charles in the spring, and yet, this season still makes me happy. The warmth of a literary stroll…especially with a companion." I see her smile as she looks up to the trees.

She says, "Do you have friends in Paris, Catrine? Besides that Freddie person."

"Not since she kicked me out." But then I think of Odette. "Well, maybe one..."

"Any young men? Surely you've attracted a few."

I feel my cheeks flush. "Actually, there is someone. Vincent. He took me to dinner on my first night in Paris and went on the disastrous beach trip I told you about. We get along really well and for a short while I thought he might like me, but I haven't seen him in weeks." I shrug. "I don't have a good history with men, though. I mean, I don't really have any history, to be honest."

"Maybe this Vincent is the start. Where has he been these past weeks?"

I shake my head. "Freddie told him I went back to the US. I don't know how to reach him, unless I ask Freddie, and I won't do that. I'm sure she told him we fought—her version of things—so even if he knew I was still here, he'd probably avoid me. And then of course, I moved…"

Madame laughs. "So, from his perspective you've disappeared entirely and Freddie's thrown dirt over your tracks. No wonder you haven't seen him."

I think about this for a moment. "Well, that one girlfriend I mentioned—her name's Odette. I saw her a few days ago and she told me he was away on business, but that when he got back, she'd tell him she saw me. She knows how to contact me and said she would pass that on."

Madame voices my next thought. "But until she sees him, even if he wanted to find you, he couldn't?"

"I suppose not. Not until Odette tells him the truth."

"Well then, by all means leave your fate up to someone else's whims."

"You think I'm not doing enough?"

She shakes her head. "It's not for me to say. But sometimes I wonder if we each have to take a bit more responsibility for our own loneliness."

I reflect on what she says until she slaps her knee and stands, her voice stern, her face all business. She taps her cane on the sidewalk. "Time to go. Can't sit here all day."

"And you Madame? What are you doing about *your* loneliness?" I ask as we cross the boulevard.

She gives me a sly look. "Making a new friend, what do you think?" She finishes with a wink.

I smile at her sideways compliment. Yes, we're becoming friends, and unlikely as our alliance may be, it's helping me feel like I belong in this city.

"Madame," I say. "Do you have many friends?"

"Years ago. My fellow professors and I were close and saw each other often. But when Charles got sick, we lost touch. Many retired and moved to their ancestral homes in the country. Others died or keep to themselves. Charles and I were quite content to have each other."

We turn right onto the *rue de Fleurus*. "Are we going to the Luxembourg Gardens?"

"Not that far." She stops after a few more steps. "Number twenty-seven."

A stately nineteenth-century apartment building of ivory stone and iron balconies, just like so many other Haussmann-era structures, stands before us. The face of an old, bearded man is carved above the door and its white numbers on a blue square are to the side. I note the plaque that says Gertrude Stein, her brother Leo, and her lover, Alice B. Toklas, lived there.

"Oh my God! This building's in *A Moveable Feast* too. Gertrude Stein's salon. She's the one who called Hemingway and the other expat authors 'The Lost Generation.'"

Madame nods. "How she loved those writers…so disillusioned after the first war." She shakes her head. "And not only writers, but artists like Picasso and Matisse." Her words take on a professorial tone and I picture her at a lectern. "Stein surrounded herself with them and became their mentor and cheerleader. I like picturing her in her big chair by the fireplace draped in her brown corduroy suit, commanding attention, and encouraging her devotees' experimental expressions."

"Sounds like you sympathize with her."

"I guess I do." She leans on her cane, one hand atop the other. "Many of my students were writers and took inspiration from the masters. Some showed promise but lost confidence. I did what I could to encourage them."

I take a step towards the building and press my face to the glass door, overlaid with a decorative iron screen, to peer through the entryway. Past a wall of mail slots, I see a slice of inner courtyard—lush grass, the edge of a flowerbed, and the leafy branches of trees. I wonder who lives in Stein's apartment now.

As I pull away, a voice tinged with an affected British accent, reminiscent of Eleanor Roosevelt, calls from around the garden wall. "It is inevitable when one has a great need of something one finds it. What you need you attract like a lover."

"Did you hear that?" I spin around to face Madame.

"Hear what?"

"Those words from inside the courtyard. 'It is inevitable ... something, something ... like a lover.'"

"Must have been Ms. Stein herself. 'It is inevitable when one has a great need of something one finds it. What you need you attract like a lover.' It's one of her most memorable quotes."

I think for a moment and then say, "I'm sure I've never heard it before. Not until now. But it does remind me of something my father used to say. 'Always be searching—what you don't look for will never be found.' Maybe it was him I heard." Before considering how Madame will react I add, "I've never told anyone, but this isn't the first time I've heard a voice no one else does."

She smiles. "I hear literary voices all the time."

Shocked, I say, "You do?"

"Perhaps it goes hand in hand with reading others' words so diligently."

"But you hear them as if they're speaking to you directly? Not just that their words float through your mind, perhaps as timely memories?"

"Does there have to be much of a difference? If you're listening, why not expect to hear something useful from time to time?"

Maybe she's right. Hearing things is a natural consequence of living alone, always in my head, my attention so often in a book.

Madame says, "I repeatedly told my students everything you learn is tucked in a corner of your brain, there to draw upon when you need it."

"But I never heard voices until I arrived in France. Where were they when I needed them back home?"

"Maybe you were so filled with yearning in America that you weren't receptive. The voices were there, but other concerns drowned them out."

I step forward and again grab the iron grill, my face between the bars, listening.

Silence.

I'm feeling gutsy, so I turn and tell Madame about my encounter with Monsieur Baudelaire. I end with, "One should always be drunk. That's all that matters."

Madame Arnoux finishes it. "'With wine, with poetry, or with virtue, as you choose. But do get drunk.'"

Her head falls back as she laughs and I join her.

"My, my…from your love of a children's book about Brittany to channeling Baudelaire on a Left Bank bench." She shakes her head and adds, "Baudelaire never failed to express himself, so I'm not surprised he revealed himself to you." There's a new pleasantness in her voice.

"You don't think I'm crazy?"

"Aren't we all a little? Baudelaire and Balzac both speak to me often. I even summon them when I need someone to talk to—particularly now when no one else wants to listen."

"Really?"

"I'm alone a lot these days. Eugène is always busy." Her smile fades for a moment but then she perks up. "But not too busy to be a busybody. That's an English expression, *non*?"

I nod. "I guess he must wonder where you are." I check my watch. "I really should get you home."

"I am tired and probably walked more than enough today. I'll take the bus on Raspail. It goes right to my corner."

"I'll walk to the stop and wait with you."

"You're very kind. I've not enjoyed a day like this in a long time. But before we go, may I ask you to consider something?"

I look at her and nod.

"Perhaps you will keep hearing these voices until you find your own."

I don't know what to say, so I shrug and simply nod again.

She takes my arm as we cross the boulevard. "I would love to see you again," I say. "If you're up to it."

"I have a few doctor's appointments this week, but how about Saturday? It's supposed to storm, so we should plan something indoors. Eugène is coming in the morning to help me clean, so perhaps coffee that afternoon? Two o'clock at Chez Papa?"

"Coffee it is." We arrive at the stop as her bus pulls up, brakes hissing. I watch her leave and am suddenly blue, like a child when Christmas is over.

As I head to my flat, cutting through the Luxembourg Gardens, my steps are slow as I'm unable to shake Gertrude Stein's words. "What you need you attract like a lover." Why hasn't it worked with a job?

And then from nowhere I hear, "*N'être plus écouté: c'est cela qui est terrible lorsqu'on est vieux.*" To no longer be listened to: that's what is terrible when you are old. Albert Camus echoes exactly what Madame said. But she also said hearing voices isn't so strange, so I pay Camus no mind and continue across the park, reflecting on what she said. Are the voices trying to help me find my own?

Chapter Twenty-Three

I've sent Mother a letter every week but have yet to receive one from her. The afternoon after my outing with Madame, guilt nips at me until I can't ignore it. I don't really want to speak to her but duty wins out. I decide to call her from La Poste to check on her before she leaves for work.

"I haven't heard from you in so long," Mother says when she picks up on the first ring.

"Aren't you getting my letters? You told me not to call."

"Of course, I am. I keep thinking one of them will say you're coming home."

Why does she want me back so badly? Does she really miss me and not just my rent?

"I'm actually looking for an au pair job—"

"A what?"

"Taking care of a family's children in exchange for room and board. So I can stay."

"A job in Paris? Aren't you tired of it all yet? Sounds like you've already been to every museum and church and park. One museum would be too many for me."

"There's still so much to see. All over France."

"Beyond Paris?"

I can almost feel her shudder through the phone.

"Your letters make you sound like a social butterfly—out and about all the time. What do you wear to all these glamorous outings?"

"They're hardly glamorous."

"It's not what Rose Marie from Catholic Daughters said. She went to Paris two years ago and everywhere she went, people were dressed up."

No matter what I say, she'll believe a Catholic Daughter over her own daughter.

"I'm glad you called, Cat. I got a letter from Walter, Aunt-Dagmar-who-moved-to-Germany's husband. She may be close to meeting our Lord."

"Is she sick?"

"She's had heart troubles since we were little and now she's having complications. I called her when I got Walter's letter."

Mother spent money to call Germany?

"They're in a convalescent home in their town—in an apartment together—to prepare her for surgery and then recovery. Unless she dies first."

"Are you going to see her?"

"I can't."

"Why not? You're her only sibling. Why didn't you ever tell me about her heart?"

"Telling everyone everything can be complicated."

I brace myself against the back of the wooden booth "Mother, you need to come to Germany to see Aunt Dagmar. It's your responsibility. You're the one who always talks to me about my family duty to you."

"You know very well I don't even own a suitcase."

And I was born with mine packed.

"But she's your sister and you say she might die."

"I can't travel that far, especially alone." She sounds wistful for a moment. Remembering my father? But then she perks up and I'm sure it's rehearsed. "You go, Cat. Germany's close to France, isn't it? You'll go for me."

"I can't—"

Mother barrels ahead and insists I write down Uncle Walter and

Aunt Dagmar's address. I take down the particulars but stiffen as I consider her request. I want to go to Germany to meet my family, but on my terms. This is her obligation. "I can't afford it right now, Mother."

"I'll pay," she says, as if it releases her. "Will be a lot cheaper than me flying from Virginia. I'm sure Walter could get you a room for a few days."

"At the convalescent home?"

"Might be a nice getaway."

"What do you know about getaways?" I mumble, holding the receiver so tight my nails dig into my palm.

"What was that?"

"Nothing, Mother." I pause, feigning calm while drawing my free hand into a fist. I hold the receiver, my head against my neck, to scratch at my eczema. "Goddamn it. She's your sister, for Chrissake."

"Language!"

"You, Walter, and I are all she has left. Don't you want to see her?"

"I'll wire you the money to visit Dagi—sorry, Dagmar."

The operator holds up a finger.

"I have to go, Mother."

"Well, I'm glad we're agreed. I'll send the money this week."

I end the call and sit quietly in the wooden booth to settle. It's not that I mind going to Germany. Dagmar and her husband Walter are family after all and they send me a birthday card every year. The card always includes a check and a chatty line or two of news, and I dutifully write a thank you note. Mother says I'd met them when I was little, but I don't remember. For years I wished Mother would take me to Germany to see them, and when she didn't, I promised myself I would visit one day.

But right now, I want to stay in France, I need to find work, and I don't want Mother thinking she can still boss me around. But while I'm in the phone booth, I might as well call them right away. Maybe Aunt "Dagi" isn't as sick as Mother says and can hang on until I figure things out.

I arrange the call with the operator. A minute later, an English-speaking receptionist answers and tells me my aunt and uncle are with the doctor. She'll tell them I called. Before leaving La Poste, I buy a postage-paid mailer and dash off a note to my uncle.

> Spoke to Mother. I really want to see you but a visit in the next few weeks will be tough. But I will try.

I write my return address on the back flap and seal the envelope.

Walking home, I reflect on how little I know about Mother's family. Whenever I asked, she told me my grandmother, her mother, fled Germany in 1931 to escape crushing unemployment and became a housekeeper in America. She married a German farmer in Virginia. Dagmar was born shortly thereafter, and Mother came along years later. In the 1950s, my grandparents returned to Germany. Mother refused to fly, but Dagmar went often. On one trip, she met Walter, and eventually moved there to marry him.

Mother always ended the story with, "Dagmar should have stayed in Virginia with me. Her baby sister." Her pout told me she still resented it.

I did manage to engage her one Saturday night when I was ten. We were watching "The Carol Burnett Show," one of few things that made her laugh. Out of the blue I asked, "Who was your best friend growing up?"

"Aunt-Dagmar-who-moved-to-Germany," she said without hesitation. "Me and her were inseparable."

She and I.

"Did you ever visit her after she moved?"

She got a faraway look in her eyes. "Things happened. Difficult things."

"Like what?"

She looked down at her hands, chin trembling, and wouldn't look up. I knew better than to push so I repeated my first question. "So, you never visited?"

She shook her head. "Too expensive. And too foreign." She paused to wipe her eyes. "They all spoke German but I didn't even try. I'm no good at languages. Not like you."

It was the first compliment she'd ever given me. I was so distracted that I hardly noticed her get up and disappear into another room. But later I wondered about the things she hadn't wanted to talk about. What had been so difficult?

Chapter Twenty-Four

The weekend dawns dreary, just as Madame had predicted. A soft rain falls all morning, freckling the puddles along the rue Monsieur le Prince. Perfect for turning inward to my journal. I've so much to think about since my call with Mother. Her family has always been in shadows. Just a few black and white snapshots of two girls in front of a white clapboard farmhouse in the Virginia hills and annual birthday cards. But there was something about Mother calling her sister by her nickname, Dagi, that brought my aunt to life—a very real girl who grew up with Mother and is now sick and only a train ride away. I really should get there as soon as I can.

I leave my flat in plenty of time to meet Madame for our Saturday afternoon rendezvous, anticipating a few cozy hours over coffee. But as I cross my building's courtyard, the heavens open and needling rain drops in sheets. Madame Vauquer waves from her window and calls me over. I'm sure it's about next month's rent, due yesterday. I've been putting it off, reluctant to tell her I'll only be staying three more weeks and magically thinking I'll find a way to extend.

I step into her mudroom, rain dripping from my hood. I say before she has a chance to tell me, "I know about the rent. I'll get it to you tonight."

"*D'accord,*" she says, handing me a paper towel for my face.

I wipe the rain and pause for as long as I can before I voice the inevitable. "And I'm afraid this will be my...my final rent payment for you."

"Well, I'll be sorry to see you go. You're a good tenant." She sits to open her green ledger on the kitchen table, already moving on. She turns to look up at me. "You're sure?"

I nod. "I can stay for three more weeks. Through June twentieth." At least I'll still be in Paris on the sixteenth—my twenty-third birthday.

"I'll need to find a new lodger as soon as possible. I'll post it tomorrow."

My voice breaks. "I don't want to go back..." I start to say, "home," but choke on the word. "...to America. But I must." I turn to the courtyard before she can see my eyes have filled with tears.

I snap open my umbrella but the minute I pass through the entryway to the street, it detonates in the wind, beyond salvage. I stuff it in the nearest trashcan and pull up my hood against the elements. Thunder rumbles and rain pummels. Maybe this isn't the best day to meet Madame. Given the weather, will she even venture out? Mercifully, as I cross through the cemetery, the wind quiets, the downpour eases, and I'm able to walk upright without clutching my trench to my throat. A thick fog settles and people, trees, and cars become the gray shadows of charcoal drawings. The welcoming light of Chez Papa on the corner emerges from the gloom, and after veering to avoid the rain sluicing over the awning, I push open the door.

Inside is a fog of cigarette smoke and humidity, wet clothing, and the burn of the radiator. I'm transported back to third grade wearing my sleeveless wool jumper dress that I always wore over a white blouse. The gray fabric was soaked after I walked several blocks to school in the rain. Mother had brushed aside Dad's concern about dark morning clouds and sent me off without a slicker. The dank fabric made my thighs prickle with an allergic reaction. My teacher sent me to the health office with a red rash traveling down my legs. I sat on the cot behind the white privacy curtain, scratching furiously.

"Try not to scratch, okay?" the nurse said. "Let's see what I can find you to wear, But my, you are a tall one."

I took off my soaked jumper and damp white blouse and folded them neatly. The nurse pulled back the curtain, applied a white cream to my legs, and then helped me into a too-tight tee and too-short sweatpants from her lost-and-found. She took the yellow emergency contact card from my file, left the manila folder on my cot, and closed the curtain. I heard her call Mother, asking her to bring me a new outfit. From what I could tell, Mother was reluctant to leave work, but the nurse was firm.

Waiting, I finished the book of La Fontaine fables I'd brought with me and then flipped through my health history file. The last sheet had basic data written by Dad: name, address, birth date, and phone number. Under next of kin, it listed mother but beneath her name was my grandfather's: Étienne Gray. Why had Dad written that?

Mother arrived in a huff, swept back the curtain, and dropped a paper bag of clothes on the floor next to me.

The nurse stood to greet her. "Hello, Mrs. Gray. Catrine will be fine without her wet jumper. Look—the swelling and rash are better already. She'll go back to class soon and I'll send her home with some salve."

"Good," Mother said. "I have to get right back to the office. There's a pile of letters to be typed." She looks down at me. "And you know my boss."

She then turned to leave, unapologetic.

"Mother," I said, catching the tail of her coat from where I sat. "Why did Dad write my grandfather's name on this form instead of his?" I waved it in front of me.

She grabbed it, took a glance and harrumphed. "Your father probably filled it out after an all-nighter and wasn't thinking straight." She handed the form to the nurse.

"See you at home." And she was out the door. No hug, no kiss.

Yes, my rash had calmed but the eczema on my hand was raging.

Chapter Twenty-Five

Two o'clock comes and goes while I sit at Chez Papa, sipping my *café crème* by the fogged window. I'm still damp and shivering at two-fifteen. The weather is evil so it must be delaying Madame. When she fails to arrive by two-thirty, I'm sure it's the weather that delayed her.

I order another coffee and take out a book of French poetry. I'll give her until three, in case she mixed up the time. I do my best to lose myself in my favorite poems but can't concentrate.

The café door slams open and bangs shut. A stocky man with a balding pate and glasses stands and looks around. He's well-dressed in gray slacks, dark peacoat, and wingtips. A slight paunch strains his button-down blue shirt. What remains of his thinning hair is wet and drips onto his shoulders. He takes off his fogged glasses and wipes them with a handkerchief. After replacing them, he scans the room and catches my eye. He makes his way to my table. Towering over me, he looks me up and down and says in French, "You are Catrine?"

"Yes, I'm Catrine." I pull my cardigan tight. "And you are?"

"My name is Eugène and my mother was to meet you. But she cannot." He bends forward, his jaw clenched tight. "Not in this weather."

"Oh, I see. I'm sorry she can't come today. Is she okay?"

"When she told me how far she walked with you the other day—past Montparnasse—well, that is crazy. She's a seventy-nine-year-old widow with epilepsy, or did you not notice?"

His irritated tone is drawing looks from other cafe customers. I gesture for him to sit, which he ignores, and says calmly, "I've seen her brief seizures. I like your mother and enjoy her company. She seemed to enjoy our walk."

"Well, you were mistaken, young lady," he says. He picks up the spoon from the setting across from me and slaps it down. "My mother is fragile—has been since my father died—two years now. I worry about her all the time, living by herself and taking care of that apartment, which she doesn't do well, I assure you. I can't have the extra stress of worrying about her being out with a stranger."

I meet his gaze. "I'm not a stranger."

He drops the irritation and turns to an appeal.

"Look, she was still in bed when I arrived at ten this morning. She never sleeps so late. But once she told me about your outing, it made sense. It was too much for her."

"I understand your concern and don't want you worrying about your mother. I promise we'll shorten our walks. But she is lonely and we're becoming friends."

He raises an eyebrow. "Friends? Why would a young woman like you want to waste your time with a difficult old woman?"

"We have a lot in common actually."

He rubs his balding head as if it helps him think. "Listen, my mother was upset when I told her she couldn't come today. And was furious when I said she shouldn't see you anymore."

"Why would you say that?"

"I cannot have you taking her all over Paris to God knows where. She could have a seizure, fall, or get hit by a car and I wouldn't even know."

"But I would be with her."

He offers a weak smile. "I can see you are a 'friendly American,' but in a month or two you'll be back in the States and I'll be stuck with an invalid mother grieving her lost friend. At least give her some time to recover."

Before I can argue, he strides to the door, and disappears into the fog.

Back in my apartment, Eugène's visit has me rattled and I toss and turn all night. What if his anger had turned violent à la Freddie? I decide I'll give him some time to cool off and will delay my next visit with Madame. But despite my fear, I won't allow him to end my newfound friendship.

Chapter Twenty-Six

Desperation to stay in Paris has me branching beyond au pair positions. I spend all day Monday crisscrossing Paris answering ads for a waitress and getting through a frustrating interview with a harried single father looking for an au pair who speaks French and Italian.

By Monday evening, I'm spent and call Odette about getting together. She apologizes and says she can't until the following weekend. "I'm working a book signing Wednesday and I'm super-stressed because the author is one of our VIPs and there are so many details to sort out and my boss and colleagues won't be there to help."

Odette is speaking really, really fast, her words running together.

"Don't get me wrong, I want to do it because he's a brilliant writer and really famous but I'm so nervous and there'll be lots of press, and what if I screw up?"

Odette sounds like she's falling apart. "I want this signing to be perfect because I'll be in charge and it might actually lead to a promotion if it goes well, and—"

"Whoa," I say. "Alone? For such a star?"

"Most of the office is at a book convention and, fine, I'll admit it. The guy is really cute and I kind of have a crush on him and so I told my boss I could handle it by myself. Which might have been a mistake—"

"A crush?! So he's not the pompous, pointy nosed professor type I'm imagining?"

"*Oh mon dieu, non*!!" She laughs. "You should see him, mysterious, handsome, charismatic…" I think I've momentarily made her forget her stress, but then it's back.

"*Mais, putain*! What if he's furious I'm the only one there. What if he expects more fuss? They say he needs special treatment. One of the editors calls him Tartuffe because he's so aloof and full of himself. But I thought he was sweet when I first met him. And, he is *si si beau*. I wish you could meet him—" The line goes dead quiet. Then Odette practically screams my name.

"Catrine! You can help me! Can't you? Can you?…"

I parrot back, "Can I?… " I'm so curious about her job and it would be a dream to meet a famous French author. "When is it?"

"In two days, on Wednesday."

"I'm free, so I can definitely help, if you want. I mean, if you show me what to do."

"Of course! *Merci mille fois*, Catrine. Three o'clock at Les Editeurs in Odéon but I have to be there in the morning to set up at ten o'clock." When she gives me the address, her voice is a touch lighter.

"I'll be there," I say, a mixture of fear and excitement gathering in my gut. A real book signing with a real French writer in a fancy café. And it's right around the corner from my flat. Finally, I'll hear an author's real voice instead of one in my head.

Two days later, I stand under the red and white awning of Les Editeurs, a fashionable café on the Carrefour de l'Odéon in Saint-Germain-des-Près. I read in *Let's Go* that the quarter is home to many publishing houses and that Les Editeurs is crawling with literary types. Even without the description, I could have guessed from the look of the place: red leather barrel chairs and wall-to-wall mahogany shelves filled with hardcovers.

I shift from one foot to the other until Odette arrives in a black skirt and blouse and a red beret that matches the chairs. Her clipboard rests in the crook of her left arm. I'm relieved I chose to wear my black dress and ballet flats, because our complementary attire makes us look like we really could be coworkers.

We work together all morning making reminder calls to the media (I spoke to a reporter at *Paris Match*!), hanging signs (I stenciled two myself), setting up tables, chairs, and a lectern (my palms are blistered), and piling books in careful spirals (I'm dizzy looking at them). Odette explains how the program will work: introductions, an author talk, Q and A, and then the signing. All that's left is for the author to arrive. I shake my hands to stop their trembling.

Odette pulls a cigarette from her bag, lights it, takes a long drag, and blows perfect, sluggish, smoke-rings. "I can't thank you enough for helping. I was crazy to think I could do it alone," she says, flicking the ash.

"I'm having fun and learned so much already."

She takes another long drag. "Hey, forgot to tell you. Vincent's back from Frankfurt and I'll see him at a party tomorrow night."

She must see my look of hope and then worry because she says, "Yes, Freddie will be there. But I'll tell him privately you're still in Paris and he should see you soon." She gives me a sad face. "You know, in case you have to go back to America."

My stomach flips but I have no time to respond because Odette cries out, "*Putain*—he's here!" She drops her cigarette and grinds it into the pavement. She turns to me, "But, *merde*! He's half an hour early!"

A sleek black sedan pulls up and stops in the middle of the street. I see a profile in the back seat.

"It's him," Odette says. "Christian. Wait till you meet him! I am so damned nervous." She crosses her arms, hugs her clipboard close to her chest, and grips each side with her hands.

We wait for the door to open, but when he doesn't appear after several minutes, I suggest that Odette rap on the back window. But her face is flushed and she looks like she's going to be sick. I knock for her, but when there's no response, I go to the front window. The pane slowly comes down. The driver says, "He told me to drive away. Doesn't want to get out."

"What?" Odette says. Overhearing the driver has snapped her back to attention. Her voice rises as she says, "He has to get out. All these people are here to see him." She points to the gathering crowd behind us. "Is this a publicity stunt?"

I lean on the front door and poke my head in. I turn toward the dark interior of the back seat, where the author sits with his face held in his hands. "I can't do it," he says.

I immediately recognize what we're dealing with. If this man were simply being rude, I'm sure Odette could handle him. But this poor guy is twitching with anxiety, something I'm quite familiar with. "Please come inside, Monsieur," I say. "We won't start until you feel comfortable. I promise." My words have no authority but I also know if he doesn't get out of the car, Odette will have a nervous breakdown.

As I step back, several photographers along with a few pedestrians approach the car, still mid-lane. Traffic has backed up behind the sedan and horns blare.

"What should I do, Catrine?" Odette asks, tears about to spill.

"Get those folks back on the sidewalk." I say before leaning back through the window. "Monsieur, I'm sure you don't want a scene with the media here." He lifts his head, pulls a handkerchief from his pocket, and wipes his nose. I say, "We'll whisk you past them. To a room in the back." I pause to catch his gaze. "Please?"

Christian unexpectedly exits the back door. Café patrons and those Odette has driven back stare. He's in jeans, black leather slip-ons, a gray UCLA T-shirt, and a black sports jacket. He's about forty, on the short side with tanned, boyish features and wavy blond hair. He doesn't even look at Odette as she steps forward to greet him. He bounds up the stairs and hurries to the back of the restaurant. Odette turns and gestures furiously for me to follow before trailing him up the stairs.

She catches up with Christian and unlocks the door to the room we've stocked with water, Perrier, coffee, and a fruit platter. She ushers us in and closes the door. He sits hard on a red chair looking at the floor, his hands glued to his knees. Odette opens her mouth, but nothing comes out. She's flushed and still looks like she's about to vomit.

I step in, pretending I know what I'm doing. "Something to drink?" I ask Christian.

He doesn't look at me, but shakes his head. I see his right leg shaking. One hand rubs his thigh as the fingers of his free hand tousle his hair.

"Or, I could get you something from the bar?"

Christian looks up and manages a half-smile. "I've had three coffees and two Cocas to get me ready, but they haven't helped. How about a Cognac."

Odette blows out a sigh, finds her voice, and says, "Add it to my tab. And make it two."

Christian's eyes close and his hands shake as he sips his Hennessy. He crosses his legs and then crosses them again the other way. He rolls his shoulders and gets up to pace the room with his drink, his free hand on his neck. He's a nervous wreck and Odette isn't far behind. She swirls what's left of her drink, having already taken a gulp. "You'll be okay, right?" I imagine she's picturing her promotion circling the drain.

But the cognac does its work of loosening and relaxing. For both of them. Over the next ten minutes, we learn our companion suffers from debilitating stage-fright. He almost never does appearances, but his editor pleaded with him to do this one prior to his new novel publishing in September.

"Everyone thinks I'm a snob because I'm such a hermit. I do almost no public speaking because I hate it. What I have to say is in my books."

Odette sits up straight. She's regaining her composure the more Christian speaks.

He says, "But people misunderstand and say I'm testy. Arrogant even."

I nod. It's what Mother always said about me. If you don't talk, people will think you're a snob. "It hurts when people misjudge you," I say.

He nods, takes another sip of cognac, and pulls a set of index cards from his pocket. "I prepared a talk but can't do it. It's been a bad, jumpy week and an even worse day. I'll sign books but can't speak."

Odette slumps back down.

I know exactly how he feels. Freddie did all our high school French presentations and so the first time I had to present a paper in college—on Maupassant's use of imagery—I was terrified. I spoke to my professor and she understood. She agreed to a format as if I were defending a dissertation. I sat in front of the class, she asked questions, and I answered.

"When did you start writing, Christian?" I ask.

"I was young. Maybe ten…"

"What did you write?"

"Short stories. I wrote my first novel at university."

"And where did you get the inspiration for your new book?" I hold up an advance copy.

"In the village where I grew up. From one of the families there."

"And how about the last one you published?"

Christian's confidence seems to inch back as he answers my questions. Odette catches on and adds some of her own. His responses are soon fluid.

"Look at me," I say, pulling over a chair to face Christian.

He takes the final sip of Cognac and puts down the snifter.

"What if Odette introduces you, you come out and sit at the table with me. In some easy chairs. We'll get rid of the damned lectern. I'll ask you a few questions, like I just did. And then Odette can field questions from the audience. You can sit and respond for maybe fifteen minutes, exactly like you've done with us. And then we'll jump right into signing books?"

He rakes his hands though his hair and rubs the back of his neck again.

"Christian?" asks Odette.

He clears his throat. "Sounds good. I can handle questions."

Odette looks at me and mouths, "Thank you."

"*Putain de merde*!" Christian says, patting his pockets. "Forgot my lucky pen."

I take a deep breath. One more hurdle. "What kind is it?" I ask, standing. "There's *une papeterie* down the street."

"Navy, with blue ink—a fountain pen."

"Be back soon with one blue pen and two more Cognacs."

In the packed salon, attendees spill into the bar area. I interview Christian for a few minutes and then Odette calls on raised hands in the audience. Christian answers dozens more questions while I sit beside him, and afterward, he signs more than one hundred books. The media swarm, photographers capture the event, and Odette and I are asked to pose with the author.

Christian's black sedan returns to swoop him back to his hotel and Odette treats me to dinner at Les Editeurs. "Catrine, you are beyond a good friend," she says, raising a glass of red. And I hear the proverb, "*Au besoin on connaît l'ami.*" When you need something, you find out who your friends are.

I look around. But this time the voice is Odette's, beside me.

Chapter Twenty-Seven

A few days later, Odette reaches me on Madame Vauquer's phone to pledge her eternal gratitude for a successful signing. She says she saw Vincent at the party and he asked for my address and phone number. There's no guarantee he'll call, but I float across the courtyard on the possibility. My spirits high, I venture back to the cemetery just before noon to find Madame. It's been over a week since my encounter with her son.

She's there on her bench and is back to wearing black. From behind a tree, I see no sign of Eugène. The church bells toll, she sits in the hollow silence that follows, and then, leaning on her cane, walks towards the gate. I follow at a distance, still on the lookout. She crosses at the light, turns left past Chez Papa, and continues for two blocks. I shadow her from across the divided boulevard until she stops before a wrought-iron filagree entry, inserts her key, and enters.

I peer from behind a blossoming lilac to take in the apartment building. Because of how she dressed the first couple times we met, in tatty clothing and with little care, I hadn't expected such a fashionable address. Though perhaps not wealthy, she must have some means.

I wonder about her life behind those walls. Is she sad there, the place still filled with reminders of Charles? Or is it comforting to be surrounded by mementos of their life together? I hear something from behind me and jump, fearing Eugène. I hear, "*Ce qu'on peut voir au soleil est toujours moins intéressant que ce qui se passe derrière une vitre.*" What one can see in the sunlight is always less interesting than what goes on behind a windowpane. *C'est vrai*, Monsieur Baudelaire.

As I continue watching the building, the corner shutters on the second floor open. Madame leans out to water the flowerbox and leaves the window ajar. As I cross the street, scanning left and right, anxiety niggles. I reach her door and push the bronze button above her name: "Arnoux."

Madame is surprised to hear it's me at her door but she immediately buzzes me in, I go up the stairs, and she opens her door. She takes my hand and squeezes. "I worried I might never see you again." She smiles. "How did you ever find me? Eugène certainly didn't share my address."

At the mention of his name, my breath catches. "Let's just say I'm observant. And curious, as you know."

The foyer is redolent of lavender and sad strains of guitar music come from beyond. A soft male voice sings about loneliness becoming his friend. "*...avec ma solitude*."

But there the appeal ends.

The source of the fragrance, a candle in a jar, sits on the hallway table next to an unruly pile of magazines. Above the table is a gilded mirror but smudges distort my reflection. On either side of the table are yellowing piles of what seem to be every issue of *Le Monde* ever published. One pile has fallen over and trails into the next room. A vacuum cleaner sits in a corner, a dry cleaner bag of clothing hangs by the closet and kicked off shoes lie askew beside the front door. My goodness, Eugène was right. This place is a housekeeping disaster.

Madame says, "My son was so angry with me. I'm sure he was terribly rude at the café."

"He did scare me, otherwise, I would have tried to find you right away. He insisted I let you recover from our walk." She takes my trench and hangs it on a rack overburdened with coats and hats. I look left to the salon and to the right to a hallway, which must lead to the bedrooms. "Seems he was worried about whom you spend time with."

"Come," she says, leaning on her cane. We brush past a half-dead houseplant as she leads me into the sitting room. She drags a laundry basket filled with clothes from the sofa we're to sit on, one of two overstuffed black and white damask sofas facing each other in the room's center. A glass coffee table sits between them, and a silver chandelier hangs overhead.

Paraphernalia is everywhere. Heaps of opened bills, grocery flyers, and miscellaneous household items—a battery, playing cards, and a corkscrew—litter the end tables, and look about to topple over. Clothes are draped over several chairs. Daisies droop in a vase and pollen dusts the coffee table. But despite the mess, being with Madame makes me feel so calm. I look around and mentally declutter the place, doing my best to find something pleasant to say. I ask Madame about the candle in the entry as we take a seat.

"Lavender. Eugéne brought it yesterday, along with some sachets. Told me my place smelled like an old lady and that I need a maid. I won't repeat my reply, but it wasn't nice. I don't appreciate him criticizing my home."

I've no idea how to respond so I concentrate on envisioning the cozy space it must have been before Charles got sick. How could she have let the disarray get so out of hand?

Madame says, "Do you know what de Beauvoir said about keeping house?"

"I can only imagine."

"Few tasks are more like the torture of Sisyphus than housework, with its endless repetition: the clean becomes soiled, the soiled is made clean, over and over, day after day."

"She does have a point."

Madame smiles. "So, what did Eugène say to you?"

I gulp, fearing she'll acquiesce to his ultimatums.

She leans in to catch my eye before I reply. "Whatever he said, ignore him."

I give her a sly grin. "I guess I already have since I'm here."

She pats my knee. "He can say what he will, but this is my life and I'll make friends as I please."

Hearing her call me her friend makes a smile tug at my lips before I can stop it.

"We will continue seeing each other and yes, he'll scold me about all that could go wrong. But our walkabout in Montparnasse made me happy. My legs were sore, but they recovered, and I will keep venturing out whether he likes it or not." She juts out her chin. "I can be very stubborn."

I nod and smile.

"Besides, Eugène's bark is worse than his bite." She stands. "Something to drink?"

I stand too. "Yes, please. But I can get it."

"No, no." Madame waves her hand. "You stay and relax." She heads through the formal dining room at the back of the apartment and into the kitchen to the right, the double-hinged door swinging behind her.

The crisp scent of lemon oil wafts from the dining room and I see the surfaces have recently been polished. More of Eugène's olfactory efforts? All Madame's furnishings appear of high quality, but thin layers of dust cover the lampshades and I spot cobwebs along a corner baseboard. My hand goes to my mouth to suppress a sneeze.

I remain standing to look around. Soaring white bookshelves, the salon's most prominent feature, reach the ceiling, crammed with hundreds of volumes. A sliding wooden ladder for the upper reaches is pushed to the side. Evidence of her well-read life. The shelves straddle a fireplace with an elaborate marble mantel.

I turn toward the street side of the room where floor-to-ceiling windows framed by gossamer white curtains between pale blue silk draperies held back by heavy tasseled ropes let in the light. I glance out over deep pink geraniums to the leafy boulevard below and see the lilac I hid behind. How different from the view out the windows back home in Virginia—a muddy creek glimpsed through tiny panes.

A burled writing desk sits by the front windows. It's covered in a whirlwind of file folders and paper, and beside it, last year's calendar, its edges curled, is thumbtacked to the wall. I glimpse the keys of an old Olivetti typewriter under the piles.

When I turn back, I see dust motes play in the sunlight streaming through the sheers. A cerulean rug hides much of the wooden herringbone floor and two oversized landscapes echoing the blue hang on the wall opposite the bookcase. It's an extraordinary space but for the chaos.

How different this home is from Mother's sterile abode, where she tolerated few family artifacts and absolutely no clutter. Daily, she vacuumed and dusted, including the signed, framed photograph of JFK, the first Catholic president and her hero, who lorded over our dining room. She paid bills the day they arrived; charity solicitations were torn and tossed unread; Christmas cards were pitched the day after the holiday (except those from Aunt Dagmar, saved in a special box). When I asked about getting a puppy, Mother said, "Too dirty and with fleas." I once brought home a turquoise candy dish I'd made in art class. Mother held it up. "Well, isn't that unique." She put it on the sideboard that evening but the next day it was gone. Several Saturdays later, I saw it in the car, next to ratty dishtowels and my old winter coat, all jammed in a box bound for Saint Vincent de Paul.

I shake the memory, knowing my turquoise dish would be welcome in this home. "May I look at your books?" I call.

Madame props open the kitchen door. "Of course. I'm sure you will find much of interest."

I approach the shelves, many of the volumes bound in leather, some upright and some on their sides. I scan the authors shelved in no discernible order: Flaubert, Hugo, Sagan, Balzac, Rimbaud, Molière, and all the many names I would expect, with one notable exception.

Instinctively, I pull books from the shelves and blow dust from their tops. I start rearranging them alphabetically by last name, hoping to come across the short story master so I can place him between Malraux and Mauriac. But after rearranging half a dozen titles, I check my compulsion to organize. These aren't my books and this isn't my home. I drop my hands to my sides and switch to simply scanning the titles. I make it all the way to the bottom shelf.

She pokes her head from the kitchen. "Almost ready."

"Where's Maupassant?" I ask, stifling a sneeze.

"Behind you, *ma petite*. In his own place of honor."

I turn and see a finely carved display case with glass doors against the opposite wall. How could I have missed it? "What a gorgeous piece of furniture. Is everything inside by him?"

"Either by or about him. Take a look. This isn't a museum." She retreats to the kitchen.

I run my fingertips along the glass front of the case, undo the latch, and pull open the doors. In contrast to the mishmash on the shelves, this collection is protected and in perfect order. No dust. The top shelf is filled with antiquarian editions by the author—burgundy, brown and rust leather volumes with gold lettering. I squat to see the titles on the bottom two shelves. Organized by author, they start with multiple volumes by Charles Arnoux.

At the far end of the bottom shelf is a blue and green marbled box. I touch the label on the lid, "Manuscript," and then open it: a messy pile of double-spaced papers. I flip through and find the cover page, the title centered in bold type: Maupassant—My Take. I put it on top and then pat the stack so the edges line up, even though many pages are upside down.

Madame calls from the kitchen. "Help me, Catrine?"

"*J'arrive.*" I replace the pages, cover the box, and close the doors.

Chapter Twenty-Eight

The simple white kitchen with a black and white tiled floor is spotless. Half a baguette, carefully wrapped in a dishtowel, sits on a square enamel table with two black chairs in the middle of the room. There's a single plate and a single cup and saucer drying on a rack by the sink. Apparently, Madame is capable of care and cleaning when food's involved.

"This is when I eat my lunch, so I made us some sandwiches. Ham, Beaufort, and butter."

"I'd love a sandwich. If you don't mind, of course."

"Would I have offered if I minded?"

I grin.

She adds, "We'll eat at the little table in the dining room. The light is better." She hands me a fistful of silverware.

I hesitate, thinking of dust, but then recall the lemon oil.

Madame grabs a bottle of Evian in one hand and leans on her cane with the other. I follow her out of the kitchen to a lacquered game table next to the open window that looks over the building's tidy courtyard at the back of the room.

"You sit, Madame. I'll get everything else." I scoot back to the kitchen for the plates and glasses and make a second trip for the sandwiches and napkins.

We settle into mahogany buttoned-leather game chairs, and I look over to a courtyard edged with green hostas and a variety of colorful flowers.

"Do you usually eat here?" I ask as I take a sandwich.

"Charles and I did. But I eat my meals in the kitchen, so I don't have to carry things."

"Is that Charles?" I nod towards a photo of a distinguished man with thick black hair and a carefully trimmed beard going grey on the credenza behind her.

"It is. Twenty years ago in the Bois de Boulogne, long before he got sick." She swings around, stares at the photo for a while, and then turns back with a beatific smile.

I wonder at the love in her gaze. Will someone ever look at me the way she looks at her husband?

"When I close my eyes and think of Charles, that's what I see." Madame sighs and says, "We used to love walking in that park and then going to a book fair or museum."

I point at another picture. "And is that Eugène in the pearly frame?"

She nods.

I squint. His face has a look of accomplishment and joy. "How old was he?"

"Maybe seven. On vacation at Lake Annecy. Back then he was always so happy. Constantly in motion and always wanting me to read to him—fairy tales, adventures, and eventually, the classics."

Madame is animated talking about her young son, but there's a wistfulness in her voice. I can't help noting the contrast between Eugène in the café and this adorable boy.

"When Eugène was born, I was obsessed with his perfect, pudgy self—his fat, dimpled arms and downy hair."

While I can picture a younger Delphine Arnoux cradling a baby version of the boy in the photo, I'm unable to picture Mother caring for me as an infant. Maybe because there are no photos of my first year since Mother said they lost that scrapbook in the move to our house. In fact, only two photos are displayed in our living room: Mother and Dad's wedding portrait and my college graduation shot. Nothing of me growing up.

I say out loud before I can stop myself, "Mother says picture frames are dust catchers."

Madame laughs and looks around. "I guess they are. And I have plenty. Maybe Eugène is right and I could use some household help."

"That's not what I—"

"I know, *ma cherie.*"

To cover my embarrassment I point to another photo behind her. "How old is Eugène in the photo on the wall? He's quite handsome with his long hair."

She turns. "Twenty-two. Before he stopped swimming and taking care of himself." She ponders a moment. "He started to change when he went to college, he wasn't interested in literature anymore. And all he reads now is *The Financial Times*. Says literature is about the past and he's interested in the future. He became obsessed with business and his friends who only cared about getting rich. He's stuck there, now letting his paycheck dictate his life." She shrugs. "And I thought a preoccupation with success and making money was American, not French. Sorry, *ma petite américaine.*"

"It's fine, I know what you mean. some Americans are obsessed with money and all things material." I sigh. "If I had money I'd use it to stay here in France."

Madame laughs. "*C'est vraiement une bonne idée!*"

She takes a healthy bite of her sandwich and I dig into mine. I chew and swallow as politely as I can before exclaiming, "My God. This cheese is delicious. So buttery and..." I struggle to describe the taste.

"Nutty?"

"That's it—nutty. So good." I take another bite.

"Beaufort, from Savoie, in the French Alps."

"I can't forget to record it in my journal."

We sit quietly, enjoying our lunch, until my eyes drift back to the photos.

"And you, Madame? Why no pictures of yourself?" My tone is teasing but I trigger more wistfulness.

Because I'm old and don't like being reminded of who I was and am not anymore. Slim, attractive, at the opera with Charles, and with a son who adored me." She pauses. "Young people don't understand—I certainly didn't when I was your age. Now, I prefer to focus on the present. And I do my best to avoid mirrors." She pauses. "Faded photos with torn corners remind me of how miserable I've been the past few years, unable to make peace with the face looking back at me from the mirror. I don't recognize myself anymore and feel anger I can't explain. It's not easy getting old alone, with no one to share memories with."

She takes a wedge of lime and squeezes it in her glass. "I'm not necessarily upset about aging, but I wonder about some of my choices. Was it my mothering that turned Eugène into such a malcontent? What if I'd insisted Charles see a doctor sooner? And should I have retired?"

"We can torture ourselves with 'what ifs…'"

"How could you possibly have regrets? Your whole life is ahead of you—nothing but potential. My years have already been judged." She looks out the window.

I decide to keep my own 'what ifs' to myself. What if I'd spent more time with Dad? What if I hadn't been so reticent all my life? What if I'd come to France right after college?

"Enough of regrets," says Madame, pushing aside her crust-strewn plate. She catches sight of a brown sparrow landing on the sill. "Would you like some crumbs, *mon petit*?" She places her plate on the sill. She continues to watch the tiny bird, its head twitching. "Eugène must find his own way, but it makes me sad he's so stressed, so unhappy." She heaves a sigh, looks down, removes her glasses, and pinches the bridge of her nose.

I add my crumbs to the plate and watch the sparrow peck. When I glance back at Madame, I see tears in her eyes. And then from the courtyard floats, "*Il y a des silences qui en disent long comme il y a des paroles qui ne signifient rien.*" There are silences that mean so much, just as there are words that mean nothing.

It's Edith Piaf. The Little Sparrow. But it's not the time to ask Madame if she heard her.

Madame finally says, "Do you know what they say about bird visitors?"

I shake my head.

"They're spiritual messengers announcing news to come."

"This is your home, so he must be here for you."

"But he landed right next to you, and there he stayed." And with that, the sparrow pokes one final time and flies away.

Chapter Twenty-Nine

Walking home, I'm cheerful in my step. Madame seemed pleased I visited, making me promise to come back soon. But a thought pulls me from my delight. How painful it must be for her, having a son she doesn't like much. Is that how Mother feels about me? And then I'm yanked further down by a poster advertising a July fourteenth concert in the Bois de Vincennes. Might I be back in the States when France celebrates its independence? My bright walk slows as I feel a pull deep inside, as if someone plunged a hook between my shoulders and jerked me from behind. I catch my breath at the thought.

The likelihood I can stay in France is now paper-thin, but I refuse to book a ticket home. I have two interviews tomorrow and must do well on at least one or I'll be heading back to Virginia in a couple weeks. I sit down hard on a green metal bench, a shiver runs down my spine, and I drop my pack to the dirt. I take a long look down the Boulevard Saint-Michel and then up at the leaves rustling in the plane trees. I cannot fathom leaving this city.

After making my way back to my building's courtyard, an agitated Madame Vauquer scurries toward me in her housecoat and then slows to a waddle. She waves a thin paperback above her head. It's clear she's been awaiting my return.

"There was a man. Looking for you. A French man, a few hours ago."

Oh God, Eugène. My legs weaken and my hand itches. How did he find me? "I hope he wasn't rude," I say, my voice unsteady.

She shrugs. "He was a businessman and left this for you."

She proffers the book but my arms remain at my sides. Why would Eugène go to the trouble of finding me to give me a book?

"What did he look like?"

"He had glasses."

"And...?"

"He was handsome. *Alors*, he is your new French lover, yes? I told you your new hair would find you a monsieur."

I don't know whether to be insulted or laugh out loud. She thinks Eugène is handsome and could be my boyfriend. "Definitely not."

"*Ah, tant pis*. You two would make an attractive couple. Both of you with such lovely hair."

"Hair? He wasn't bald?"

She doesn't understand, so I rub my head.

"Yes, beautiful hair, I told you."

I frown. "Did he say what he wanted?"

She thinks a moment. "Only asked if Catrine Gray lived here. When I said you were away—remember? I saw you leave this morning—he asked me to give you this." She jiggles the book, and I reach to grab it. I run my fingertips across the book's cover. French Quotes for the Literature Lover.

I blink a few times. Vincent...? Vincent! "Thank you, Madame!" I turn before she can ask questions.

"There's a note inside," she calls as I head for the stairs. "Did I mention he was very handsome?"

One turn up the spiral stairway, I sit on the step, bite my lip, and open the book.

> Catrine,
>
> Odette gave me your landlady's number. I called, but no one answered, so I came to see you. Your landlady said she would give you this—a gift from my grandfather I keep in my brief-

case. I want you to have it. Call me.

Vincent

Under his name is his phone number and address and below is an asterisk and a page number. I flip to it. "*J'entends ta voix dans tous les bruits du monde.*" I hear your voice in all the world's noise. – Paul Éluard

The Surrealist poet.

I lean my head on the stairwell wall. And then I remember the sparrow. My spiritual messenger. I consider calling but it scares me. I run up to my room and dash off a note.

Vincent,

Thank you for finding me. I must return to Virginia in two weeks unless I find a job (I'm trying hard…), so we should see each other soon. Leave a message with Madame Vauquer and I'll meet wherever you say.

Catrine

I rush to La Poste to mail it before losing my nerve. He'll likely get it tomorrow. I put thoughts of Vincent aside to focus on impressing two families the following day.

My future in Paris hangs on one of them liking me.

Chapter Thirty

The first couple interviews me in their cluttered kitchen, half-eaten breakfasts on the table. The man pulls out a pack of smokes, gives one to his wife, takes one himself, and they both light up in the middle of asking about my education. If the charmless modern building in the eleventh arrondissement near the Charonne metro weren't bad enough, the acrid stench of their Gitanes makes me gag. They have one little boy, but the hours would be long as they're both lawyers, though not well paid by the looks of their apartment. The au pair's room is tiny with a futon on the floor, two long shelves, and no closet or dresser. I'm not crazy about the set-up and I'm sure they can tell as I look around. I see Madame Arnoux standing in the corner, telling me I can do better. She isn't there, of course, but it soothes me to think she is, and she's right.

But I needn't worry about deciding. On my way out the door, they say they'll be offering the job to someone else.

An hour later, I stand on the sidewalk in the fifteenth arrondissement, a block south of the Champ de Mars, clutching my Eiffel Tower key chain and looking up at where I'll have my second interview. I ascend the stairs to the second floor of a nineteenth century building with soaring ceilings, like Madame's.

They're a French family—the husband in finance and the wife a doctor—and want their little girl and boy to learn English from an American. They interview me in the cream-colored salon. I learn the position comes with its own room and a bathroom shared with the children. Don't get your hopes up, I tell myself, but the woman does seem to like me. She tells me she's impressed with both my studies and my French.

I leave the interview hovering on hope.

As I make my way east through the city, I decide to stop in at Madame's to tell her about my interview and Vincent's note. She's happy to see me and sets about making us coffee. Before she pours, she retrieves a bowl of fruit from the *frigo* and sets it on a tray.

"So, did you land a job?" she asks as she pours the coffee.

"Maybe?" The hope is still there as I carry the tray of fruit and coffee out to the salon but I don't want to jinx it. "May I tell you about Vincent first?"

As we settle into our seats, I take the book he left me from my pack and fill her in on what I wrote to him.

"But why didn't you call him? You must go after what you want."

"I just didn't know what to say and it was so much easier to write. I think I'm still so embarrassed about the beach. And about breaking his glasses."

"Getting what we want is not always easy. But we shall see. And so, your story continues," she says, smiling. "You know, you can always call him from here. You still have his number, yes?"

"I do... I'll think about it. I just need some courage."

"If he's that important to you, you'll find it. Why not call right now? Before you have time to be nervous."

I reach down, pull Vincent's note from my satchel, and jump up full of energy. "I'll do it!"

Madame says, "Go right in. The phone is on the nightstand."

My fingers tremble as I dial. The phone on the other end rings and rings. I hang up and let out a long breath I didn't know I was holding, though something inside me sinks even as the tension drains away. I return to the salon. "No answer. I'm sure he's still at work."

"Maybe you can come over first thing and call again tomorrow. Now, about your interviews..."

"The first one didn't go well but fingers crossed for the second. I think they really liked me and the woman said she'd call by the weekend."

"How many days a week?" She picks up a juicy blueberry and pops it in her mouth.

"Six." And then the details tumble. "I'd have Sunday off and they'd pay me a stipend and I'd get all my meals and I can take my vacation with them in La Rochelle in August and I can use their car and the kids are only four and six so they'd need me for a few years, meaning…" I hear a drumroll in my mind. "I can stay in Paris!" I grin like a fool.

Madame straightens her glasses, a twitch I've come to recognize as annoyance. "Did you hear what you just said? One day off a week. To see all of France? Certainly, your wages will not be sufficient to pay for much travel." She shakes her head.

"Well, maybe I could take the job for a year, save up, and then look for something else?"

"Maybe," says Madame dismissively. She's back to being a grump and her words and attitude deflate me.

She points to my cup. "More coffee?"

I nod and twist my napkin hard. "I'd do almost anything to stay in Paris. I don't want to go home." The word feels hollow, stale in my mouth. Virginia isn't home anymore. Not without Dad. I feel a huge sob build in my chest.

Madame hasn't noticed my state. She says, "Let's start with more coffee and then dissect your problem."

"Fine. More coffee then." I follow her into the kitchen. She lifts the pot from its cradle and fills my cup and then hers. But as she lowers her cup to its saucer—crash!—it drops to the floor.

"Madame!" I rush to her side. She stares ahead, over the sink, eyelids slack. I allow the spell to pass, my palm pressed lightly to her back for support.

When she comes to, she bends to pick up the pieces. "How stupid. It's the first time I've broken anything in a long time."

I help her up, take her hand, and see blood. "You cut yourself!"

"*Merde, alors*. Clumsy old woman. But do stop fussing. I'm fine. It's only a nick."

I point to the blood trickling from her thumb to her palm and pass her a paper towel. "I know it was an accident and you're all right, but you could have burned yourself. Do you have a Band-Aid?" She directs me to the bathroom. "Don't move," I say.

I return with a bandage from the cluttered medicine chest and wrap it around her finger.

"You sit and I'll bring our coffee." I carefully sweep china shards from the floor into the dustpan and dump them in the trash. I now understand Eugène's concern. I take a new cup from the cabinet, fill it with coffee, and carry both cups on their saucers to the salon.

"Okay now?" I ask, sitting down. She nods as she slices a *pain d'épic-es*. I catch myself before saying, Careful with that knife. Don't want to be a scold like Eugène.

"It was nothing. And as I said, I haven't dropped anything in ages."

"What's ages?"

She ignores me, dipping a sugar cube in her cup, watching it fill, and bringing it to her mouth. I imitate her, but my cube dissolves and I end up wiping my sticky fingers on my napkin.

Madame covers her mouth to hide a yawn. I should keep my visit short. She needs her rest. She takes a bite of cake and then a sip of coffee. I take an orange and peel it, releasing its sweet citrus scent. She loosens the pins from her chignon, lays them on the edge of the table and gently ruffles her hair. It falls below her shoulders, the ends brown and dark, gradually lightening to gray at her scalp.

"Your hair!" Instinctively, I reach to the back of my neck and for a moment, I ache for mine. I force my hand back to my lap. "I've only seen you with it in a knot and had no idea it was so long. It's beautiful."

"Oh, Catrine. I just remembered what Fréderique did to you. I am so sorry. Taking down my hair was insensitive."

"Don't worry. I've decided I like it short. For now."

"Well, thank you about what you said about my hair." She sweeps the hairpins into her palm. "I never wear it down because it's wiry and gray, not silky like before. Charles liked it long and I haven't had the heart to cut it since he died." She stifles another yawn. "We women feel strongly about our hair, don't we?"

"We do, indeed."

Madame says, "I hope you won't think me rude, but I'm especially tired today and need a nap. Not unusual in the afternoon."

"Of course. I actually should be going..."

"Please don't. I like having you here. Will you stay until I'm up? An hour or so is all I need. You're welcome to look at anything in my library."

I waver, but the offer is tempting. Is she being sincere? "Of course," I say. "But one question. Would you mind if, well, I organized the shelves for you? Put everything in alphabetical order by author?"

She looks at me and presses her lips into a line. "You don't like my librarian skills?" She's angry, I know it. My request was insulting. I feel my face redden. But then her lips curl into a smile. "You're right and are courageous to suggest it. And it's not only my shelves that need organizing. But it would be a start."

I clutch my fists to my chest. "I promise I'll be careful, Madame, and I'll treat your books like the treasures they are."

"Organize whatever you'd like." Her cane helps her stand and she heads to her room.

While I clear the coffee and fruit and wash the cups and saucers, I think about Vincent. If I hadn't been such a coward about calling, I might be looking forward to a drink with him tonight. But now I must wait for him to get my note and respond.

I wipe my hands on the dishtowel and then glance down the hallway to check on Madame. Her bedroom door is ajar. I take a few steps closer, lean my hip against the wall, and listen to Madame's soft snuffle and the ticking of the living room clock. Outside, a motorbike revs and then vrooms by on the street below. Church bells chime two o'clock.I tiptoe back to the salon to have my way with Madame's books.

Chapter Thirty-One

A warm breeze billows the curtains over the windows but all else is still. I tilt back my head, roll it side to side, and fully relax. I'm exactly where I should be, spending the afternoon in front of a wall of literature and hearing Jean-Paul Sartre. "*Tout ce que je sais de ma vie, semble-t-il, je l'ai appris dans les livres.*" All that I know about my life, it seems, I have learned in books. He knows me well.

I have a hard time concentrating on the books with the room in such disarray. Madame did say to straighten what I'd like, so I poke around in the kitchen pantry and foyer closet and find several cardboard cartons, a box of garbage bags, and cleaning supplies. After fifteen minutes, each is filled with trash, piles of magazines, newspapers, and miscellaneous items. All furniture surfaces in the salon and dining room are clear of debris and I've polished away the dust Eugène's cursory efforts missed.

The bookshelves are next. I brush them with a feather duster, thinking of yesterday's sparrow and humming *La Vie en Rose*, Edith Piaf's signature song, as I go up and down the ladder.

Loose grime gone, I withdraw a slim volume with a black spine and red lettering and touch its title—*Bonjour Tristesse*—and then open to the copyright page. It's a first edition of Françoise Sagan's coming of age novel. I bought an old copy for pennies at a yard sale and devoured it in junior year of high school. Seventeen-year-old self-absorbed Cécile joins her handsome, philandering, widower father and his current mistress for a desultory summer on the French Riviera. How I loved reading about a teenager's life so unlike mine.

I remove the balance of the books, one by one, wipe them and the shelves clean, make piles by author last name, and then return them. After an hour, the bookcases are in perfect order, and Madame is still asleep.

With a feeling of accomplishment, I go to the beginning of the author alphabet and pull out a leather-bound copy of *Le Père Goriot*, gently open it, and note what's written in faded pencil on the flyleaf: The Sorbonne, September 1929. I imagine Madame reading the book as a young woman and wish I knew the timeline. Was she an undergraduate? A graduate student? Or was she perhaps already teaching? I replace the volume and, author by author, select books to browse. I focus on my favorites: *L'Étranger, Madame Bovary*, *Les Misérables, L'Avare*, *À La Recherche du Temps Perdu*. I carefully turn the yellowed pages of each and take time to read the notes in the margins, still legible after so many years.

At the far end of the lowest shelf is Émile Zola. I page through *Germinal*—the gritty tragedy about French coalminers in the nineteenth century. The main characters' ill-fated love affair, which plays out against the backdrop of the slag heap, still haunts me.

The final work I open is *Thérèse Raquin*, a scandalous, tawdry tale of adultery, desire and murder. As I move to the sofa to savor its pages, from the book's empty slot on the shelf I hear, "*Si vous me demandez ce que je viens faire en ce monde, je vous répondrai: je viens vivre tout haut.*" If you ask me what I came into this life to do, I will tell you: I came to live out loud. Zola always spoke to me through his writing, but now I'm hearing his voice. I listen for more but he is quiet while I endure the piercing shriek of an ambulance siren passing. When calm returns, I resume reading.

I slip off my boots and lean back against the arm of the couch, extending my legs and stocking feet. I flip through the pages and then turn to the front. Inside the cover is an inscription:

My darling Delphine,

My love and devotion on your birthday and forever,

Charles

16 June 1932

I gasp. June 16th. Is it true? Madame and I share a birthday? "Birthday twins," as Freddie would say. Oh God, do not bring her into this. Birthday mates? Sisters? That's it. Birthday sisters.

Madame and I were born on the same day of the year, and despite the gulf of decades and living worlds apart, we're two planets in similar orbits finally crossing paths. We're already connected and now have another bond. My thoughts drift to possibilities for marking the day together. Perhaps this once, my birthday will arrive with celebration. If I help Madame enjoy the day, maybe I'll enjoy it too.

I prop open the book and a yellowed, deckled-edge snapshot slips out. It's Madame in sepia, her derrière leaning against a wooden door, one elbow out, her hand behind her tiny waist. Her other hand hangs beside her. She's slim in a dark pencil skirt, white blouse, and black stilettos, one toe poised on the floor behind a shapely calf. Dark, wavy hair spills over her shoulders. Beside her is a seascape on an easel, its full width truncated by the photographer. I examine the picture closely. Her right hand holds a paintbrush pointed at the floor. Is Madame an artist?

I return my attention to *Thérèse Raquin*, but the phone rings. I look at the clock. Four p.m. already. Madame slept for over two hours. I hear her answer the phone.

"Hello Eugène." A pause. "Of course, I'm fine. I was napping," she says, followed by silence. She's likely being scolded. "No more long walks. And no traveling on the metro or bus. I told you that yesterday and the day before as well." More silence. "Her name is Catrine." Pause. "No more public transportation for me at all. Agreed. Speak to you tomorrow."

Madame's bedroom door creaks open. Her steady steps and the soft thump of her cane approach. "Seems I needed a long sleep, but it was the strangest thing. I dreamed we went to Normandy. To Rouen."

"Why Normandy?"

"I don't know, other than that college friends and I went there to paint. Following in the footsteps of Monet, I suppose."

"You are an artist!"

Her smile fades "Let's just say I used to paint."

"No longer?"

"Not for years. Don't have the inclination. Or the inspiration."

"Maybe your Normandy dream is telling you something."

She looks at me and lowers her head. "It was simply a silly dream."

We sit for a moment, and I show Madame the photo. Of her with the paintbrush.

"Charles loved that picture. It was before we met." She looks away, lost in thought.

"I hope you don't mind, but I saw what Charles wrote for your birthday." I hold up the book, waiting for her reaction.

She turns her gaze to the window. "You know my feelings about the past."

"But June 16th is a lovely day for a birthday," I say. "It's also mine." I know I'm too chirpy, given her mood.

She finally smiles at me. "What are the chances?" And then she sighs. "Birthdays mark time passing and at my age, I don't want to celebrate being another year closer to death."

"But it also celebrates another year of being alive."

"Charles always made my birthday special. I've been dreading it for weeks."

She stops, off again in thought, and then continues. "On June 16 two years ago, I was still at Eugène's. In mourning, in a fog, or maybe shock, so I didn't even realize the date. I have a vague memory of Eugène making a cake…"

An image I can't conjure.

"And last year, I told him I wanted to forget the day and be alone." Pausing, she inches to the edge of the couch to take her cane and get up.

She heads for the kitchen.

I let her go away on her own, understanding how she feels. I've often tried to forget my birthday because Dad was usually away, and Mother never made a fuss. But I do remember my tenth. Dad gave me a Duc de Berry's *Book of Hours*—fully illustrated in color, with French translations beneath the English. I couldn't put it down for weeks. Mother gave me new sneakers, which she had to buy me anyway, and some rosary beads she got at the church fair.

Madame returns to the salon studying her desk calendar. I thank her for letting me spend time with her books. As I get up to leave, she asks if I can come back tomorrow. For an outing.

"An outing? But, Eugène…"

"Leave Eugène to me. I do not break promises."

Chapter Thirty-Two

The following day, I arrive at her door by eight a.m. Madame stands in her foyer with erect French formality, chest high, arms close to her waist, hands atop her cane. It's a posture I haven't yet seen from her, except in the yellowed photo. She's petite and trim in her navy-blue belted dress (Madame, you still have a figure!), matching pillbox hat, and pale blue sweater over her shoulders. The outfit accentuates her now clear blue eyes. Her ankles aren't nearly as swollen as when I first saw her in the cemetery, her nails are filed and painted pearl, and she's wearing a touch of pink lipstick.

Her eyes brighten when she sees me.

I look down at my navy tee and jeans, swallowing. "Are we going somewhere fancy? If I'd known..." Should I have made more of an effort?

She shakes her head. "Special, yes, fancy, no." She looks at me for a moment. "Wait here. I have something."

She returns from her bedroom with a paisley pashmina, indigo and pale blue woven with gold thread.

"There," she says, draping the wrap around me. "You do know we French love our accessories."

"It's gorgeous. The colors are perfect. Thanks for letting me borrow it."

"It is a gift, *ma petite*."

I protest, but she cuts me off.

"I haven't worn it in years, but I know you'll make good use of it."

I relent, happily. "Thank you, Madame. I've never had something so lovely."

"Come sit. I'd like to share an idea before you try Vincent." She puts her arm through mine like we're old friends and her cane leads us into the salon. She sits on the couch and pats beside her.

Her eyes twinkle. "Any more interviews this week?"

"Not so far, but the Champ de Mars mother called me last night. She didn't offer me the job, but asked if I could start next week if she hired me."

There's sudden pounding on the door. Madame seems unfazed by the interruption, but frowns.

"I'll get it." I stand and head to the foyer.

"I'm sure it's—"

The door opens. "*Maman.*" It's Eugène, When he sees me in the hall his face turns crimson. He slams the door hard enough the salon windows vibrate and then stiff-arms me out of the way. To his mother he's says, "What is she doing here?"

Madame's facial muscles tighten but she remains seated, one hand on her cane and the other straightening her dress across her lap. "Please settle down. You're overreacting."

Eugène paces, jiggling the change in his pocket. "You told me you wouldn't see her. Were you lying?"

I stand next to the Maupassant collection, still and stiff. I wish the floor would swallow me up. Eugène exudes anger as he turns to me.

Madame says. "I didn't lie."

Eugène ignores her and says to me. "And you. You promised you wouldn't see her."

"Actually I—"

"Calm down, Eugène," Madame says with verve. "I said no more long trips. Not on foot and not on the bus; not by myself and not with Catrine. But I never said I wouldn't see her. Those are your words."

He stops pacing and stands in front of his mother, nostrils flaring. "You're all dressed up. Where are you going?"

"On an excursion. In a taxi."

A vein in his forehead protrudes as he tries to hide his irritation. His jaw is firm, but he finally lets out an exasperated burst of air and drops into a side chair. He spreads his knees and clasps his hands. "I asked you months ago to take taxis, but you said you like the bus."

"I do prefer the bus, but I wanted to agree to something you asked. I can easily part with extended walks and public transportation, but I will not surrender my friendship and outings with Catrine."

Eugène turns to me. "She's had thousands of students across dozens of years and never once did she bring one home. What makes you so special?"

"We're friends," I say and then look to Madame.

"Catrine enjoys our friendship and isn't looking for a grade or a reference or a grad school recommendation. She wants nothing but my company, literary conversation, and…" Madame stops and strokes her thighs. We both hang on her words but I realize, and Eugène must too, she's having a spell. I go to sit beside her. I put my hand on hers until she comes to.

"My God, Maman," Eugène says. "This is why I worry about you living alone. When Papa was here—"

"Well, he's not, is he?"

Eugène sighs as he rubs between his eyebrows with his thumbs. "I know..." I detect a twinge of sadness in his voice. He recovers quickly and leans forward. "What about my proposal? You need someone—an aide of some sort—to come check on you and cook you a hot meal. Maybe stay over during the week."

"You'll be pleased to hear I've considered it."

He sits up straight, hands on his knees. "And?"

"I've found someone. She'll be my assistant and help with the apartment and cooking. And, she'll organize your father's writing." Madame pauses to look at me. Her lips curve into a smile and her head tilts when our eyes meet. "My new friend is moving into your old bedroom, aren't you, *ma petite*?"

My mouth drops and I'm speechless.

Eugène stares. "You barely know her."

"You don't want me living alone? Fine. But I get to choose my housemate and I choose Catrine."

I'm too stunned to speak, but I manage to close my mouth. A slide show of images flickers behind my eyes. Mother in the rearview mirror. Blink. Freddie kicking me out. Blink. My sixth-floor walk-up. Blink. Endless job interviews. Blink. The woman will call by the weekend. Blink.

Eugène points at me. "Did you put her up to this?"

Eugène, I haven't even—" says Madame.

"Let her speak." He waits.

I gulp, sit up straight, and find words that match what's swirling in my mind. "It's actually the perfect solution. I need a place to stay, your mother needs help with housekeeping, and…"

"But are you even qualified to help with the… the elderly?"

"Eugene, please!" Madame's eyes spark. "I know I'm getting older but you're out of line."

"I'm worried about you—

"I think you're more worried about the apartment's upkeep. Well, look around."

He does.

"That's her handiwork from yesterday."

He eyes me. "Okay, fine." He turns to me. "How many seizures have you been around for?"

Madame scoffs, and I give her a worried glance, but she just shrugs, as if surrendering, so I meet Eugene's penetrating gaze.

"Including today, four or five." He seems surprised. I add, "I can handle them. And I watch for them, too. I can call an ambulance if that's ever needed."

Madame bows her head, as if defeated, but then she raises it proudly. "You see, all the boxes are checked."

Eugene seems to be considering as Madame adds, "She's perfect company for me, but besides that, what I'm really hiring her for is to help get Charles's manuscript published."

This is news to me.

Eugène may be in the same boat as he glances warily at the Maupassant desk. "It's a pipe dream, Maman." He gets up from the chair and starts pacing again. "He spent years on that book but publishers won't touch it."

"I think they will," says Madame. "With some help." She smiles at me.

I turn to Eugène "Your father was an expert, wasn't he?"

He stops pacing and jingles his change. "He wrote many books for libraries and professors. But this one is different. The academic world told him it was simplistic. Too 'common.'"

Madame says, "We'll find a way."

"I would love to help," I say. "Really. It's a dream come true, actually."

Eugène looks at us, from one to the other and back. Finally, he throws up his hands. "I surrender. Do what you want. You always do anyway, Maman." He glances at his watch and starts towards the door. "I'm in a rush and have to go."

"Eugène, *mon petit.* Why did you stop by? Apart from wanting to argue, of course."

He turns back. "Right. I forgot. Your car's back in its parking spot in the garage, all inspected and re-registered." He drops a set of keys on the coffee table with a jangle. "And since you won't let me sell it, it can sit and gather dust for another year."

"*Merci, mon fils,*" Madame calls in a sing-song voice as he leaves, slamming the door behind him.

"What was that?" I ask, lightheaded as I break the silence. "It all happened so fast."

"I did plan to work my way up to the offer, but Eugène forced the issue." She puts her hand on my knee. "Will you accept?"

She waits while the ramifications ricochet inside me.

She adds, "Weekends are yours. And maybe we can go on some

trips together. To see more of France." She reaches for the car keys and shakes them. "You can drive can't you?"

I can in theory, but in France?

"We'll be able to go places." The twinkle in her eye is back. "What do you say?"

"Yes...Yes! But I must pay you some rent…"

There will be no discussion of that. You'll help me with cleaning and… health issues…and get room and board in exchange. I will pay you wages to work on Charles' manuscript."

Wages too? The ease of things going well is almost as powerful as things going wrong. Madame takes my hand and I nod, afraid saying anything more will jolt me from this dream.

She says, "Having you here will help me as much as it helps you. I haven't had the heart to work on the book myself because it makes me sad, thinking about his disappointment with every publisher rejection." She pauses to wipe her eyes. "It's the only project he didn't let me edit. Said it wasn't scholarly enough."

I'm finally able to speak. "What needs to be done?"

"Organization. By someone who knows Maupassant. And then we need a publisher." She pauses. "Right before Charles died, yet another rejection letter arrived but I never showed it to him. I was so furious about how condescending the editor was that I picked up his manuscript and threw the pages across the dining room, followed by the box he kept it in."

"No."

"Paper was everywhere and I left it all on the floor until Eugène came by a few days later. He collected it in no particular order and managed to fit it back in that box." She points to a corner of the dining room table as she stands.

The pretty blue and green box that was on the bookcase's bottom shelf.

Madame walks to the dining room, opens the box, takes out the paper stack and pats it lovingly. "Charles's '*chef d'oeuvre.*' But since the day Eugène gathered it up, yesterday was the first day I touched it. To move it to the table to show you. Your French is excellent, Catrine. You even said that reading and writing French is your forte."

"But—"

"No more buts. You can no longer keep all you know and love to yourself."

I call the family in the fifteenth to tell them I found another position and they're disappointed. Turns out they had planned to offer me the job. I look skyward. Thank you, Madame Arnoux.

I think about calling Vincent before we leave, but it's now too late as I'm sure he's already left his flat for work. He'll probably receive my note today and since I'm not leaving Paris, I can give him some time to respond.

Chapter Thirty-Three

Our "special but not fancy" outing is a visit to Parc Monceau. When I told Madame I hadn't yet been to the park, she said I couldn't call myself a Maupassant devotee until I had.

So, that afternoon, we find a bench beneath the lilacs near the Parc Monceau's gilded gates. The air smells faintly of blossoms. Around us, the neighborhood unfolds in quiet elegance—rows of *hôtels particuliers* several blocks northeast of the Arc de Triomphe. The townhouses' tall, narrow façades stand shoulder to shoulder, their shutters freshly painted and their wrought-iron balconies spilling over with pots of geraniums. Across the gravel path sits a bust of Maupassant atop a pedestal, a swooning, sculpted muse reclining at the base, forever caught in admiration. It's one of many statues of writers and musicians in the English-style park, less formal than most Parisian landscapes. Madame's head drops forward, bobbing slightly, for a quick snooze.

I look over at Maupassant's handsome face with its grand moustache. I think about how Charles's desire to make the writer's work easily understood should have been a good thing, but clearly academia wasn't right for it.

Madame awakens from her nap and we take a gentle stroll on meandering pathways. She tells me Monet did several paintings of the park's trees and broad lawns, work I'm not familiar with. "Did you paint here as well?" I ask.

"Once, when Eugène was little. He played and I painted."

"Do you still have the canvas?"

"I do," she says but then quickly circles back to Monet.

She continues giving me my own private art and architecture seminar as we walk in mellow sun under beech trees, over the mini-Venetian bridge, and through the Renaissance-styled archway, a relic from Paris' eighteenth-century city hall.

"This is a special place," I say. "Thank you for bringing me." I add Maupassant's statue to the things that connect me to him.

She loops her arm through mine and leads me out the gates to the *boulevard de Courcelles*. "On to our next stop."

The cab leaves us on the busy *boulevard Diderot*, across from the Gare de Lyon. When I ask where we're going, she says I'll know when we're there.

We turn onto *rue de Bercy* and walk two blocks to a narrow, cobblestoned street. It's lined with terraced houses, like English cottages, and each is painted in a different pastel: yellow, lilac, pink and blue. Not a Haussmann structure in sight.

"Oh my God," I say, smacking my forehead. "It's the *rue Crémieux*, the street on my journal! You said it was real and it is." I put down my pack, unzip it, and pull out my journal. I walk to the center of the sleepy street, hold it up, and compare the sketch to reality. I half expect a carriage to round the corner or a princess to appear at one of the windows, her gown fluttering in the breeze. A car beeps and I scoot over to join Madame on the sidewalk.

"I'm happy I could show it to you. Although it wasn't always like this."

"What do you mean?"

"Over a hundred years ago, the Imperial Arena was here—a huge public space for races, carnivals, and such. When the quartier was no longer fashionable, developers tore it down and built working class housing."

"Well, it certainly has become charming."

"The current owners have really spruced them up and I can't imagine their price."

"Can we look closer?"

"Would we have come if we couldn't explore?"

I shoot her a look.

She scowls and then narrates our stroll down the lane. "These thirty-five houses were designed like workers' residences in England. Each is only one room deep with two floors and the kitchens in the basement."

"Adorable." I stop to study a pale blue one with bright yellow planters out front.

"I do love this little street. I'd forgotten about it until I saw your notebook. A world away from busy Paris."

"Did you and Charles escape the city much?"

"We visited many historical sites, especially in summer with Eugène before university. When he actually liked spending time with us. We French are very proud of our *patrimoine* and want to pass it on to our children."

We stop to consider a colorful facade crisscrossed with a trompe l'oeil painting of flowering vines.

"But a few years before Charles got sick, his eyesight was failing and he couldn't drive at night. So we did day outings to Giverny or Fontainebleau or Chartres."

"Have you taken trips on your own? Eugène said you have a car."

There's no response. Madame has stopped, both hands on the cane in front of her. She glares. "You really think they would give an epileptic a driver's license?"

I feel my face flush, and I step back to join her. "I'm so sorry. How stupid of me..."

She adjusts her glasses. "I accepted not being able to drive a long time ago."

"Then why keep a car?"

"For some reason, it gives me a feeling of freedom. Maybe I thought when Charles died I'd still find a way to use it. Eugène certainly doesn't understand." She stops to look as a young couple approaches, his arm around her shoulder, her arm around his waist.

"It is a romantic street," I say, watching them pass.

She looks at me. "Since we're talking romance and now that we'll be housemates, tell me more about Vincent."

I blush and hesitate. Mother wanted to hear nothing about the opposite sex, not that I had anything to tell, and so I'm uncomfortable with the subject. But Madame encourages me, and I find that once I've voiced his name, I can't stop.

"Well, it sounds like this gentleman likes you. You may give him my phone number, of course."

My belly flutters as I thank her.

We reach the end of the street, head back to the Gare de Lyon, and catch a cab. Madame asks as we speed along the Seine. "When you bring your things over on Friday, you can use my car if you'd like. Do you drive a stick-shift?"

"I do. My dad taught me in his delivery trucks, but I definitely won't need your car." I chuckle about how little I have.

She looks skeptical but I reassure her.

"Well, if you don't have plans, why don't you come for dinner and stay tonight. I had a good feeling you would accept my proposal, so your room is all ready—fresh sheets, towels, and a lavender candle."

I smile. "I do love good French food. If the taxi leaves me at my flat, I'll tell my landlady I'm moving out Friday, and be over this evening." And I'll stop on the way to get a *tarte aux abricots.*

"Well then. Another reason we're a good pair. I love fine food too but hate eating out alone. Going to La Rotonde was the first time I'd had a restaurant meal since Charles died, even though he and I ate out often."

"What were your favorites?"

"When we were young, we tried all the best-reviewed places in Paris, but as we got older, we kept going back to those we liked best." She goes on to list their favorites—Chez Papa, Tout Va Bien, Lapérouse, and Roger La Grenouille—and describes the dishes they loved best—*confit de canard, galettes de Bretagne,* and *cuisses de grenouilles à la persillade.*

"Perhaps you and I will try them one day. Or perhaps Vincent will take you."

The taxi drops me at Madame Vauquer's and she calls from her kitchen window when I enter the courtyard. "Where were you all day? That handsome man called but you missed him again."

"Vincent?"

"I hope you weren't out with someone else." She raises an accusatory eyebrow.

I shake my head. "I was with a friend—a girl friend. Please don't worry about someone replacing Vincent."

She disappears and steps out her door. "Here," she says, handing me a piece of paper. "I wrote down exactly what he said."

"Thank you, Madame. I appreciate it."

"Oh, I did it for him, too. How could I refuse?"

I glance down, scan the message, and can't help grinning at the restaurant name. One of Madame and Charles's favorite restaurants.

Madame Vauquer says, "You'll say yes, won't you? Dinner with a man like that in a place like Roger La Grenouille on a Saturday night doesn't happen every day."

"Can't imagine I'll turn him down," I say as I wave the note above my shoulder. "And Madame. I'll actually be moving out on Friday. I found a roommate and am staying in Paris." I hand her my new address and phone number.

"So, someone can move in Friday? But you've already paid and I said no refunds."

"I figured, but yes. On Friday." I turn to cross the courtyard.

"Thank you, Catrine. You're a good tenant. And I do hope you will keep seeing that handsome Vincent."

"And so do I," I say.

"But wait," Madame Vauquer says. "I almost forgot. There's also a letter from Germany."

My heart stops and I take a moment before turning back around. With a crooked smile, I step towards her.

She must see the change in my mood. “Is Germany bad news?”

I look down at the envelope. “Not sure.”

“Open it then. Get it over with.” Madame Vauquer crosses her arms, all serious and practical.

I’m anxious to hear the news, so I slip my finger under the sealed flap and pull out the notecard from Walter. He’d like me to visit after Dagmar’s surgery on June 30—a couple weeks from now.

“Not bad news. But I have to make a trip to Germany later this month.” I hope Madame Arnoux will understand why I must be away for a few days. With one note in each hand, I thank Madame Vauquer again, race up the stairs and flop back on the bed to consider next steps. First up, pack. I’ll worry about Germany and Madame tonight.

Chapter Thirty-Four

At Madame's apartment, she shows me to my room—*my* room—and retreats to the kitchen, *tarte aux abricots* in hand.

A silvery fluted mirror hangs over a long white dresser, its corner anchored by a set of gray porcelain pots. I stand in front of the mirror and am startled by my image. There's no mirror in my flat, so I haven't had a good look at myself in weeks. My jawbone seems more angular, and who knew cutting my hair could give me cheekbones? My brow and forehead have relaxed, and my hair is straight and shiny with none of the waves that twisted before Freddie cut them off. I look down at the scar on my hand, soft and pink. No hint of inflammation.

There's a lightness in my chest as I drop my pack at the foot of the white, wood-framed bed, a scallop shell carved into the headboard. A fluffy gray duvet and a tumble of slate blue pillows grace the bed. Fresh blue cornflowers stand in a wide-mouthed ginger jar on the night table beside a lit lavender candle. I couldn't love the room more, bright with slats of sunlight from two tall windows on the far wall. Pale blue silk drapes hang from the ceiling and puddle on the parquet floor. Next to the dresser, there's a walk-in closet filled with cardboard boxes, trunks, and clothing hanging on both sides, everything in its place.

I open the door to the left of the bed and gasp. My own bathroom? It's big, airy, and covered in glossy white tile. Growing up I shared with my parents, then with Freddie at her flat, and with other tenants at Madame Vauquer's. I take in the luxury of it all and picture myself getting ready for dinner on Saturday night…

I have to tell Madame my news. I race down the hall, find her in the salon, and blurt, "Vincent asked me to dinner at Roger La Grenouille! Of all the restaurants in Paris..."

She claps her hands and smiles. "Clearly, he wants to make an impression. I like this Vincent already."

"Oh my God, I have nothing to wear!" I pause. "And may I share a secret?"

"I'm listening."

"I'm twenty-two years old and this will be my first date. Ever."

"But you already had dinner with him…"

"It wasn't a date. He was only being nice when I arrived in Paris. And Freddie joined us halfway through." I cringe, thinking about how she overtook the entire evening.

"Could you tell he liked you then?"

"A bit, but it was mostly when we went to the beach. We talked a lot. About wine and art and literature. It was so easy. Of course, Freddie wasn't happy he paid me so much attention."

"My, my. Wine, art, and literature—impressive. I wouldn't worry about that cousin of his."

"All I know is I'm comfortable with him and he's interested in what I like." I push my hair behind my ears. "But I'm so nervous to see him." I wonder about his glasses and whether he replaced them. And then I recall the awkward end of our beach day and wish I could erase it.

Madame pats my knee. "You must order the frog legs at La Grenouille. Their specialty. Lightly fried and delicious."

"When in France..." Wait till I tell Mother.

Madame describes the rest of the menu and I take notes: terrine for my starter and Paris-Brest for dessert. "As to what to wear, come with me."

We head to my bedroom, where the closet's double-doors are open and a pile of clothes lies heaped behind a box. "I was making room for you," Madame says. She steps inside and pulls a blue-beaded cord to light the bulb. "I started this morning but haven't gotten far. I took out

Eugène's things but can't part with Charles's suits." She runs her fingers over the fabric of a jacket and leans forward, breathing in its scent.

"Eugène helped me empty his drawers and donate his things last year, but what's still hanging, I can't say goodbye to yet."

"You should keep what you want for as long as you want." I touch her shoulder, recalling how Mother's haste for tidiness found her shipping Dad's things to Saint Vincent de Paul weeks after he died.

"Maybe a little longer then..." Madame sighs. "So, a dress for dinner. Have a look. You'll see I can spare a few." All along the right side is a rack of dresses, long, short, and in between, in every color of the rainbow, plus black and white. Along the back wall are two columns of cubbies filled with meticulously folded tops and pants.

"It's like a designer boutique." I caress a cashmere cardigan. "Did you get dressed up often?"

"I used to. Not much anymore. But, like Charles's suits, I can't seem to part with my dresses. Some go back to 1928, when we got married."

"So, there are over fifty here!"

"Fifty-one. One for every year we were married, in chronological order. Charles bought me a birthday dress every year and I wore it when we celebrated. He never missed one, including the year he died. He had Eugène go to my favorite shop and pick one out."

"Did you get to wear it?"

"I did. A little early because we knew he didn't have much time. We ordered take-out and ate at the little table in the dining room. Charles was in his bathrobe, and I wore my new dress. He insisted." She picks up the hanger closest to the door—a navy blue jersey wrap-around. "This is the last one he gave me, and I only wore it that once."

She holds the dress up against her and looks down at her slippered feet, as if lost in memory. Yet barely a moment later, she says, "But, we are not here to talk about me. Let's find you a dress."

She replaces the hanger. "Try on a few you like and then come model your choice for me."

She leaves the room and I take my time choosing, looking through those with frills and flounces for something simple with no fripperies.

When I step from the bedroom and head to the salon where Madame awaits, I'm in a sleeveless claret A-line dress from the sixties, modest and unadorned, its silk lining lusciously soft. It fits perfectly, apart from the hem, which likely hung below Madame's knee but rests an inch above mine. I enter the salon with a twirl. "What do you think?"

She cocks her head. "Oh, Catrine." Her voice catches and her eyes well. "The length is so flattering. It accentuates those legs of yours."

I put my hands on my hips and pose at a quarter angle.

"You are so lovely without knowing it and that makes you even more beautiful."

I feel my cheeks redden, not accustomed to compliments.

"And that color makes your eyes look even deeper brown."

"Are you sure you don't mind me borrowing it?"

"You must wear it. I insist. But we need to get you some shoes. Those clunky boots of yours won't do. I know just the ones." Madame starts to push herself up from the couch but sits back with a heavy sigh.

"You stay," I say. "I'll get them. Tell me what they look like."

"Beneath the dresses are some black slingback flats. They were always too big for me. I'm sure they'll fit fine if you loosen the back straps." As I walk back down the hall, Madame adds, "But no rummaging around. Just find the shoes."

On my hands and knees in the closet, I push aside the parade of hems and uncover a row of fancy footwear, all lined up, toes to the wall.

I find the slingbacks and try them on. Slightly small. I inch my toes forward to make them fit. They squeeze a bit but are fine once I fix the straps. They're prettier than any shoes I've ever worn, so I won't even notice the pinch.

Before standing, I glimpse some painted canvases in the back right corner. I crawl over and pull back the dresses to reveal a framed pastel of the Parc Monceau. In the corner is a signature: Delphine. This is Madame's artwork! It's so beautiful… But she told me not to rummage. Does that mean she doesn't want me to see them? Why?

I start to stand but something else, at the base of Charles's clothing on the left, catches my eye. I kneel back down, push aside the jackets, and uncover several more paintings, landscapes, leaning one against the other. I recognize the views: Étretat and its coastline. Next to them is an upright row of rolled canvases, each tied with a black ribbon. One roll has no tie and I gently unfurl it. It's actually two canvases, one of a young man resembling Eugène but with an elongated face and sad, droopy eyes. Like an El Greco portrait. The other is similar, but it's a young woman, billowing blond curls framing her face. She too looks hauntingly sad. I'm startled by the images' rawness, in stark contrast to the cheerful pastel of Parc Monceau. Did Madame paint these too? Maybe on a bad day?

"Catrine." Her voice is harsh.

I swing around, still on my knees. Madame grips the closet door, jaw clenched. "I said no poking around."

"I'm sorry, Madame. I was just—."

"No excuses."

"I'm really sorry. It won't happen again." My chin quivers.

"Make sure it doesn't."

"Yes, Madame."

She seems to realize the severity of her tone because for a moment, she looks sheepish. But then she hands me a quilted Yves Saint Laurent clutch. Black with a gold monogram. "I came back here because I found this for you."

A designer purse? "I couldn't, Madame."

"You must have a proper purse. You're always lugging around that rucksack that looks like it's been through the wars."

I run my hand over the purse's soft leather.

"I see the look on your face, but don't worry. It's an imitation. Bought it at the flea market years ago. Wouldn't dream of paying the fortune they want for a real one."

I hold the purse against my hip. "You're being so generous—"

"None of that. And take these too." She hands me a pair of gold knot earrings and a soft black shawl. "Now you are ready for tomorrow night." She turns to leave but stops. "And by the way," she says over her shoulder. "All the clothes in this closet and on the shelves are yours. If you want them. The slacks may be short on you, but everything else should be fine. I'd rather you have them than donate them to people I don't know."

Before I can thank her and repeat my apology, she's off down the hall.

I move to the bed, slip off the slingbacks, and from the closet comes a voice. "*On n'est point toujours une bête pour l'avoir été quelquefois.*" Being a fool sometimes hardly makes one a fool all the time." Monsieur Diderot coming in from the eighteenth-century court right in time to make me feel better. I was a fool to ignore Madame's wishes. I'll try to be more respectful.

Her full closet beckons and I can't resist. I slip on a black skirt with a black sleeveless sweater and cinch it with a gold belt. I see myself in the mirror, amazed that for once, although all in black, I don't look like a holy sister.

I return to the salon with my best runway strut. "How about this?" I ask, hands in the pockets.

Madame looks delighted. "I must say, your first try at an outfit is a hit."

"Not too monochrome?"

She laughs. "You're a femme fatale. Chic and minimalist. A perfect *Parisienne.*"

Chapter Thirty-Five

Feeling like royalty, I slip off my new black outfit and walk into the bathroom. *My* bathroom. I set my toiletries on the sink next to a fresh bar of soap, turn on the shower, and step behind a panel of glass and into the tub to wash up for dinner. I hold the shower hose over my head, as there's no hook to hang it on, and open my mouth to the steady, hot stream. I push my hair back with my free hand. My longest, most luxurious shower since arriving in Paris.

I don the plush pink robe hanging on the door to unpack and dress. My clothes folded in the dresser and my plastic-wrapped braid tucked away in the nightstand drawer, I put on my jeans and a black long-sleeved tee. I head down the hall and into the kitchen, warmer than the rest of the house and filled with the scent of garlic. Madame tosses a dish towel over her shoulder and smiles. I see she's set the kitchen rather than the dining room table to make dinner easy as both of us are dragging from our day.

We sit and Madame swings around in her chair, opens the fridge, and grabs a bottle of Sancerre. She twists in the corkscrew, pops the cork, and pours. Dinner is simple: pasta with olive oil, tomatoes, and porcini mushrooms followed by a green salad. When I admire the cobalt, and obviously handmade, ceramic bowl filled with grated Parmesan in the center of the table, Madame tells me it's Eugène's childhood artwork. I tell her what a good mother she is to have used it all these years, and then share the story of my candy dish Mother gave away.

"You poor thing. That was cruel." She reaches over and pats my hand. "Eugène was a very good potter growing up. Some of my favorite pieces are in your room."

"The gray pots? I noticed them first thing."

She leans in to wipe a bit of cheese from my sleeve and then dabs at it with the corner of the napkin she'd dipped in her water glass. The intimate gesture makes me feel cared for. Mother would have scolded me about the stain.

"Do you like your room?" Madame asks as she dunks a piece of baguette in the garlicky sauce and I bite into a forkful of pasta.

"I'm sorry. I should have told you right away," I say, covering my mouth as I chew. "I love it. The colors—blue, gray and white—are beautiful. And this is the first time I've ever had my own bathroom. It's all perfect." I twirl my pasta, stab a tomato, and before taking my next bite, add, "You're an excellent decorator and cook."

"I was never interested in cooking until Charles and I spent hours doing it together." She looks up at the sky. "Such long romantic evenings that started in the kitchen..." She closes her eyes and takes a slow drink of wine. "I do miss cooking with him."

I watch her for a moment. Her love for Charles seems to radiate from her.

Before I realize I'm speaking my next thought aloud, I've whispered, "I hope I love someone so intensely one day."

Her eyes snap open. "Of course, you will. You're a lovely, interesting young woman and you have plenty of time. And there is Vincent..." She raises her glass and takes another sip.

I do too, while crossing my fingers she's right about him. Then I set my glass down and get up to clear and wash our plates—Mother trained me to never let a dirty dish sit—but Madame insists I leave them in the sink.

"They can wait. I'm anxious to try that gorgeous tarte. I'm touched you remembered it's my favorite."

I cut into the apricot pie and bring two slices to the table. She takes a forkful of its flaky, buttery crust. "*Délicieuse.*" We sit with our dessert and drain our glasses, each of us now speaking with a Sancerre slur.

"Thank you for agreeing to live with me," Madame says quietly. "I hope you won't change your mind." She turns to look out the open window.

I say, following her gaze and say, "Please don't think that. I won't."

We listen to the final unhurried calls of the swifts at dusk as they rise and fall in the cool air of the courtyard, careening towards their nests under the eaves. Once again, it's *l'heure bleue*, and tonight it marks the end of a miraculous day in Paris.

Chapter Thirty-Six

"Mother," I say from the phone booth the following afternoon. "I heard from Uncle Walter."

"About time. It's been two weeks since I told you about Dagmar."

I try to visualize her on the other end of the line, but her features are fuzzy, as if the longer I'm away, the less substantial she is.

"Spit it out. What did he say?'

I tell her about Dagmar's surgery date. "I'll visit right after in July."

"But you'll be home by July. You said so last time you called."

"I said no such thing. I found a job. I'm staying in Paris."

Silence. Then with annoyance she says. "Watching children's not a real job, you know. You made such a fuss about college to become a babysitter?"

"I won't be babysitting. I met a woman—a professor—who needs someone who speaks French to work on her husband's manuscript about Guy de Maupassant, the French writer."

There's no response for several seconds. Then, "If that's what you want." She pauses again. But I'm sure there's more. "I'm surprised, that's all. I thought this going to France nonsense was just that…"

I hear a sniffle. "Well, at least you'll be there to see Dagmar and Walter. My only family."

"You also have me, Mother. Or are you writing me off since I'm not coming home?"

"Of course, I have you. But Dagi's my sister and—"

"So why don't you visit her?" Part of me is angry about her intractability and another part sad that Mother won't have the solace of seeing Dagmar.

Another sniffle. "I want to, but I'm too scared to fly. What if I have a heart attack? Or get sick from the food?"

"Why can't you get over your xenophobia—"

"My what?"

"Your fear of everything foreign. Leave it behind to see your sick sister."

Silence.

"They need you more than they need me right now," I say.

Nothing.

"Well, since you're too scared to fly, and can't seem to muster the courage to do something for someone else, your sister of all people, I'll go. Dagmar and Walter are my family too. It's the right thing to do."

I hang up and sit for a moment, letting my eczema and anger ease. I hated hearing her style of words come out of my mouth, but wasn't it about time she heard some blunt facts? As I open the door to the booth, Colette speaks to me. "*Il n'est pas mauvais que les enfants remettent de temps en temps, avec politesse, les parents à leur place.*" It is not a bad thing that children should occasionally, and politely, put parents in their place.

After the phone call, I pick up some groceries at the busy Raspail market, vendors trying to make themselves heard above the hubbub, knowing I now have a fridge in which to put them. I walk back to Madame's, press the buzzer, and then run up the stairs two at a time. I'm breathless when she opens the door.

"Catrine, I made you some keys," she says as she lets me in. She drops two in my outstretched palm. "Now you can come and go as you like."

"They'll go right on my Eiffel Tower key chain."

"I guess this makes it official."

Chapter Thirty-Seven

I can't remember having ever felt this happy before. I have a new place to call home and a date with Vincent tonight. Having tossed and turned all night with jitters about our date, I get up with the first glimmer of dawn to take a walk, leaving a note for Madame.

I cross the Boulevard Saint Germain and make my way towards the Seine on the *rue de l'Éperon*. I realize I'm around the corner from Roger La Grenouille on the *rue des Grands Augustins*. I pass in front of the narrow restaurant and cup my hands to look in the dark window. I take in the brightly tiled floor and lace curtains and see myself sitting at a candlelit table across from Vincent. My heart catches. I walk around the corner to a café and order a pain au chocolat and grand café crème to celebrate.

My hand shakes as I raise and then put down the full cup. I hold a sugar cube over the rim and let it fill with coffee, à la Madame. This time the sweet square makes it into my mouth. A good omen. And again, Colette speaks to me. "*Il y a souvent plus d'angoisse à attendre un plaisir qu'à subir une peine.*" There is often more anguish in expecting a pleasure than in undergoing a pain. Exactly, Colette. Exactly.

I try calming my nerves, reminding myself that at least I'll look ready for my date. My perfect Parisian outfit will complement Vincent's always-cool attire and, as much as I hate to think of her, I'll use the tricks Freddie taught me about makeup. And yet, my stomach tightens.

I devour my warm, flaky pastry and gulp down coffee, too nervous to sit for long. I leave some francs on the table and head back to Madame's.

While we're sitting in the salon reading, I realize I never told her about Dagmar. "With all the excitement about my date with Vincent, I totally forgot to tell you I must go to Germany at the end of the month. To a little spa town called Bad Neuenahr-Ahrweiler." I fill her in on Walter's letter and my call to Mother.

"I'm so sorry about the surgery, Catrine. But I'm sure your aunt and uncle will be happy to see you."

Madame stands and says she's off to do some errands and to visit Charles. "Why don't you take the time to try on more of my clothes."

I give her a thumbs up, head back to my room, and pretend I'm in a department store as I go through her closet and lay several pairings on the bed. Madame voices her approval when she returns from the cemetery and sees what I've accomplished.

By late afternoon, it's time to get ready. I spend hours showering, shampooing, and doing my hair and makeup as I've never done before. Madame gives me her approval, multiple bisous, wishes me luck, and I'm off.

I step out of the cab, right on time, and wait for Vincent outside Roger La Grenouille. After ten minutes, I cross my fingers hoping reality won't be ruined by expectation. The tuxedoed maître d' at the door suggests I come in. "It's a nice evening, mademoiselle, but you would be more comfortable inside."

I hesitate but then agree.

"And the reservation is under …?"

"Lanier. Vincent Lanier."

"Ah, Monsieur Lanier. Yes, he is a very good client. If you are his date, you must be very special. I will bring you to his favorite table."

He has a favorite table? As the gentleman leads me to the back corner past frog-themed bric-à-brac—photographs, sculptures, and musical instruments—I'm wondering how many "special" women Vincent has brought to this romantic place. The table is nice. Private, with a view of the whole restaurant. I take my seat, but I'm nervous as I wait, not feeling special at all.

The maître d' brings a menu and the house aperitif—a kir. "*Santé, Mademoiselle,*" he says with a slight bow.

I sip the kir, a pale shade of pink that complements my dress and calms my nerves. A stylish woman in a business suit walks by my table on her way to *les toilettes*. "Your dress is fabulous," she says. I blush, thank her, and hear the suggestive voice of Françoise Sagan. "*Une robe n'a de sens que si un homme a envie de vous l'enlever.*" A dress makes no sense unless it inspires men to want to take it off you." My blush deepens and I stifle a giggle. What is taking Vincent so long?

The waiter approaches and brings a second kir. "Perhaps you'd like to look at the menu while you wait?"

"*Merci,*" I say, happy for the distraction. Resisting the urge to look at my watch, I carefully read the menu, heavy on frog specialties and other French classics. I promised Madame I'd try the frog legs.

As I watch tables fill, a twist of trepidation makes its way from my belly to my throat. When one empty table remains, I become impatient and finally check the time: seven-thirty-five. The excitement in my stomach curdles into disappointment and a drum in my head beats loudly.

Did I get the time wrong? The day?

No, the maître d' would have said something. The waiter returns. "Would you like another drink while you wait?"

"*Non, merci,*" I say, my voice trembling. "But may I ask if Monsieur Lanier called?"

He leaves and returns promptly. "I am afraid not, *mademoiselle.*"

"I see. I'll wait just a bit longer."

"As you wish." He smiles with a quick bow.

My heart pounds, keeping me on the edge of my seat, and the minutes tick by—ten and then twenty more. And then, all my past nights of self-inflicted chastity bubble up at once and any poise I had at the beginning of the evening pools at my feet.

When I can no longer bear it, hot tears spill. I open my purse to pay for my drinks, but the waiter catches my eye and shakes his head. "They are on the house," he says.

"*Merci,*" I manage to whisper as I pull up my shawl and then hasten to the exit, eyes on the floor. The maître d' opens the door. "*Désolé, mademoiselle. Bonne soirée*. Perhaps I will see you again soon." I give him half a smile and flee.

Chapter Thirty-Eight

I look down at the cobblestones and then up to the sliver of night sky above the narrow street. Where are my guides? Speak to me, please. Tell me what to do. But all is silent, the voices mute. I think about how carefully I'd gotten ready and with so much anticipation. What a fool. How could I have thought Vincent would fall for someone like me?

My knees wobble and I fear I'll collapse. I must sit for at least a few minutes and pull myself together before returning to Madame's. I can still taste the kir, but I wonder if maybe a glass of wine—elsewhere—will help steady my nerves and numb my heartbreak.

I make it around the corner before Simone de Beauvoir finally comes to my aid. "*On lui coupe les ailes, et on déplore qu'elle ne sache pas voler.*" Her wings are cut and then she is blamed for not knowing how to fly." Simone, you understand.

I slip into the café from this morning. It's all lit up with artificial blue-white light, bustling with a Saturday night crowd. I scan for a table, spot a huddle of girls at one end of the bar, a conspiratorial cluster of young men at the other, and see someone wave from the side banquette. Wave to me. I squint and see it's Odette, alone near the window. Any other time, I would love the company, but after being stood up? I can barely breathe. I consider pretending I don't see her, but that seems even more foolish, so I force myself to walk over. She tells me Freddie was supposed to come for a drink but left a message that she had to cancel.

As I feel my shoulders relax, she insists that I sit, saying it's a sign. "I planned to call you tomorrow to see about getting together and now here you are."

So, I slide into the seat across from her. I'd still like a drink before going home.

"Catrine, you look so beautiful tonight. My God, that dress is stunning on you!"

She's cheerful and happy to see me, while I can barely collect the composure to be cordial. I dig my teeth hard into my lower lip, taste the tang of blood, and look at the ceiling, trying hard not to cry.

"Are you okay?" Odette reaches to take my hand. Her touch releases a torrent of tears. Softly, she says, "No, you're not okay." She squeezes my hand as I try to speak but choke on the words.

"Take your time." Her kindness only makes me cry harder. "You need a drink." She signals for the waiter. "*Encore un verre, s'il vous plaît.*" She turns to me. "You don't have to say anything, but I am a good listener."

I dry my eyes, wipe my streaked makeup, and breathe deeply. My wine arrives and I take a long gulp. "Vincent," I say.

"Is he all right?"

"He asked me to dinner but never showed."

Odette looks stricken on my behalf. "No! And you looking so gorgeous... Are you sure he's not just late?"

"I waited an hour..."

"I'm sure something happened because the Vincent I know would never do that."

"Maybe you don't really know him. Maybe I don't either."

"Listen, as I told you, I saw him the day after the book signing, and well, the smile on his face when he heard you were still in Paris said it all. There's no way he decided not to show up."

"What other reason could there be?"

"I've no idea, but we'll find out." She raises her glass and I halfheartedly clink.

Odette's words stem my tears and although the wine soothes me, it's going to take a couple more glasses to loosen the knots in my empty stomach. I ask, "But Odette—why are you in this bar." She reminds me she works down the street, near where I saw her and Gaston, and tonight, even though it's Saturday, she had to work late on a media report. "This is my favorite spot to wind down."

Conversation with Odette makes me feel better already. She orders two more glasses of wine. She asks where I found my beautiful vintage dress and I tell her about Madame, her apartment, and how I'm starting work on Charles's manuscript. "It all happened at the perfect time because I was almost broke."

Odette leans in. "So, you're staying in Paris after all?"

"For as long as Madame will have me."

"That's great news. After seeing how you managed Christian, organizing a manuscript, and getting it published seems perfect for you."

Odette's affirmation brings a swell of pride, like a swirling of leaves. "It's about Maupassant."

"Who's the author?"

"Charles Arnoux."

"I remember reading something by him at university. He wrote a lot about Maupassant, right?"

"Yes, but this one's not scholarly. More for general readers. It's unfinished but I have some ideas for pulling it together."

Our waiter brings our wine, but I'm not sure I can handle any more.

"You know, our office had a meeting this week. About a Ministry of Culture initiative. They're encouraging publishers to do books about artists, architects, and writers for the public. Accessible writing to help promote cultural pride. Funding's available and..." Her voice trails off and she sits back, her eyes widening, her face corpse-white. She leans left, staring past me.

"What?" I ask. I push back from the table and half-turn around. Freddie.

The sight of her sets my teeth on edge and my heart pounding. My eyes narrow as I reach up to touch the back of my neck. I twist back to

Odette. She shakes her head and appears genuinely surprised.

Freddie approaches our table and I get up to leave before I do or say something stupid. But she blocks my way, smirking. "Well, look at you, Scaredy-Cat. Out with my friend Odette, and all dolled up, I see." She gives me the once over.

Odette says, "She was meeting Vincent and—" She claps a hand over her mouth, realizing her slip. I turn to her and she looks like she wants to disappear, her head in her hands.

Freddie scoffs. "And of course, he didn't show. He's been with me all night." She laughs, her eyes raking over me. "And you just waiting there, all dressed up and pretty." Her gaze grows icy. "Didn't you know that was his plan all along? How pathetic. You really are a sucker."

I feel numb, flinty, beyond the pale of rage, and shame. I pick up my barely touched glass of wine and splash it in her face.

She screams as red stains blossom on her white peasant blouse.

"Enjoy the wine, Freddie. It's a really nice Syrah."

I disappear out the door.

Chapter Thirty-Nine

The following morning, I stare in the bathroom mirror, my eyes a puffy mess. I splash my face, brush my teeth, and crawl back into bed. Propped up on a pile of pillows, I take a long drink from the glass of water Madame left for me on the nightstand, attempting to swallow the sadness tightening my throat.

There's a gentle knock at my door. "*Oui*," I say.

Madame enters with a tray of steaming coffee and a warm croissant.

"*Bonjour*," she says, fussing to put breakfast on the bed. "I heard you in the bathroom and couldn't wait to hear about last night. You did have the frog legs, didn't you?" She sits on the end of my bed, pats my shin, and looks at my face. Her face knots with concern.

"Oh no. What's wrong, *ma petite*? Tell me."

I tell her everything.

"I am so sorry," she says. "There could be many explanations for what happened, but I'm sure it was a terrible disappointment for you." Madame opens her arms to me. It has such a calming effect when I fold my shoulders into her cushioned embrace. How quickly she's become my safe space.

"When I saw Freddie and heard what she said, I was crushed. And I don't know about Odette. I feel like a fool."

"Is it possible you overreacted? Vincent hasn't yet had the chance to explain—"

"But Freddie! Why would she say all that?" My tears are back. "You weren't there and didn't see her face. She was awful. So vindictive."

Madame pats me again gently and stands. "Simply consider the possibility of another explanation, *ma chérie*."

"Maybe," I say.

She touches my shoulder, turns, and tap taps down the hall.

I sit in bed sipping the coffee, nibbling the croissant, and rehashing last night's café scene. Freddie clearly still hates me, and maybe she'd say anything to hurt me, but Vincent didn't show up. And he didn't call the restaurant. If he was with her…

After fifteen minutes of ruminating, I get up and shower, scrubbing my face to remove whatever traces of last night's makeup tears didn't wash away. Watching the soap bubbles circle the drain and disappear, I decide to focus on the future. I'm with Madame, in a perfect place in Paris, with an interesting job. I convince myself that for now, it's all I need. Besides, there are other *poissons* in *la mer*. Though it's harder to convince myself of that.

I step out of the shower, dry myself, dress, and join Madame in the kitchen. I put my breakfast tray on the table, sit, and take the last bite of croissant. "Even if it turns out there's another explanation, a romance with Vincent was probably just a sentimental dream. I have to move on."

Madame refills her coffee and says, "I have an idea, Catrine."

"Hmm."

"Do you want to hear it?"

"Anything to distract me."

"Remember I told you I dreamed we went to Normandy?"

I nod.

"It got me thinking about our birthdays. Maupassant lived in Rouen for a time, was born to the north, and lived in Étretat when he was a boy."

"Where I went to the beach." And where those closet landscapes were painted, but I say nothing about that.

"As I'm sure you know, it's a literary region. Gustave Flaubert is Rouen's most famous son and Maupassant went to high school there.

His mother introduced him to Flaubert who became his literary godfather. We wouldn't have Maupassant without Flaubert."

Madame leans across the table and takes my hands. "Let's go to Normandy for our birthdays. You and I both need a change of scenery. We'll leave tomorrow, stay in Rouen, and have dinner at *La Couronne* on the town square. You can wear the claret dress and replace last night's memory with a happy one."

I didn't think I had a smile in me today but immediately, one wells up.

Chapter Forty

We're going on a road trip. A welcome distraction to help me get past the previous night, and a wonderful way to celebrate our birthdays. My first one in France.

That afternoon, Madame sits at the formal dining room table unfolding road maps and making notes in her Michelin Guide. She goes to her room to make some calls and I overhear her reserve a hotel room. The phone rings while she's still in the bedroom. Eugène must be ahead of schedule today.

"*Oui*," she says. "*Mais non. Pas d'excuses*." She sounds upset. "*D'accord. Je vous écoute*," she says after a long pause. She's quiet as she listens and then softly closes the door. I'm sure it's more about me living with her and I'm grateful I can't hear what's said.

When she returns, she's carrying a small navy bag. "*Tiens*. Your suitcase." She sets it beside the couch next to where I sit. "I refuse to let you go to the venerable Hôtel Le Flaubert lugging that old satchel."

"Thanks so much. Was Eugène scolding you?"

"Oh, the call. Nothing new." She throws a sweater around her shoulders. "I'm going to do some errands before our trip, including a stop in the cemetery. I need to tell Charles we're going away, so he knows why I won't be visiting for a few days."

She takes her wheeled shopping cart from the front closet. "And I'll get us something for dinner."

"Do you want me to come with you?"

"*Mais, non*. I'd like to go alone."

Before she leaves, she points to the navy suitcase. "Don't forget to pack."

I nod. The door closes.

But before we go, before I even start packing, I want to make a small dent in the editing job Madame has hired me for, as I must earn my keep. Perhaps if Eugène can be convinced that I'm useful this way, he'll stop giving her such a hard time.

I sit on the salon floor and am soon floating in a sea of paper, losing myself in Charles's writing. But the sheets aren't numbered, so putting them in order seems impossible. How will I ever make this confusion of five-hundred-plus pages into a discernible whole? Normally, I relish this phase of a project, when everything's a mess and I've no idea which way to turn. But this time, the stakes feel high—I want to please Madame.

Focus, Catrine, focus.

I sit up straight and fill my lungs. There's only one way to start and that's by plunging in, page by page, word by word. I quickly flip through the sheets to see what's there and make random piles to feel like I'm accomplishing something. But my eyes blur as I can't even find two pages that follow each other. I read several paragraphs and see that the writing is indeed accessible, rendered beautifully in plain language anyone can understand. And some of the pages include line illustrations. No wonder the academic world rejected a book written for ordinary, non-scholarly readers. Charles sent it to the wrong publishers.

I chew on my pencil and tap it on my lower lip like a schoolgirl. After a few minutes, I get up to make coffee. Perhaps some caffeine will fuel my manuscript puzzle skills. I return with a steaming cup and take tiny sips as I sift through the white sheets. Those with sketches, I set aside. I continue with my coffee and a drop falls on the page in my lap, right on the word, "Fifi." *Mademoiselle Fifi*. One of Maupassant's short stories, this one a tale of fantasy revenge.

And then, as if in relief, the names of stories rise from the pages around me. Did Charles organize his book by individual story? Why didn't I notice before? I put down my cup and furiously begin highlighting titles, and then making piles with the same names, alphabetically by story, a total of twelve. I pause to read one page about *The Necklace*—an easy-to-digest analysis. Charles has written he believes the story is Maupassant's *chef d'oeuvre*. I smile. He agreed with me, but I won't tell Madame.

I'm still surrounded by piles of paper organized by story but none of the pages are sequential. Another hour passes and finally, patterns reveal themselves. Charles focused on themes, not stories, to organize the book. Life under the Prussian occupation of France, the noble prostitute, class barriers, reputation versus hearsay, and social ambition—all depicted unflinchingly. I take a marker and make blue checks that help me start reorganizing the story piles into themed ones. I fall back, arms above my head, and rest on the Persian rug. I'm finally making progress but enough for today.

I decide to grab a slice of *tarte aux abricots* to reward myself.

Just as I'm becoming concerned about where Madame has gone and wonder if I should have accompanied her, the front door opens and she waltzes in with her grocery cart.

I stand and my mouth drops open. "Madame—your hair!"

"You think you're the only woman who can change her look? It's about time I got some color."

No longer dull and brittle, her hair is now a gentle chestnut highlighted with silver, similar to the style in the pencil skirt photo. It's trimmed, but still long, and pulled into a flattering French twist. Her eyes look different too…

"What do you think? I tried your budget salon. And I got some new glasses." Her clunky black frames have been replaced with soft gray ones. She touches them with her finger. "I ordered them last week."

"Your hair is gorgeous. Your eyes are gorgeous. You're gorgeous! But you walked to the Sorbonne?"

She rolls her eyes. "You sound like Eugène. I visited the cemetery and then took a taxi to the salon, did some shopping, collected my glasses, and took one home."

"Why all this today?"

"We are traveling, *ma cherie*. To wonderful Rouen. And since I have not been out of Paris in years, I was inspired by Coco Chanel. 'A woman who changes her hair is about to change her life.' Have you heard this, Catrine?"

Part Two

BEYOND PARIS

June 1981

Chapter Forty-One

The next morning, Madame insists we leave promptly at ten. On our way down to the garage, I say, "Eugène is fine with this?"

"This is our getaway. Not his. We're going to enjoy ourselves on our birthdays and that's what matters."

I longed for French adventure and here it is.

I lift our matching navy bags into the back seat of her yellow 1971 Citroën Dyane. She eyes me from the passenger side of the car. "You did say you're comfortable driving stick?"

I assure Madame I'll have no trouble with the gearshift, but a shudder about driving in such a big city wriggles up my spine.

We climb in. I depress the clutch and turn the key. The motor roars, the car convulses, and I grip the dark indents in the tan steering wheel, imagining Charles's hands wore them into the leather. Out of the garage, our rattletrap ride has some fits and starts and then settles into a low rumble I feel under my seat. The uneven rattle as we drive over cobblestones is a pleasing surprise.

Madame consults her map and says. "It'll be four hours to Rouen. The autoroute would be faster, but we'll take *le chemin des écoliers*,"

"The what?"

"The one taken by students not eager to arrive at school. In other words, the scenic route through rural Normandy."

For three months I've been in Paris and now, finally, I'll get to see another part of France—some of its pastoral countryside. My stomach fills with butterflies. Madame will worry about the details and I can simply enjoy. *C'est parfait.*

We struggle to make it through Paris traffic and then its suburbs, drivers beeping the minute lights turn green, cars cutting across the roundabouts, and motorbikes splitting lanes. It's a roller derby, French style.

Eventually, we're out of the city's environs and heading northwest. The tangerine sun shines against a pale, bleached gray sky and the twisty byway slices through fields of green dotted with red poppies. My shoulders loosen and I relax. I guide the Dyane through flaxen fields, and then slow her to a crawl on lanes cutting around corners of stone villages lost in time. Cypress trees stand tall along tidy property lines, now and then the rock walls of a chateau emerge through the trees, and the occasional outline of a fortress tower crests a hill.

We sit in companionable silence, two for the road with miles passing beneath us, until we're beyond Madame having to consult her map. Now, at even innocuous junctions, signs mark directions for both neighboring hamlets and distant waypoints, including Rouen.

"What a system," I say turning the car sharply to the right to veer off a roundabout. "So logical, so simple, and well, so French."

"We French are nothing if not logical." She points to a dirt tractor path in the middle of nowhere. "Let's pull off here for a minute. To roll back the roof. It's getting warm, don't you think?" Madame talks me through unhooking the canvas, folding it back, and securing it.

Jumping back in, I tell Madame how beautiful her hair looks reflecting the sun. She pulls her pink silk scarf over her head and ties it under her chin, Marilyn Monroe-style. Then she dons a pair of oversized sunglasses.

"You look like Simone Signoret in *Chère Inconnue*," I say.

"Charles used to say I resembled her."

"He must have felt proud with you by his side."

She pats my knee. "As I feel with you, *ma petite*."

"This is my first time in a convertible," I admit as I pull back on the road. I look over at Madame, basking in the sun, her cheeks pink. We slow as we enter yet another sleepy village, stopping to let a shepherd and his wooly wards cross the lane from one field to the next.

"Madame, I am so enjoying this. It's like we're in the nineteenth century. Peasants tending the land in a Millet painting or a Hugo novel."

We speed back up, the wind whipping my hair. I add, "And now we're in that Claude Lelouch movie from the sixties—the one where they're always in a car heading to Normandy."

"Since I'm in a scarf, I'll be Anouk Aimée, and that would make you—"

"Ha! Jean-Louis Trintignant." I belt the theme from *Un Homme et Une Femme*. A Man and a Woman.

"*Comme nos voix ba da ba da da da da da da.*

Chantent tout bas ba da ba da da da da da da..."

Madame throws her head back and joins me in singing.

"Perfect, although you're much taller than he was." Madame's chuckle turns into a snort, and we laugh until our stomachs hurt. She turns her face to the sky. "Let's thank God we have a beautiful day and don't need the windshield wipers. It was always raining in that film."

"A sign for Giverny!" I say. "Can we stop?"

"It's somewhat out of the way and we need to get to Rouen. Maybe on the way home?"

I do a furtive watch-check. Why the hurry? I look over and see the tiny, now familiar, movements that signal a spell: a jerk of her leg and the slight drop of her head. When she comes to, she straightens her shoulders and smiles her Simone Signoret smile.

"Tell me how you're feeling, Catrine. Is Roger La Grenouille still hurting?"

There's a pang in my chest. "I'm doing my best not to think about it, actually, so I can focus on traveling with you."

"Have you considered giving Vincent a chance to explain?"

"I don't know." My voice cracks and I swallow hard, unable to shake the hurt.

She twists in her seat to look at me. "Do you like this man?"

"Doesn't matter now."

"Of course, it matters. What you want matters." She lets her words linger. "If someone you like presents himself, don't let him get away." She pauses again. "And there's no need to run the Dyane into the ground. She's ten years old and hasn't been out for a country drive in years."

The speedometer says my foot is made of lead. We're going 120 kilometers an hour—about seventy-five miles fast. "Sorry, Madame. I didn't realize..."

"You're upset. The question is, what will you do about it?"

I check my speed. Much better. "Right now, I don't know."

"Okay then. Start by telling me what you like about him."

I tilt my head and think before answering. "He's intelligent, interesting, and well-read. He makes me laugh because he finds the same things I do amusing. He's charming and self-assured but is earnest and silly at the same time. And he's very tall...taller than I am."

"And you're a smart, funny, generous, warm, attractive young woman. You're curious and have spirit. Why not go after what you want?"

"Hasn't he already rejected me by not showing up Saturday night?" I grip the steering wheel and my speed ratchets back up.

She pats my knee. "I still think there could be an explanation, but you'll have to be patient." She adjusts her headscarf slightly. "I've learned a few things about relationships in my years. First, nothing hurts more than being treated like you're disposable, so I understand that."

I nod.

"And, you must never accept someone if he or she doesn't appreciate you."

"I agree. So, why should I consider giving Vincent another chance?"

"The next thing is the most important. Misunderstandings happen and the other person deserves a chance to explain."

We slow at a crossroads in a dense apple orchard, the arrow for Rouen pointing right.

Madame says, "The mistake many make is thinking they're strong by refusing to listen, but they're actually being foolish."

I frown as I make the right turn. "You think I'm foolish."

Madame says, "*Il n'est pire sourd que celui qui ne veut pas entendre.*" There are none so deaf as those who will not hear. Do you know this proverb?"

"You're telling me I should listen."

"What harm can it do?"

We round a sharp curve, and Madame cries out, waving at a roadside stand. "Here, Catrine. Turn. They have Calvados—the famous apple brandy of Normandy. We must get some. Right from the producer."

"Aren't we in a hurry?" I say, pulling into a dirt lot.

"It'll just be a quick stop for some Norman specialties." She checks her watch. "A few minutes ahead of schedule, thanks to your speedy driving." She marches up to the man in overalls, points to a bottle and says, "We'd also like a basket of apples. Some *Reine des Reinettes*, if you have them." He gives her a nod and she turns to me. "My favorite apple. Crisp and juicy."

The farmer starts filling a paper bag with apples from an oak barrel, but Madame stops and points. "How about one of those pretty baskets? Fill one and I'll pay for the basket as well."

"Anything for you, Madame." He gives a little bow and wanders off to retrieve a basket.

I say quietly, "He's being very nice."

"When you are clear about what you want, people respond."

As we get in the Dyane with our apples and Calvados, I wonder about what she's said. Her clarity hasn't seemed to work with Eugène, but I decide not to bring that up right now. I turn on the ignition and get us back on the road.

Madame takes a ham, Brie, and butter baguette sandwich cut in two from the plastic bag at her feet. She wraps each half in a napkin and hands one to me.

"Do you want me to pull over? I know eating on the run is not very French."

"It's fine this time. We should keep going." She turns to me. "You have a way of getting me to do many things I'm not accustomed to. Like taking off for Normandy with a day's notice."

"Me? This was your idea." I smile.

"I suppose it was," she murmurs. "It's wonderful to be overcome by a sense of spontaneity and romance."

Her words remind me of Vincent, but I don't want to think about him just yet. Though his rebuff still hurts, I refuse to give up believing in romance.

"Tell me about Charles, Madame. What was the attraction?"

"Above all, he had a wonderful sense of humor. And we could have long, intellectual discussions and disagree without rancor."

"And, he was handsome?"

"You saw his picture. He looked like Yves Montand. Do you know this actor?"

"I fell in love with him when I saw him in that movie with Barbra Streisand. *On a Clear Day You Can See Forever.*"

"So, you understand why he caught my attention."

"I do." I think back on all the movies set in France and all the French actors I saw as an adolescent and teen. I was already a Francophile, but they set my passion aflame.

"And Vincent? Is he your Yves Montand?"

My jaw clenches and I shake my head.

"No?"

"I'm just not ready to talk about him."

"I see." She frowns but doesn't press the point. "*D'accord.* So, tell me more about your mother."

I finish chewing my sandwich, hand Madame my empty napkin,

and heave a big sigh.

"She did her best to make me think having my own dreams made me evil."

My dramatic delivery makes Madame laugh. "Nevertheless, you came to France. All by yourself." She reaches over, pats my forearm, and leaves her hand there with its warmth.

Thoughtfully, I add, "I finally took Madame de Stael's words to heart. '*Le plus grand bonheur est de transformer vos sentiments en actions.*'" The greatest happiness is to transform one's feelings into action.'"

"*Bien sûr*!" Madame's hand lifts off my arm to reach into the basket behind her.

She hands me an apple and I take a big bite. She carefully slices another with a Laguiole pocketknife on a dishtowel in her lap.

"The pain of parental disappointment is stitched inside you. Mothers should shield their children from life's harms but not draw the curtain on life itself."

"It's been exhausting fighting her. The way she looked at me, I might as well have been from Mars."

"Maybe she uses disdain to mask the fear that you would leave her behind?"

"Maybe." I go on to tell Madame things I haven't shared with anyone, opening like a morning glory on a summer day when I discover the ease of sharing freely while facing forward in a car. "Growing up, I assumed all mothers were fixated on religion, afraid of sexuality, and manic about money. But by high school, I knew something was wrong. Her religious compulsions—watching to see if the priest said the prayers in the right order, for example, weren't normal. Once, we had to go back into church after mass to repeat the dismissal prayers because the priest forgot to say, 'Go in peace.' Another time, we got to mass three minutes late. She made us stay for the next one as well to be sure we heard every word."

"Definitely obsessive. She's neurotic about money too?"

"Everything in her life is related to what she spent or what she saved.

She carried her budget and lists of what she'd spent that day, that week, and that month in a notebook of green accounting paper. To this day, I can't look at that paper without feeling ill."

"God knows raising a child is difficult, but I think your mother suffers from scrupulosity. A fixation leading to pathological guilt about sinning. It's a form of mental illness along with her obsession about money. I had students with compulsive disorders who worried about grades or typing perfect term papers with no erasures."

I'm quiet, wondering if I'm ready for Madame's diagnosis to absolve Mother for treating me like a mistake needing fixing.

Madame leans her head back on the seat and closes her eyes.

Chapter Forty-Two

Waking from a half-hour nap, Madame asks, "Where has our glorious day gone?"

The clouds have gradually gathered over the past thirty minutes to darken the sky and make the hills cast gray shadows across green fields. I stop the Dyane to reattach the roof when the wind whips up and a light drizzle begins.

"'Rouen, the watering pot of France," says Madame when we're again en route.

"Guy de Maupassant. *Mademoiselle Fifi.*"

Madame chuckles. "I'll stump you yet." She raises her arm to again glance at her watch

"Are we in a rush? You're awfully fidgety."

"I told the hotel to expect us by two, but this storm will certainly delay us. Unlike many of my fellow citizens, I do not like to be late."

I didn't think hotels cared when you arrived. But what do I know? "Madame, may I admit something else? I've never stayed in a hotel before. A hostel, yes, a hotel, never."

She smiles. "*Alors*, this is a trip of firsts for you. Your first time outside Paris, your first convertible, your first hotel. Might there be other firsts?"

"My first time seeing the Cathédrale de Rouen towers!" I cry as a zigzag of lightening slices into the inky sky. "When I read Madame Bovary, I could picture exactly where Emma met her lover inside the cathedral..." Before I can finish, the cloud bellies burst, releasing diagonal

Norman rain. The downpour slows us to a crawl, the windshield wipers at full throttle swooshing rivulets of rain. Whoosh-thump. Whoosh-thump.

"Wish we were inside the cathedral right now." Madame looks at her watch. "We're going to be late."

"For what? The hotel's not going anywhere."

Madame sighs impatiently.

While I focus on keeping the car on the road, Madame watches for signs for the *Centre Ville*. She directs me right, across the Seine. We splash through a puddle that blinds me. The car bobbles on the cobblestones, skids against the curb, and then veers back into the lane. I slow further, more concerned about arriving intact than tardy.

Entering the city, Madame directs me to our hotel, Le Flaubert, a 15th-century mansion turned boutique hotel. It's around the corner from the central square, *la Place Du Vieux Marché*, where nineteen-year-old Jeanne d'Arc met her fiery fate in 1431 at the hands of the English in the Hundred Years' War.

The streets are deserted. I pull under the porte cochère, jump out, and help Madame to the door. The bellman takes our bags and says, "Park behind the hotel. There's an entry in the back."

Madame hands me an umbrella from her bag. "I'll get us checked in."

Under teeming rain, I swing around the building, maneuver into a space, and grab the umbrella. I slip out of the car and struggle with the thing as I run for cover, splashing through muddy pools. Thank God I wore my jeans and boots and not Madame's expensive clothes, safe and dry in my suitcase. The umbrella pops open when I reach the door.

I stamp my feet in the back foyer and then clomp my way down the hallway to reception. Rain drips from my chin and hands, and the bottoms of my pants are so wet they darken the crimson carpet once I stand still. My hair is sopping, hanging in my face and my white T-shirt is soaked to transparency. I shiver as I take in the details of the dark-wooded barrel-ceilinged lobby. I look for Madame, but there's only a young woman behind the registration desk.

"Catrine?"

I spin around pushing clingy, wet hair from my forehead and see a tall figure rising from a chair by the lobby fireplace. My chest constricts.

"What are you doing here?"

Chapter Forty-Three

Vincent crosses the lobby to the front desk. "A towel, please," he asks the clerk who disappears behind a door. He turns back to me. "You *did* cut your hair..."

I'm speechless, but inside I'm trembling, churning with emotion. Vincent's wearing a soft chambray shirt with chocolate colored corduroy blazer draped over one arm. His distressed leather boots make him look more French Marlboro man than Parisian banker.

The clerk hands me the towel. After dabbing at my face and hair, I press the towel to my chest, which Vincent has been staring at. I look down and see the outline of my pink lace bra. I feel ever more foolish and blush. When I look up, he's blushing too.

"Why are you here, Vincent, and where is Madame Arnoux?"

He looks uncomfortable, his cheeks deepening their pink. "Let us sit. By the fireplace. You must be freezing."

I move towards the fire, hissing and seething behind its brass. I drop the towel on the table, no longer caring if he or anyone else can see my bra.

"Madame said she will meet you in the room."

"She knows…She knew you were coming?" I turn away. How could she—

He takes my arm. "Catrine, wait. I want to explain what happened. Madame thought—"

"Madame thought... What does she have to do with this?" I fake a look around. "What, no Freddie?" I'm instantly ashamed of my sarcasm, but my emotions are feeding a ball of fury.

Vincent calmly takes my hand and holds it firmly when I try to step away.

"Madame would like us to talk and so would I. *S'il te plaît.*"

He draws me closer to the fire. I see the glint in his blue eyes, and now notice the cotton candy-colored tulips on the table. I ignore both and remain standing.

"She told you to be here? At two?"

He pushes his hands deep in his pockets and looks down at the carpet. "I need to tell you about dinner—"

"And why Odette made me sit and have a drink until Freddie waltzed in? Was it all planned that way?"

Vincent's brow furrows. "You think I planned that?" There's a wounded look in his eyes.

I'm suddenly shivering uncontrollably. His face softens, and he takes off his jacket. "Put this over your shoulders."

I wrap myself in the jacket. It's warm, smells like him, and I want to bury my face in the cords. I'm afraid I'll cry but manage a whisper. "It hurt, Vincent..."

He steps towards me, his arms open tentatively, as if he's about to embrace a wild animal, but I don't attack and so he comes closer. His hands rest on my shoulders. "Let me explain and I will make it up to you."

I lean in but say nothing.

"You will be more comfortable in dry clothes. You change and I will wait."

I raise an eyebrow.

"As long as it will take."

I walk away with his jacket. Collateral of sorts. The desk clerk hands me my room key. I make my way to the elevator and the fourth floor. When I open the door, Madame sits at the end of the twin bed on the far side of the room by the window. She looks sheepish.

"Who knew you were so conniving?" I say.

"I knew you would refuse to see him if I suggested a more normal way..."

I move past her to look out the window over steaming slate roofs to the wet pavement below. The rain has stopped, but the skies remain leaden, and water still trickles from the rainspout. Just as Madame said. The watering pot of France. "Yes, I would have."

"Then I will allow Voltaire to speak for me. '*Le doute est un état mental désagréable, mais la certitude est ridicule.*'" Doubt is an uncomfortable condition, but certainty is a ridiculous one.

I continue looking down on the old city, trying to remain belligerent. But my chin trembles and my resolve crumbles. "What do you or an eighteenth-century philosopher know about me?"

"Maybe more than you know." She joins me at the window and hands me a tissue.

I dab at my eyes.

"I've seen you light up when you talk about him and heard your voice. People who make us feel that way are rare. That I know."

"I want to trust you—I really do—but what if you're like Mother and Freddie, thinking you know better?"

"Nobody knows better than you, Catrine. But when we've been hurt, we can lose perspective."

I lift my head but can't look her in the eye. "I'm so tired of people hurting me."

"Vincent didn't mean to hurt you. He called for you yesterday right before I went out. I told him we were going to Rouen for our birthdays. He must have gotten my number from your landlady."

Vincent's jacket falls from my shoulders.

Madame quickly picks it up and puts her arm around me. "And I didn't mean to cause you pain. Cruelty hurts, but love can too." She pulls her arm back. "You're freezing, *ma petite*. Get out of those clothes and warm up."

I grab some things from my suitcase and disappear into the bathroom for a steaming shower. Vincent said he would wait.

Chapter Forty-Four

Thirty minutes later, I'm dry and pink, my limbs loose and finally warm.

Madame says, "I could tell you what Vincent told me about Saturday night, but it would be more meaningful coming from him."

I buckle my belt, brush my hair, and meet her gaze.

She continues, "I know you'll say no right now, so don't decide until you speak to Vincent. I'd like him to take my place at *La Couronne* tonight."

"But it's our birthday dinner. Vincent arrives and everything changes?"

After mountains of words and repeated assurances, Madame says, "Please go with Vincent as your birthday gift to me." With a maternal touch, she tucks my hair behind my ears. "It would make me so happy. Tomorrow is the sixteenth—our actual birthdays—and I promise, we'll spend it together."

I leave without a word.

As I return to where Vincent waits, Voltaire's words about doubt and certainty ricochet. I sit carefully on the tapestried chair, but its old frame groans anyway, as if warning me away. I'm close to the fire, in a white sweater, jeans, my black flats and damp hair. Vincent looks uncomfortable, like a schoolboy at his desk, knees together, feet on the floor. I slip off my shoes and tuck my legs under me, composed and calm. I'm sure it's warmed outside, but the lobby remains damp and cold. The cup of mint tea Vincent ordered while I showered warms me further as evergreen wood smoke wafts from the hearth.

"Catrine," he says, looking up from the floor. He offers me the pink posy of apology I saw earlier. I can't take my eyes off his strong, tanned hands but make no move to accept. "Thanks for the chance to explain."

The fire pops beside us and I lean forward to finally accept the flowers. We're back to speaking French. Before I can catch myself, I tell him how much I love tulips and add, "Thank you, Vincent. They're very pretty."

He runs his hands through his hair. "I'm sorry for surprising you, but I was sure you wouldn't see me unless I did."

I lay the tulips beside me and sip my tea in silence.

"I'm also sorry I didn't let you know I couldn't make dinner. I called the restaurant, but you'd left." He stops and our eyes meet. "I know how you must have felt. And I'm sure it was even worse afterwards, seeing Freddie." He turns away to stare at the fire.

I break my silence. "You can't imagine how I felt waiting so long. And then, seeing her brought back every big and little putdown she'd ever lobbed my way. It was as if she were still holding that knife to my neck."

"What do you mean?" Vincent scoots forward. "Like a proverbial knife?"

"Odette didn't tell you? And, of course, Freddie never would. She always needs to be the hero of every story, so she made me the crazy one." I sigh. "She said I cut my hair, right?"

He nods slowly. "You didn't?"

"No." I shake my head. "Freddie did. Came at me with her bread knife—"

Vincent looks confused. "She attacked you?"

"Grabbed my braid and hacked it off." My eyes brim with lingering hurt as I clasp my palm to the back of my neck. Vincent comes over to sit on the arm of my chair. He takes my hand and guides it up to rest on his thigh.

"Why would she do that?"

My voice falters. "Because of the beach. You seemed to like me and she was jealous. We were talking and laughing and it set her off. I had your attention and she wanted it back."

"Freddie's always been—"

"Please, no excuses about your cousin. I'm sure she told you I flipped out because I couldn't handle being in France. But she's the one who lost it."

"She could have seriously hurt you." He touches my neck gently and a tear escapes the corner of my eye. He wipes it away.

"She told me you went back to Virginia."

"And you believed her…" I take my hand from his thigh and he returns to the seat across from me.

"Probably believed her too easily. We're family and I took her word. But I should have tried to reach you. To see if you really had left."

"I wanted to call you. But Freddie threatened me. I was so afraid of what she would do if she found out I contacted you or your mother." I push a lock of wet hair from my face and shift in the chair. "And after the beach, with the keys disaster and all, I thought your feelings had changed."

Vincent leans over, elbows on his knees. He says quietly, "A rough ending to a really nice day. I was a jerk at the end, though. Not helping you with your stuff. I thought about reaching out to you but was sure there was no chance you still liked me. Freddie said you told her I was bothering you in Étretat. I distracted you and that was why we lost the keys."

"She's a liar."

"And the next week, she said you'd gone."

"Another lie." And in that moment, Voltaire's words about certainty slice through my hurt and expose fresh longing.

"You have no idea how happy I was when Odette told me you were still in Paris."

He blinks and clears his throat. He folds his hands in front of him, and then looks up at me, firelight reflecting off his glasses. His voice catches as he takes a deep breath and starts speaking in hoarse fragments. "The evening of our dinner. Just as I was leaving my flat to meet you my mother called. My grandfather, who had been visiting her in Paris for a few days, had been rushed to the hospital. I'd had lunch with him that afternoon." He smiles. "I told him about you. Said we were having dinner that night. Anyway, when I got the news, I jumped in a cab without thinking. I needed to get to the hospital. I was so afraid of losing him." He pauses. "Once he was stable, I realized the time and found a phone. But it was too late."

I swing my legs forward. "For your grandfather?"

"To reach you. He's okay but he'd had a heart attack. He's doing well now, except for the exhaustion. He looked awful Saturday night—sallow skin and puffy eyes. The hospital kept him overnight." He takes off his glasses and rubs his face. "He was released, yesterday morning and insisted my mother and I drive him back to Normandy. To his farmhouse. I told you he lives there, in a village on the way to the beach."

"So, you've been here in Normandy?"

He nods. "It's why Madame suggested I meet you here."

Feeling confused, I wonder aloud, "Wait. Is that why she wanted to go to Normandy in the first place?"

Vincent smiles. "No, that part was a coincidence. I reached her only yesterday."

It brings me some relief to realize Madame has been opportunistic rather than manipulative. And also that fate had a hand in placing Vincent in my path again. I'm sure Madame would quote Napoleon, telling me, "*Il n'y a pas d'accident, seulement une incapacité à reconnaître la main du destin.*" There is no such thing as accident; it is fate misnamed. But then I return to his reason for being here. "Your poor grandfather. Is he better today?"

Vincent nods. "We stayed last night and my mom is there now."

"I'm sure you were so worried. Still are."

The bellman appears and begins to stoke the fire. We pause while he kicks up fragrant pine smoke and coaxes the flames to leap higher.

Flushing from the heat, I push my hair from my face. I regret now that I jumped so easily to false conclusions about Vincent, but I do need him to clarify one more thing.

"So, why was Freddie with you at the hospital in Paris?" And for the first time in months—perhaps because Vincent has admitted guilt—it doesn't sting when I say her name.

"She met us there. He's her grandfather too."

I look at him, suppress a laugh, and shake my head. "I forgot. I totally, completely forgot."

"But I will say I was surprised she came when I called. She's not close to him and never liked visiting Normandy when we were kids." He goes on to say that once his grandfather was asleep for the night at the hospital, he went home with his mother. By then it was after nine and too late to call Madame's apartment.

"I don't know what Freddie did after we left the hospital. She must have gone to meet Odette."

"Odette. Oh God, I have to apologize…"

The desk clerk approaches to ask if we need anything. We shake our heads, thanking her.

Vincent says, "I still can't believe she cut off your hair. You think it was because of me?"

I hesitate, shifting in my seat, and uncrossing my legs. "She said she was furious about me losing the keys and embarrassing her, but I'm convinced it was mostly because you'd been so nice to me." I stop for a moment, biting my lip. "You do know her feelings for you go too far, right? I mean, isn't it odd to have that kind of crush on your own cousin at her age? I don't have any, so I wouldn't know, but Freddie's almost obsessive about you."

"I guess I've been blind to it. Chalked it up to playful bantering. It's how she's always treated me."

"She believes she has you wrapped around her little finger."

"Not anymore. Not after what she did and the lies she told. Odette called me late Saturday night. She likes you a lot, by the way, and thinks it's horrible how Freddie treats you. Odette helped me see the situation more clearly." He stands, shoves his hands in his jacket pockets, walks to the fireplace and turns. "Freddie's always been manipulative, and I thought I could handle it, see through it, but I never realized how badly she treated you."

"I needed to hear that."

"I wish I hadn't listened to her. About you leaving Paris." He shakes his head and sits.

I pick up my tea and finish it. "We both made mistakes."

"Can we start over, Catrine?"

I nod. "As long as we're honest from now on."

He looks so relieved. His smile is a magnet.

I stand. It's now my turn to sit on the arm of his chair, the look in his eyes drawing me there. "I'm sorry for being so angry. And for overreacting. It was childish." I take Vincent's hand. "I apologize for not trusting you. Forgive me?"

"Only if it goes both ways. Freddie influenced me too much and I believed her too easily. From now on, I trust you." He tucks a renegade strand of my hair behind my ear and his fingers linger.

I lean down to take his other hand, my balance shifts, and I slip to his lap, his hand on my hip. His face is close, his arms strong, the kiss inevitable, his lips warm. My body tingles all the way to my toes, my mouth a circle of surprise that melts into a smile. Another first.

Vincent whispers. "You act like you've never been kissed before."

My cheeks redden. "I haven't."

He looks amused and puts his palm against my cheek. "May I tell you, Catrine Gray, how pretty you are when you blush?"

Chapter Forty-Five

I've changed into my claret dress and black slingbacks and Vincent has reclaimed his corduroy jacket. "You look lovely," Vincent says when we meet in the lobby.

"And I might say the same."

As we leave the Hôtel Le Flaubert, the sun breaks through the clouds and warm mist rises from still damp streets under the evening sky. Instantly, it's a pleasant evening and I'm happy for the mild June breeze and the promise of summer as we walk hand in hand to *La Couronne*. The festive restaurant on *La Place du Vieux Marché* blends with the string of half-timbered medieval buildings—four- and five-stories high—on the town square. We walk by the spot where Joan of Arc was killed and I recall reading that she too heard voices—unlike mine, hers were from heaven. Quick anger flares as I remember what Freddie said about me going all "Joan of Arc crazy" with my hair.

From the moment we enter the restaurant's tiny foyer and then the dining room, we're surrounded by the world of gourmet dining, its soundtrack a mix of murmured conversation punctuated by the tinkle of crystal and fine china. Warm, tawny light from shaded table lamps bathes the room, intensifying the deep yellow of the table linens. Autographed pictures of famous guests line the amber walls. With quiet efficiency, the maître d' seats us at a corner table by a window framed with thick crimson drapes. Behind Vincent is a large black-and-white photo of Audrey Hepburn from *Breakfast at Tiffany's*, her left-slanted signature under her image.

I look across at my date, his cheekbones chiseled, his forehead furrowed, and a faint sheen on his brow. He fidgets with his jacket's lapel and runs his fingers through his hair.

"Are you all right?" I ask.

"I'm a little nervous, I admit. I have so much to make up to you."

"Surprising me in Normandy and taking me to dinner for my birthday is a good start."

He reaches across the table. "It makes me happy to be here. With you." His touch is soft against my palm as he lifts my hand and kisses it. His touch is electric and hearing him speak, I recall how smitten I felt when we first met.

Our waiter is a tanned, six-foot two doppelganger for beach boy Johnny Hallyday, the French pop icon, sophisticated with a warm smile and a twinkle in his eye. He wears black slacks and his white shirt is pressed to perfection under his gray vest and red tie. He hands us the leather-bound menus. "*Un aperitif, mademoiselle*?"

I order a kir. Vincent does the same.

"Very good," says Monsieur Hallyday, with a dignified nod.

"Have you been here before, Vincent?"

He shifts in his seat. "I have."

I lean in with a smile. "Tell me."

"It was five years ago and it was a very special dinner." He pauses as I sit back. "I was here with Chef."

"Chef?"

"My grandfather's nickname. Like chef de cuisine."

"He likes to cook?"

"No. Far from it. He was a high school teacher. He's a brilliant storyteller about France's history. Normandy especially. You would like him." Vincent tells me his mother, Mathilde, dubbed her father "Chef" when she was a teen because though terrible in the kitchen himself, he loved to watch others cook, especially his wife. And then when Chef and Vincent's grandmother visited Freddie's family in Virginia, he saw Julia Child's show, *The French Chef*. He loved her style and became her biggest fan. Before Chef discovered her, he was content with simple country fare, but it took an American to get him to appreciate his own country's fine cuisine. His English was very good, so Vincent bought him Child's book, *Mastering the Art of French Cooking*.

"And then he started cooking?"

"Never! But thank God my grandmother was keen to try the recipes and was happy to indulge him. After she died, he read the recipes to Maman and me, and we made them for him."

"*Mademoiselle. Monsieur.*" We sit back as our server places our drinks. He bows slightly. I stifle the urge to say, "*Merci*, Johnny."

Vincent raises his glass. "May I propose a literary toast in the words of Marcel Proust?"

I lift my kir.

"*On ne reçoit pas la sagesse, il faut la découvrir soi-même après un trajet que personne ne peut faire pour nous.*" We must discover wisdom for ourselves after a journey only we can take.

We clink and sip as I hold his gaze.

"And I'll propose one of my own. Also from Proust. *Soyons reconnaissants aux personnes qui nous donnent du bonheur; elles sont les charmants jardiniers par qui nos âmes sont fleuries.*" Let us be grateful to the people who make us happy; they are the charming gardeners who make our souls blossom. Again, our eyes and glasses meet.

"You do surprise me. I love that quote."

"When you were here five years ago, what was the occasion?" I ask.

Vincent smiles and looks up, summoning the memory. "It was my twenty-first birthday and we'd lost my grandmother a few months earlier. Chef wanted to take me to France's oldest restaurant—here since 1345—to boost our spirits."

"That's even before Joan of Arc."

He nods. "And it was one of Mrs. Child's favorites."

"Really?"

"When Julia and her husband Paul came to France in 1948, they arrived by ship at Le Havre. On their drive to Paris, they stopped in

Rouen at La Couronne. That lunch inspired her culinary career and she often came back."

"I wonder what she had." I pick up the menu.

"They still serve it. The Julia Child prix fixe. Oysters on the half-shell, *sole meunière*, green salad, and *fromage blanc* with berries."

My mouth waters and the names dance as I read the menu: *belles huîtres de la manche, carré d'agneau rôti, bouillon de coquillages, filet de boeuf à la sauce bordelaise*. I look to the next table as a couple chooses cheeses from an enormous tray.

Our waiter returns, pad and pen in hand.

Vincent leans in. "Shall I order for you?"

"Actually, I know exactly what I'd like." I smile, wink, and turn to the Monsieur. "But I do have one question."

"Of course, Mademoiselle."

"Is the *foie gras* the warm escalope or the pâté?"

"The latter, fresh daily from La Dordogne and served with a glass of Sauternes."

"Then, I'll have the *foie gras, les filets de canard, sauce pommeau*, and the *plateau de fromages*." I look across the table at Vincent. "Shall we share the cheese plate?"

He nods slowly, wide-eyed.

"And for dessert?" asks the waiter.

"*Le Soufflé Grand Marnier de Normandie, s'il vous plaît.*"

"Excellent, *Mademoiselle*." He smiles. "*Monsieur*?"

Vincent leans back in his chair and lays his menu on the table. He chuckles as he looks at me. "My companion has made things easy. I'll have the same."

I tilt my head and smile.

"Very good." The waiter collects our menus, looks at me and then at Vincent. "And would Monsieur like to choose some wine?"

"I have a feeling Mademoiselle might like to decide."

I give a crooked smile. "How kind of you, *Monsieur*." I turn to the waiter. "Perhaps you can recommend a nice Burgundy?"

"Of course, *Mademoiselle*. I will send the sommelier straight away."

Vincent puts his hands in his lap. "My, my, Miss Gray. It appears you are no longer the tentative American girl who arrived three months ago."

The sommelier brings the wine list, points, and suggests a *Côte de Nuits-Villages* Burgundy. I look at Vincent nodding and say, "Perfect."

And then from between the wine list's covers I hear, "*Si nous descendons en nous-mêmes, nous constatons que nous possédons exactement ce que nous désirons.*" If we go down into ourselves, we find that we possess exactly what we desire. Vincent smiles, unaware that Simone Weil has spoken to me again, as she did at my first dinner with him. Her words give me a rush and I'm sure my cheeks are pink.

Conversation with my date runs unbroken across hours, multiple courses, and the bottle of wine. Vincent is observant, considerate, and curious as we speak about our childhoods, French art, and U.S. history. Both our fathers died young but while he's very close to his mother, I have to stretch to find a few nice things to share about mine. I love classic rock and he loves jazz. The American Civil War fascinates him, French politics intrigue me, and yes, French literature has a hold on us both. He's never seen the Dordogne's caves at Lascaux, and I tell him I hope to visit Brittany's coast to hike along *La Côte de Granit Rose*.

"There's so much ahead, Catrine. Perhaps so much we can share."

Chapter Forty-Six

It's not yet dark when we step from La Couronne. Normandy is north of the US mainland, and so mid-June's dusk seems endless. The sun hangs on the horizon, reluctant to set, keeping darkness at bay until well past ten. We stop to watch the magical murmuration of starlings in the twilight, shadows swooping, expanding, contracting, and then swelling again and again. I unconsciously rub my hands up and down my cool arms as we watch.

"*On se promène un peu?*" Vincent takes my hand.

"*Mais oui, monsieur,*" I say, knowing I would walk with him till dawn if he asked. But while I want the evening to last and already dread saying goodbye, I'm also impatient for a goodnight kiss.

The town square buzzes with revelers. The restaurant terraces, whose red umbrellas match the geraniums overflowing their boxes, are full. Chatty teens line the squat masonry walls crisscrossing the plaza, and the buttery smells from a stand selling freshly made crêpes float through it all. We pass the shuttered stalls of the open-air market and the modern *Église Jeanne d'Arc*, its roof a sweeping curve of slate.

I never imagined my first night beyond Paris ending this way—strolling through a medieval town with Vincent, grateful the yearning for male attention I've kept locked up for so long has broken open. Most girls learn to flirt in their teens, but I turn twenty-three tomorrow and had my first kiss this afternoon. And as I've come to expect, I hear a voice. Anatole France. "*Si le chemin est beau, ne nous demandons pas où il mène.*" If the path is beautiful, let us not ask where it leads.

Vincent suggests we continue to the vaulted arch of the *Gros-Horloge*—The Great Clock. I agree, even though what I really want is to kiss him again and again, and then move on to whatever comes next. We turn off the square onto darkening feudal streets and approach the Renaissance arch and the still-working six-hundred-year-old clock with its brilliant blue and gold face. Vincent tells me that as a child, he dreamed of being an architect. He wanted to design timber-fronted houses like those on either side of us.

"When I turned twelve, Chef let my brother and me help him build a medieval-style barn at the farm. The facade looks like these buildings but inside it's a guesthouse for eight. His house has only two bedrooms, but with the barn, all his grandchildren could visit together."

"Did all the cousins go?" I squeeze his hand.

"Most summers, to work on the farm. And yes, Freddie came sometimes, but never for long. She got bored and preferred staying with my mom in Paris. I never understood because the countryside is so gorgeous."

"Sounds like a special place." I look up at his face, but all I see are his lips. And my lips can barely form a question. "So, tell me about what you want to build with your grandfather."

"Chef is an excellent carpenter and he taught me a lot, but for now I'll focus on banking and keep designing and building as a side pleasure. I'd love to show you all my sketches and blueprints for homes and schools and—"

The urge is now irresistible. I pull Vincent into the shadows under the arch, my back against the wall. My hands move under his jaw, drawing his mouth to mine, and then I cup his face with my hands. He kisses me back, slow, soft, and warm. By the time he breaks away, I'm breathless.

He looks at me and says, "So, you knew what you wanted at dinner, and now here in the dark..."

"I want you."

"You know that in France, men take charge of many things. Especially when it comes to romance." He runs his fingers through my hair. "But maybe I disagree. I think I like this American way."

He puts his arm around my shoulder and pulls me back into the street. We continue under the arch and then around a corner on a well-lit pedestrian street where a noisy German beer garden is filled with revelers celebrating a soccer victory. I catch a whiff of yeasty beer spilled on the terrace. "*Prost*" calls Vincent, pretending to raise a stein. He shares some brief banter with a fan.

"You speak German?"

"My biggest clients are German. I see them every month."

"Maybe you can teach me a few things before I visit my family there."

"You have family in Germany? Tell me more."

"It's my aunt and uncle. I met them when I was little, but don't remember. Aunt Dagmar is my mother's sister and she's sick. Walter is her husband. I'm going to visit in early July after Dagmar has surgery."

"I'm so sorry. Where exactly do they live?"

"In a little town south of Bonn—Bad Neuenahr."

"I know right where that is."

"They have a cottage in town but are staying in a convalescent home for now."

"Is your mother going?"

"I tried to convince her, but she refuses to travel."

"But not until July, right?" He squeezes my hand when I nod and leans over. "I'm all yours, *Fräulein*, if you'd like me to teach you some German." His breath tickles my ear and he kisses my cheek.

I whisper back. "*Danke, mein Herr.*"

We've walked in a big circle and are back on the market square. We sit on a stone wall, our hands entwined in my lap. I sidle in close and look up at a slim crescent moon, dazzling in a now navy sky sprinkled with stars. "It's hard to believe those are the same moon and stars above my backyard in Virginia."

"The sky over Chef's farm is even better. You can see the Milky Way and sometimes shooting stars."

We sit awhile without words, his arm lowered to my waist, watching passersby and listening to a street violinist play Debussy's *Clair de Lune.* I breathe out, long and satisfied, relaxing into him. "You have to go back tonight?"

"Yes." He checks his watch. "*Maman* has been with Chef all this time and must be exhausted." He strokes my hair. "It's a half-hour drive, so I should go. But I wish I didn't have to."

I won't let him go just yet. I curl up close in his warmth, breathing deeply, filling my nose with his spicy scent. So, this is what I've been missing.

Vincent stands slowly, pulling me up with him. Hand-in-hand, we stroll across the square and say goodnight at Le Flaubert's front door. Gently, he runs his fingers up my neck, takes a handful of my hair, and tilts my head back. The kiss is long and sweet, making my knees weaken, and my heart quicken. His mouth tastes earthy, like the Burgundy at dinner.

Vincent murmurs, "Catrine."

I look up, expecting another kiss, but he grasps my shoulders.

"Let me show you the best Normandy sky. Come to my grandfather's farmhouse. Tomorrow." He's excited, full of energy. "And yes, bring Madame."

Chapter Forty-Seven

I float to the elevator, thinking about the drive to Chef's, and ready to crawl into bed.

As the elevator pings its imminent arrival, I hear my name. Startled, I turn and see Eugène coming from the bar. He's in jeans, a black T-shirt, and loafers, and his head is shaved, the comb-over gone. A much better look for him.

"Why are you here?" I ask, crossing my arms over my chest and expecting a reprimand and a demand that Madame return immediately to Paris.

Instead, he offers a charming smile. "I intercepted a message for you."

"For me?"

"May I buy you a drink to explain?"

The last thing I need is another drink, especially with Eugène, so I shake my head.

"I promise it won't take long. It's important." He cocks his head and adds softly, "I left my drink inside. Join me?"

"All I need is the message."

"Please?"

Since when does he ask nicely? I follow him into Emma, the narrow bar lit by small, amber-hued lamps with mica shades. We sidle up to the bar.

"*Un Perrier, s'il vous plaît,*" I say to the bartender as I slip onto the high leather stool.

"My mother told me you had dinner at La Couronne." He looks down at his hands. "It's a special place."

"You've been?"

"Many years ago." He lifts his beer.

The bartender pours my mineral water and drops a slice of lemon and a spoon in the glass. As Eugène sets his beer on the bar, I see an ugly, raised scar on the inside of his forearm that a sleeve must have always concealed. I can't help pointing. "What happened?"

He glances down, then moves his arm.

"Another time." He rubs his head.

"The message?" I sip my Perrier.

"This morning I stopped at my mother's to see if you'd brought your things. No one was home, so I let myself in. Your backpack was there, so I checked the garage. No Dyane. Angry, I went back upstairs. I couldn't believe you'd both gone off without a word."

I was sure Madame had told Eugène, but maybe I'd misheard. "We weren't trying to hide anything. But how did you find us?"

"There was a map of Normandy and my mother's note about this hotel in the dining room. The phone rang and it was your Uncle Walter."

My heart skips. "Why didn't you call the hotel or come find me the minute you got here?"

"*Calme-toi.*" He pulls a paper from his back pocket and unfolds it, takes his eyeglasses from the bar, and reads. "They operated on your aunt sooner than expected. All went very well so you may come to Germany when it's convenient."

Eugène hands me the note. "Walter's contact information is on the back." I start to slip down from the leather stool, but Eugène holds my arm. "There's nothing you can do about it tonight."

I look down at his neat, French-schooled handwriting.

"They'll release your aunt from the hospital tomorrow morning. Tuesday. Walter suggests you arrive on Wednesday if you can. He hopes you have enough notice."

"Thank you, Eugène. If you hadn't been there to take the call..." My thoughts are a jumble while I sort out logistics.

"I'm sorry about your aunt." Eugène closes his eyes and pinches the bridge of his nose.

"We'll drive back to Paris tomorrow, and I can take an early train Wednesday morning."

"Maybe you should take the Dyane from here. Is my mother going with you?"

"To Germany?" I lift my glass and finish my Perrier in one gulp. "This is sooner than expected, so I haven't asked her. I assume you wouldn't approve?"

"Catrine, I'm not concerned about her traveling with you. Your friendship is clearly good for her. Anyone can see how she's changed since she met you. She's sleeping better, cares about her appearance, and has her sense of humor back. I had dinner with her tonight and she hasn't been this happy since before my father got sick."

"I'm happy to hear that."

"If my mother doesn't want to go with you, I can always drive her back to Paris. You can still take the Dyane." It's unexpectedly generous of him to offer. Then he adds, "If my mother says it's okay with her, of course."

I smile and slide from the stool. "I'll ask her what she wants." I pick up my purse with one hand and rest the other on the bar. "But, Eugène...You came all the way to Rouen to tell me about Walter? Why didn't you just phone the hotel?"

He stares straight ahead into the mirror behind the bar. Both hands grip his beer. "Walter's message was a timely excuse."

I wait for him to continue.

He grabs the back of his neck and says, "I wanted to go to the beach. To Étretat."

"On a whim?"

He turns to face me. "May I ask you something? The watercolors in the dining room. Did you put them there or did my mother?"

"The watercolors in the dining room... " I remember finding them and how angry Madame was when she caught me snooping. "The only canvasses I saw were in my bedroom closet. Why didn't your mother keep painting? She's a brilliant artist."

Eugène drops cash on the bar and stands. "I'm glad you liked the paintings, but they're not hers."

"How was dinner?" Madame asks when I enter our room. She's propped up in bed, the light low.

I cross to the armchair, kick off my slingbacks, and lean down to rub my toes. "It was quite the evening."

"Tell me."

I reach back to unzip my dress, stand to let it drop to the floor, and then carefully drape it over the chair. I move to my bed, slip on the t-shirt on my pillow, and sit cross-legged on the bed across from Madame. I share everything, including that I spoke to Eugène in the bar.

Her eyebrows knit together. "He told me about Dagmar and I have an idea." She smooths the bedsheet across her lap. "We'll stay in Normandy tomorrow for your birthday surprise. The following morning—Wednesday—we'll drive to Germany together."

"Really? You'd come with me?"

"I'm getting the hang of this road-tripping business." She winks. "And I'm not ready to go home yet." Madame yawns. "I think Eugène's finally discovered the fine line between caring for me and overstepping. He also admitted his father's death wounded him more than he realized and that as my only child, he felt a huge responsibility. Balancing duty with the demands of his job was difficult." She yawns again. "But he wanted to be with me on my birthday tomorrow, especially because it's a big one. Eighty. He got a room in the hotel and will stay with us."

"He told me he also came to visit Étretat."

Madame doesn't answer and I see she's leaned back and closed her eyes.

"Madame?" I murmur.

She opens her eyes and turns her head. "I'm so tired. Can we talk in the morning?"

"It's about tomorrow. What would you think if we stop at Vincent's grandfather's farm? He invited me and when I said you and I were planning to spend the day together, he invited you too. I'm sure it would be fine if Eugène came along."

"The grandfather who had the heart attack? He has a farm?"

"He's recuperating there and Vincent said having company would cheer him up. His village is Tourville-sur-Arques, maybe sixty kilometers—"

"As long as it won't ruin tomorrow's surprise," she says, yawning. Then she laughs softly. "Actually, it might fit our plans perfectly…" She pats my hand. "Of course, we can visit Vincent's grandfather. Now let's both get some rest."

Chapter Forty-Eight

It's before dawn when I awaken and am soon deep in thought about turning twenty-three and my night with Vincent. Everything has changed since yesterday.

I roll to my side and watch Madame sleep. Ours is not an average friendship, but I do know I want to be near her whenever I can. She's lived her life among words, atop volumes of stories for eighty years now, and she's taught me more than I thought I could absorb. I met her in a cemetery, at the end of a bench, under a tree on a chilly day. How lucky we are to have found each other.

I hear Madame rouse. "*Joyeuse anniversaire*," I say as I spring from bed. "*Que tous tes désirs se réalisent*." May all your dreams come true.

Morning sunlight streams in the window as Madame and I sing happy birthday to each other. She quickly dresses, looking smart in her belted dress and pillbox hat. Her outing attire.

I hop in the shower.

"Vincent just called," Madame says when I come out in a towel. "He gave me his grandfather's phone number and driving directions. Lunch is at noon. When I mentioned Eugène had driven up from Paris, he said he could join us before I even asked."

"I'm so happy you're okay with going."

"Some socializing will be good for us both."

"Why don't you go down and get us a table for breakfast?" I say. "I'll dress and call Walter to let him know we'll be there tomorrow."

Twenty minutes later, I join Madame in the bright yellow breakfast room as she finishes her last bite of croissant.

"Did you reach him?" she asks as I sit, a giant pen-and-ink sketch of Flaubert's face on the wall beside us.

"I did. But Walter sounded strange for a man whose wife had surgery. Upbeat even."

"Dagmar must be doing well," says Madame as she enjoys a coffee-filled sugar cube.

"I hope so."

"Would you like the *pain au chocolat*?" Madame asks, lifting the breadbasket. "I saved it for you."

"Thanks, but I'm a little nervous about meeting Chef–his nickname–and my stomach is upside down."

"I understand. But I know you'll make a great impression." Madame wipes her fingers on her napkin. "*On y va.* We have almost two hours before we have to leave for the farm and I want to show you some sights."

It's a bright, cool morning as we leave for our literary hopscotch of Rouen. The cathedral is first. Madame says, "So, this man, Chef. How can he know so much about cuisine but not cook?"

"I guess he's a cuisine voyeur."

She laughs.

"We'll ask him at lunch," I say. "But tell me about last night's dinner with Eugène."

"Did he tell you why he's really here?"

"For your birthday and to go to the beach."

She stops walking and turns to look at me. "You remember those paintings in your closet?"

"Yes."

"Well, they remind me of a terrible time for our family and I wanted them to remain hidden. But then, when you left for Roger La Grenouille, I couldn't help going back and dragging them out. And then the following day, I was so excited about planning our trip that I forgot to put them back." Madame pauses abruptly, rubs her sides, and stares ahead until the spell passes.

I say, "Eugène saw them after we left."

"Yes, those of Étretat and the portraits. They upset him and it's part of why he drove here." Madame shakes her head and resumes walking. "The paintings, all but the couple on top, the ones of Paris, are Eugène's. He painted them after university."

"What? Eugène was an artist?"

"Is an artist. I refuse to say was because your talent may hibernate but it does not disappear."

"Why did he stop?"

"Her name was Manon. She and Eugène were at university together for three years. They met on the swim team. Charles and I hoped they would marry. They were so good for each other.

"Right after graduation, she moved home for the summer. South to Montpellier. She asked him to visit many times and her parents even offered to have him stay with them if he got a job down there. But he'd found a good position in Versailles and didn't want to take time off. Even in August when everyone was *en vacances*. They paid him handsomely to work through the summer and promoted him when their biggest client liked his work."

"So, business before love."

Madame nods and continues to say that a year after graduation, Manon came to Paris for her birthday to see if she and Eugène had a future. He was still living at home and she stayed with a friend. After several days, seeing him only at night because of work, she asked him to take time off to go to Normandy. She wanted to get him away from the office and told him she would leave him if he didn't. He agreed and they made plans to visit Rouen. Dinner at La Couronne was Madame and

Charles's birthday gift for Manon. "You see, *ma petite*, special dinners at La Couronne have a history in our family." She pauses to watch a young couple walk by. "They spent several days in Étretat in a seaside cottage. Manon was a very good swimmer and wanted to be by the water."

The past tense plus my water phobia makes me shiver.

"As I said, Eugène swam too. But she was the superior athlete and won many meets."

I picture Eugène and his girlfriend dropping their clothes to the sand and bronzed Manon striding into the water, the striking stone formations beckoning. I see her strokes, cutting through dark, briny waves, Eugène far behind.

Then Madame stops and I assume she's having another spell, but when I turn, I see tears. I take her elbow and guide her to a bench. I sit beside her while she continues.

"Manon was accustomed to swimming in the Mediterranean, not the powerful Channel. He told her not to go far but she underestimated the currents. The undertow sucked her down. Eugène went after her but a wave slammed them both into the rocks below the arch."

I gasp, my hand to my mouth.

"Eugène lost a lot of blood from the gash and was in the hospital for days." She stops to take out her handkerchief and dab at her eyes. "Manon's body was recovered a day later and Eugène had to identify her."

I reach over to touch her knee. "I am so sorry."

She puts her hand on mine. "Her poor parents were devastated. For me and for Charles, it was terrible too, but Eugène went into a black hole. We all went to Montpellier for the funeral but he couldn't forgive himself for not moving there. Yet, when we returned to Paris, rather than change how he lived, he threw himself further into work. He hasn't painted since or had a serious girlfriend I know of. I don't think he's dealt with what happened in any meaningful way in thirty years."

"Maybe coming to Rouen and going to Étretat are first steps."

"Maybe," Madame says, nodding. "Maybe."

She stands and holds my arm to continue. We arrive at the cathedral, the tallest in France, with its three spires, the highest nearly 500 feet. She guides me to the plaza and the rooms across the way where Monet painted the cathedral's facade.

"What brilliance," I say. "Turning heavy, gray stone into impermanence and light." While I would normally be thrilled to stand and study the exterior's lacy sculptures for hours, I am haunted by Madame's story.

She says, "Let's go in and say a little prayer and light a candle for Manon."

"And for Eugène," I say.

Inside, we sit in the nave on rush-seated ladder-back chairs, craning our necks to take in the soaring ceilings and stone ribbing.

I think of Emma Bovary linking her arm illicitly with Léon's. As we stand to leave, I hear Flaubert's voice from the elaborate stone pulpit and then repeat the Madame Bovary quote aloud. "*Au fond de son âme, cependant, elle attendait un événement*." At the bottom of her heart, however, she was waiting for something to happen.

Madame says, "I was thinking of those very same words. Both of us summoning Monsieur Flaubert because something's on the horizon."

"Maybe, but I actually heard him."

She gives me a sly smile and puts her arm around my waist as we head to the back, light two votives, and exit.

"They're magical, these voices," I say. "They scared me at first, but I've grown to welcome them. They always capture what I need to hear."

"Keep listening. They're a blessing. I told you, I hear literary voices all the time."

We move to the red-awninged Métropole Café, where, apparently, Simone de Beauvoir breakfasted daily. "I had no idea she lived in Rouen," I say as we peek inside.

"For four years. See her bust next to Sartre's on the shelf? The café's most famous customers. De Beauvoir taught at the *Lycée Jeanne d'Arc*. She lived up near the train station, where every weekend she met Sartre. He also taught high school and came from Le Havre to see her."

"This town is a literary treasure trove."

"And we haven't even seen the birthplace of its most famous sons yet. But we'll have to skip Pierre Corneille's home." Madame lifts her watch.

"I must admit, I'm not a big fan of his plays. A little too 17th-century for me. And his name is impossible to pronounce... for me at least."

"On to Flaubert's home, then. Maupassant's mentor."

We leave the medieval center behind and quickly cover the few blocks west past creamy stone residences lined one after the other to Flaubert's birthplace: a stately eighteenth-century home and former hospital where his father was a surgeon. Most of the building is now a museum of anatomical curiosities and archaic surgical instruments. We enter its cozy stone-walled courtyard of soaring pines and a garden filled with yellow-flowered vines and alliums like lavender snowballs.

Madame says, "If we had time, we would see the room where he was born, but we must meet Eugène and be on our way. As you know, I don't like to be late."

I step from the courtyard and hear Monsieur Flaubert, as if commenting on Madame's punctuality: "*Soyez régulier et ordonné dans votre vie, afin d'être violent et original dans votre travail.*" Be regular and orderly in your life, so that you may be violent and original in your work.

Chapter Forty-Nine

After miles of rolling Norman landscape, we approach a low-slung farmhouse made of gray stone with a moss-furred roof and periwinkle shutters. It sits at the end of a long dirt drive lined with apple trees. Vincent waves from beneath cascades of purple wisteria surrounding the doorway and points to where I should park by the half-timbered barn. Eugène pulls in beside us.

"*Bienvenue*," Vincent says. He gives Madame and me enthusiastic *bisous* and I hand him the flowers we bought in town. Eugène gets a handshake and offers a box of fine chocolates from the hotel gift shop.

As he leads us toward the front door, I whisper in his ear, "Freddie's not coming, is she?" He assures me she is not. My neck and shoulders loosen.

We follow him through the door and into the entryway. Immediately, I smell cherry tobacco. An old red bicycle leans on one side and a mackintosh, pea coat, and anorak hang on the other. Wellington boots and work shoes neatly line the wall. The main space—a great room with an open kitchen, dining area, and living room—is flooded with sun from skylights in the wooden ceiling high above. I'm immediately struck by the homey smell of butter and sugar and the strains of a guitar ballad from the turntable. *Avec Ma Solitude*, in Georges Moustaki's evocative voice. The same song I heard when I first visited Madame's.

"Is your mother here?" I ask Vincent.

"She went for some groceries in the village. Should be back soon."

A long, rough-hewn farmhouse table, set for lunch with red gingham napkins, sits in front of a floor-to-ceiling bookcase spanning the length of the far wall. Thick woolen rugs warm the terra cotta tile floors, chunky-knit blankets drape over two well-worn leather couches, everything in the muted colors of sunrise—orange and yellow, red, rose, and gray.

Madame looks around and says, "What a magnificent room."

I look to the right, at the fireplace dominating the front wall. A massive black and brown dog sleeps on the slate hearth, his head on his woolly paws, too tired or too old to get up. The whole place feels warm and welcoming.

A handsome elderly man with a certain raffish elegance despite his florid complexion sits to one side of the fireplace. Chef. He has an untamed mane of salt and pepper and a hint of Vincent's angular face pushes through softened lines and gray stubble. On the table next to him is a pipe, the source of the cherry tobacco. Eugène closes the door behind us and heads right for the snoring giant dog, bending to pat his back and pull at his ears. The dog wakes with a start, his head and ears shoot up, his mouth opens, tongue out. He gives Eugène a good long look, gets up, and stands by him. When Eugène moves closer to Madame, the dog follows.

Vincent says to Chef, "This is my friend, Catrine." He gives me a huge smile and puts his arm around my shoulder. "She knows Freddie from Virginia."

"*Enchantée*," I say. "Vincent has told me so much about you."

The old man looks up, his glasses perched on his nose, but stays seated. He watches me warily over the top of his broadsheet. Then he puts his newspaper down and raises an eyebrow. "You know Freddie, do you? She never told us about you."

He sounds almost suspicious. Why didn't Vincent warn me? I'd imagined being instantly charmed by Chef, and him by me, but now I feel on the back foot. Does he assume I'm like Freddie and that's why he's cold? But I dare not say anything negative. Family is family, after all.

"I do know Freddie," I say tentatively. A "but" hangs in the air and I think Chef senses it. I see the barest twitch of a smile on one side of his mouth and a glimmer of curiosity in his eyes. Could we possibly share a slight antipathy towards Freddie?

Vincent continues his introductions. "And this is Madame Arnoux and her son, Eugène."

Chef's curious gaze slides toward Madame and his face lights up. Grasping the arms of the leather chair with his hands, the gnarled hands of a farmer, he stands slowly. He approaches Madame, takes her gloved hands in his. He seems reluctant to let go and she doesn't appear to mind. He never gets around to shaking Eugène's hand or mine. "*Enchanté*," he says. "I'm happy you could come." He adds, "Balzac is pleased to meet you as well." He looks at Eugène, the dog rubbing against his leg. "Especially you it seems, Monsieur."

"Isn't he marvelous," Madame coos, her purse over her arm like the Queen of England. "I must say he looks like his namesake. That face. What is his breed?"

German Shepherd-Bulldog mix," Chef says.

"Where'd you get him?" asks Eugène.

"He was abandoned in the village as a pup," Chef says. "He looked like old man Balzac even then."

Eugène squats to Balzac's level and scratches the pooch-with-the-face-of-a-writer behind the ears. The dog's tail thumps on the tile floor. Eugène smiles as he stands to ask about *les toilettes*.

"Come," says Vincent. "I'll give you all a quick tour." He leads us past the dining room table to a hallway running parallel to the back of the house. Balzac remains close at Eugène's heels, tail wagging.

"Looks like I have myself a buddy," says Eugène.

Madame stays behind, leaning over the record player, saying something to Chef about Georges Moustaki.

"*Les toilettes*," says Vincent opening a door. "Between Chef's room at the far end and the guest room, there." He points. "My grandfather added this part of the house when he and my grandmother moved in. Before that, the plumbing was outdoors and the beds were in the big room."

Eugène disappears into the bathroom. From the front of the house, the door slams, and I hear a female voice. Oh no. *Merde.* Is Freddie visiting her convalescing grandfather after all? I peek my head around the corner. I breathe a sigh of relief as Chef greets his daughter, Mathilde, standing with grocery bags beside nested cardboard boxes. "You look terrific, Papa," she says. "Your color is back and you're standing on your own. Your visitors are helping."

Chef nods as we all return to the front room from the back hallway. "Vincent is taking good care of me, and his friends are a breath of fresh air."

Mathilde gives Vincent and me *bisous*—three each—and introduces herself to Madame and then Eugène. "It's so nice of you to visit. My father's had a tough few days and I know he enjoys the company."

I look over and see that when Chef sits back down, it's on the couch, next to Madame. Vincent leans in. "He never sits on the couch." I'm happy Mathilde has everyone's attention as I can see Madame staring ahead. Another spell. Chef appears not to have noticed, his eyes on his daughter.

"Lovely to see you, Catrine," says Mathilde. "*Joyeux anniversaire*! Vincent told me you and Madame Arnoux are both celebrating birthdays, so I'm so happy we can make you a special lunch."

"Good to see you too." I wish seeing Mathilde didn't make me think of Freddie.

"How nice you look. A new haircut and new clothes. That black skirt is perfect with your yellow blouse and earrings." She winks.

I thank her and then move behind Madame to make sure she's okay. I rest my hands on her shoulders and she reaches up and touches my fingers. She gets up from the couch and says, "I'm pleased to meet you, Mathilde. Catrine told me you're a designer with a lovely boutique."

"It's so nice to meet you as well," says Mathilde and then leaves to collect more provisions from her car.

Opening the refrigerator, Vincent asks me to help with the salad.

He hands me some radishes, fresh from the ground. I wash and then slice them. At the far end of the room, Eugène, followed by his new furry friend, slips out the French door to the stone terrace. His hands in his pockets, he appears lost in thought as he gazes beyond the garden.

Vincent puts a plate of strawberries on the counter next to the sugar bowl and passes me some freshly whisked vinaigrette. I dress the salad with a wooden fork and spoon. He comes up behind me, puts his chin on my shoulder, takes the biggest, juiciest strawberry, dips it in the sugar, and raises it. I open my mouth and slowly bite. He pops the other half in his mouth and reaches around to wipe a bit of sugar from my lip.

I look over and see Chef watching. "*À table*," he says abruptly as he pushes up from the couch. He offers his hand to Madame and they move toward the table. "Time to eat," he repeats. "The quiches are warm, the salad is ready, and I'll slice the bread."

Madame says, "No, no, Chef. You must sit down. Allow me."

He turns to her. "It was a *little* heart attack. I'm fine. But you must use my proper name. Henri. And when you finish with the bread, you, the birthday girl, will sit right here." He lowers himself into the ladder-back chair at the head of the table and pats the seat perpendicular to his.

"As you wish, Henri. And you will call me Delphine." She touches his arm as she makes her way from the dining table to the kitchen.

I look across to Vincent, donning black oven mitts, and then to Mathilde, putting bags of groceries and a cold bottle of Champagne on the counter. They each return my smile.

Vincent says, "I hope you don't mind, but since we're going on a field trip this afternoon, I thought we would have a lighter lunch."

A chorus of approval circles around the room.

Mathilde says to Chef, "You'll be happy to know I'm taking those things of *Maman's* you set aside for me in the barn. The market gave me some boxes and it should all fit in my car."

"In your puny little Peugeot?"

Eugène returns from the terrace and says, "If you don't have room,

I can take some things in my car and drop them off to you in Paris in a few days."

"Let's see what I can fit in my *puny* car." She rolls her eyes in Chef's direction.

Eugène turns to Vincent, "Anything I can help with?"

"Keep Chef company at the table?"

Eugène sits, Balzac flopping at his feet with a harrumph. "Your home is beautiful," he says to Chef. "The garden is gorgeous and you can smell the ocean from the terrace. Have you lived here long?"

"I grew up in this house. My grandfather built it 150 years ago."

"Your grandchildren are lucky to visit you here in your ancestral home."

Vincent hands me a bottle of Alsatian Riesling and grabs pitchers of lemonade and sparkling water. As I lay the wine and corkscrew next to Chef, he looks up at me. "Vincent tells me Freddie is your friend, but it is hard to imagine. You are very different. For one, you speak lovely French, doesn't she Mathilde?"

"It's a refreshing change to hear an American speak *comme une française*."

The compliment makes me blush.

Chef says, "My granddaughter was never interested in our heritage and never liked Normandy. Always running back to Paris to see her English-speaking crowd. And yet, here you are." He looks at me with a curious gaze.

Madame reaches for the salad utensils and says, "They're no longer friends."

Chef's eyes twinkle at Madame's bold interjection. I'm worried he'll ask why, but he says, "Well, thank God for that. Vincent said you lived together and I feared you were close."

"I realize now we were never close. I've known her a long time, but in fact, we have few things in common. France, of course, but we have very different perspectives."

"You finally admitted it," says Mathilde. "I never did understand your bond."

"Let's just say, I finally saw the light."

Chef turns to me. "Lemonade?" he asks, gesturing towards the pitcher. "Or wine maybe?" he adds as he uncorks the bottle.

"Riesling, please."

He fills my glass and then grins at Madame as she puts the basket of bread on the table. When we're all seated, Vincent next to me, conversation kicks in. We talk about the farm, the sea, and what Madame and Chef have in common as we pass the salad, take slices of baguette and quiche, and refill our glasses.

Well into our meal, the phone by the front door rings and Vincent gets up to answer it. My stomach tightens. I left this number with the hotel in case Walter called.

Chapter Fifty

Vincent returns and looks at me. "For you, but don't worry. It's Odette."

Instantly, I relax. At least nothing has gone wrong with Aunt Dagmar. I go to the phone in the entryway. "Odette!"

"*Bon anniversaire*! Vincent told me you would be there. I'm so sorry about the other night. Did Vincent explain?"

"He did and I'm so sorry I doubted you."

"That's all behind us. When you get back to Paris, I'm taking you out. Some place fun. I never thanked you properly for rescuing me at the book-signing. And we can talk more about publishing. If you're interested, who knows? I may even be able to get you a job here."

"For real?"

"After your job with Madame Arnoux, of course. At our staff meeting yesterday, my boss announced we can hire a couple interns this fall. Think you'll be free by then?"

My chest flutters. "I'll talk to Madame and—"

"You're the first one I thought of, Catrine. You said publishing sounded intriguing and I knew you were looking for a job. You know so much about literature and Vincent says you love to write. I could help you learn the ropes."

"That would be amazing, Odette. Can't wait to see you back in Paris."

"Vincent said you're having lunch, so I won't keep you. Again, *joyeux anniversaire*!"

I return to the table, beaming.

Chef says, "What's got you so happy? You're radiating sunshine."

"It was a really nice birthday wish from Odette."

Madame says, "Now she sounds like a real friend. One you should keep."

"So, how about my grandson's quiche?" asks Chef. "Spinach, ham, and cheese. My favorite."

I pat Vincent's knee.

"It's *délicieuse*," says Madame. "Creamy with perfectly crisp crust. But I understand you don't share your grandson's culinary talent, Henri?"

"I enjoy fine food and watching its preparation. Years ago, I tried making *coq au vin* and *crème brûlée* and nearly destroyed the kitchen. The chicken exploded and I incinerated the dessert. It really was *brulée*." Burned. He throws back his head with a hearty laugh. "My wife, told me I was banned from cooking after that."

Vincent leans over. "It's so good to see him happy instead of sad when he mentions her."

Eugène helps himself to a second wedge of quiche and asks, "Do you have a favorite meal, Chef? I'm told you like Julia Child."

Chef rests his fists on the table, his knife and fork upright. "Yes, Mrs. Child is one of my heroes. She helped millions appreciate French cuisine, unlike so many of my elitist culinary countrymen. And my favorite meal is one Julia made often: *escalope de veau à la crème avec pommes de terre rôties*." Veal cutlet with cream sauce and roasted potatoes.

"I often make that," says Madame. "And for dessert?"

I'm back at my first lunch with her and her sweet tooth at La Rotonde, her face like a little girl's as we ate our *tartes au citron*.

Chef says, "It's so simple even I can make it. *La glace à la vanille avec des marrons glacé*. And *chantilly*, of course. For me, it is Proust's madeleine..."

"*Maman*," says Eugéne. "Do you remember when we used to have ice cream in Étretat? That was always my favorite. When I imagine the chestnut and vanilla, I'm back at the beach with you and Papa." They exchange smiles.

"You spent summers at Étretat?" Vincent asks.

Eugène nods. "At a cottage on the cliffs."

"My brother and I did too. We stayed here with Chef but went to Étretat on weekends."

"I haven't been since university. But I'm going this afternoon." Eugène pauses to sip his wine. "I'm going back to paint."

I look at Madame, her fork frozen midair.

Chef asks, "You are a painter, Eugène?"

"I was. Once." He looks across the table at his mother.

"He is," she says.

"Not for thirty years. Haven't even thought about it since the last time I was at the shore. But it's time to go back. My mother convinced me."

Madame nods.

"Might be a good idea for you too, *Maman*," he says, first glancing at his mother and then turning to Chef to add, "She paints as well."

Chef raises a surprised eyebrow as Madame scoffs. "I used to paint," she says, "but my son has the talent." Mother and son exchange a warm look. I appreciate the shift in Madame's relationship with Eugène and can see how much it means to her.

Chef folds his napkin, looks at Eugène and then Madame. He steeples his fingers in front of him. "The drive to create is what makes one an artist. Creativity is a gift we all need."

His teacher's tone touches me.

"Without the passion to create..." He pauses to look around. "...we are like a bicycle without pedals or, or...a love affair with no desire." His gaze rests briefly on Madame. "I believe in writing and art, music and photography, as some believe in God and cathedrals. For me it is always writing. I pick up a pen when others run for hymnals."

I'm filled with affection for a kindred spirit. "What do you write, Chef?"

He picks up his napkin without answering.

Mathilde stands to refill the water pitcher. "My father is a modest man, but I can tell you that much of what he's written has been published."

Chef seems to recover his poise. "I write about local history, including short stories, but recently, I'm drawn to poetry."

"My, my," says Madame. "A historian and a poet. What a combination, Henri."

"We're all artists in our own way, aren't we?" says Mathilde. "Adrift unless we create."

Vincent says, "My mother designed much of what's in her shop. I have vivid memories of her stenciling patterns and cutting fabric when I was a boy. And I know when I'm drafting a project, I don't want to be anywhere else."

"I felt that when I painted," says Eugène. "Like I was inside my canvas and wanted to stay." He folds his napkin, puts it on the table, and pats it. "Lunch has been delicious, and I can't thank you enough, Chef."

"*Mais non*!" he says. "You can't leave now. It's time for *le dessert* and we're having something special for the birthday girls. A few more minutes?"

Eugene nods. "Sure." He stands and helps clear the dishes.

Vincent pops open a bottle of Veuve Clicquot, compliments of Mathilde. He fills six flutes and sets them on a silver tray.

"Before we toast," says Chef, "Vincent, will you present *la pièce de résistance* to crown our meal?"

"You made a cake?" I say, genuinely surprised. No one has ever made me a cake.

"Vincent, you shouldn't have," says Madame.

"My grandson is brilliant in the kitchen," says Chef. "But even I had my doubts about this enterprise. He started when he got home last night and was up at dawn to finish."

"And you insisted on getting up to read me the recipes. We pulled it off together."

Vincent disappears down the hallway and emerges holding the most beautiful confection I've ever seen. He places it carefully on the table, between Madame and me.

"*Un croquembouche*," says Madame. "Haven't seen one in years."

"That's what I smelled when we got here!" I say. "Bubbling sugar, melted butter, and caramel."

I'm captivated by its conical shape. The tapering tower of small, crisp, cream-filled profiteroles piled one on top of the other is a regal assembly with a caramelized sugar filament drizzled up and down the sides to hold it together. Tiny sugar flowers and pink candles dot the syrupy cone. "It's...it's gorgeous!" I say.

"We make them for all important celebrations. Like birthdays, especially two on the same day," says Vincent.

The sulfur whoosh of the match whisks me back to when I was twelve. To the countries-of-the-world birthday party I rode my bike to and the keychain that left an Eiffel Tower imprint on my palm. I never could have imagined one day being in a Norman farmhouse celebrating my birthday.

As Vincent leans in to light the candles, I hear the crunching of wheels in the driveway. Vincent blows out the flame. "Bad timing," he says.

"Probably the postman," says Chef.

A door slams and a car pulls away.

Mathilde gets up. "I'll go see." We wait a moment and then hear Mathilde. "What are you doing here?"

"To see Chef. And get the stuff I left. If I knew you'd be here, I wouldn't have come."

Oh, God. It's Freddie.

Chapter Fifty-One

"Your timing is impeccable." I hear the sarcasm in Mathilde's voice. "We're in the middle of—"

But Freddie pushes her way in, her peasant skirt swooshing, the door slamming behind her. Her brow wrinkles as she catches my eye and she glowers at Vincent when she sees the Champagne in flutes.

"Well, well. Isn't this the perfect family party. Forget to invite me?" She walks towards the *croquembouche* and points. "And what is that thing? My going away present?" She looks across the table at Madame and then Eugène. Her voice rises. "And who the hell are you two?" She hits her forehead with her palm. "Wait, you must be the old lady Cat's living with." She turns to me. "An old woman? I mean, really."

Balzac growls, his tail between his legs.

"Stop this nonsense now," says Chef, standing and slapping his palms on the table. "If you cannot behave, you will leave my home." Chef's face is crimson. He turns and heads for the hallway.

"I swear to God, I always was too much for the old man." Freddie drops her macramé bag to the floor with a thud and glares at Mathilde. "You tell everyone?"

Mathilde glares back, her arms crossed. "It's your story, Frédérique."

Freddie jabs her finger in Mathilde's direction while scanning the room. "Do you believe it? She fired me. Her own niece!"

She turns to Vincent. "She tell you?"

He nods.

"What a sad little shop," Freddie says, turning to Mathilde. "And the pittance she paid me after working there for years. So what if I took a few things? Nothing I didn't deserve."

"I put up with your *mauvaise* attitude for so long," says Mathilde. "All those calls you made to America without asking, showing up late, and calling in sick too many times to count. But to steal from me. *C'était la goutte d'eau qui fait déborder le vase.*" The final straw.

"You never liked me, Mathilde. You hired me to make my mother happy."

"That's right. I did it for my sister, but you never appreciated it."

Freddie helps herself to a glass of Champagne and chugs it.

"*Ça suffit,*" says Vincent, moving towards her. Enough.

"What? Ruining your little party, Vincent-who-does-no-wrong? You always were the favorite, weren't you? Your mother's favorite, Chef's favorite, and now you're Cat's favorite." She gives me a side-eye.

Chef returns with a duffel bag. "Your things," he says, tossing it on a side chair. "I said nothing when you and your entourage drank a case of my best Bordeaux when you stayed last month. Think I wouldn't notice? You must leave. Now."

Freddie stares at him, her eyes daggers. "You never had time for me, did you? Not you and not *grand-mère.*" She turns to me. "And you, stabbing me in the back. Taking over my family and Odette. None of them will speak to me. And now you and Vincent think you're the perfect couple: the blond American and the handsome Frenchman. But you're a joke." She motions towards us with the empty flute, droplets spiraling.

She bangs down the glass and as she takes another, she hits the remaining flutes and they topple like dominoes. Vincent grabs her arm before she can drink. "Stop, Freddie." He takes away the glass. Eugène steps in, takes the glass, and removes the tray.

Their eyes lock, her mouth a hard line. But then her chin trembles and her eyes well. She shakes her head and turns back to me. "So, no more Scaredy-Cat. Now you're Cat-the-Coquette?"

"Enough." I step towards her, heat rising up my spine, but she turns back to Vincent.

"I hope you're happy with your American prize, cousin. But don't forget, it's all my doing. I'm the straw that stirred the drink. I'm the one who brought you Cat Gray." She looks around the kitchen, at the pile of lunch dishes, and then focuses on the *croquembouche*. Her eyes tighten. She whispers, "Not without me."

"Freddie!" I grab her wrist hard and she jerks back. She struggles and frees herself but I position myself between her and the caramel concoction. "You will not. Ruin. Our day."

Eugène has maneuvered beside her. "Your grandfather told you to leave. If you won't go willingly, I'll be happy to escort you."

She steps back, eyes wide at first and then sullen. Eugène releases her arm. Defeated, she leans down to scoop up her bag and then stomps to the couch. She picks up her duffel. With her forearm, she pushes back hair falling in her face and tries to stand tall. As she retreats towards the door, she kicks at Balzac who bares his teeth and growls.

"Go to hell. All of you," she says. Blindly turning on her heel, she slams into the red bike against the wall, loses her balance, and arms flailing, crashes hard. She cries out in pain as she hits the floor.

At first, no one moves. Then I jump up. "Freddie!" I dash over, crouch, and pull her to a sit, her legs splayed on the floor. She leans forward, arms covering her head, and starts sobbing. She then tries to push me away.

"I'm trying to help, Freddie."

Vincent steps over her and walks the bicycle outside to make room. She rocks and whimpers, her arms now across her torso, holding what must be badly bruised ribs.

"Mathilde, a wet towel," I say as I use my napkin to dab the blood blossoming on her leg and then dripping to the floor. "And some ice. The rusty fender slit her calf."

The gash is jagged and raw, livid with blood against her pale skin. Freddie digs her teeth into her lower lip and squeezes her eyes closed, her face white. Fat tears fall when she opens her eyes to look at her leg, grimacing. My anger softens as Mathilde hands me a plastic bag of ice chips and Freddie some tissues. Vincent returns and I kneel with the towel he hands me.

Freddie looks up at her cousin and then down at my ballet flats. I see her face harden as she lifts her eyes slowly, tracking my legs to my skirt, up the buttons of my blouse, and then higher to my face. Her eyes lock on mine and she shakes her head. "Really, Cat?" she says, her voice huskier than usual. "That stupid yellow top again..."

I ignore her and say, "That's a pretty nasty cut. She may need stitches."

Vincent says, "Eugène, help me get her up."

"I'll pull my car to the door," says Mathilde, "and take her to the hospital in Dieppe.

Mathilde dashes out the door, kicking pebbles in her wake. Balzac barks behind Eugène. I hold the iced towel to Freddie's leg. Vincent moves behind me and puts his hand on my shoulder.

Chapter Fifty-Two

Mathilde and Freddie leave for Dieppe. Those of us remaining speak briefly about what happened until Chef sums up how I feel. "Friendships need understanding and intimacy, neither of which Freddie is capable of."

We decide we're not in the mood for immediate celebration. The *croquembouche* will wait for the evening because Madame promised a birthday outing and she will not be deterred. Eugène mops up the spilled Champagne and then he and Balzac are off to Étretat. Madame, Chef, Vincent and I squeeze into the Dyane, the top down. I'm at the wheel, having insisted on driving. Vincent sits beside me.

As I maneuver down the driveway, Madame passes everyone an apple from the basket beside her. "This will have to do as dessert for now."

At Chef's direction, I turn left when we reach the road. "It's not far," he says, as we make slow progress behind a tractor hauling hay. "Right, Catrine. Here, where the road bends." We start down a narrow lane between dense thickets and a sign appears: ornate white script on a forest green signpost. *Château de Miromesnil.*

I pump the brakes and then jerk the car to a stop. "Maupassant was born here! I knew it was in Normandy, and Vincent, you said it was near Chef's." I turn around, laughing. "Madame, what a wonderful surprise."

Chef chuckles. "Sounds like you're the granddaughter I should have had."

Madame leans in from the back seat to touch my shoulder. "I've thought about bringing you here ever since we spoke in the cemetery. I'm so happy to share it with you. With all of you, in fact."

We wind down the long driveway around several sharp turns lined by trees and finally pull into the gravelly parking lot. Thoughts of Freddie evaporate as I look up at the soaring sycamores watching over the property. I shut the car door and it echoes off the tall brick barrier laced with climbing roses—red, pink, and white—ringing the castle. We skirt the wall to reach the broad green lawn leading to the main entry. Two turrets flank the ornamental Louis XIII facade and brick chimneys rise from every angle.

"This is like the chateau in Nanette's story," I say. "That was Brittany and this is Normandy but it's exactly as I imagined."

"Haven't been here in years," says Chef. "Not since Vincent and his brother were boys. The original building is from the late sixteenth century, this wall was built in the seventeenth, and the front elevation came later. Everything's held up well, I'd say."

I step onto thick grass, taking it all in. What was this home like when a literary giant played here as a child over a century ago? "How long did Maupassant live here?" I ask Madame.

"His family rented the chateau for only a few years. Then they moved to Étretat and eventually Rouen. He died in 1893, in Paris, at only forty-three."

Vincent says, "So young. How did he die?"

"Syphilis," I say. "He called it his dark valley."

Vincent puts his arm around me. "A sad way to go."

The mid-afternoon sun is now intense. "Let's walk around back," says Chef. "A two-hundred-year-old cedar shades the yard and if we're lucky, the lawn chairs will be free." Madame offers her arm to help him walk and he holds tight around her elbow.

As we round the chateau, the lawn chairs are indeed free, and Chef says, "Perfect. All to ourselves."

I inhale the pungent, citrusy smell of the cedar as Madame helps Chef sit in the shade under branches reaching as wide as the chateau.

"Why don't you two young people explore inside?" says Chef, pulling a tarnished gold watch from his pocket. "Delphine and I will sit for a bit. Shall we meet in say, a half hour in the *potager*?" The kitchen garden.

"Please go ahead," adds Madame. "I could use a little rest."

"I wish we could have explored upstairs," I say. "But I guess it's for paying guests only. I mean, the ground floor was gorgeous—all those wood panels and upholstered antiques. But I'd like to see the bedroom in the rear. Where Maupassant was born."

"We'll have to come back. The caretaker is Chef's friend and I bet he can arrange a special visit." He reaches around my waist, pulls me to face him, and lifts my chin. "Maybe even an overnight in the turret?"

The very idea makes my legs weaken and heart pound. "That, Monsieur Lanier," I whisper, "would be lovely." I lean in for a long kiss.

He sighs and takes my hand. "And that, Mademoiselle Gray, makes me very happy." He leads me through the archway into a walled potager, where a profusion of flowers, herbs, and vegetables grow side by side, their bright petals and green leaves open to the sun. The garden is structured and symmetrical, bordered by perfectly pruned privets and brick masonry.

"I could live in this garden," I say as I stroke velvety Lambs Ear leaves between my fingers, careful not to bruise them. "Despite Freddie's interruption, this is a birthday I won't soon forget." I grab Vincent's arm with both hands and pull him close.

We amble through the multihued quilt of parcels, each edged by spongy grass. Purple artichoke thistles protect tender hearts bursting through celadon petals, and noisy bees dip into hydrangeas with radiant blue blooms. The sun beats down and dragonflies hover. I think about Mother's lush angel garden of foxglove and lily-of-the valley, tucked in a corner of our back yard, and am grateful for all she taught me about flowers.

My face and arms are warm and my hint of summer tan will surely darken today. We wave to Madame and Chef who have moved to a cozy wooden seat under a blossoming tree on the far side of the garden. But they fail to wave back, having slouched into sleep, leaning one onto the other on the back of the bench.

Vincent says, "Chef and I planted an apple tree behind his house when I turned six. Like the one they're napping under. Chef said it would always be my tree." He looks to the sky and digs his hands deep in his pockets. "I've always felt so attached to this corner of Normandy."

"I can tell."

"It's where my ancestors were born and died for hundreds of years, and I spent so much time here growing up. It's where I want to start the business I told you about. The smell of the soil and the air itself make me feel I'm home. Do you feel that about where you grew up?"

"I'm afraid I have little affection for Virginia, and while I'm curious about where my mother's family lives in Germany, I doubt it'll grab me. Even as a child, all I ever wanted was to be in France."

I stop when I catch sight of a trio of rabbits nibbling on lettuce. "Don't scare them off," I whisper, taking Vincent's arm to turn down another path. He bends down to break off a leggy-stemmed daisy, and I pluck a sprig of lavender. We exchange blooms, our fingers fragrant. I touch his lips, his cheek and kiss his temple. He kisses my mouth. A dance of color rises from the flowers behind him, and I laugh as a butterfly lands on his hair.

"Can we stay here forever, in this place you love?" I ask. Then I shake my head, remembering. "But Madame and I must leave for Germany tomorrow."

He stops and takes my hand, entwining his fingers with mine. "Catrine. Take me instead. I'm supposed to see clients in Bonn next week, but I'll see if they can meet early. It's so close to where you're going."

I hesitate. "I've already asked Madame. She's looking forward to coming with me, and it is her car..."

Vincent's shoulders drop.

"Catrine."

I turn and see Madame approach.

"Chef invited us to stay tonight. In the barn guest rooms. You and Vincent can drop us off and then drive to Rouen to collect our things. I'll make us dinner. Eugène will be back from the beach and he already checked out of *Le Flaubert*."

Vincent's checks his watch. "It's only five o'clock and we can be back by six-thirty."

"One more thing," Madame adds, looking at Vincent. "You speak German, *ja*?"

He nods.

She turns to me, inclining her head. "Would you be horribly disappointed if Vincent went with you to Germany and I stayed here with Chef?"

Vincent says, "You're sure you want to miss Germany?"

Madame smiles. "I think I'd be more disappointed to say *au revoir* to Henri so soon."

Vincent puts his arm around me as we head back to the car, "She got exactly what she wanted."

"She always does," I lean into him. "And so did I."

Chapter Fifty-Three

Madame and Chef are on the couch when we return from Rouen with our suitcases, he puffing on his pipe.

"Freddie will be fine," calls Mathilde from the kitchen. "After we left the hospital, I took her to the Dieppe station and put her on the train to Paris."

Chef says, "She left her things." He waves towards the duffle on the chair. "*Tant pis.*" Too bad.

As Madame helps him stand and walk to the table, Mathilde tells us about the hospital visit.

"They gave her some stitches, a tetanus shot, and antibiotics, and the doctor said she'll have a nasty scar. She barely said anything to me except she's had it with France. Apparently, my sister got her a job back in America as a restaurant hostess, so she's flying home next week."

"She'll probably be much happier doing that," I say.

"I'm sure she blames us all," says Mathilde, going to sit next to her father.

I head into the kitchen to slice the baguette. Vincent stirs the sauce on the stove. "That is her way, isn't it?" I hip-bump him gently, and he leans over and tries to nip my ear with his teeth but I shimmy away, laughing.

Madame enters the kitchen, a twinkle in her eye. "Everyone hungry?" She winks at Vincent before bending to take the potatoes from the oven.

The six of us sit for a dinner of *escalope de veau à la crème* and *pom-*

mes de terre rôties. Vincent pinches his fingers together and blows a chef's kiss. "*Délicieux.*"

"How'd you manage to whip up Chef's favorites so quickly, Madame?" I ask, unfolding my napkin.

"Our host has a well-stocked kitchen, thanks to Mathilde." Madame gives her a little clap. "So, not difficult at all. Eugène brought some Chablis and you and Vincent picked up the baguette. And finally, we'll have our *croquembouche.*"

"In case anyone hasn't heard," says Vincent, biting into his veal. "Catrine and I are going to Germany together. First thing tomorrow."

Eugène looks up, a mushroom on his fork. "I thought *Maman* was going with you."

"That was the plan," says Madame. "But since Vincent has business in Germany, Chef suggested we switch places. I'll stay to take care of him." She looks at Chef who winks with a mischievous smile. She adds, "And you, Eugène? Want to stay as well?"

He takes a slice of baguette to mop up the rich sauce. "I wouldn't mind. To take some walks with Balzac." He leans over to stroke the hound sniffing at the table. "But I'm heading back to Étretat. Called my boss and told him I'm taking the rest of the week off. I rented a room with a view over *les falaises.*"

Madame's eyebrows rise and she beams at him from across the table.

"Balzac does like the beach..." says Chef.

"So, he'll come with me." Eugène slips Balzac a bite of veal. "I always painted best with company."

"I'm also leaving tomorrow morning," says Mathilde. "To interview replacements for Freddie. Fingers crossed. It's been tough handling the store by myself."

We're now in evening shadow. Conversation hums and I feel I'm at home in this place, with these people. I wish I didn't have to leave so soon.

"Cake time," announces Mathilde. Eugene lights the candles and then places the tower of caramel and cream in front of Madame. My face is one huge smile as I stand beside her, her eyes glowing in the soft light. We lean in to blow out the candles together after everyone sings.

Vincent comes up behind me and nuzzles my neck. "*Bon anniversaire*, Catrine." He holds a sticky cream puff to my lips and I bite.

We linger over the *croquembouche* and what remains of the Champagne until Mathilde stands and announces, "Calling men with muscles. I have some heavy boxes of my mother's things in the barn—pictures and pottery mostly—and I'm finally carting them back to Paris."

Vincent and Eugène need no further muster. They're out the door with Mathilde, leaving me at the table with Chef and Madame. "Shall I make some coffee?" I ask Chef.

"Please," he says. "But while you're doing that, would you tell me about this book you're working on. Delphine mentioned it earlier."

I can't get used to Chef calling her Delphine, I think, heading to the kitchen to get the coffee brewing. Then I sit back down next to Chef to fill him in on Charles's manuscript.

"The way he wrote about Maupassant is straightforward and yet, amusing at times. It seems best suited for general readers. His rendering is written beautifully but in non-scholarly language everyday readers can understand. It's no wonder academia rejected it."

Chef knits his eyebrows together. "How is it organized?"

"By theme—class barriers, the noble prostitute, loneliness. I'd like to add the annotated text of one story to his exploration of each. I already edited one chapter about stories exploring resistance in the Franco-Prussian War." I look over at Madame and, as expected, she looks skeptical, sitting back with arms crossed. "But I'm not sure Madame approves."

"I don't disapprove." She sits forward. "But you haven't persuaded me yet. I need time to get used to the idea of Charles writing for the masses."

"Have you read the manuscript?" Chef asks.

"No. He didn't want me to see this book until it was finished." She shakes her head. "But then he got sick..." Her voice catches. "And I haven't had the heart to look at it since he died."

I reach across to touch her hand.

"So much has been written about Maupassant," says Chef. "What's the plan for publication?"

"Vincent's friend—our friend—Odette, who works in book publishing, said the Ministry of Culture announced an initiative promoting French literature. They're funding projects that are easy-to-digest and help average citizens appreciate France's writers. Including high school students."

Madame gets up to retrieve the pot of coffee. "What do you think, Henri?" She fills three cups and brings them to the table, one by one. "Could you have used such material in your classes at the *lycée*?"

"Definitely. There are children's picture books about writers and many for universities, but few between the two. The idea has merit." Chef sips his coffee. "But I have an additional thought. You mentioned a story for each theme. What if the book focused on Maupassant being from Normandy and included only stories that took place in this region? He was so adept at describing settings and making readers feel they inhabited a story."

I add a sugar cube to my coffee. "I like that idea because his writing showed such love for his birthplace. He always depicted the Norman people with dignity without idealizing them."

"Exactly." Chef nods. "And the book could include historical background from when Maupassant lived here." He turns to Madame. "All in layman's terms."

She looks at Chef. "So, you would add the perspective of place?"

Chef grips the arms of his chair, pushes himself up slowly, and reaches to the bookcase behind me. He pulls out a well-worn paperback and puts it in front of Madame. He taps at his name on the cover, smiling broadly.

Surprised, she says, "It's one of yours, Henri."

He winks at me as I read the title out loud. "*Une histoire concise de la normandie au XIXe siècle.*" A Concise History of Normandy in the

Nineteenth Century. His eyes never leave Madame as he sits. "Perhaps Catrine and I could collaborate?"

"You're offering to work with me on Charles's book?"

"*Bien sûr.*"

Madame stands, picks up his book, and walks to the terrace door.

My eyes follow her. Eventually, she turns back and approaches the table as she studies the cover. She tucks a stray hair behind her ear and looks at me. "Would you like Henri to work with you, *ma petite*?"

I sit up straight, my hands on the table. "I would."

She sits and sips her coffee. "I'm still not convinced."

I heave an audible sigh. But, undaunted, I get up, pull a manila folder from my pack, and put it in front of Madame. "This is what I have so far as the first chapters. I thought I'd have time to work on them in Rouen, but..." I glance up at Vincent as he rejoins us. "I've been distracted."

"Maybe you can look at what Catrine's done while they're away, Delphine," Chef says.

"That'll work," says Madame. "You and I will read it together."

Chapter Fifty-Four

Vincent and I stand on the terrace, my head on his chest. The sky is clear and the waxing crescent moon, high on the horizon, shines a path across the fields. Crickets hum and moths are frantic in the golden glow of the porch lights, their bodies pinging against the bulbs. Anticipating Vincent's touch is delicious torture as my breath quickens. I lift my head and he grazes me with his lips behind my ear. A shiver of desire courses down my back. He takes my hand, walks me through the garden, and kisses me under his apple tree. We continue far into the dark, open field where we spread a quilt his grandmother made him when he was a boy so we can watch the stars from our backs. The sky he promised reveals itself—a wondrous black carpet sprinkled with more stars than I've ever seen, the translucent white of the Milky Way painted across the sky.

And of course, a shooting star.

From that star, Francis Cabrel's clear voice sings, "*Je viens du ciel.*" But then I turn and see it's Vincent I hear. "*…et les étoiles entre elles ne parlent que de toi.*" I come from the heavens, and the stars speak only of you.

My head rests on his outstretched arm and I smell the wet trace of earth beneath us. I roll towards him and extend my arm across his chest, leaning in to hold his face in my hands. My thumb traces a line across his brow and then another along his mouth. We're breathing in perfect unison. I dig my fingers deep in his hair. He draws me closer and cups my warm cheek with his cool palm. His fingertips trace the side of my face and I feel a familiar ache.

The years I've waited melt into a pleading sigh that touches his lips. He whispers my name and I feel his breath on my neck. My hands tremble as I open his shirt slowly. One button at a time. He unfastens my blouse, slower still, his lips warm on my skin. When his fingers slide to my breasts and then around to my back, I can barely breathe. Heat rises between us as his hands slide under the waistband of my skirt to pull my hips against his. His magic hands touch me everywhere and his mouth soon follows. No one has ever touched me there. Or there... My eyes remain open, willing the night, our need for each other, and the tenderness of his fingers to go on and on. I unbuckle his belt, feeling him stir beneath my touch. Then he pulls me on top of him and I sink, melt into his body, his hands aligning our hips, my chest against his. I hesitate and then let go of all control. I wince and then soon, feel the warmth of a pleasure I've never known.

Chapter Fifty-Five

In the morning, I pass by Chef holding his pipe and Madame sipping morning coffee at the farmhouse table. I push open the French doors to the terrace. Soft with happiness, I join Vincent in the cool morning air as the sun rises through the trees. My thoughts swim in the miracle of last night. I put my arms around his waist from behind and we stand under the terrace awning, listening to early birdsong. A dewy dawn gilds the fields and a rabbit hops from beneath the bushes.

"I don't want our visit to end," I say, pressing my cheek into his back. "I'm afraid leaving will break the spell."

"We'll be back. Soon. Let's see how things go with your aunt and uncle and then look ahead to a few days at the *Chateau de Miromesnil* before returning to Paris."

"Mmmmm, that sounds divine." I say. I shift my position to his side, tucking myself under his arm. "But I have to say…I'm a little nervous, actually… about my family. I don't remember meeting them and they're going through a stressful time."

"They've asked you to come, so I'm sure they'll be glad to see you."

"Would you like to meet them?"

"You drive down first. I have my meeting in Bonn this afternoon and a client lunch tomorrow, but then I can take the train and meet you in Bad Neuenahr. If you think it's okay."

I nod. "Sounds good."

"There's a nice little *weinstube* in my hotel and if we leave now, we'll get there in time for a late lunch. The *jaeger schnitzel* is excellent."

The *jaeger*-what?"

"My favorite German dish. You'll find out soon enough."

Eugène and Mathilde join us on the terrace. He's leaving with Balzac for the beach and she's returning to Paris, both their cars packed with Mathilde's boxes. "Why don't the four of us get together when we're back in Paris?" Mathilde says. "Dinner at my place?" She looks at Vincent. "It's been ages since I made my son a proper meal."

Everyone agrees and we say our goodbyes. Eugène and Mathilde go to the driveway and Vincent and I sneak a look out the window. We catch them mid-*bisous*. "Maybe dinner for two will come first," I say.

Madame and Chef linger over breakfast. Madame stands and says, "Do not worry about us while you're gone. Chef will rest and I will take care of him. It's as simple as that."

Quietly, I say to her, "And your seizures—"

"Henri knows everything. He's prepared."

She looks at Chef and he gives her a salute. "You heard what the lady said. Take your time in Germany." He winks at Vincent as Madame walks around the table to stand behind him, her hands on his shoulders. "Do not return until you are ready."

Part Three

BEYOND FRANCE

June 1981

Chapter Fifty-Six

The Norman farmhouse and miles of highway behind us, we cross into Belgium, so like northern France, and then into Germany, where everything changes. We stop at the border for passport control and then at a bank to exchange francs for marks.

"Everything looks and feels different," I say. "The architecture, the highways, and even the landscape." What I don't say is that I'm dwelling on the country's World War II history, and it leaves me uneasy.

We make it to Bonn in time for lunch. While Vincent checks into the hotel, I take in the *weinstube*'s decor—dark, heavy wood, arched, latticed windows, and deep peach walls stenciled with red flowers—and the smells—vinegar, sausages, and baked pretzels. He returns and orders for us both in what sounds like flawless German. After months of French immersion, I'm not sure I'll ever get used to how harsh German sounds, even coming from his perfect mouth.

I tell him that indeed, *jaeger schnitzel* is delicious, goes perfectly with our wine, and that although yummy, I prefer French breads to German varieties.

"No, Germany is not France," says Vincent as he winks. "But it does have its charms."

"You mean like the fact that you have an empty bedroom upstairs?" I look at my watch. "When's your meeting?"

He answers without looking at his wrist. "Plenty of time." He stands, leans down, kisses me, and takes my hand.

On the half-hour drive to Bad Neuenahr, I think about the past few miraculous days, including the half hour in Vincent's bed for urgent lovemaking. Mother never even hinted about the pleasures of sex and that it isn't only men who enjoy them. I abandon the thought as André Breton steps in. "*Je vous souhaite d'être follement aimée.*" My hope for you is that you be loved madly.

I respond out loud, "I'm on my way, Monsieur Breton. Loved, indeed—madly at that."

With some effort, I turn my thoughts from Vincent to Walter and Dagmar. I'm anxious to meet them again, though I don't remember the first time. I truly regret Mother will miss out on being with family.

Soon enough, I turn off the autobahn and follow the local directions I noted on the map to the convalescent home. I drive through the wooded grounds surrounding the facility, a looming six-story Bauhaus building shrouded in fog. Sharply sloped bright orange and pale blue awnings alternate over apartment terraces, making the facade appear tiled. It's nothing like the timber-framed *bauernhaus* I'd imagined.

I park at one end of the parking lot next to a broad duck pond scattered with lily pads. Then I make my way to the main entrance.

My hands are steady as I push open the heavy glass entry door. I check in at reception, the light fluorescent and everything the same blue and orange of the exterior, the furniture laminated, plastic, and metal. Thank God the clerk speaks English. The braids coiled on top of her head in a milkmaid hairstyle contrast with the modern decor. She makes a call and points down the hall. "You may go up, Miss Gray."

The elevator pings and takes me to the fifth floor. Will my aunt be anything like her sister? What if she is? Then I gulp. What if she's worse...? I haven't thought of that ahead of time. I've always imagined a better, kinder version of Mother.

I walk down the silent, brightly lit corridor on industrial carpet—well-worn and orange—and stop at apartment five-thirty. The front door is wide open but I pause before knocking. Dagmar may be asleep. I step inside and peek into the room on the right. My aunt is propped on the hospital bed, the sheet draped to her chin, her head drooped forward, like a sunflower at noon. A slight, bald man sits in a plastic chair, gazing at her, holding her hand. Uncle Walter. A chunky knit beige cardigan hangs on his thin frame over a button-down shirt and brown corduroys. A skinny gray cat, its tail in the air, walks by, looks up at me without stopping, and glides into the bedroom.

I knock gently on the doorframe. Walter turns and, as he stands, bumps over a box of saltines on the nightstand. The cat jumps on the bed. Dagmar lifts her head.

"Catrine," Walter says, reaching to right the box. He beckons and I enter. He takes my hands, looks me up and down, and envelops me in a tight hug. The warmth of his embrace is overwhelming, and I feel tears well.

I look at Dagmar, her limbs mere suggestions under the sheet. Her face is markedly thinner than what I remember from pictures and much more heavily lined. I see my mother's face in hers. The cat slinks up the bed and settles into Dagmar's lap. She says, her voice raspy, "Catrine. You've come. You look like him...those big brown eyes." She winces, her own eyes flutter shut and her head lolls back into the pillows.

I turn to Walter and ask quietly, "Who does she think I look like?"

He hesitates and then says softly in heavily accented English, "She's been in and out since the surgery. It's the pain medication. Everything went very well, but I was so worried." He wrings his hands and then pulls his earlobe.

I turn to look at him, focusing on his long, thin neck accentuating his Adam's apple. Despite his smile, I see his apprehension, his eyebrows drawn together. I say, "Tell me more."

"They operated early because she was losing weight and they needed her strong. The day after surgery, she wouldn't get up to walk." He dabs at his eyes with his handkerchief. "But when I told her you and ..." He pauses, as if remembering something. "...that you were coming, it was the motivation she needed."

Dagmar pulls a thin arm from under the sheet and I see the IV in her hand. She tries to pat the bed beside her. The cat lifts its head.

Walter says, "She wants you closer."

As I approach Dagmar, there's a knock at the door. A nurse comes in pushing a stainless-steel cart. She's young, zaftig, and blond with bright white teeth. It occurs to me that she and I are the only things in the room not emaciated. She says something to Walter in German. He nods and she turns to me. I can barely understand her English, but I catch the words "family" and "picture." She checks Dagmar's vitals and replaces the empty bag hanging from the pole on the far side of the bed. Again, she speaks to Walter in German and he responds in English. "Yes, the little girl in the photos."

"Lover-ly," she says and gives me a big-toothed smile.

Dagmar has fallen asleep, so she hands Walter a paper cup of pills and gives him instructions. He responds, "Yes, when she wakes up."

"Nice I meet you," says the nurse as she wheels her cart from the bedroom.

Walter takes my arm. "Come. Let's sit in the living room where we can talk more easily." He leads me into the next room, cramped, with only one small window for natural light. There's just enough space for a sofa, coffee table, console television, and hutch. A pillow sits atop a pile of neatly folded sheets and blankets on a red-topped Formica dinette table with four aluminum chairs with matching vinyl seats. Walter must sleep on the sofa, as it seems there's no second bedroom. Didn't he say I could stay with them?

Walter says, "It is so nice to see you after so many years. But you must be tired after your long drive? Some coffee or tea?"

"I'd love some tea. And would you mind if I use your phone to let my friend know I've arrived? I know she'll worry."

"Of course." He points. "On the wall." He disappears around the corner into the galley kitchen. "Milk and sugar?" he calls.

"Please."

I pull Chef's number from my pocket. The phone is next to the hutch, so I walk over and gaze at its shelves packed with framed pictures. Family photos, finally.

"Are all these your pictures, Uncle Walter?" I call.

"They are. Dagmar insisted we bring them to remind us of family while we're here. Take a look, Catrine."

I'm taken by a formal black and white wedding portrait of Walter and Dagmar on the top shelf, a Gothic church portal behind them. I scan the images of my aunt and uncle through the years—hiking up a trail, wading at the beach, and posing in front of the Eiffel Tower—and the succession of my school pictures Mother sent every Christmas. I shake my head at the black turtleneck I'm wearing in every single one. No new picture-day outfits for me. Though each turtleneck must be a size larger.

On the top shelf is a picture of two adolescent girls laughing, one on the other's lap, their arms every which way. Must be Mother and Dagmar. Why was she so resistant to come to Germany? And as if in response I hear, "*Il est difficile de libérer des imbéciles des chaînes qu'ils vénèrent.*" It is difficult to free fools from the chains they revere. I silently thank Voltaire for his reminder.

Looking at the lowest shelf, I notice a black and white snapshot of a baby in a tarnished silver frame. There are no other children in the shot. I lean in, looking closely. Those look like my big eyes… It's my baptism, I'm sure of it. I'm wearing our family's smocked white gown, the one Dad showed me once, and I'm in the arms of a tall man who resembles my father. He stands next to a woman, also tall, but I don't recognize her. She's pretty, though, with long, straight hair a shade darker than mine. The couple seems about forty and they smile as they gaze down at...me? Now I'm not so sure. The baby's tiny hand holds tight to the woman's finger. If it is me, who are these people? Godparents maybe? If so, I never knew I had them. I study the couple, the man in particular. Is he related to my father? He looks so like him, but older. Dad was only twenty-one when I was born.

Walter returns from the kitchen and places a tray with two cups of tea and Lebkuchen on a flowered plate on the coffee table. "Did your call go through?"

"Haven't even dialed yet. Was distracted by the pictures."

He points to the one I've been staring at. "It was one of just a few pictures we had of you—until your mother started sending school photos."

"But who—" There's a rap at the door.

"Walter?" A female voice.

"Excuse me," Walter says. It's the building manager. She's going to open a vacant apartment down the hall for you—they're giving us one complimentary—and I want to be sure it's ready for you. I'll give you some privacy with your call." He opens the door and disappears.

I lift the receiver and dial, still perplexed by the photo. The phone rings multiple times. Where are Chef and Madame? At first I fear the worst, but then imagine what they might be up to... I suppress a giggle.

Madame finally answers. I barely say I've arrived safely when she announces she's decided.

"Decided what?" I ask, my mind elsewhere.

"Charles's manuscript. Chef and I reviewed what you've done, and I finally understand how different it is. It is for general readers and I saw how you added some explanatory history. And the quotes you included at the beginning of each chapter, well...they're brilliant. How about this for a title? *Guy de Maupassant: Le Fils de Normandie*." The Son of Normandy. "It places him right where he was born and lived."

"Whoa, Madame—" I say, but she continues to rave. "Henri agrees."

Why am I not surprised? Chef agreeing with Madame. Exactly what she wants.

"Henri says you did a good job highlighting Charles's writing while adding some of your own. You write well, Catrine. The way you pose rhetorical questions and then answer them is very clever. And Henri has some ideas for more historical context…"

I lean against the hutch, beaming.

Chapter Fifty-Seven

My call over, I wait for Walter. I look in on Dagmar, but she's still asleep, along with the cat, so I return to the pictures. There's one of me as a toddler on Mother's lap on our front stoop and one of the three of us at an amusement park, Dad holding me. Mother looks pretty, and Dad is tall and handsome, as always.

But I keep going back to the christening photo. I pick it up, cradle it in my palm, and try to will it bigger to see it clearer. Why would Mother and Dad have kept my godparents from me?

Dagmar whimpers, her voice weak. "Walter?" And then something in German. I scoot to her side in the bedroom. Her head is back, the cords of her neck visible, her body arched.

"Aunt Dagmar? What can I do?" I say.

"Catrine," she says, pulling her head up. "Forgot...you were here." Her words are staccato, and she pauses for a breath. "Pain meds..."

I move the frame from my hand to the nightstand. I carefully empty the paper cup of pills in Dagmar's palm and hold the plastic mug of water. I bend the straw to her mouth.

"*Danke*," she says, her eyes closing. "Sit. On the bed. Close."

"Okay if I shift you over a little?"

She nods but then her head drops back. I shoo the cat from the bed and walk to Dagmar's other side. I pull back the sheet, spade my hands under her slight form, and slowly draw her towards me. I pull over the sheet and tuck her in. Looking carefully at her face, so like Mother's but softer and thinner, makes my eyes brim with tears for all the years lost.

How can it be that when I finally see my aunt, she's sick and in such pain?

Walter pops his head in the door. "Everything okay?"

I nod. "I gave her her meds."

"Thank you." He goes to Dagmar to kiss her forehead. "Room's all ready. I'm going downstairs to order dinner in our room. Back soon."

I skirt the bed and sit carefully as the cat jumps back up and rubs its nose on my thigh. I take my aunt's hands—cool with veins protruding—and place them between mine for warmth. Her eyes remain closed, but she asks me to fluff her pillows and help her roll to her side. "Easier…to breathe," she says and then winces as I shift her.

"Paris," she says. "Tell me. We went...years ago."

For the next few minutes, I quietly fill her in about the last three months. She smiles faintly and her voice is less strained, soft as a whisper, as she relaxes into medicated relief. "Paris was your mother's dream."

I shake my head. "Not my mother." Must be the meds talking. But then she adds, "So sorry. About your brother."

"Aunt Dagmar. I don't have a brother." I stroke her hands gently, hoping she's not slipping into some kind of delirium. I wish Walter would hurry back.

She continues. "I wish…he could have visited you…in France." Her eyes are at half-mast.

"Dagmar," I say quietly. "I think you may be imagining things. I'm Catrine, your sister's daughter. I don't have a brother. And Mother never had any desire to go to Paris. Ever."

"I know who you are, Catrine. And, yes…you do have a brother. You have Stephen, like I have my sister, Hildy."

I've rarely heard Mother's first name said aloud so it takes me aback. Dad always called her "Hon." But Dagmar's making no sense and I'm worried. I wonder if I should try to find Walter.

Dagmar says, "Étienne. He would have taken her. To Paris if he could."

"You mean my grandfather, Étienne?"

She looks at me. "Grandfather? Father."

What is she talking about?

"Get me the picture."

Darting around the room, my eyes settle on the silver frame. I pick it up.

Dagmar rolls towards me and tries to sit. "Show me."

I turn the frame towards her.

"Yes, you see? Your parents. Étienne and Catherine. Your baptism. Did you see the picture with me? You held my finger."

I look down and see she's reaching for mine now. She holds tight and I help her inch up against the pillow.

"I don't understand," I say, as flashes of childhood memories bang into one another.

"I helped Hildy and Stephen. They moved. From that dingy apartment to the house." The cat jumps to Dagmar's other side. She releases my hand to stroke it. "All she wanted was a baby. A house. And Stephen, of course."

Her words are flowing more easily, more lucidly, so I ask, "But the people in the picture. Étienne and Catherine. Aren't they my grandparents?"

"Your grandparents?" She chuckles. "No." Then her face dims. "When Hildy had a miscarriage at five months, she was devastated."

"Mother lost a baby?"

"Her doctor said she couldn't have another. She was only nineteen. Stephen twenty-one. Married eight months. I quit my job in DC. Moved in with them in Virginia. She was so depressed. Cried all the time. Wouldn't eat. The only place she got out of bed for was Mass. Every morning."

"Yes, that would be Mother." I scratch my head.

"Then you arrived. A few months later. Her depression led to delusion and then fantasy. She thought you were her baby."

"But I was her baby. Wasn't I?..."

"When she finally accepted the truth, she became resentful. Of you.

God knows it wasn't your fault. But she saw the little girl she lost every time she looked at you."

Quiet tears start running down Dagmar's cheeks, her eyes still closed. I take a tissue, wipe her eyes, and put the tissue in her hand.

"Tell me again who the people in the photo are."

"Étienne and Catherine. Your parents. There was an ice storm. And a horrible crash. They died, leaving you an orphan. Not even a year old." Her gaze holds mine with a fierce intensity. "How they adored you." She wipes away fresh tears with the tissue.

Panic rises as I nudge Dagmar. "What happened next?"

"They did what they had to. Cared for you as their own. Called you their daughter." She stops to blow her nose. "But you were Stephen's sister...it wasn't right not to tell you..."

"Stephen's sister?…"

I look at the baptism photo again, feeling like a cubist portrait, my eyes at uneven angles, my lips and chin on one side of my head. But then, like a puzzle, the pieces click. All the clues I never acknowledged now break the surface like bubbles. Things that always confused me begin to make sense. Mother's contempt and distance, her angel garden, my lack of resemblance, my hair and height and eyes like Dad's, the dearth of photographs. Images emerge, slowly at first and then scrolling. From them flow others, memories merging, recollections rushing. Of course Dad looks like the man at my baptism. It's his father—and mine—holding me, his daughter.

"They never told me…"

Dagmar says, "I always thought you should know." She releases a sigh, as if letting go of an old, heavy burden.

And for a moment, I feel threads inside me being cut, what will replace them unknown. I drop the frame to the floor. The glass shatters along with all the limitations I thought had held me back. Finally, I understand.

Chapter Fifty-Eight

I have no idea how long I sit on the couch, trying to breathe, the small, cramped room pressing in. Two minutes? Twenty? My head hammers and eyes throb. Questions and judgments churn around the secrets Dagmar shared. A simple snapshot has blown open the door to my past, putting an end to everything I've known to be true.

Dagmar moans and I go in to adjust her pillow. I crouch to retrieve the photo from beneath the glass shards and look at it for a long time, drinking in the faces of my birth parents. I move to the kitchen, put the picture on the counter, find a broom and dustpan in the closet, and softly sweep up the mess next to Dagmar's bed.

As I dump the glass splinters in the kitchen garbage, I hear footsteps and quickly slip the snapshot into my pocket. Walter enters and asks about Dagmar.

I have to clear my throat several times to find my voice. "We spoke a bit, but then she drifted off."

"That's nice. You had a chance to catch up." He starts to say something about dinner, but I interrupt.

"If you don't mind, Uncle Walter, I could really use some fresh air before we eat."

"Of course. The grounds are lovely. If the rain holds off, you take your time."

I stand, feeling for the edge of the photo in my pocket before slipping out the door, down the hall, and out the building.

My head feels light and heavy at the same time and I barely notice the cool drizzle outside. I sit on a wooden bench, cross my legs, hands open on my knees. The roots of my life have been ripped from under me, the narrative I've believed for twenty-three years all wrong. If I let go of my memories and see my life through a new lens, will it change who I am? What am I thinking? It's changed me already…

I feel an immense wave of grief rise up. Tears flow, as if my body is grieving without thought, without reason. Feeling the heartbreak I've been carrying all along without knowing it.

But how can I mourn two people I never knew? I take a few steadying breaths. I imagine I'm in yoga—breathing deeply, letting go. I hear Madame whisper: *Calme-toi, ma petite. Calme-toi.*"

Her voice in my mind has a settling affect. She's been my dear friend of late, even though she has her own difficulties. I think of her and Eugène having dinner in Rouen, talking and enjoying each other's company. They managed to reconcile but will that be possible with Mother? My stomach lurches at the thought and I push off the bench to stomp down the path past-an ivy-covered trellis flanked by beds of yellow marigolds. I can't. It's too soon.

But Madame whispers again, "This will not destroy you, Catrine. But you must do your part. So get your anger out now."

I stand and stride towards the duck pond, feeling long time fury and fresh betrayal pour out through hot tears. I have a childish impulse to launch into a primal sprint to escape to the woods, limbs pumping until all I can hear is my heart pounding. But I keep my pace steady as I pass two noisy swans, their necks entwined, but in a strangle rather than an embrace.

An errant branch hits my face and I break it off, hurling it beyond the swans. I skirt the water's edge until I turn to follow a narrow, fast-moving stream. It mesmerizes me as it hurtles over fallen boughs and unruly rocks. I lose my balance, going down on all fours in the shallow icy water, my tears falling in the flow. I find a foothold, pick myself up, and then drop to a log on the bank. Soaked and trembling, I yank off my flats, roll up my pants, and plunge my feet in the cascade. I lean down, rinse my hands, and splash my face, hoping it will bring clarity.

Is my life story still mine or must I redefine it? Am I still who I've been for twenty-three years? Does what I've learned change everything or nothing at all? I wipe my hands on my pants and pull up my shirt to dry my face.

Catherine and Étienne, who I thought were my grandparents, are actually my parents. It was Catherine—my mother—who passed along her books as well as her love of France. And my brother—Stephen—took me in and became my dad.

When I look up again, a mother duck, ducklings in tow, waddles beside the pond in my direction. She sees me, quacks, and turns quickly to the water, her babies behind her.

I think of Mother, and I'm still shocked to realize this woman I've known all my life is in fact my sister-in-law. And though I can't forget how she treated me, in a strange way, the fact that she's not blood is liberating, lifting a weight I've long carried. It explains why I felt such distance and how we could be so different. Though there's no shared biology, she did raise me, and the truth is comforting and heartbreaking at the same time.

I turn and my gaze follow the wake of the mama and her ducklings to the bank. They've made it safely across the pond.

I look down at my feet and kick up a splash. Dammit. How could they not have told me? But then shrill laughter erupts as I think about my epithet: a curious-intellectual-with-a-streak-of-rebellion. I was forever asking questions, but they kept me in the dark.

I remain at the water's edge, dangling my feet while the stream and the truth eddy around me. And then I remember how it all began. The mother and father who gave me life lost theirs on an icy road while their son and his wife cared for their baby daughter. I look up through the canopy of rain-dripping trees and ask the parents I never knew, "Does who I've become make you proud?"

Feeling as if everything I've ever known is melting, running through my fingers, I'm desperate for something or someone to cling to. I flash to Vincent, Madame and Chef, Eugène, Odette, and Mathilde. They've made me feel I belong and will help me through this. They'll be waiting for me in France when I get back.

Feet frozen, clothes clammy, and drained of tears, I tug on my flats that won't easily slide onto wet feet and roll down my pant legs. Retracing my steps through delicate mist, I scratch at the trace of eczema that's been quiet for days. Work on letting go, Catrine. Focus on surrendering and looking forward instead of back.

For the second time today, I push open the weighty glass entrance door and walk by the front desk. The plaited clerk waves.

"*Fräulein*—a message." She tears a sheet of paper from a pad.

"*Danke schoen*," I say.

> Catrine,
>
> Finished today's meeting but client canceled tomorrow's lunch.
>
> Will take the morning train to Bad Neuenahr and a taxi when
>
> I will arrive. I miss you.
>
> Vincent

I stare at the note, wishing his arms were around me. I fold the paper and tuck it in my pocket, next to the picture of my parents.

I step to the elevator, reach forward, hand trembling, and push the button. The doors open as words swim and ricochet. Parents. Hildy and Stephen. Birth parents. Mother and Dad. Grandparents. Brother and sister-in-law. This morning, the labels were so clear.

Chapter Fifty-Nine

Walter looks from the apartment doorway and down the hall as I approach. A woman peeks from behind him. It can't be…

"Catrine," he says. "There's someone who just—"

"Mother? How did you—? Why didn't—?" I can't complete a sentence.

"Cat, your hair! You said you cut it but I couldn't imagine—"

"Please! Call me Catrine."

She lifts her eyebrows.

I turn to Walter. "You knew she was coming? Why didn't—"

"I thought you'd be pleased by the surprise." He looks down at his feet, sheepish.

Mother sniffs and tugs at her hair that she's let grow longer since I've been gone. "I thought you'd be pleased too." She approaches with a sour smile and gives me one of her wooden-armed embraces, my limbs limp, hanging at my sides.

Neither of them knows what Dagmar has told me. And right now, it's all I can do not to explode. But I squash my anger, speak calmly, and suggest we sit on the couch. Blowing up will not help us discuss the inevitable.

Walter says, "Before we sit, Hildy, let's see your sister. Dagmar's sleeping, but we can look in on her quickly."

When they return, Mother-who-is-not-my-real-mother is saying, "It's very upsetting seeing her like this. Especially when we've been apart for so long."

I'm sitting at the dinette table while they move to the couch. I manage to keep bitterness from my voice. "You've been apart because you wouldn't travel. Until now. In my wildest dreams, I never thought I'd see you here."

She looks at me for several seconds before replying. "Well, I'm here now. Obviously."

"Why?"

She clasps her hands and looks at her lap. "What you said the last time you called." Her voice catches and quavers with her next words. "About Dagmar being my sister and doing the right thing. It made me feel so guilty."

Well, this is unexpected. Mother being emotional, feeling guilty.

Walter reaches over and takes Mother's hand. "Whatever the reason, we're happy you're here, Hildy. How was your trip?"

My head pounds as Mother prattles on about her flight and I wish she would stop. And then I hear Napoleon himself. "*N'interrompez jamais un ennemi qui est en train de faire une erreur.*" Never interrupt your enemy when he is making a mistake. That may be fine mid-battle, but I'm wrestling with all my questions for the woman in front of me.

Finally, she ends with, "More terrifying than I thought. So bumpy and long. Took forever to get here. Everyone was speaking German and I was stuck between two men who spoke no English. Can you imagine?"

I can't help myself. "And you speak no German. Imagine that…"

She gives me a half-hearted smile. "Father Ceinture encouraged me and said Jesus would want me to go. He lent me a suitcase and drove me to the airport, actually."

"Jesus or Father Ceinture?" I ask.

Walter chuckles. Mother gasps. "Not funny, Cat. It's disrespectful."

"Oh, really?" I stand, too agitated to sit quietly anymore. I take the photo from my pocket and slowly, deliberately, lay it on the table, facing Mother. "And what might Jesus say about this?"

She takes a quick glance and looks away.

"Would he say you're not my mother? Would he tell me you're my brother's wife?"

Walter's eyes widen, he frowns, and then tugs at his earlobe. But then he stands and clears his throat. "I'll be with Dagmar if you need me." He disappears into the bedroom, noiselessly closing the door.

I tap the photo. "Tell me the truth. Who are these people?"

She looks down at the photo, not meeting my gaze, and says, "It seems you know already. Was it Dagi who…" She closes her eyes tight and swallows hard. "Of course, she must have or…

"Or it would have remained a secret forever? That you and Dad took care of me when my real parents died. A secret meant to protect me?"

Her mouth is taut, eyes now glued to mine. My cheeks heat up under her hard stare, which suddenly softens, betraying pain and fear. She looks away.

Then she whispers, "We thought it best."

"Did you ever think I might have wanted the truth about my life?"

She's silent for a while. Then she picks up the photo, gives a quick look, and drops it. Tension drains from her face and her features melt. She buries her head in her hands. Her voice muffled, she says, "We always intended to tell you…but then your father, Stephen…and then I couldn't…"

She pushes away tears running down her face. I pass her a box of tissues from the kitchen table.

"At first, we thought you were too young. And then the years slipped by… Before we knew it, you were a teenager. We, especially your father, your—Stephen—thought the truth would hurt too much at that age. Those were difficult years for you." She wipes her cheek and sighs. "What do you want to know?"

"Everything. I want to know everything. From the beginning."

Mother rubs her forehead, crosses and then uncrosses her legs. Finally, she says, "You were ten months old. Stephen and I were babysitting you and…and there was a storm." For the next fifteen minutes, she explains about my parents, that they lived close, the details of the accident, and how back then family confidences remained secret. "It was the 1950s. People didn't question certain things."

My eyes sting as I reach across and pick up the black and white photo. I feel my parents' absence in my gut, a gaping hole I never had a name for until now. I touch the image and want to believe that from the sole likeness I've ever seen of my mother and father, their love will make its way through my fingertips. I slip the photo back in my pocket.

I say, "That's a heavy burden to carry. And for so long. Why did you keep it a secret?"

"Back then, people didn't mention adoption. Barely said the word. In some ways, a stigma was attached."

I lean forward. "Is it true you lost a baby?"

She looks to the window, tearing at a hangnail until it bleeds. She takes the crumpled tissue from her lap, presses it to her thumb, and nods with a fresh flow of tears. A mother's tears. "Yes. A little girl."

I feel compelled to reach across the table to put my hand on hers but stop myself. I'm not ready. She's now weeping, sobs swallowing the final words of her sentences. "I convinced myself…taking care of you… would ease the pain. I was nineteen. What did I know?"

I always forget she was still a teen when she became a mother and is now only 42. "You were so young."

"We tried to do what was right. For you and for us."

I'm so emotionally drained I can no longer speak. No one does. It'll take time to digest it all, especially without Dad's—Stephen's—side of the story.

Mother finally breaks the silence. "I need a few minutes. To splash my face." She gets up, still pressing the tissue against her thumb.

I point toward the bathroom and say, "Take the time you need."

Chapter Sixty

Mother and I sit quietly in the living room on opposite ends of the sofa. She holds a damp washcloth to her forehead. Walter comes from Dagmar's room and offers me an orange afghan to put across my lap.

"You're still wet. You must be cold," he says. I take the blanket with appreciation.

"May I join you," he asks.

Mother and I both nod. Walter sits between us, and I turn to Mother. "Please tell me why you came to Germany. Was it really guilt alone?"

She continues looking ahead as she runs the damp cloth down her cheeks and then coils it in her hands. "When Stephen died, I had my job and the church. And you were there. It all distracted me from being sad and I wasn't living alone. But then you left. So suddenly."

She breaks down again, her face scrunched in pain, tears falling as if all the emotion she'd bottled up for years had been uncorked.

"I lost a baby. I lost Stephen's parents. I lost Stephen. And then I lost you. I was so alone." She takes a moment to blow her nose. "I needed you and I needed my sister."

Walter takes her hand and pats it. I do feel sorry for her but am annoyed by her martyrdom. "I understand all that, I do. But you could have made different choices."

She dries her eyes but keeps her head down. "I guess I was too focused on my own pain." Her tears begin again. "I don't have close friends, never did, and didn't know what to do with myself alone."

"And those Catholic Daughters?"

She closes her eyes, breathing hard. "I thought they were my friends. But then, two weeks ago, we had a meeting. They'd started early and were talking about me. Rose Marie said, 'She sure can type but I don't want to hear any more about her crappy little house.' Someone else said, 'Can't she just be our secretary?'" Mother pauses to wipe her eyes with the washcloth. "And then the new president said, 'Don't worry. We'll never meet at her house again. Those vanilla air fresheners made me gag. And those awful little white bread sandwiches…'" Mother fidgets with the cloth.

"I'm sorry. That must have hurt," I say.

She nods, refuses to look at me, and brushes invisible crumbs from her thighs.

"Some water?" I ask, getting up for the pitcher on the dinette.

She thinks a moment, chewing her nail. She finally looks at me, pauses, and says, "I think I'd like a glass of wine."

I slowly put down the pitcher. "You want a glass of wine?"

"There's some in the fridge. I bought two bottles at the airport because Dagi likes it."

"You spent money on wine?"

She nods and I can't suppress a chuckle.

"Father Ceinture got me a ministry deal on my flight, so wine for my sister fit my budget."

Walter goes to the kitchen and returns with a bottle. He pops the cork and pours three glasses of Riesling Spätlese.

"Not that I know much about these things, but don't we say cheers first?" Mother asks.

Walter says, "Let's toast to Dagmar. To her improving health."

I raise my glass. "*Santé*, Aunt Dagmar."

Mother echoes me as our glasses clink. "*Santé*, Dagi." I watch as the wine touches her lips and then she takes a bigger taste.

"Your first?" I ask, watching Mother gingerly hold the stem with both hands as if the glass might break.

"The first," she says, her voice soft. "In over twenty-four years. Since I lost our baby. In those days, having a drink was fine for expectant mothers. So, Stephen and I went to dinner every weekend and toasted being pregnant with some wine. But once our little girl died..." Her voice cracks.

"I'm so, so sorry," I say. "But wait, you and Dad went out to dinner?" I try to imagine them on a date, spending money to enjoy themselves.

"We did. Payday Friday every month, usually at Renato's, the little Italian place near work. We always had a carafe of red. How I looked forward to those dinners..."

Mother takes several swigs of wine in succession. She empties her glass, puts it down on the table, gets up, and walks to the window. I watch as she turns, leans on the sill, and looks up at the ceiling. I stay quiet as it seems she's about to say something important. Her chin trembles.

"When we lost the baby, I thought it was my fault."

I glance at Walter and he nods.

"Your fault?"

She continues her confession. "Stephen tried to convince me it wasn't. But I was sure something I did caused her death. And then there were complications and I had a hysterectomy. I was sure that was my fault too."

I'd often imagined having a sibling. But I knew Mother would have compared us. And perhaps it's what she'd always done—compared me to the daughter she lost.

"Days after my surgery, I saw Father Ceinture. He told me I wasn't to blame for what happened. But I knew how important having children was to the Catholic Church and there I was, barren, my womb empty and gone—unable to contribute..."

I've never seen her look so despondent. "It's such an ugly word: barren," I say. Please don't think of yourself like that. What did Father Ceinture say?"

Mother dabs her eyes and returns to the sofa. "He told me God works in mysterious ways and not to blame myself. He said when one door closes, another one opens."

I grimace. A *Sound of Music* bumper sticker. "And what did you think?"

She shakes her head. "I couldn't think anything back then. All I needed was someone to tell me I'd be all right." She blows her nose. "A couple months later, the accident happened and there you were."

I wish she would acknowledge the tragedy of me losing my parents. And apologize for all the lies and the hurt they're causing me now. I turn away, my foot jiggling.

"Stephen and I were taking care of you while your parents went to dinner for their anniversary. At the Auberge Chez François, during a terrible storm. The temperature dropped, that twisty road I refuse to drive on got icy, and well, I got the call."

I reach over to touch her arm. This time I follow through.

"Stephen dealt with the police and the hospital and all the paperwork, and I took care of you. We both took leaves of absence from work. They were going to put you in a foster home—"

The words slap me, my wagging foot gone still. "A foster home? But you and Dad..."

"We *never* would have let that happen. Stephen had to go through all the legal rigmarole, especially because we were so young. The judge wanted to be sure we had the means and maturity to take care of you. So, we hired a lawyer, filed the paperwork, and adopted you."

I sit, playing with the ends of my hair, listening carefully to her words, absorbing what she and Stephen did for me. Our glasses empty, Walter retrieves the wine from the fridge. He pours refills without asking and leaves the empty bottle on the coffee table. I get up to sit on the dinette chair, facing Mother.

What she's shared, along with the wine, have eased my hurt of minutes ago. "I always thought you hated me...hated my love for books... hated that I looked so much like Dad and not you. I was different but you wanted me to only make decisions you agreed with."

She looks at me. "When you arrived, I believed my prayers had been answered and was so grateful to have a little girl to take care of. I tried to protect you from the world and steer you towards what I thought God wanted."

I'm able to say calmly, my anger having dissipated, what I've wanted to say all my life. "But you never loved me for who I was. Your affection was conditional. It depended on me being who you wanted me to be. It hurt so much..." It's now my turn to cry. Walter gets up to put his arm around me.

Mother says, "All I ever wanted was a safe, normal life—nothing new, everything familiar. But all you ever wanted was to explore the world and see new things and I didn't know what to do with a daughter with such curiosity. I wanted security and you wanted France."

We sit quietly as I make a mental list of all I want to know about my parents. I start with, "What was my mother like? And my father?"

Mother thinks for a moment and then leans forward to look me in the eye.

"Your parents were wonderful people and loved you so much. They met in college and were both so funny, so smart, and so in love. They married sophomore year. Stephen came along quickly and your mother left school. They kept trying to have more children, but it wasn't to be. Until Stephen turned twenty and you were born. Such a surprise as they were new parents at forty. They believed you were an unexpected gift from heaven. I was especially close to your mother and she was very good to me when I lost the baby." She pauses. "We had dinner together every Sunday. Catherine knew I didn't like to cook, so we always ate at their house. Do you remember the little yellow colonial by the high school?"

"Of course. I always loved that house."

"At first, we thought we'd move into their house, since you and Stephen were their only heirs. But we found out soon after they died that they were actually renting and owned little. Your father spent every minute he could with you and often worked half days so he could take you to the park. He had a small office supply business and apparently, he was a much better father and husband than businessman."

I nod.

"Several months after the adoption, maybe because I finally realized you weren't the baby I lost, I went into a black hole. I was smothered by guilt and it took me a long time to crawl out. Stephen said it was when my obsessions started. To help me try to control my life."

She's admitting compulsions. It's a start. "Why didn't you tell me any of this before?"

"Father Ceinture said not to. It was a time when people didn't talk about such secrets. He said we should pretend your birth parents were your grandparents and the less said the better. He convinced us that in the end it would be healthier for you."

"But I would have understood—"

"You say that now. Now that you're all grown up and accomplished and living in France. But would you have understood as an adolescent or a teen? I don't know. Maybe... But those years were difficult for you."

"I never thought you noticed. It seemed all you wanted was that I work at the warehouse and earn money."

She shakes her head and crosses her legs. "I thought that would be best because it's all I knew." She looks at me and folds her hands on her knees. "I hope you know Stephen adored you as both a father and a brother."

I'm unable to handle her words sitting down and must stand. I walk to the window and look over the parkland. Her admissions allow me to let go, exhale by exhale, of the rage I've felt for so long. I have no space inside to carry it around any longer. I've always known the woman who raised me is flawed but I must acknowledge that at nineteen, she and her husband lost a child and his parents, one right after the other. And they turned their lives upside down and sacrificed much to raise me. I may not agree with how they did it, but I can try to understand and forgive. As Madame recently told me, forgiveness is a process.

My thoughts are interrupted by two more words I've never heard from Mother. "I'm sorry," she says.

I turn away from the window to meet her gaze. Tears well in her eyes.

"I'm so sorry for all the pain. No, I never understood you, still don't in many ways, but I do recognize you're not me and that's okay." She sips her wine, takes off her sweater, and drapes it over the sofa arm. "It was always so hard for me to accept you as my child because our differences were so clear, constantly reminding me." She stands. "But I'd like to make things right between us."

She crosses the room to pick up a shoebox sitting next to Walter's bed linens, now in a corner on the floor.

"We have something for you. Something I let Dagi and Walter bring back to Germany years ago after they visited us. Walter reminded me he still had it and brought it here to show you."

"What is it?"

"You were their only niece and they put together a 'Catrine' box. You drew some pictures and gave them one of your favorite barrettes, they took one of your first pairs of socks and a pair of slippers you'd outgrown, and of course, some photos." She gives me the white box covered in crayon-colored flowers—drawings from my little self.

I take off the cover, look at photos of me as an infant, none of which I've seen before. I run my fingers over the socks and slippers, hoping they'll trigger memories. I pick up two crayons, one yellow and one gold, and a construction paper card. "For Aunt Dagmar and Uncle Walter. July 1962." Apparently, I could write at four.

At the bottom of the box is a waxed paper sleeve. I carefully pry it open. A faint memory bubbles up…Mother being so mad and I couldn't understand why. And then it all pops back into awareness and I throw back my head and laughter bursts from deep within. "Oh my God! Now I have two!" I gingerly take the braid—a towhead's thick plait—and lay it flat on my palm. It's almost as long as the one I left in Paris.

Mother says, "You cut it off when you wanted to look like Madeline."

"I remember," I say, still giggling. "I'd forgotten but I remember now…I can't believe I did that…"

Now Mother laughs. "You had a mind of your own, Cat—Catrine Gray. You always did."

Dagmar calls from her room with more verve than I've heard since I arrived. "I remember that cut. Walter and I were there. We'd just finished reading *Madeline's Rescue*. Your favorite."

Walter gets up to join Dagmar.

"That's right," Mother says. "You disappeared into the bathroom while we made dinner. You went in with hair to your waist and came out with crooked bangs and hair chopped to your neck. I was furious but everyone else thought it was adorable."

I continue to laugh, shaking my head as I put my braid back in its sleeve and then back in the box. That horrible morning with Freddie seems so long ago…and I feel so much less fragile.

"What's so funny?" asks Mother.

"Too long a story for now, but let's say it reminds me of my introduction to Paris."

Walter returns from the bedroom. "It's getting late you two. And Dagmar wants you with her while she eats, Hildy. Would you mind helping her to the living room while I heat up what the kitchen delivered? Egg noodles with mushrooms in brown gravy."

Mother stands, and we see Dagmar peep around the bedroom door.

"You're walking again!" says Walter. "But be careful."

"Let me help you," says Mother, rushing to her.

Dagmar says, "I still can't believe you're here, Hildy. And that you finally told her. It's about time. Are you okay, Catrine?"

I nod. "It's not been the day I expected, but yes, I'm fine."

Mother helps Dagmar to the couch and I say, "Talk more in the morning?"

Mother stops and looks back at me. "Sure. And by the way, Catrine. Your new haircut is pretty. You look very...French."

Chapter Sixty-One

Mother strokes Dagmar's hand, tender as a lover, a gentleness I never thought I'd see. While they huddle in conversation between bites, Walter grabs a photo album and he and I take our plates down to the end-of-the-hall apartment where I'll spend the night. He puts the album on the coffee table and suggests I'll like the pictures of me as a child. We sit at the small dining table, he with his stein of beer, and I with my wine, nibbling at our meals.

"Has Mother always been like she is? Obsessive about money and crazy about Catholicism?" I say, relieved I can voice my questions.

"She did always focus on money, that is true. Maybe because her parents constantly spoke about how bad things were in Germany in the thirties. It's why they left. And when they got to America, Dagmar said they had to be careful with finances. Your mother was always afraid of being poor." He chuckles. "I do know her money obsession about drove your poor father crazy. She counted every penny that went in and out of that household. Twice."

"And is Aunt Dagmar the same?"

He shakes his head. "She was years older and maybe not as impressionable as Hildy."

I take a forkful of noodles.

"Dagmar begged her to get help about her fixations. I suspect Dagi's concern is part of why Hildy never visited all those years. Afraid we would gang up on her."

"But how about the religious thing? Were their parents that way?"

"They weren't devout at all. But Hildy wasn't either until she lost the baby. Stephen told us that at first, she stayed in bed for weeks and wouldn't talk to anyone, including him. And then suddenly, she became angry. He heard her cursing God and swearing at the crucifix above their bed. 'Why did you let this happen? I hate you!'"

"But then Stephen asked Father Ceinture to visit her. I don't know what he said in the hours he was there, but the next day, she insisted on going to Mass. And just that first return to church ignited the devotion that soon blossomed into full-blown mania. She reached for religion as if it were a lifeline—becoming compulsive about daily Mass, covering her head with a mantilla long after that rule went away, going to confession a couple times a week, saying the rosary, and following the church's rules exactly. It was like she was doing penance, making up for her guilt about losing a child and being unable to have another. It was clear to us all, including Stephen, that it was a way for her to control her life so nothing else bad would happen. She even admitted once that the Catholic Church made life easier because she didn't have to think. Just follow the rules."

"*L'homme naît libre; et partout il est enchaîné.*" Man is born free; and everywhere he is in chains. Jean-Jacques Rousseau speaks to me and I can't get his words out of my head.

"How did my dad—Stephen—put up with it all?"

"He tried to get her a therapist, but she wouldn't spend the money. All she agreed to was talking to that parish priest."

"Father Ceinture."

"Yes, he's the one. Stephen said he was a good guy. Helped ease her obsessions and gave them a name. Said he'd seen it before in varying degrees. Scrupulosity he called it."

Exactly what Madame said. I recall the times Mother insisted I wear a hat in church and how she refused to see a doctor unless he or she was Catholic. "And she refused professional help, other than the priest?"

"Said the Church was all the help she needed." Walter tugs on his ear. "Stephen asked their doctor for a prescription to calm her fixations."

He gulps his beer. “Of course, Hildy didn’t think she needed pills, but Father Ceinture told her they might help.”

“Did they?”

“Stephen said they did. We visited a few months after Hildy lost the baby. She was quite happy because you had arrived. A blessing from God.”

I try to picture her happy and nurturing but can’t.

“She stopped the medication, saying it made her too drowsy to take care of you. And she feared taking medication would make God angry with her. Of course, the daily church visits started again and all she talked about was keeping you safe and from sinning with boys when you got older.”

I laugh. “Well, no danger there. She got what she prayed for in that department.” I finish my wine and noodles, take the photo album, and flip through. “So, did you visit often, Uncle Walter? I don’t remember you in Virginia.”

“Only until you were about four, when Hildy said some terrible things to Dagi. About not being a good sister because she left and went to Germany. And for not practicing her faith.”

“Sounds like Mother.”

“But the final straw was when she said we were selfish for not having children.”

“What?”

“She was just parroting Catholic teaching. And maybe because she couldn’t have a child, she couldn’t understand why anyone would choose not to.”

I shake my head. “What a terrible thing to say.”

“It hurt Dagi deeply. Hildy scoffed when we told her the doctors said we shouldn’t stress her heart with a pregnancy. Anyway, we cut our final visit short and returned to Germany. Never went back.”

“So how’d they heal the rift? They’re getting along so well.” I look over my shoulder towards the hallway.

“It took years of letters and phone calls and then recently, when

Dagi's condition worsened, I think they both realized how important they are to each other."

"I'm glad," I say.

Walter picks up our dishes and gets up. "They're bringing a cot for your Mother to Dagmar's room and I have to set it up. They insisted they sleep next to each other and Hildy didn't want me paying for a room." He laughs and hugs me good night. "And she certainly wasn't going to pay for one herself."

I chuckle as I watch him walk down the hall, bald pate shining as he tugs at an earlobe. Dagi is lucky to have him.

After fifteen-minutes of yoga and a long shower, I sit on the bed, the photo album on my thighs. As I turn the acetate-covered pages of the binder, studying every image, I see that my eczema welts have calmed. Many are of sights in Washington, DC and the Virginia countryside, but I focus on those of Walter and Dagmar, Mother and Dad, and me. Walter and Dad are handsome young men, and I'm astonished by Mother's cascade of shiny brown curls falling to her waist. Dagmar's hair is cut short and both of them are pretty. In many photos they're together and giggling, but the smiles have disappeared on the final pages. Dad, Walter, or both stand between the sisters.

There are a handful of loose snapshots of me at the back of the album: several from my baptism, a couple of me in a sandbox and at a park, and there's a five-by-seven of me on Dad's shoulders, both of us laughing. Mother stands several feet away, her eyes looking beyond the photographer, her face forlorn. And today I understand. Because today, I've finally been told. Today, I've learned the truth.

That night I dream. I conjure the past, even though I remember nothing anyone said or did.

A freakish spring ice storm. A car skids off the road.

An explosion, and a fiery crash.

A deafening crunch of metal on metal.

Shattering glass leaves a mosaic on the asphalt. Shards dig into skin.

Flickering lights as a car flips over and over again.

A woman moans, "Catrine," but then silence. Stubborn silence until broken by sirens.

Fire trucks and paramedics work for hours in the reflection of bright red strobe lights.

An emergency crew and the jaws of life.

But there are no lives left to save.

Chapter Sixty-Two

The following morning, the four of us have a simple breakfast of butter and orange marmalade on pumpernickel toast in the apartment. Walter drizzles honey into a cup of tea and hands it to Dagmar, propped up with pillows on the sofa alongside the cat and her sister, Hildy, my mother. She no longer seems like the pet-disdaining, scowling, fearful, judgmental woman I've always known her to be. She's softer. They're telling stories about the past and my parents, and I'm listening attentively.

The phone rings, and when Walter answers it, he gestures to me subtly, without disrupting the sisters' reminiscing. I slip over to the phone and hear Vincent's voice on the other end.

"I'm at the station," he says.

"Already?"

"I took the earliest train because I couldn't wait to see you."

He insists he'll take a taxi, so I give him the address and tell him I'll meet him in the lobby.

Uncle Walter knows Vincent's coming to meet me here, but Mother and Dagmar have no idea. I'm pretty sure Dagmar won't mind, but to Mother, Vincent represents a trifecta for her mistrust: He's French, has an accent, and is a man.

I freshen up my outfit of red capris and a sleeveless white blouse with a silk leopard scarf and then scurry out of the apartment on a feigned impulsive desire to take a brief walk. I ignore Walter's raised eyebrow, but he doesn't give me away. The sisters are too far down memory lane to say more than, "Sure you won't need a sweater?"

My stomach flip-flops like a schoolgirl's when I see Vincent step out of the taxi. He's in jeans and a white button-down shirt and carries a bakery box tied with red string in one hand and his leather overnight satchel in the other. I open the lobby door and he greets me with a long, soft kiss.

"It was only one day, but I missed you so much," he says.

"I missed you too, and I've got so much to tell you." I drag him over to the orange leather sectional in the corner of the lobby.

Under the harsh fluorescent light, I tell him what Dagmar told me about my childhood. As I hear myself speak, it all sounds so logical. Naturally, they took me in. Of course, they adopted me. Yes, I lost the mother who gave me life but she didn't choose to leave me. What's important is that my brother and his wife accepted me as their daughter and cared for me, no matter how imperfect our bond.

Vincent asks perceptive questions as he assures me he understands how what I now know leaves me off kilter.

"What you must remember is who you are inside." He lightly touches his fingers to my chest above my heart. "You are not defined by who raised you, where you grew up, or the terrible things that happened to your family. All of that shaped you, yes, but they are not who you are."

I nod. "I'm still trying to absorb it all but I know it will take some time."

"Have you called your mother since finding out?"

"Called her?" I suddenly laugh. "You won't believe it, she's here."

He looks confused. "In Europe?"

"Upstairs! She came to see her sister after all." My eyes are wide with renewed shock.

"But this is good news, yes? You're happy to see your Mother, no?" He checks himself. "Not your real mother but—"

"I must admit, she's still 'Mother' to me…"

"And I'll get to meet her now?"

I bite my lip. "I know it's a bit sudden, a bit early in our…" I'm not even sure how to refer to whatever we are, whatever we're doing.

He laughs now. "If you can handle your sudden shock, I think I can handle this little surprise."

"But now that you know the story, are you sure you want to meet her?"

"You and your mother have had difficulties, but she's part of your life, so of course I want to meet her." He pulls me onto his lap and nuzzles my neck. "And I have a surprise for you as well, *Mademoiselle* Gray."

I press my hand to my cheek, "I'm not sure I can handle any more surprises."

"I think you'll like this one." He winks. "Though we'll have to see if it can still work out with all these new events...Hmm...Maybe it won't. I don't know."

"Stop stalling." I lightly punch his shoulder "Tell me it's something good."

"I thought we could go back to Normandy…"

"That would be good." My stomach flutters as I remember our night under the stars.

"My boss gave me a few extra days off. So, I spoke to Chef last night and he put me in touch with the guy at the *Chateau Miromesnil.* His caretaker friend. And guess what? We can have one of the turret rooms at the chateau this weekend."

"*Chouette*!" I say. Cool. I lean in to kiss him again.

When I sit back, he says, "But first things first. Let's meet this Mother/not Mother of yours."

He stands and pulls me to my feet. "You take the pastry box. Should be enough for everyone." The string on the box is the exact same shade as my pants.

Walter, Dagmar, and Mother are lined up on the couch, hands in their laps, like a jury. Dagmar's in the middle, bolstered by her husband and sister on either side.

I introduce Vincent.

"*Enchanté*," he says, reaching across the coffee table to shake their hands.

Walter stands. "*Enchanté*," he says. So does Dagmar.

But Mother is transfixed. She offers her hand and slowly pulls back once Vincent releases it. Returning it to her lap takes forever. Her eyes are riveted and I can't tell if she's staring because he's French and foreign, or because he's so handsome.

Finally she says, "So you're Freddie's cousin?"

"Please do not think of that against me." He gives her a crooked, boyish grin as he steps back to reach for the white pastry box dangling from my hand. He sets it on the coffee table. "An apple strudel."

Dagmar claps. "My favorite!"

Walter says, "Your appetite is back? It seems you've turned a corner since yesterday."

"I feel so much better. Having my sister here is such a gift. She gives me energy and makes me hopeful." She pats Mother's thigh.

Walter says, "*Danke schoen* for the strudel. I'll slice it and we'll enjoy it while it's fresh." He picks up the box and heads for the kitchen.

Mother's eyes remain on Vincent, but she's hardly said a word. When we gather to sit at the dinette, she positions herself so she can look right across the table at Vincent.

"*Monsieur* Vincent," Mother says. "Remind me how long the two of you have known each other."

"No *monsieur*. Please." He laughs and looks at me. "There are four months since we met. On the day she came to Paris, but it seems I have known her very much longer."

Mother gives a slight nod. "I see." Her eyes narrow. "Tell me about your family, Vincent."

"There are three of us, we all live in Paris, and we are close. Especially since my father died ten years before. My oldest brother is an engineer and my mother has a boutique."

"Where Freddie used to work," I say.

"Ah," Mother says. She proceeds to question him more about his family and his job, and he asks her to tell him about her flight and what she thinks of Germany. I see her shoulders relax and imagine she's realizing conversation with Vincent is like conversation with anyone else. Yes, he's handsome; yes, his accent is intoxicating; and yes, he's also as good at conversation as an American. As she loosens, she smiles, strokes her neck, and leans forward. There's a hint of flirtation in her manner. Never thought I'd see the day.

"You will stay long in Germany, *Madame* Gray?" Vincent asks. "Or you must get back to America?"

"Please call me Hildy."

Vincent smiles and reaches across the table to touch Mother's hand. "*Avec plaisir.*"

Mother flashes her biggest smile yet once she recovers her composure.

Over the course of the morning, Walter refills our coffee and tea multiple times. We speak about Mother's house in Virginia, Vincent's business in Bonn, Walter and Dagmar's move into the care home, Madame Arnoux and Chef, Normandy, and Charles's manuscript.

At the first lull in the conversation, Mother takes the last bit of pastry from the plate and pops it in her mouth. She sits up straight, clears her throat, and addresses the room. "Before I left home, I told my boss about my sister." She turns to Dagmar, gets up and sits next to her. "I hoped he'd understand why I had to leave so suddenly. When I told him I still missed my husband and gave him details of your surgery, he got it." She stops, her voice breaking. "He told me to take the time I needed, especially because I hadn't taken a vacation in years."

Mother always painted her boss as a tough taskmaster, but might she have been listening to the one in her head?

"So, I bought a one-way ticket—it was cheaper that way." She sits on the couch next to Dagmar.

Vincent and I share a smile. Mother is confirming all I've told him about her and money.

"At first, I thought I'd take a couple weeks—three at the most. But now that I'm here, now that I'm with Dagi again, I'm not sure I can leave so soon."

"And I don't want you to," says Dagmar, now patting Mother's hand.

Walter stands, opens the window, and leans his bottom on the sill. "I haven't told you this, Catrine, but the manager called last night. She offered us the apartment for as long as you're here." He chuckles. "And according to the doctors, it looks like we'll only be staying another week or so."

Dagmar turns to Mother. "Once we leave the care home, you'll stay with us at our home."

"As long as you need me. I came all this way, after all. My boss said I can take a leave of absence if I want. With all my vacation time, I won't miss a paycheck for months."

Vincent squeezes my hand under the table and I give him a look that says, "See?"

"And you, Catrine? When are you going back to America?" Walter asks.

"I've been wondering that too," Mother chimes in. "When are you going home?"

For many months now, when Mother mentioned home it was to provoke guilt. But as I feel Vincent's grip, the word has lost its hold on me. My world is now big and exciting and filled with possibility, and I can't imagine returning to a place that diminishes that, even if it is called home. I think about my life as I now know it: being raised by people not my parents, my often-absent father and emotionally unwell mother, my love for France and my intellectual curiosity, meeting Vincent, Madame, and now my aunt and uncle. If any of that had changed, would I be here in Germany, six hours from Paris, where I live with a woman I admire and like? With a good man who appreciates me, a man I'm beginning to fall in love with?

"Actually, I'm not going back."

Mother stares, her eyes blinking. She looks to Vincent and then back at me.

"I take it you like Paris," says Walter.

"Did you see the picture of me and Walter at the Eiffel Tower?" Dagmar asks, pointing to the hutch. "I understand why you love Paris so much. We'll go back someday, right, Walter?"

He nods. "Yes, *mein Schatz.* We will go, my darling. But let's get you healthy, first."

"The cardiologist said she's surprised to see I'm doing so well, didn't she?"

"She did. And she wants you up and walking this afternoon and to cut back on the pain pills if you can."

"I took two last night, but only one this morning, and I'm feeling okay."

"The doctor said it'll take about five weeks for you to be back to yourself."

"I have an idea," says Mother. She scoots to the edge of the couch. All eyes turn to her.

"Because you're doing so well, Dagi, and because Cat—Catrine—will be in Paris, and because I've decided to stay, and because I'm curious..." She pauses her litany.

"Hildy? What?" says Dagmar.

"Well, I know it will be expensive and I know you must get stronger, but maybe we could go to Paris together? We'll visit Catrine and she can be our tour guide."

I can't believe what I'm hearing. She's interested in my life? In France? "You want to go to Paris?" And I think, to that den of iniquity?

She turns to me. "We'll also meet your French landlady."

"She's not just my landlady, Mother. *Madame* Arnoux is a retired French literature professor, and she's also my friend."

"Then we'll meet your lovely French friend. Your *Madame* Arnoux."

Dagmar says, "Hildy! What's happened to you?"

"Well, I've changed my mind. As long as I'm here..." She gets up to add a spoonful of sugar to her coffee, stirs and sits back next to her sister. "Dagi and Walter liked it there, you obviously love it, and well..." She turns to the dinette. "It would be a shame not to see Vincent again. If people in Paris are as pleasant as you, I'm sure we would have a lovely time."

Dagmar is practically bouncing with glee, like a child on her birthday. "Walter, can we? Something to look forward to." But then she winces, her hand on her chest. "Ow, that hurt. Getting ahead of myself, I'm afraid." She sits back, resting her head on Mother's shoulder.

"Easy," says Walter, getting up to reposition Dagmar's pillows and pull her blanket across her lap. "Let's get you stronger and stable and then we'll think about traveling."

"It can't have been comfortable sleeping on a cot," I say to Mother. "So Vincent and I are going to head back to Normandy today. That way, you can have the apartment and Vincent won't have to stay the night in a hotel."

I'm waiting for her to object, but she says, "Agreed. My back has been bothering me and the cot didn't help. I'm still awfully jet-lagged but after a good night's sleep, I'll be better help for Walter and Dagi. And you need to get back to France."

Is it possible we're both finally finding our places in the world and can no longer let anyone or anything hold us back, including ourselves?

Chapter Sixty-Three

The clock ticks towards noon. Vincent says, "It was very nice to meet you all." Everyone but Dagmar stands. Vincent shakes Walter and Dagmar's hands, but when he goes to Mother, he stops. He takes her shoulders. She blushes. "*Au revoir*, Madame Gray. Hildy." He leans in and kisses each cheek.

She says, "I hope we will see you and Cat—Catrine—in Paris. *Au revoir*."

He turns to me. "I'll leave you to say goodbye to your family," he says in French, "I'll get the car."

I hand him the keys from my purse. "Should be easy to spot the yellow Dyane. I'll be down soon."

He touches my arm, picks up our bags, and leaves with a wink. I see Mother wide-eyed, as if she's realizing for the first time that I actually do speak another language.

Walter says to Dagmar, "You look tired, my darling. Let's get you back to bed."

She nods, her eyes closing, and manages to stand with a little push on her lower back from Mother. Walter's arm around her waist, he guides her to me. "Goodbye, Catrine," she says. "You're so close now. An easy train ride."

"Bon voyage," Walter adds as he and Dagmar turn to the bedroom.

Without a word, Mother stands, walks around the coffee table, and puts her arms around me. For the first time, she embraces me for real and my arms lighten, no longer leaden at my sides. I slowly lift them to embrace her. She pulls back gently, glances down, and then looks up again, still holding my hands. She says, "You do know I love you."

It's the first time she's ever uttered these words to me. My long-held anger crumbles and I let my tears fall. I recognize in that moment that forgiveness is no longer something I must learn or that Mother has to earn. Faced with an impossible decision, she and my brother chose me so I could go on to choose my life.

"I'm grateful to you and Dad for raising me," I say, looking her in the eye. "Thank you. I love you too."

It takes her a long time to let go of my hands. I don't resist. She steps back, smiles, and folds her arms across her chest. "You've changed. It really is remarkable. Your hair is different and your clothes, of course, but there's something else..."

I run my hands through my hair. "I'm happy, Mother, I'm actually really happy. Happy to be in France, happy to be with Vincent, happy to have met Madame Arnoux. And I'm so happy to be doing interesting work." I nod towards the bedroom. "And it looks like you're happy to be with your sister. With your family."

She nods.

"*Au revoir*, Mother," I say as I give her goodbye *bisous*.

"*Au revoir*," she says in her best French accent. "But now that you know the truth, do you still want to call me that?"

I look her in the eye and nod. "Can't imagine changing after twenty-three years."

She smiles and adds, "What's round your neck is very pretty, but it looks awfully expensive."

I reach up and touch Madame's silk scarf. I shake my head and let out a loud, genuine laugh. "It was a gift, Mother. But, I'm sure it was." I turn to leave but then turn back around. I untie the scarf. "Here. You keep it. A little piece of Paris. From me."

I slow my steps as I walk down the hall to let what's happened in Germany settle. There's a mirrored wall in the elevator and I stare at my reflection. I'll learn to accept the truth of my past and I have so much to look forward to. While I've moved far away and started a new life, having fashioned it rebelliously from my dreams, I'm still the same little girl who looked out her bedroom window with such yearning over twenty years ago. Reading told me there was a big world out there and Dad told me I could find it. And yes, in the deepest, most secret corner of my heart, I always knew my life would be what I made it and I would eventually find my place.

I push past the glass door into the warm afternoon to where Vincent and the Dyane await. He offers to drive, but I insist on taking the wheel. I close the door behind me and press the starter button. We cruise through the parking lot, down the driveway, and onto the road. First, we'll go north towards Bonn, head west across the German border, through Belgium to the French border, and then all the way to Normandy.

I shade my eyes as we move into brilliant sunshine, the motorway unfolding before us. I'm like a bird, soaring high, surveying it all. How far I've come—from the suburbs of Virginia and that little white house, across the infinite ocean to Paris, Normandy, and Germany, for the amalgam of circumstances, events, and people that put me in this car, at this very moment, with Vincent, feeling brave about the future.

I press on the accelerator. The past is behind me. I don't know what will happen next, but I finally know who I am and am doing what I want to do, rising to Coco Chanel's challenge: Be who you want to be.

The wind whips my hair. I sit back as Vincent turns up the radio and sings along with Edith Piaf, exaggerating her nasal warble. I'm back with Dad in the coffee shop in Virginia as I translate in my head: All the good things and the bad, they're now all the same to me. I join Vincent in the chorus. "*Non, je ne regrette rien...* "

As we merge onto the motorway, I hear bright laughter followed by my favorite French proverb: "*Dans le voyage, il n'y a pas de certitude, seulement de l'aventure.*" When traveling, there is no certainty, only adventure.

Vincent turns to me. "Catrine, did you hear that voice? About traveling?"

I glance over, catch the twinkle in his eye, and say, "Indeed I did."

"I've never told you, but voices speak to me sometimes."

I smile. "Welcome to my world, Vincent. Are you ready? Ready for some adventure?"

He puts his hand on my thigh. "As long as it's with you."

La Fin

Acknowledgements

When Paris Whispers is shaped by my love affair with France. It began in high school French class with Monsieur Stefanik, continued through college, and deepened during the year I lived there as a graduate student. With every return visit, my love for the country and its language is renewed and enriched.

Every book that finds its way between two covers is a collective effort, and I am deeply grateful to all who helped bring this one into being.

To my husband, Joe—the best companion ever, through life and on the road.

To our children, Chris and Caroline and our children-in-law, Ashleigh and Luke, for whom my love knows no bounds.

To my grandchildren, Noah and Lily—I can't wait to take you to France.

To my rescue dog, Snap, who sat faithfully beside me as I wrote, and loves traveling to France with me.

To Melissa Carrigee and her team at Brother Mockingbird, who took a chance on this first-time novelist.

To Annie Tucker and April Bosshard, editors extraordinaire, whose insight, encouragement, and care made all the difference.

To my dearest friends—Cher, Nancy and Noreen; Didi, Jackie and Jill; and Davida. I am so grateful to have you in my corner.

To my fellow writers—Andrea, Ariela, and ElJean; Ann, Art, Elizabeth, Jeannie, Joan, Libby, and Rina—members of my decade-old writing group, with whom I trade blunt but loving criticism. You have my deepest thanks.

To Dolly's Bookstore and the Barnes & Noble in Park City, Utah, for your steadfast support of local writers.

And finally, to my readers who take the time to send kind notes to mariannecbohr@hotmail.com. Your generosity and thoughtful reviews mean more to me than I can say.

About the Author

Marianne C. Bohr is a published author and award-winning essayist with a lifelong weakness for faraway places. A former travel blogger for T*he Huffington Post*, she married her high school sweetheart—now her favorite travel partner—and they have been hitting the road together ever since. Her first book, *Gap Year Girl: A Baby Boomer Adventure Across 21 Countries*, grew out of a yearlong sabbatical she and her husband spent wandering across Europe. Her second, *The Twenty: One Woman's Trek Across Corsica on the GR20 Trail*, chronicles hiking across Europe's toughest footpath. After years in publishing and teaching middle school French, Marianne now lives in Park City, Utah, with her ski-instructor husband, where she skis, hikes, and writes—sometimes all in the same day.

***

I hope you enjoyed *When Paris Whispers*. If you did, please leave a review on Amazon, Goodreads, BookBub, or all three. A review can be as brief as a single word or sentence, and it helps other readers decide whether this book is for them. It is one of the greatest gifts you can give an author.

www.ingramcontent.com/pod-product-compliance
Lightning Source LLC
Chambersburg PA
CBHW031134100926
51231CB00042B/669
* 9 7 8 1 9 6 0 2 2 6 3 4 1 *